Betrayal

Book One of The Wielder Series

By David Gosnell

Betrayal

Book One of the Wielder Series
David Gosnell
Fourth Edition

Find out more at:
thewielder.com or on Facebook at The Wielders Place

Special thanks to my wife Beverly - my life, my love.

Beginning

North Carolina, 1934

"Kid! He done it again," Bigs says, breaking into the room.

Durned fool. At least I already put my dick away. The girls are still on their knees, their smiles wiped away by the large man's news. But the evidence of my earlier pleasure hasn't exactly been.

"Damn, Bigs, can't you see we're having a moment here? Couldn't you tell Uncle Ardan about this? We're celebrating my marriage, you know."

"You're so bad, Kid," Lucy says, running her hand up my thigh.

"Kid. You know the old man'd kill the fool," Bigs says.

"Damn," I say, knowing he's telling the truth. Uncle Ardan warned him once. That's all the warning you get with him. "Bigs, give me a moment to finish up with these fine ladies here, right?"

I take another pull from the mason jar because that's what I do.

"Okay, Kid. I'll just wait out here."

He leaves the room. He may be one huge man, but he ain't that bright. I guess I could have told him to go deal with Geoff Franklin, but the truth is Geoff is just as large as Bigs, but a whole lot meaner.

"Don't go get yourself hurt now, Kid," Sabrina says, wiping a little of my seed from her chest and bringing it to her mouth. "Give me a sip to wash it down?"

I turn the mason jar carefully, and she opens her mouth like a baby bird. I flow a nice drizzle into her willing mouth.

"You going to kick his ass, Kid," Lucy asks. "What he did to her last time wasn't right."

"Now, now. You know I'll deal with it. Don't you fret your pretty brown behind. The Kid has this all under control."

She buttons my fly. I appreciate that. She's a damn fine whore. One of the best my Uncle Ardan has. She'll do anything. And she'll do more for me because I'm The Kid.

I leave them behind and join Bigs out in the hallway, making sure to close the door. I gesture for him to follow me and about halfway down the hall, stop. First to take another sip of this fine corn whiskey, second to ask a question.

"How bad he mess her up?"

"Not as bad as last time, but bad. She's crying, and her face is messed up."

"Well, why didn't you just beat the shit out of him?"

"He's scary. I need someone having my back in case he gets on me."

I shake my head at Bigs in disappointment. Then I laugh. He's a mountain of man coming to me. I'm at least half his size. But I have a reputation for being a little … unpredictable.

"I got this. But if he gets on me, you damn well better have my back. You hear me?"

"Yeah, Kid, yeah."

I head to the bar area trying not to weave around too much. After all, it's where he'll be. That's what he does, beat our whores then drink our whiskey. At least he pays.

Entering the room, I see his back and take in my surroundings. I take another sip from the mason jar and a plan forms. A simple plan, but simple is all I'm good for right now. I walk to the bar and grab one of our stools, pulling it over to me.

"Geoff," I say as nicely as I can. "You can't keep damaging our stuff; Uncle Ardan's talked to you about that."

I set my mason jar down on the bar.

"She was mine. I paid for her. Go shit yourself, drunk-ass Kid."

He doesn't even bother to look at me. I know how to fix that. I shove him off his stool.

Geoff immediately starts to get up to pound me into a fine pulp. I grab the mason jar, and he gets one hundred twenty proof right in the eyes. Stepping to the side, I take hold of the stool and rather than putting it upside his head, I slam it right against his shin bone as hard as I can.

He goes back down. I slam my knee into the side of his head since it's in range. Broken bar stool leg in hand I flip it around and jamb it down on the big man's collarbone. Then I shove it into his throat.

Not far enough in there to kill him. Uncle Arden has influence, but not enough to get me out of murder.

Cold-blooded murder anyway.

"Yeah, you just make a move, and I'll end you here, big man."

I pull the stool leg from his throat and drive my knee a few times into his head. He's a big guy. He can take it. He starts to get up again. There's an easy answer there. I bring my foot down to the side of his leg with a crack. He screams.

I take a step back. He's less an arm and now a leg. He has a face of one hundred twenty proof. I could set him on fire. That'd be a hoot.

Wait … still in uncle's bar. Best not to start fires here.

"I'm going to kill you, Kid," he screams out.

"Really?"

"Tell you what, big man, how about I just mess you up, drop you off at your house, tuck you into bed and then burn the whole goddamn place down, huh? Sounds like fun to me. You like to beat our girls? I think I might have to pay your mother and sisters a visit."

"I'll …"

He doesn't get to finish that statement thanks to the blunt end of the stool leg I jam into his mouth.

I pull it out as quickly as I jammed it in there. He pukes all over.

This is fun. I'm thinking of the next thing I'm going to do to him, when the words, "What the hell, Kid," come bellowing from the side of the bar.

Uncle Ardan arrives.

The regulars playing cards give us a little attention.

"Uncle, this piece of shit beat on our girl again. Then he mouthed off to me about it."

Out of the side of my eye, I see Geoff starting to realize the seriousness of the situation. Uncle tends to bring out the serious.

"He did what?" Uncle asks.

Geoff is now concerned.

"She was mine. I rented her," Geoff says.

Ardan walks up to us; I step back.

"You rented her, but I own her. You think it's all right to break my property, boy? I warned you."

"It won't happen again, Mr. Mac. No way. I understand, sir. Yes, I do."

"That's what you said last time, you good for nothing sack of crap. I've of mind to let my nephew here, pay your family a visit in the middle of the night. He does like to set things on fire."

I do like to set things on fire. Yes, I do.

"Tell you what, Geoff," Arden says with a smile, "You're going to pay me for the damage to my merchandise." He turns to me, "How bad is she?"

I turn to Bigs, "How bad?"

"Her face is messed up."

"Well, I figure a week then," Uncle Ardan says. "You owe me one week of what she'd make me with that pretty face. You got a problem with that? I figure a hundred fifty."

"Hundred fifty dollars?" Geoff protests.

"Fine then. Gentlemen, please leave the room, private matters are about to take place you do not want to be witness to," Ardan says to the men playing poker.

"Listen, Mr. MacInerny, I'm just saying that's a whole of money."

The men and bartender hustle out of the room, leaving our fine establishment.

Once we're clear of onlookers, Ardan looks over at Bigs. Then he pulls out his Colt.

"You may want to step out too, Bigs. I can't have you puking all over after I spray his brains across the floor. I know how you get about this kind of stuff."

"Hundred fifty dollars, sure! Please, Mr. MacInerny, I just get carried away. Please, you ain't going to kill a man over no whore, are you?"

That makes me laugh.

"Hey, Geoff," I say to get his attention. "He'll damn sure kill you over his whore you dumb-shit. She's his. And you ain't."

Geoff goes into a panic when Ardan pulls the hammer back on the gun.

"Please, I'll pay it back. I will."

"Yes, you will, big man. You'll pay me for a week's wages in a week. If you can't, then we're adding twenty percent to the balance you owe. That's twenty percent every week you're late. You understand?"

"Yes, yes."

"And you ain't ever, ever, coming back here again. You lost your privileges boy. And if you get any funny ideas, I'll send the kid here out to pay you a visit. He may not be your size, but trust me, you won't see him until it's too late. Kind of like tonight."

"Yes, sir," he says, his eyes locked on the Colt.

"Good. Pay me quick, and we're done. Pay me slow and owe me a long time," Ardan releases the hammer on the Colt and holsters it. "Bigs, get his arse out of my business. Kid, you're with me."

"Sure thing, Uncle," I say hopping across the bar to grab myself a new whiskey. It's not the special stuff that was in my mason jar, but it'll do. Got to have my whiskey… I figure I'm in for a butt-chewing.

I head back into the hallway, and Ardan is waiting for me, patiently leaning against the wall.

"You should have sent Bigs to deal with him, boy."

"He was scared, Uncle. I dealt with it."

"Yeah, you did. Listen, we need to talk about important things."

That's interesting.

"Like what, Uncle?"

"Like your new family. You and your Dorothy. She's with child. That's why you got married, remember?"

"Shotgun wedding."

"That ain't the point. What I'd give to have a family. And trust me, I've tried. I'd marry any of these whores if they'd give me a child. You have a blessing, Arthur. Maybe it's time you considered something outside of this life I lead."

"But I'm damn good at this."

"Yeah, you are. But you got a family on the way. This ain't no life for raising a family. Hell, we all thought you and Dorothy would end up together anyways. Remember how you two used to play and get in trouble when you were so young? I'm sorry for you losing your mom. I'm sorry your paw couldn't handle it."

"He ain't nothing," I say, regretting it immediately.

Ardan bolts forward and slams me into the wall His forearm is in my throat. My mason jar drops. I can't breathe.

"That's my brother. Your father. You will show respect, or trust me; I'll beat it into your drunken, crazy arse. You hear me, boy?"

I can't say a word. I nod yes, emphatically.

He releases me from the wall, and I take a well-needed breath.

"I don't enjoy doing that. You know that – right?" he says to me. "Your father loved your mother. When he lost her and your sister in childbirth, I think it broke him. That's why he went and tried to hang himself. I know it ain't been easy. We'll talk more tomorrow—when you are thinking clearer. Hear me?"

"Yes, sir," I say. To say anything else may get my ass kicked thoroughly.

"Have yourself together tomorrow," he says to me. "We'll talk when maybe you can better understand what I'm telling you. What I'd give to have a child, a family."

"Yeah, Uncle. All right. I'll take the truck home and drive it back for deliveries tomorrow. Gonna need me a new jar."

"The only jar you get is your Paw's medicine. You've had enough. Bring the truck back in one piece lad," he says. "And on time."

The damn thing bounces all around the road, but it's better than a horse. The lights barely cover the road, but I still keep it on track. Then the engine goes out.

Damn it. I thought I had enough fuel. I know I did.

I step out of the vehicle. I hear moaning, a keening.

I stand there taking it in, It calls out, "Help. Help me …"

I walk up the hill toward the voice and see something inside a glowing circle. I walk forward, and it acknowledges me.

"You! Release me, please. The witches laid this trap for me. They're going to let the sun burn me away," says the smallish four foot something, devil-looking thing.

Speechless. I am struck dumb. That must have been some special hooch I was drinking. I take a moment and rub my eyes. Yeah, he's still there.

"Yes, I'm real. Please, you have to help me. If you help me, I can reward you."

"You're a devil. They warn you about making deals with devils."

"Please. It's not a deal. It's a kind gesture. The witches wanted to use me for evil," he says, leaning in. "But I said no. So now they're out to destroy me."

"What kind of devil doesn't want to do evil stuff?"

"You can't believe everything you hear, young man. That's like saying all people are good."

"Humph. "The little devil makes sense. "How do I know you won't try to kill me or do some devil crap on me?"

"You'd leave me here to die? To burn away in the morning light? A cruel death indeed."

The devil looks at me with sad puppy dog eyes.

"All right. But we ain't making no deal. So how do I get you out of this … thing?"

"Just rub your foot across it. Break the seal."

I walk over carefully and rub my foot into the glowing circle. The light goes out, and the devil rushes out of the circle.

"Free! Thank you, Arthur, that was quite kind."

With the light from the ring gone, my devil friend looks more like a shadow now that anything. But I don't have to see him to know something's amiss.

"How did you know my name?"

I can tell by the pause he wasn't expecting that question.

"It's a devil thing."

That makes sense as much as any of this does.

"I see the lack of light has hampered your sight, let me set you at ease," with the grumbling of a few harsh words I can't understand, and small globe of light appears in his hand. He directs it with his finger to float in the air above us.

The orb casts a bluish light. I examine my new friend. He's maybe four and a half feet tall, with thick tubes coming out of the back of his head, that must be something like hair for him. He has yellow eyes and a big friendly smile. His skin seems to move.

"Well, my new friend, Arthur, I am Maldgorath. Set yourself at ease, you're much larger than I. There are gifts for you. I think you'll like them."

"No deals, remember?"

"Pfft, please. This is not a deal. It's me being thankful. Please come close so I might share my thanks with you."

"I don't need no devil gifts, it's all right."

"But I have to repay your kindness. It's kind of like law, young man."

"I don't know …"

"Oh, please. If you don't take the gifts, then you are insulting me. You don't want to insult a devil, do you? That would lead to very bad things. And not the kind of bad like letting your uncle's whores pleasure you only days after your … what do they call it? Yes, shotgun wedding."

"How did you know that?"

"It's a devil thing."

He's pretty good with those devil things. I'm not thinking insulting him is a smart move. Besides a devil gift could be kind of neat. Maybe I'd get a flaming dagger or a ring of invisibility or something.

"Yeah, devil thing. Well, I don't want to insult you, so gift away. You wouldn't happen to have any fine corn whiskey?"

"None finer than your uncle's, Arthur, but I may be able to send something your way. Yes. Roll up your sleeve friend and give me your arm."

I'm confused. But I do it anyway.

He takes my arm. His touch is warm. With his other hand, he reaches to his forearm and pulls off a writhing, squiggly black mass. He holds it up in front of me, and it unfolds into some kind of pattern.

"This is your first gift – a temptress. You think your uncle's whores are fun? This one will do anything for you. And I mean anything. Once you have sampled of her talents, all others will pale in comparison. Beautiful, strong and oh, so willing. We call her kind succubus."

He lays the pattern on my arm, and it sinks in. My head rushes. My entire body tingles as if some unseen energy courses through me. I get dizzy. Maldgorath's hand on my arm steadies me.

"The gifting of a soul is quite an experience, isn't it? I have more for you," my new friend, Maldgorath says.

I look at my arm and plainly realize that the pattern is actually a script. It says "Silithes." The word absently rolls off my tongue.

"Yes. That is her name. To call her, merely run your finger along her sigil and call her to come by name. But wait … there's more."

He reaches to his skin and pulls another wriggly-squirmy from himself.

"This one is a sorcerer of great might. His might is yours to wield. But more so, he will guide you in the ways of arcane power."

"What?"

"Magic. Magic, Arthur. He'll teach how to use powerful magic so no man might stand against you."

"Wow, magic. Hey, umm, you might not want to use all those big-city words."

"Apparently so, Arthur."

He lays the sigil on my arm and the overwhelming sensation returns. He keeps me falling backward. I look at the sigil knowing clearly it says "Arixtumin."

"Steady, Arthur. Now everyone needs some muscle to protect them. This one is strong and fast and willing to give its life without hesitation."

He lays the sigil upon my arm and again holds me from falling. I look down and see it reads, "Vetisghar." The taste of alcohol in my mouth grows stronger. My vision blurs.

A gentle slap on the cheek brings me back.

"Come now, Arthur, we're not done yet. Every boy needs a dog. I grant you this Hjuul, this hell-hound: strong, vicious, smart and loyal. It will set fear into the heart of your enemies."

He takes my other arm and lays the sigil on it. Next thing I know, he's helping me up from the ground.

"So much power, Arthur, can you feel it?"

"Yeah, I think so, but I don't know how I think I'm feeling drunker."

"Your body is just reacting to the new energy. Here's another – a spy and a thief. He also has this never-ending flask, it refills itself. You'll want that after your corn whiskey burns off. Wonderful magic. The trick is to separate it from him."

"Huh?"

"Hold tight, Arthur, here he comes."

The feeling washes over me again, and I concentrate, trying not to pass out like last time. The feeling is a good one. It's just intense. I look at the sigil on my arm, and it reads "Pffiferil."

"He's a leprechaun, Arthur. And for your last gift, I present you with a scout, huntress, and warrior. Not to mention she's a treat between the sheets if you know what I mean? You should use her often and sell her services."

"She's a whore?"

"She's whatever you want her to be, Arthur. She's a fairy and a rather pretty one. Pretty willful and disobedient also, but that's another thing."

I'm confused.

He pulls the writhing mark from himself and places it on my arm. Dizziness overtakes me; I think he's laughing.

I hear the sounds of birds chirping and the sunlight tears at my eyes. I sit up, expecting my head to be pounding from the inside. But it's not. Actually, I feel pretty darned good.

I see I'm in the woods and remember my strange encounter last night. It must have been a dream or the corn whiskey. I figure I have a long walk home given that the truck stalled out.

Uncle Ardan's going to kill me. He said not to mess the truck up or to be late. Oh, yeah, he said to have myself together. I feel pretty together. In fact, I feel very together. Taking a deep breath to collect myself, I stand up.

That's when I see the tattoos. Sigils, Maldgorath called them.

Damn, it happened. I freed a devil. It gave me these things. I remember what he said about how to call them. I start to reach for the temptress' sigil and stop.

Dorothy is probably wondering where I am. Dad's medicine needs a refill. I have to go home. Hopefully, it's not too late in the morning.

Dorothy. Boy have I messed her life up. I knocked her up and got her kicked out of her own family – and married into mine at the end of a shotgun. I remember when days were better. Before mom passed in childbirth. Before my paw tried to hang himself and failed. He's been wrong ever since. Not that hanging yourself is right any way you look at it.

So many thoughts. I make my way to the truck, still at the side of the road, hoping the walk will take my mind away from them. Everything seems so clear.

I am a terrible person – an apprentice moonshiner, debt collector, murderer, and I don't think I've had a sober day in more than two years. But with an endless supply of the best hooch in all of the Carolina's why would I?

The sight of the truck clears those thoughts away. On a lark, I put the key in the starter. The truck turns over. Well, if that ain't something. Maybe I will make in time for deliveries and uncle's "talk." I close the door and in the confines of the truck realize I still smell faintly of the girls.

How's that going to make Dorothy feel? Funny, I didn't seem to care last night.

I pull up to our house. I see Paw on the porch. He probably hasn't moved all day. It's sad. He used to be such an active, happy man. Now he just sits there, mumbles, cries or throws a fit. Uncle Ardan's medicine has helped with the crying and fits.

I have no idea what's in that crap, other than hooch.

I pull the truck to a stop and take the mason jar with the dark fluid. I make my way to the front porch where he's sitting.

"Hey, Paw," I say.

He looks at me with blank eyes. He smells. Damn, he's crapped himself again. This is where I'd normally yell at him and make a scene. That's not going to change anything.

"Got you some more medicine," I say, opening the jar and pouring some liquid into his mug.

He takes it and drinks it down. It brings a smile to his face. He deserves a smile.

"Your maw is making biscuits, son. You know I like her biscuits."

He means Dorothy. I'm not going to correct him.

"Yeah, Paw. I'll be back to clean you up in a bit."

I step in through the door and set his jar of medicine on the table next to the door. I smell the biscuits. Dorothy is cooking. I walk across the living room and into the kitchen.

There she is, doing something, chopping vegetables. She doesn't look at me.

"Do I want to know," she says.

I take a moment to consider her tone and my response.

"Probably not."

She looks over her shoulder at me, then away. I see the mouse under her eye has receded. I did that. What kind of a man does that?

"Your paw crapped himself. I'm not cleaning him again."

Well, that's history repeating itself all over again. That's why I hit her. I made her do it. She doesn't have to look at me for me to know she's afraid; afraid of me.

"I'll get him."

She looks back at me trying to mask her surprise and then goes back to chopping her vegetables.

I walk across to one of the cabinets, open it and pull out the mason jar of moonshine. I unscrew the lid.

"Kind of early to be starting on that."

"Yeah … it is," I say stepping over to the sink and pouring the jar into to the drain.

"What are you doing, Arthur?"

"It feels like I'm starting over," I say, turning around to sit down at one of the chairs at our small dining table.

"You're not making sense. Did you kill someone? Are the police coming for you?"

"No. I didn't kill anyone … well, almost. But that's not it."

"What did you do to your arms, Arthur MacInerny?"

She had to notice. I hold my arms out for her to see. I want to see them too.

"Gifts from a devil, Dorothy. A real devil."

"How much did you drink last night? If you keep this up, you're going to end up dead or worse. This is crazy talk you …" She silences herself. I see the fear creep back.

"I know how it sounds. And yeah, I was drinking – a lot. But it happened. And now, it's hard to explain, but I feel like I'm seeing things clearly for the first time, in a long time. I know it's clear because I really don't like what I see. I've done wrong by you, Dorothy. More than just hitting you, all of it. You deserve better."

She's not sure what to say to that. Given my past performances, I understand.

Finally, she says, "Yes. I do deserve better."

"I'm going to try."

"Tell me what happened," she says. "Tell me about this devil that gave you tattoos. Maybe we can make some sense of this."

"I ran into this thing in the woods. It said some witches trapped in this strange looking circle of light. It asked me to let it go and said it would give me a gift if I did. I did. I let it go."

"You released a devil into our world?"

"I was drunk. Yeah, I did. It gave me these tattoos, each one is supposed to be a thing I can summon to do what I want with."

She takes a few steps toward me.

"Let me see."

I hold out my arm. Dorothy takes it and examines the sigils.

"They don't look like fresh tattoos."

"This one is for a Silithes. She's supposed to be some kind of loose woman that will do anything. I think he called her kind, succubus."

"I don't like the sound of her."

"Yeah. This one is for Arixtumin. He's supposed to be some kind of sorcerer thing that will teach me magic."

"Magic?"

"Yeah, I think he said something like the ways of arcade power."

"I think he said arcane and it sounds evil."

"Now that you mention it, yeah. This one is a warrior, named Vetisghar. On my other arm, I have this Hjuul, which supposed to be like a hell-hound."

"That sounds dreadful and scary."

"This one's a Leprechaun. He's like a thief or something and has a never-ending flask of hooch."

"That's just what you need."

I chuckle, and it seems to set Dorothy at ease.

"The last one is supposed to be a fairy. I'm not sure what to think about her. He said she was pretty and warrior and … a whore? This all sounds so crazy. Do you think I've snapped?"

"Honestly, Arthur, yes I do. Which is funny because this is the first time I've heard you … sounding of right mind in so long. If this all wasn't so crazy."

I turn around and sit back down on the chair.

"We need to summon one," I say to her. "That way we'll know for sure."

"I suppose. That makes sense, sort of."

"Which one, Dory?"

"You haven't called me that since we were kids."

"Sorry," I say, not sure why that name slipped out. "So who you do you think?"

"Not the succubus thing," she says quickly. "And a hell-hound sounds dangerous." She takes a moment to consider. "The sorcerer could be evil too. And I hear Leprechauns can be tricksters."

"That leaves the fairy or the warrior."

"The fairy," she says. "Call it a feeling. They're supposed to be nice. And if she is a whore, maybe it's because someone forced her into it. Like your uncle does."

I'm not going to argue the point. Uncle Ardan never forced anyone into service that I know of. Now, leaving his employ, that could be a thing …

"Okay, the fairy. Here we go."

Remembering what Maldgorath told me, I run my finger along the fairy's sigil while saying "Sheyliene come out."

The air ripples before us and a golden-haired fairy with butterfly-like wings appears.

Dorothy gasps. I try not to pee my pants. The fairy looks around in seeming panic. She clutches herself.

"It's a cruel joke," she says. "He just wants to make me think I'm free, then he'll swoop down and reap you to get me back." She looks around in panic. "Where is he? You're in danger. So much danger."

"He's not here. He gave you to me last night because I broke him free from a witches circle. We're all right."

"No! A witches circle could never hold him. You don't understand. You can't understand."

"The little guy is gone. You're safe here with us."

"He's not little," she says back to me. "You're humans… Are you good humans?"

"We think so," Dorothy says. "Some of us maybe more than others."

Sheyliene falls to her knees, trembling and crying. Dorothy rushes to her, wrapping her in a gentle hug.

"It's going to be okay little one," she says comforting her, running her fingers through the fairy's hair. Dorothy looks at me, her gaze full of questions and worry.

"Hey Sheyliene," I say quietly. "He gave me some others, do you know them?"

Sheyliene looks at me with welled-up golden eyes.

"I'd have to look," she says.

Dorothy helps her up.

"You're nice," Sheyliene says to Dorothy, takes a few steps over to me. I hold my arms out.

"Mr. Pffiferil is all right, I think. I don't really know the others. Except her." She points to Silithes' sigil. "That one is bad news." Sheyliene turns to Dorothy, "She'll steal him away from you."

I give a little laugh. All eyes are on me.

"I'm not sure she'd mind. I haven't been that great to her up to now."

Chapter 1

Nothing is redeeming about this day. Yes, it's sunny and beautiful. Yes, I am surrounded by loving family. The grass is so very green.

But today, I bury my wife.

My love. My lover. My confidant. My voice of reason. My reason for being. The mother of my child. My partner for the last seventy-six years. Now I stand by while we lay her here to rest eternally. I stand here with little hope of joining her soon because of a "gift" given to me. A gift that assures me agelessness. A gift that grants me the privilege of watching those that I love age, decay, and die.

I look at my aging son, his wife, his sons and daughter, their children, their children's children. It washes over me that I will outlive them all. Unless I decide to eat a bullet, or some other unfortunate event occurs.

That might not be so bad.

Dorothy was the better part of me. Even in these last hard years her grace and her beauty never diminished in my eyes. She was sharp to the end, though her body could not keep up with her spirit. What I would give to be making her morning tea and toast right now. To hear her voice telling me… anything. Telling me, I should spend more time out. Telling me rabbits were eating the garden. Telling me, she needed help to the restroom. Telling me, she loved me.

My eyes well up with tears. I want another seventy-six years with her. Ninety-four years is too young for a woman like her to pass.

There's this distracting sound – a buzzing almost. I come to the realization that it is Pastor Robert Williams. The pastor is saying his words to give us all peace and reassurance that in the end, it's really the beginning. I look up from the green grass and try to pay attention. She would want me to – for everyone else.

God, I can hear her… "Be strong for Jerry, Marge, and the babies."

"I will, Dorothy," I whisper to myself, and before I can turn my attention back to the ceremony, I feel a strong, reassuring hand on my shoulder, and look over to see that it's our son Jerry. He must sense something.

I need to get it together for them.

Pastor Williams is in the midst of John 5:24-29; "For just as the Father has life in himself, so also he gave his Son the possession of life in himself. And he gave him power to exercise judgment because he is the Son of Man. Do not be amazed at this because the hour is coming, in which all who are in the tombs will hear his voice and will come out, those who have done good deeds to the resurrection of life."

I won't be in those tombs anytime soon. This "gift" I've been given... six entities that respond to my command also leach into me their endless power, so aging is not an issue. Or disease. Or hope that those I cherish most can walk the whiles with me. Nobody told me agelessness was part of the gift; I had to find that out later.

That is why I am here as distant cousin Arthur, caregiver to Dorothy MacInerny in her twilight years. Dorothy planned for all this. After all, how do you explain that the nineteen-year-old man taking care of you is really your ninety-four-year-old husband? You don't. You can't. We made Jerry, and the grandkids pledge that future generations would only know me as a loving, distant relative. She thought of everything, and God knows I didn't even want to acknowledge those things, much less deal with them.

She was so, so, good to me. And now I can't even stand at her interment and proclaim my love for her as her husband.

I was her husband! I want to scream it. I want her, God, and the world to hear it. I want it to reverberate through the valley. But I can't. She was right; it's too much for the little ones. It was hard enough with the grandkids. So I stand here, unable to acknowledge our love, our years, and our bond other than in the broadest of platitudes.

Jerry's hand brings me back to the moment again, and he whispers "Arthur, it's time for you." It's time for me to say words as her ever-present caregiver for the last ten years. Those ten years since we moved just flew by. Pastor Williams beckons me to join him and greets me with a hug. I wipe my eyes, take in a breath, and get ready to say the words I have prepared.

The first sentence comes out okay enough, "Dorothy was an incredible woman." But then, shortness of breath stops me. My hands tremble and my eyes well up. Torrents of sobbing come out of nowhere, and I collapse to my knees. I know nothing, but this stabbing, sickening feeling of despair and loneliness. She is gone! I am gone. I want my Dory. All I can think is I want my Dory. Dory's not here. She'll never be here.

Dory....

I feel hands upon me again and realize that Jerry and Pastor Williams are consoling me. I hear Jerry say, "It's okay." His strong hands take me under the arm and offer to lift me, and I oblige, still sobbing.

"Let's find you a chair," he says, and he takes me to the gallery to sit me down. I feel a warm kiss on the top of my head and a pat on the shoulder. I try to wipe the tears from my eyes, but they just keep coming. My body heaves with each sob.

I hear Jerry pick up from where I left off. "Yes, she was an incredible woman. She touched us all so deeply, and we know that while we all may have had to look after her in her later years, she is now looking over all of us with love. We pass thanks to Arthur MacInerny, who gave the last ten years of his life in service to my mother, as if she was his own – there is no question of his love for Dorothy. Or ours for her also."

Dammit, he said what I couldn't say, and that brings something of what may look like a smile on my face through my sobbing. He is so like her; there are things he just knows. I work to regain my composure and nod to him an acknowledgment. I look to his children and try to pass on that inside "know." I make myself sit up straight and pay attention.

Dory would not want me to look weak like that. Jerry comes and sits next to me, draping his arm around me. I want to break down again. I won't. Instead, I look into his eyes to let him know I love him. I try to look strong.

Pastor Williams begins the prayer for the family. "Heavenly Father, you have not made us for darkness and death, but for life with you forever. Without you, we have nothing to hope for; with you, we have nothing to fear. Speak to us now your words of eternal life. Lift us from anxiety and guilt to the light and peace of your presence, and set the glory of your love before us; through Jesus Christ our Lord. Amen."

Amen.

Jerry pats my knee and stands up to greet family and friends. He is so strong. I stay in the chair. I don't know what else to do. Marge, Jerry's wife, and their kids come by with hugs. When Marge whispers to me, "hang in there old man," I damn nearly lose it again.

Instead, I just say, "Thanks."

I overhear Pastor Williams comment, "He sure was attached to her, wasn't he?"

Jerry replies, "You would not believe."

Dammit, everyone should know this husband's love for his wife. I watch family move off to the limousines and wave, trying to eek a smile to them along the way.

I think I'll just stay here and cry awhile. I'm not ashamed of it. I want her to know she's missed. The reception can wait. I know the caterers are ready to take care of everyone. After all, they were summoned with very specific instructions.

Chapter 2

The ride back is a blur. Originally, the plan was for me to take separate transportation with my great-grandson, Allen, but given my little episode at the funeral, family who know me for who I really am, think it best I ride with them. The company is good with Jerry, their daughter Helen, her husband, Steve, and Jerry Jr. filling out the compliment.

It's nice that they'd wait for me.

I hate that I'd made such a scene.

At least they know why. I'm very happy for that.

There is much consolation and other banter, but I can't keep up with it. When we pull up to the house, I know it is time to attempt some strength. I sit up straight and put on my best game face. Looking at Jerry and his, I smile and say, "Well, time to find out if the caterers are worth a shit."

They of course smile back, and I laugh a bit too, because they know I had left my summonlings to tend to that matter. They would be fully shape-shifted into human form, and no one would know that the people tending to the reception were a combination of hellspawn and fae beings. Each one corresponds to a tattoo glyph on my forearm – the physical manifestation of their gifts and the beacon for their calling.

We leave the limousine and are greeted at the door by a pale, tall, gaunt man with a balding pate and sunken features.

"Greetings to you, Master Arthur," he offers and bows his head slightly to the left. "And greetings to you all on this most trying occasion," acknowledging my family as they make their way by him into the house.

Jerry responds with a crisp, "Thanks, Arix," and enters with the kids. You see, the gaunt man is really a kind of demon sorcerer. A very powerful one, but still subjugated to me – one of my gifts - like all of my summonlings, as he has taught me to call them.

I chuckle at the thought of him answering the door in his natural form. He would be a man just as gaunt, with bleached white skin, unnaturally elongated hands. And a teardrop shaped head punctuated by his sideways third eye that almost always remains closed. That is until something sorcerous was going to happen. With his purple lips, large and yellow lion-like eyes, his gaze alone could be rather disturbing to the first time viewer.

Allowing family to pass, Arixtumin looks at me in his dispassionate way. "You are not well. At least be comforted that all preparations for the reception have been made and are being tended to in a way to cause no disruption or question." Arix, as I have come to call him, is more or less the ringleader of my merry band of summonlings.

And also my teacher in the arcane arts as well.

"Find strength, my wielder," he says and puts a hand on my shoulder.

I look into his eyes, but he politely turns away. And I know why; he can't relate to any of this. He just doesn't understand the concept of emotional loss. After all, where he comes from or so he has told me, love and such are viewed as weakness and almost cancerous. I imagine it has to be somewhat uncomfortable for him.

He turns back to me with a false smile.

"Myself, the Vetisghar, and Pffiferil are tending to service. The fairy is gone; she did take your mate's loss poorly. Silithes will be upstairs away from the event. I took the assumption that you did not want her prancing around provocatively amongst the mourners."

That is my man, Arix, always logical. Always taking care of business. You see, Silithes is the soul-stealing succubus that was gifted to me for my entertainment and pleasure. She has been neither. All that one has amounted to is high maintenance and a continual, needy pain in my ass.

"Thank you, Arix. Just make sure this reception goes well."

"Give it not another moment's thought – If we can't at least serve food and beverages, then we aren't worth our time here, are we?"

I thank him again with a pat on the shoulder and go inside. Jerry was being consoled by the members of Dorothy's bridge club, all of whom were much younger than Dorothy; only in their seventies. I think of how much she enjoyed the weekly bridge club and turn away before I well up again. They pay little attention to the young man who took care of Dorothy for so many years except to wave. I make my way to the hall and then to my library, opening the sliding paneled doors, then make sure to close them behind me. Walking across the room, I plop myself down in my reading chair.

It feels nice.

The quiet is good. But there is some company that I want. Hard to explain, except it is something akin to the bond between a man and his dog. Standing up I take my jacket off and roll up my sleeves. The tattooed glyphs for each of my summonlings stand out plainly.

I take a moment to consider the six glyphs on my arms. Each one represents an entity linked to me. Each one empowers me, gives me this health and agelessness. Each one is a slave to my will. Each one is a prisoner.

I strive to be a good jailor.

I look at the glyph for Hjuul. Putting my finger on the glyph for him, I send him away. Wherever he was, he is now in that in-between space that Arix calls the white – a nowhere dimension linked to me. After learning of the nature of this place, I refuse to leave my summonlings there. It is a prison of nothing, just an endless white expanse. Arix tells me that the solitude and loneliness of that dimension can break lesser beings over time.

I put my finger back on Hjuul's glyph and call for him. There is a brief rippling of the air and a distortion of the space near me, and then he appears. He is something like a mixing of the beast from an American Werewolf in London and a small bear, only much more canine than either. Hjuul's eyes glow red, and he bends his head up to howl but stops himself. His eyes fix on me, and the red glow dims. His posture softens as he steps next to me in my leather reading chair and drops his immense head in my lap. I ruffle his fur and scratch behind his ears. He makes a short, chuffing sound and settles down at my feet.

Hjuul is some form of hell-hound. A scary four-hundred-pound canine who understands what I tell him. He is also my buddy. He knows that I hurt. He also knows there's nothing he can do, except be there. So that's what he's doing.

Things with Hjuul and I grew over time. The first time we met face to face, he was quite the feral beast; vicious is the word. But over time, he's softened to me and me to him. As Arix tried to explain to me more than once, the dimension of their existence is very hard and compassion almost non-existent. Over the course of our first years, Hjuul came to recognize that Dory and I weren't seeking to exploit or abuse him and we became friends. I know he misses Dory too. The day of her death, he took up a mournful howling.

He hasn't exactly been on his feed either.

The door slides open, and Hjuul protectively looks up. Jerry enters and says, "I thought you might be back here."

He makes sure to close the door behind him, so no one gets a glimpse of Hjuul. Hjuul's massive tail is thumping happily against the wood of the floor. Jerry steps up to my hound and pets his head vigorously, which elicits yet more tail thumping and some quiet chuffs from those immense jowls.

Jerry scoots up a chair and looks down at Hjuul, "You making sure he's okay?"

My hound buddy responds, rolling over against my legs and exposing his neck to Jerry.

Jerry scratches Hjuul's neck and looks up at me. "I see you're in good paws here… Hard day, huh, Pops?"

"That is an understatement, son."

I look at him and know this is just as hard on him. He's lost his mother and is now about to watch his father go away. That was part of Dory's plan. After her passing, I would relocate and start a new life with this new identity as distant relative cousin/uncle Arthur. She accounted for everything; I used to tease her that I was more project than husband.

Her plan is simple. Set me up with a new identity using my real name and start a life away from the questions of family. We purchased properties in Austin, New Orleans, Salem, San Francisco, and Seattle throughout the fifties and the sixties. All those properties now belong to the "new" Arthur and are being managed by a fine firm in Charleston, South Carolina. I would move to one of my choosing after her passing. She thought given my lack of aging, that having multiple places would be helpful to lessen questions.

I made up my mind to head to New Orleans and take over operations of a little retail tourist trap in the Quarter called The Hidden Eye. It would be good to be a bit less of the absentee landlord for the commercial and residential tenants that my Charleston firm tends to.

The door opens again, and Marge enters. She walks over to us, gently kisses Jerry on the head and then looks over at me. She greets me in the usual fashion, "Hey old man," followed with a hug. I've told Jerry more than a few times he is almost as lucky as me. Almost.

"This is going to be hard, you know," I say. "New Orleans is a long drive from Phoenix."

Jerry chuckles. "But at least you'll be closer to Charlotte. So, you still planning to leave tomorrow?"

"Yeah, I think it's best to just to stick to her plan. She knew best, after all."

Hjuul chimes in by rolling over on his back and making a low, "hrmmmm."

That gets him a belly scratch from Marge; Hjuul is smart.

"So, tomorrow we get a rental truck and pack up my belongings, and I make the trip to the big easy."

"We'll be there to help," Marge offers.

Jerry smiles at me and pokes my shoulder with his finger. "But of course we'll leave all the heavy lifting to you young 'uns," with a wink.

That is so inappropriate, but that's my boy; quick to speak his mind, quick to call BS, and quick to be there when you need him.

"Us young 'uns are always ready to help the old and infirmed," I say, adding a wink of my own.

There is laughter, genuine laughter. I recount stories of Jerry's childhood. Jerry makes sure to remind me of a few of my more humorous shortcomings. Intertwined in all of the stories was Dory, how she put up with us, covered for us, and generally held it all together. Despite the good memories, I see Jerry's hurting. His mother is gone; his father is moving away – fading away from family, from him.

There is a pause and silence amongst us.

"I love you, son and you too, Marge. I may be moving, but I'll never be away – you know that, right?"

"Thanks, Dad."

Jerry looks away, composing himself. Marge hugs Jerry and smiles at me.

"We're holding you to that old man," she adds. It must be strange; this old man still looks like a nineteen-year-old kid.

There is a knocking on the door, and Jerry gets up to tend to it, I think relieved to break the moment. It's nice to have defenders. Though in truth, I am the one that needs to be defending them. My sullen selfishness is starting to become obvious to me.

"Come in," Jerry says, and opens the door for Pffiferil. Pffif is what most people would call a leprechaun – a small humanoid creature of the fae dimension. For the most part, he can pass as a very skinny, well-proportioned three-foot tall person except for his green hair. With Pffif being the pragmatist, he found long ago that a little hair color goes a long way. As Pffif enters the room, Jerry reaches back to his wallet and winks.

That gets a roll of the eyes from the little man and a heavy sigh.

Pffif makes his way over to Hjuul and me. He gives Marge a hug along the way.

He looks me in the eye. "She was a good woman, ana she's bein' in a better place now, ye know that… Right?"

"Of course."

"Well, I just wanna ye to know yer not alone in missin' her. She was me friend too -vera good to me. I know yer me boss and want ye to know I donna say this except that it be true. And I know ye hurt. And I say let it hurt too, so ye never ferget. Ye were more than good to her and her to ye. I be blessed to be bound to ye and havin' the joy of knowin' her."

He thumps his hand on my knee having to reach well over Hjuul's prone frame.

"Thanks, Pffif."

"I'll be leavin' ye to yer family now, ye be seeing plenty of me in the morrow, and beyond." With a wink, he turns around and makes his way out. On the way, Jerry shakes his hand, and they share a moment. That's Pffif, brief and to the point.

The remainder of the day is a veritable blur. Family who know me for who and what I am, come by to pay respects and give well wishes. I do have to make an appearance for the sake of the bridge club and others; it is more than a little surreal.

When it is over, my body screams for rest.

Despite my summonlings tending to the cleanup and preparation for the move, the house feels empty.

And I feel alone.

Chapter 3

There is no need for an alarm this morning, though the effort of getting out of bed is a bit harder than most days. Time to move. Time to go. For a dreamy moment, I imagine a young Dory standing over my bed telling me to get with it.

Makes me want to go back to sleep just so she will stay and nag me.

Someone is cooking breakfast, and it smells good. So I pull myself out of bed and drag myself down the kitchen. Good old Pffif is manning the stove from atop a chair. Eggs, bacon, and from the smell, biscuits in the oven.

"Gots to be keepin' our strength up, Master Arthur," he says. Judging by the tonnage he was making, he plans on everyone joining in too.

"Absolutely Pffiferil –where's the coffee?" I ask.

Jumping off his chair, he goes to the coffee maker and pours me a steaming cup.

"Ye know I donna care for it without a shot of the spirits meself, but who's to judge."

I raise my mug in agreement of differing tastes.

Arix already sits at the kitchen table, book in hand and still in human appearance. He raises his mug in acknowledgment. Arix does love coffee, along with red bull, monster energy drinks and most anything with caffeine, though you'd never see him jittery or jumpy. He'd probably love meth.

Note to self: keep meth and crack away from Arix.

Pffif brings that huge mound of eggs, bacon, sausage, and biscuits to the table. It smells great and cold eggs do lose their luster, so I dig in, as does Pffif. Arix takes a strip of bacon, examines it, and goes back to his book, taking dainty bites.

Then we are joined.

No doubt, the smell of food brings Vets around. Vets, as I call her, is the muscle of our group. Standing almost six and a half feet tall and muscled like nobody's business. Vets, or the Vetisghar as Arix and Silithes refer to her, is my personal bodyguard and shock troop all rolled into one. Wearing the enchantment Arix puts upon her, she is a blunt-faced Amazon woman. In reality, she is a black skinned, overly muscled warrior with catlike features, tail, fangs, and claws.

She's a true badass, with the personality of a cardboard box to boot. To Vets, as best I could tell, preparation for battle and servitude is all she knows and all she cares for. Honor is paramount to her. Duty, honor, servitude is her mantra. In our seventy plus years together, she is the one who is most like today how she was yesterday. Most of us have grown and adapted with the time. Vets… not as much.

She sits at the table and asks, "May I feed?"

Yes, feed. Of course, I say, "yes."

That takes care of most of the eggs, half of the bacon and a chunk of the sausage links. Good thing I got my plate when I did. She curls her arm around her plate, and a casts a feral look at both Arix and Pffif. Arix smiles at her. Pffif, of course, can't resist the opportunity to taunt. He ever so deftly stabs a fork at her eggs. This results in Vets hissing at him and stabbing at him with her fork. But Pffif is a slippery character and avoids the move, hopping away and taunting her by waving the fork of eggs under his nose and acting like it was the most savory morsel he would ever sample.

Vets immediately covers her plate with her body, turns to Arix and hisses at him. Totally un-phased, Arix looks up from his book stares her in the eyes and asks only one word – "Really?"

He's seen this too many times before and I think he's less than amused.

A low guttural growl emits from somewhere in Vets.

"Vets, Pffif does this to you all the time, chill out. We can make more if you are still hungry," I say.

She sits up slowly from her plate and acknowledges me.

"Yes, Master," is her only response. She begins to chow down her food, eyes darting to Arix and Pffif defensively. It always makes me wonder what dinnertime was like with her family.

"Pffif, do you always have to antagonize her like that?"

Vets' eyes bore a hole in the little guy in between gulps.

He just smiles in his usual disarming manner and says, "Now how can I pass up such sport?"

Before I can say a word, Vets responds, but not to him – to me.

"The whelp needs more lessons in respect."

She turns her glare to him while licking the last morsel of egg from her plate. With Vets, table manners have to be somewhat flexible.

Those two have been at each other since day one – mostly because Pffif finds her to be such an easy mark. And as far as lessons go, Vets has administered a few very violent ones. The last one consisted of surprising the little guy and cleaving him in two with her sword. One does not sneak up on a leprechaun easily; much less cleave one in half with a great sword. Luckily, when any of my summonlings is killed, they just return to the white and I can summon them back.

But still, who wants to experience being cleaved in half?

Vets' eyes dart from Pffif to the hall as Silithes comes sauntering in. Of course, she couldn't be fully dressed, wearing only one of my dress shirts that barely covers, much less buttons up. Upon examination, it's the shirt I wore yesterday.

"Did the Vetisghar leave anything?" she asks, making her way to the coffee maker.

Vets' eyes are following her entry into the room, and she pushes the plate of biscuits forward, which Sil acknowledges with a smirk.

Vets is decidedly carnivorous; the biscuits were safe.

Vets gets up from the table, bows her head to me, and proceeds to leave. I smile at her, goodness knows if that nicety is really understood.

Sil, like the others, is in her human appearance; jet black hair with perpetual bed-head, every inch of her a screaming a Jessica Rabbit va-va-voom. But this one wasn't drawn bad; she just is. In reality, she is just as well proportioned, accented by pale white skin, and purple lips. Punctuating all of that are, tail, wings, small horns, claws, sharp teeth and striking green alligator-like eyes.

She is an interesting mélange of the disturbing and alluring indeed.

She pours her coffee, carefully adds her cream and sugar, then eases to the table. Sitting down where Vets was, right across from me, she peers from atop both hands on her mug. A coy, knowing smile finds its way to her mouth, and she takes a slow sip.

Arix looks up from his book.

"You presume much," Arix says.

Smile not fading an inch or eyes leaving me, she says, "I always look at him that way." She turns to Arix, smile fading. "There is some consolation in routine, right?"

"As I have said… She is…"

"Incorrigible" we all three say at the same time – followed by a good round of laughter.

Sil reaches for a biscuit and some jelly, while Arix produces a clipboard from under the table.

"I took the liberty of making team recommendations and packing instructions, by room. Each room is assigned two people to ensure maximum efficiency."

He hands me the clipboard. That is Arix, always a step ahead.

"I'm sure this is great, Arix, only one change…"

"Yes, yes," he interrupts. "I will assign Silithes to someone other than you."

Sil sighs dramatically and cocks her head toward me in disapproval. "Why in the name of the…"

Arix's hand slams on the table before she could finish the sentence, jumping her and me somewhat too.

"His beloved is not a day in the earth. Show some consideration, Temptress!" he proclaims in a voice that booms and shakes the room.

Damn, it's been a while since Arix used the old voice of doom trick. It doesn't get old.

His eyes bore into her, and I am pretty sure that third one is wide open too under whatever spell he is using to appear human. Sil's expression turns from shock to sheepishness.

"Master, I mean no disrespect, my nature is well known. Sometimes I forget myself. I hope…"

I wave her off mid-sentence and look over to Arix, who has not taken his eyes off of her.

"Let me excuse myself," Sil says and proceeds to take her biscuit and coffee elsewhere.

"Be presentable for family," I call out before she gets too far.

"Of course."

"That was dramatic, Arix," I say.

Smiling, he takes a deep breath and his eyes off Sil, "This is a hard time for you my wielder; we of the Helterezen realm do not fully comprehend the depth of your pain. She needed a reminder to think with her brain, not her… man-trap."

"Man-trap… Really?"

Arix actually laughs, and his laugh was contagious enough I have to chuckle too. Arix composes himself and then looks at me with all seriousness, "perhaps I should have called it something even more descriptive; there are, after all, so many names for that particular part of the female anatomy."

More chuckles ensue, which from Arix are few and far between.

He stands up, puts his hand on my shoulder, and says, "Family arrives."

And sure as shootin', up come the cars and a big yellow rental truck. Hjuul, in a more regular wolf form, thanks to Arix, goes tearing down the driveway to greet them barking all the way.

Time to pack me up. I give a brief thanks for not having to go through Dory's things. Jerry and family will deal with that. I wonder for a moment if I am acting selfishly. But then I remember, it's all part of Dory's plan.

She's still taking care of me.

Chapter 4

The packing itself is blissfully short, and the goodbyes go by too damned fast. I should have lingered more, taken more time with the grandchildren and the great grandbabies, even though many now are approaching adults. The littlest ones would never truly know who I am. But dang-nabbit if they don't know that they're loved. We make some tentative plans for a family get-together in the fall. Marge says she will do the planning.

I plan to make sure she does. I really don't want to be away from them.

The road is tedious. There isn't much room in the front of the rental truck, so I am joined by Arix and Sheyliene. Sheyliene is in what I call Tinkerbelle Mode – a tiny, tiny little fairy with lithe gossamer wings. And by tiny I mean able to sit on my shoulder tiny. Shey, as I call her, can grow and shrink as she pleases in a cascade of fairy dust. For now, I am her seat as she lays curled up in my lap, smaller than a Barbie doll. Dory's passing hit her very hard. They were close – very close. Shey was Dory's favorite, despite the fairy's explosive temper and many-times erratic behavior. They would garden and chat and shop and cook and bother me about things I wished they wouldn't.

Thick as thieves, those two.

Shey's been very quiet. Which for her is unusual – normally she's quite the chatterbox. But I understand – I'm in no mood for idle banter either. Arix knows this; his face has been in a book the entire ride.

The rest of the crew, less Vets, is stuffed into my minivan, which was being towed off the back. Vets has no issues with being sent to the white. In fact, she prefers to travel that way, mentioning something about being able to train and meditate without interruption.

We've clocked about three hundred miles before Pffif radios in from the minivan with a request to stop soon: "The doggie is lookin' at me with hungry eyes, and he's starting to look kinda yummy too."

"Message received, Pffif. We will stop at the next restaurant."

I could just send them back to the white. It would eliminate their hunger and generally rejuvenate them. But, as Pffif has told me before – where's the fun in that? They all enjoy earthly pleasures more or less, except maybe for Vets; goodness knows what makes that one happy – decapitation of her foes?

So, my eyes are peeled, and I look for billboards, road signs, etc. for where we might take a meal.

We've just passed through Deming and goodness knows what we might find. Eventually, I spy a sign for a place called "Hondo's – home of the Hondo

Mondo Burger." I'm sold, so I radio back to Pffif that relief is in sight. That gets a Huzzah from Pffif and a woof from Hjuul.

We pull off the exit and find Hondo's bar and grill – a nondescript concrete block building in the midst of nowhere except for the gas station across the street. Painted across the front of the building is "Home of the Hondo Mondo Burger!" and another sign with changeable letters proclaiming Tuesday was karaoke night and that there were two for one pitchers before six.

But the sign that really mattered said "Open."

We all exit from our vehicles. Hjuul tears off running; I suppose nature calls. Shey, before exiting the vehicle, expands to her more normal size, by reaching up to her hair and tousling it. Then in a shimmering white downfall, she transforms fully human too. No solid gold eyes, no cute pointy ears, no silver/green luminescence to her skin – just a teeny, skinny young lady in a light, almost gossamer dress.

She looks at the building –"Burgers?" She wrinkles her nose in disapproval.

"Where they have burgers, they have fries," I add.

That gets a smile, a "yum," and some applause from her.

"Ye daft Pixie," Pffif pushes her lightly "We got to tell ye of the potato every time?"

Shey looks at him, hurt. She pouts, brushes off her dress where he touched her, then sticks her tongue out at him.

"I don't see Hondo Mondo fries on the wall – do you?"

She puts her hands on her hips as if that proves everything.

Pffif erupts in bawdy laughter while Arix just glowers at them like little misbehaving children. Arix looks to Sil for support. She just shrugs back at him, and then goes back to looking at her nails. Shey joins in Pffif's laughter for a moment. Then suddenly, something pretty and shiny catches her eye.

"Bikeys!" she exclaims and runs over to the row of five motorcycles near the entrance. She stops for a moment to look them over, with ooh's and aah's in her eyes, running her hands over the one she was closest to.

Next thing you know, she's on the motorcycle making "vroom-vroom" noises.

I look over to Arix, "I need to get Hjuul his lunch. Can you?"

"Yes, I will remove the pixie from the motorcycle and get us a table."

"Thanks, Arix."

I go to the back of the rental truck with Hjuul close at my heels. "Wish you could come in, buddy, but you know how it is."

Hjuul makes a whiney sound in response. I open the gate to the truck, pull out Hjuul's dish and reach pull out a chub of ground beef from the cooler.

Hey, he's my buddy, and he deserves good road food too.

Tail wagging, he waits patiently for me to split it open and present it to him. Rather than just digging in, he makes eye contact with me.

"No, thank you," I say. I get the other bowl and fill it with water. "You know the drill," I tell him. He does. For appearances, I attach a flimsy collar and a long flimsier leash to the truck.

It's time for my lunch, and I realize that I am hungry too. I also notice that each of the bikes has an upside down burning cross on them. I stop and consider the symbolism– does that mean the destruction of evil, the burning of the upside down cross? Maybe it just means "we want to shock you."

I conclude it doesn't matter a whole bunch; I've been around bike gangs for ages – don't mess with them, they don't mess with you.

Time to see what this Hondo Mondo burger is all about.

Chapter 5

The interior of Hondo's is just as stripped down as the exterior. It is basically an open space with a bar on one side, flanked by a small stage and bathrooms. Simple picnic tables fill the space between. Arix, Pffif, and Sil sit at one table to the wall opposite the bar. The bikers sit near the stage, obviously having a good time based on the number of empty pitchers and noise. Shey is on the other side of the stage from them in front of the jukebox with a hand full of quarters, grooving to the music.

I sit down next to Arix, back against the wall. Inadvertently, I make eye contact with one of the bikers who was apparently staring at me first. I smile and nod. He gives me the finger. I look away. No problem. No need to escalate.

The bartender comes around and greets the table. "You all may want to get the hell out of here," he whispers, followed by rolling his eyes toward the more raucous table. "Bad news, there."

His gaze sets upon Arix, as he appears to be the elder statesman of the table.

"Oh?" replies Arix nonchalantly, who then looks over across the biker's table. Not good, they were looking at him too.

I look at Arix and then the bartender. "Thanks for the advice, let's pack up, Dad."

Arix turns to me with a look that says, "Really?" The bartender turns to leave having delivered his message, then ducks as a plastic pitcher careens off the wall behind us.

"Beertender! Do your fucking job! Reload!" Mr. Middle Finger bellows followed by laughs aplenty from his friends. Our waiter was right, Mr. Middle Finger and his ratty receding hairline needed to be left far, far behind. The music shifts from Metallica to Sheryl Crow, and that is not a good sign. Shey is totally oblivious, just swaying to the music and trying to figure what to spend her next quarter on.

At that point, one of the bikers, a large, potbellied, hairy one, gets up. He slaps Mr. Middle Finger on the shoulder and begins striding to the jukebox. I look to Pffif, Arix, and Sil

I whisper the only thing I can think of, "Crap."

Beer Belly wastes no time once he gets to the jukebox in reaching out and grabbing Shey on her tiny behind.

Of course, he has to say something cheesy, "I like how you move that thing."

Shey spins around quickly into him, and by quickly I mean blink of an eye fast, knocking his hand on her rump away and with her other hand shoves him by the beer belly back two steps. It was an interesting juxtaposition watching an as-if ninety-pound girl move a three hundred pound gorilla like that. I see the tirade coming, Shey looks him up and down with disgust in her eyes. She takes a step back and lets her mouth fly.

I cringe.

"You fat fucking fuck! What the fuck do you think you're doing putting your fatty fat pig hands on me, you lard belly ugly son of a troll bitch?"

She bows up as if to say "do something and die."

As I start to say something, he moves forward suddenly grabbing her little neck in his large hand and pulling her close.

"You got quite a little mouth on you, little bitch." He looks over to his table – they apparently approve – and then back to Shey. Shey's eyes emanate rage.

"Good thing it's a purty little mouth."

The table explodes in laughter.

Shey explodes too.

Like a flash of lightning, three things happen. Her jaw comes down on his hand holding her throat, trapping it. Then her left arm darts above his arm, while the right goes under it. She turns her whole body, forcing him to turn as well. Now, having taken control of his wrist with her right hand, she hyper-extends his arm and then finishes with a blow crushing his elbow with her free left hand.

That elicits a "Goddamn!" from Beer Belly. It mobilizes his table too.

Shey immediately spins around Beer Belly and grabs both his legs out from under him, depositing him on the floor. Of course, instinct being what it is he tries to brace his fall with arms out. When the broken one hits the ground, another round of screams and curses come forth out of his mouth.

Three of the guys from the table make a beeline to Shey. Mr. Middle Finger stalks toward our table. Arix and I start to rise. We are greeted by a handgun pointed right at Arix courtesy of Mr. Middle Finger along with, "Sit the fuck down!"

Pffif is gone; slippery little guy he is; he has this trick where he can go invisible if nobody is looking at him. Sil seems unconcerned. She just smiles hungrily at Mr. Middlefinger. Arix sits down calmly.

I call out, "Pffif… No!" Someone was would end up with a knife in their back if I didn't. That earns me the attention of the gun.

"I said, sit down and shut up!"

I do.

On the other side of the room, Shey is in full on combat mode, which is not good. The first biker to arrive in her territory is promptly met with a punch to the pants followed by a grab to the belt, which spins him into the second biker to arrive. In that moment of confusion, she lithely jumps on the first guy's shoulders and grabs the second guy by his ears smashing his nose with her knee, causing his head to snap back and gouts of blood to rush from his face as he falls backward to the ground.

Shey rides guy number two down to the ground followed by a roll taking her away from the second biker. She spins around to face him, squaring her shoulders. She pulls her fist back and points at his face with the other hand, followed by a full-on charge into him.

"Bring it, little bitch," he says.

They close on each other, and at the very last moment, Shey drops into a slide between his legs. Her hands reach into her sleeves and like magic; two daggers appear in each hand. Twisting in mid-slide, she pops up behind him on her knees, and with an inside-out motion of her arms and absolutely hamstrings him.

He falls. She stands. There is a loud bang, and Shey flies back against the jukebox, her green blood spattering around her.

Mr. Middle Finger just shot her. I bolt up from my chair, which earns me the barrel of the gun again. Then he spins around again and shoots Shey again in the belly. And just like that, the gun is on me again. Shey slumps down, holding on to her new wounds.

"Dumb bitch bringing a knife to a gunfight," Mr. Middle Finger proclaims. He looks at me down the barrel of his gun, "You got a knife you want to use?"

"No."

I hold my hands up and sit back down. He looks over to his friends.

"You bunch of pussies got your ass kicked by a little girl?" He spits out at them

The front door crashes open from the force of the wolf slamming into it. Hjuul must have heard the gunshots. He slides along the slab floor from momentum, then turns to Middle Finger, snarling with teeth bared. At this point, I really wish he wasn't in a normal wolf form; it would be over more quickly. But Middle Finger wheels around, smiles, and calmly puts a bullet in Hjuul's eye socket. Hjuul rocks back from the large caliber weapon and reels. Mr. Middle Finger calmly puts another bullet into Hjuul's head and turns back to us.

Hjuul falls over then proceeds to liquefy into ectoplasm, which steams away into nothingness. That's what happens to my summonlings when they die out here in the real world.

Shey is being kicked to heck and back by Beer Belly who has picked himself up off the floor. Broken Nose Biker is getting up to join the fun. Hamstrung Biker just complains. I take advantage of Hjuul's distraction and dismiss Shey.

Beer Belly lets out a bellowing "what the fuck" and Middle Finger turns to him.

"She goddamned disappeared boss," Beer Belly says.

Middle Finger takes a bead on Arix.

"You want to tell me what the hell is going on here, old man?"

Arix looks over to me, his hands on the table in a seeming display of compliance. But I know what he's thinking… "Can I kill him already?" Of course, his looking at me gives Middle Finger the great idea of pointing the gun at me.

"Maybe I put a bullet in your boy's head, old man – huh?"

A silky voice responds, "Pu-lease don't shoot my brother mister."

Sil slowly spins one well-toned leg over the bench to face Middle Finger and looks him in the eyes. Those eyes make many promises to him wordlessly and the tongue gracing her lips is the punctuation mark. His attention is all on her, but the gun is still all on me.

Middle Finger twists a lascivious smile back at her, nodding his head in the affirmative.

"Okay, hotness, but I'm gonna fuck you right in front of your daddy there. What y'all think of that?"

The gun waves between Arix and I. Then his attention goes right back to Sil, who at this point is just piling it on; going as far as to cup one of her breasts. Then she undoes a button with a 'whoops, did I just do that?' look on her face.

Middle Finger is sold.

Arix, seizing the moment looks over at me and asks, "Why not give the good man what he wants?"

"Yea!" exclaims Middle Finger and with his free hand, he goes for his belt buckle.

Sil looks to me – for permission. Some time ago, I gave her the order to never use her talents without express verbal permission. He pops the button on his pants. That gets Sil's attention even more.

I speak up in the most sheepish little brother voice I can muster, "Could you at least take her to the bathroom? You know she's going to hold back in front of us, anyway."

Sil jumps in on that and purrs, "Pu-lease. Your guys can keep an eye on them." She stands, steps over to him and whispers "Pleeease," in his ear. She puts her hand on his belly, making little circular motions implying the promise of it sliding downward.

He is all hers.

"Jack, don't let them go nowhere."

Broken nose produces his gun and walks over to us. Middle Finger takes Sil by the upper arm and makes tracks to the men's room.

"Sil," I call out, "Don't do him to death – but enjoy a satisfying snack." She beams at me like a little girl whose daddy just bought her a pony. She had express verbal permission to do that evil thing she does. Middle Finger doesn't care. If he only knew…

They disappear into the bathroom. I'm glad I don't have to watch; it's not just the sex thing, it's the soul-eating that gets to be really disturbing. Poor bastard.

The bartender apparently took this time to grow some nerve. Pulling a double barrel shotgun from under the counter, he shouts out for Jack to freeze. Jack looks back over at the bartender.

"You better hope you can kill us all with them two shells or we're coming back with more to burn this fucking place down."

That takes the nerve out of the bartender. Damn it.

Arix leans over to me and quietly whispers "Now would be a great time for you to use the wave of shock spell we've been working on."

Leave it to Arix to think of practice at a time like this.

I lean back to him and whisper, "You first."

The bathroom door opens, and Sil comes out. There's a huge smile on her face as she adjusts her mini skirt. Jack wheels around to her and demands to know where Geezer is.

She meets his eyes, smiles and says, "He's resting up, who are you?"

Arix takes that time to stand, and projecting both hands toward Jack shouts, "Tznok!"

A wall of force slams into Jack sending him head over heels flying into the bar. The wave continues, slamming the bartender into the back of the bar, shattering bottles, and the mirror behind it.

Beer Belly, still looking for traces of Shey by the jukebox, looks over in shock at the trail of devastation. Pffif appears behind him and scoops his legs out from under him as Shey did. Again, he tries to catch himself with his broken arm. And again, he bellows in pain. Pffif scampers up to his head and promptly acquaints it with the concrete slab floor.

"See," Arix says, "no fatalities."

I can tell he's proud of himself. What a mess. I scan the bar for security cameras. This lunch doesn't need to end up on the internet. I see one, two cameras. There has to be an office, and I figure it's got to be off the kitchen behind the bar.

"Sil, get the security tapes from the office."

She gives me a little pout and saunters off toward the kitchen. I go to check on the bartender. He's breathing, and his head is lolling from side to side. I toss the shotgun away as we don't need him coming to and being armed.

I hear a door crash open followed by a crackling, dry voice. "What in the hell did that bitch do to me!"

I stand up and see who I think is Middle Finger standing there pointing his gun at Arix; he looks about seventy years old now and on very wobbly legs. Sil must have taken more than a nibble. He sees me and becomes distracted. Pffif appears behind him and takes his legs out using the same trick. Middle Finger goes down shooting, letting loose his last two rounds. One of the rounds bounces off Arix and into the wall.

Wards and shieldings. One of Arix's specialties. No wonder he seemed so indifferent.

Middle Finger struggles with Pffif now sitting on his back and manages to wiggle himself out from under the leprechaun's seat. Pulling himself up by a picnic table, he finds himself face to face with Arix, who is not pleased with Geezer at all for having graced him with a bullet. Arix drops his glamour, takes him by the chin, and forces him to meet the gaze. Arix's awful glowing third purple eye opens.

Middle Finger begins to shake and mutter "no… no... no…" – culminating in a woeful scream.

Arix releases him, and he falls to the floor, curling into a shaking, fetal position.

"Damn, what did you do to him?" I ask.

"Damn, what the hell are you?" comes the voice behind me. The bartender has come to. Crap, more to deal with.

Arix smiles to the bartender and closes his third eye. The bartender looks over to me, frozen in fear. I step over to him and put my hand on his shoulder.

"It's okay, we're not the bad guys." I guide him to a bench seat. "Why don't you just sit down? We're getting all this under control."

Arix, in his to the point way, says, "I'll need to wipe his mind like I did this one – maybe a little more gently."

"No way," says Bartender.

"It's alright, Arix won't do anything, I promise."

I summon Shey, who, after letting loose with some expletives and fully taking in the situation, looks up at me.

I whisper in her ear, "The bartender over there is a good man who needs to take a nap and not remember any of this."

She smiles and looks at me with her pupil-less golden orb eyes.

"I'll go make a friend."

She walks over to him. He is scared at first, but Shey can be very disarming when she's not having a psychotic break. I leave them chatting, knowing at some point a little kiss on the cheek and some fairy dust will make all this go away for him.

I instruct Arix to wipe the others, more gently, and I summon Hjuul. Sil comes out from the kitchen, digital recorder in hand. Arix restores his glamour and transforms Hjuul to wolf form.

I can't imagine the questions that will be running through their minds when they come to. At least most of them; Arix tells me there might not be much left of Middle finger's mind.

So we leave. Hungry, as Pffif reminds me, but, we need to put some miles between Hondo's and ourselves.

I make an executive decision; no more stops unless that exit has a chain I recognize. Local cuisine has lost its sparkle.

Chapter 6

The rest of the trip is blessedly uneventful. We stop for the night at a name brand hotel in Houston, and our meals were taken in room service. Two adjoining rooms did the trick; girls in one, guys in the other. Shey, of course, threw a tantrum having to share quarters with Sil. In her mind, it is much better to let Arix and Sil share a room.

After all, they are both demon scum in her point of view.

And it would be much better if she could snuggle with me, in her point of view.

We get an early start, so we arrive at my building just a shade under two o'clock. Our fine building complex takes up about a quarter of a block on Decatur Street. One building is rental retail on the first floor, boutique offices/studios on the second with residential on the third. The adjoining building also has retail on the first floor, but the two remaining floors are mine – all mine. The third floor is the renovated living area – more than enough apartments for our band with a huge common kitchen and entertainment room. The second floor is opened up and left mostly unfinished to serve as a work and training area.

Not to mention a little buffer from the noise below.

We pull through the very tight alley space. I get out of the truck and punch in the code for the garage door. After entering, we close the door behind us because I have to summon our heavy lifter back – Vets. We all pile out, and I send Pffif to cover the doors to make sure nobody comes out while I fetch her.

I step behind the van and roll up my sleeve. I run my finger along Vets' sigil and call her forth. The air ripples, distorts, and there she is. Clad in black spiked ornate armor with a death's head helmet. I had no idea that she was even a she for the longest while until I picked up the clues from the rest of the gang; she's just that intimidating – and I'm not one for gender verification.

I hand her a bundle of clothes – army fatigues, of course, and ask her to get changed. Arix is there to cast a spell to ensure her human appearance. I step away because I have no need to be a peeping tom.

Once we're all together, we head to the elevator, and I pull open the gate. We ride up to the third floor and pile out.

"Okay everyone," I say, "My apartment is the one with light green walls. You all figure out your quarters, no fighting… please."

I make sure to make eye contact with Shey. Pffif takes off running down the main hall, cackling something about getting the best one first.

Sil looks over at me in her usual way.

"Any with doors into your bedroom?"

"No."

Sil again gets the blank, emotionless stare.

Shey pipes up with, "Back off, slut," and steps in front of me as if I need defending.

I don't need defending. I've rebuked Sil's advances for well over seventy years. There were only a few times where I came close to falling for her succubus wiles, and those were very early on in our relationship before I truly knew what she was capable of.

Sil rolls her eyes and smiles. "Fine. But you know I won't stop until I get what I want."

Her eyes turn down to Shey, and I sense real menace there. It's like the temperature drops twenty degrees. Shey squares up, balls her hands into fists and is ready. Then Sil looks back up at me, smiles that smile of hers, laughs, and sashays toward the hall to pick her room.

Shey whips around to me. She's ready to go off. I put my finger across her lips to tell her to shush. She so wants to go off, but my finger acts as a dam to that pending river of rant. Her lips are so warm and soft, they make my finger tingle. I pull it away slowly.

"Pick a good room, Shey."

"I will!"

She skips down the hall like nothing ever happened.

From psycho killer to cutie in two seconds flat. That's our Shey.

It seems like I'm wrangling kids all over again – except for Arix and Vets. Arix has been standing off to the side, silently watching all this nonsense unfold. Vets, I can only presume, is guarding the elevator entrance. I walk to the lift.

"Arix I'm going downstairs to check out the shop. You coordinate the move and make sure the kids play nice."

"Of course, my wielder." He turns to Vets. "Vetisghar, come and select your quarters – we have work to do."

She looks over to me, and I give her a wink.

"Pick a good one."

They head toward the hallway where the apartments are.

I reach into my shoulder satchel and pull out my file on "The Hidden Eye." It has my information on staff, inventory, and of course the profit/loss statements. With that in my padfolio, I raise the gate and head back down to the garage. At the garage, I look at the rear entry door and think better of it – I should mystery shop it. So I make tracks out the back, around the block, and then down Decatur toward my little shop of horrors – my dollars go in, but they don't come out.

First things first, I take in the storefront. The logo could be bigger on the sign, the type at least. I consider the display window and find it full of all the same old tourist trap crap in every other store. I try to relate the bourbon street T-shirts and Café du Monde coffees to the "Hidden Eye" and fail at the effort.

Change the name or change the merchandising? Considering how much we paid for the dang-blasted logo, signage, and stationery that decision makes itself. So, I grab the handle and enter. I hear a brass bell chime on the door and smile – I hate those electronic customer alert, bing-bong makers. They're a bunch of baloney – and besides a good brass bell can clear the air of negative energies too if properly attuned. I quickly check the doorway for the blessings I instructed to be painted into it, and of course, they aren't there.

A sunny, happy voice greets me from behind one of the racks.

"Anything I can help ya with, hun? Our tee-shirts are all buy-one-get-one-free today."

It's Chanika Jones, one of my two store managers. She looks just like her picture – a chocolate brown cherub's face on a five-foot-two-inch two hundred and eighty-pound frame. And I love the pitch – tee-shirts are buy-one-get-one every day.

I return her smile and say, "No thanks, just browsing."

"I'm Chanika, hun. If there's anything you need, let me know."

She makes me happy; working the merchandise and the customers. I knew she was a quality hire.

So I begin my browsing of the wares, and I'm not impressed: in a word – generic. I see very little that differentiates my store versus the other tourist crap stores. The build-your-own voodoo doll station isn't there. The mysticism bookrack is tiny and relegated to a hidden rear nook of the store. And the inventory is old with a capital O.

I stand there amidst the aisles of stuff and realize that this is what happens when you leave something alone for ten plus years. I gave the managers autonomy over my store, and over time, this is what it turned into. I do a three-sixty to take it all in; I wanted a project; looks like I have one.

Chanika walks over to me looking concerned.

"You look lost, baby. Sure there's nothing I can do for you?"

"No, ma'am, but I am curious… Why is the shop called the Hidden Eye?"

"Hun, it's cause we're the Quarter's best-kept secret, all hidden away like this."

"Cool. Thank you."

It was a good answer, the wrong answer, but a good one all the same.

Chanika heads to the back, and I spy the girl attending the register across the store, texting away. Just to test the waters, I approach her and pick up a small alligator head, then stuff it into my inside blazer pocket, all the time smiling at her. No response from little Ms. Textsalot.

So I continue to approach her, taking in the register area. She at least looks the part, multiple ear piercings, a nose piercing, an eyebrow piercing punctuated with dark Goth-like make-up. I stand there in front of the register. Given her concentration on her phone, I figure it must be a game – who could text like that?

And I stand there. After what seems like minutes.

She acknowledges me with, "What?" not even looking up from her phone.

"Uh, do you have any books on...?"

Again, not even looking up from her phone, she points to the back corner and says, "back there."

I stand there for a moment, kind of dumbfounded. Then she looks up from her phone at me with a less than pleasant glare

"Want to take a picture? It'll last longer."

I bite my tongue and say, "Sorry."

I make my way back to the books, picking up a voodoo doll, a shot glass, and other smaller items along the way. Those find their way into the pockets of my blazer. I browse the book rack and pick up a copy of Voodoo in New Orleans.

I head back to the counter.

I lay the book on the counter. After a long moment, she puts down the phone, takes the book and rings it up – never looking at me once. When she does look at me, it's with a sneer.

"Eight ninety-five."

We make eye contact. I pause, seething.

"What?"

I put on a false smile and make for my wallet taking the opportunity to look away. All the time I am wondering what the hell is wrong with this generation of kids? They think they are owed a job. And any job they get is beneath them. I shoveled barns when I had to – dug trenches for sewers in the damned winter cold. And I was happy to get a hot meal and two dollars a day for it. Something, anything, to bring home. Let them live through a depression – not some downturn, but a real one.

I hand her a ten spot, and she fishes out the change, gives it to me, and then immediately goes back to her phone. I am shocked at the rudeness. So I pipe up.

"Why is this shop called the Hidden Eye?"

"How should I know, I just work here."

She gives me an icy stare intended to get me to leave.

I raise her stare with, "I would like to speak to your manager, rude girl."

"I am the manager, get out of my store."

I have to laugh, this is rich.

"Will I have to call the police?" she says, holding her precious smartphone.

"Chanika!" I call out at the top of my voice. "Ms. Jones!"

Little Ms. Textsalot blanches a bit. Chanika comes out and makes a serious beeline to the register.

Before she gets there, Textsalot goes on the offense – "This jackass won't stop hitting on me. He keeps looking down my shirt, and you wouldn't believe what he asked me to do."

Chanika is apparently a bit of a mother bear. She buys right into it. Chanika's sunshine and light turns to darkness and thunder quick.

"You are gonna leave this place right now, or you'll be thankful for the police," Chanika says.

Recognizing nothing I could say would stem the tide, I pull out the store folder from my padfolio and hand it to her.

"What the hell is this?"

I say nothing, just shrug and let her peruse the file.

"How did you get this?"

"I'm Arthur MacInerny, and I own this profitless venture."

I say nothing more just to let it sink in.

"Fuck," Textsalot says.

"You sure look a lot younger than I would have thought," Chanika says.

I guess I do, after all, I haven't aged since I was nineteen, almost twenty.

Textsalot must have felt the tide turn. She goes back on the offensive,

"Then I'm suing for sexual harassment!"

"Really?" I give her the same cold stare I give Sil when she gets pushy. That backs Textsalot up a bit. "Hey Chanika, check this out…"

I beckon her to the counter, where I unload my pockets, smiling and make a small production of each item that I set on the counter.

Resuming my cold demeanor, I take a bead on Textsalot.

"So you're rude and incompetent in watching my store. If you really think your little harassment claim bothers me, bring it. There are cameras in the store documenting everything, and my countersuit for malicious litigation will destroy what little life you have. In fact, with Chanika as a witness, I believe there may be grounds for an attempt to defraud. Who's your lawyer?"

The last was a bit of bullshit, but Textsalot doesn't know that. She stammers a bit, and I refuse to let up my icy stare. For a moment, I think she is going to run out the store crying.

"So I guess I'm fired."

"It's not like you cared about this job anyway."

I turn to Chanika before she can respond.

"Make sure she's paid every penny she's due for work through this minute." I turn back to Textsalot, "Hit the bricks, kid."

"Who's calling who a kid, junior?"

Sometimes I forget how young I look. Wish I felt that way.

As she makes her way to the door, I stop her with, "How about some free advice?"

She turns to me with a 'what!' in her eyes. I let her hold that pose for a second or two, then lay my sage advice on her.

"Try to give a shit about what you do – whatever that may be."

She tells me I am number one with her middle finger and leaves, slamming the door behind her.

Good riddance.

Chanika looks a little shell-shocked at this point.

"It's going to be fine Chanika. I'm really looking forward to working with you and listen, I'll even stay and work her shift. Hey, we're going to have some fun and make some changes to the place."

"Changes?"

"It'll be good, we should wait to talk about it with Robert too."

We make a little small talk, and I think I feel her coming to more of a sense of ease.

And that's good because I'll need her to show me how to work the register.

Chapter 7

Two weeks just fly by. The days have been great. The nights are still lonely even though I'm never alone. Having the project of turning around the "Hidden Eye" is a great distraction. Working with my managers Robert and Chanika has been energizing. Once we got them past the orthodoxy of "that's how it's done in the Quarter" and onto the task of re-imagining the store so we might make some money, they really sparkled in their knowledge of how to get things done in this city.

I proposed a total re-vamp focusing more on a blend of local trade and tourism. I would invest money into some remodeling, and we'd embark on a hybrid concept incorporating a tea bar with desserts provided from local bakeries. We'd ramp up the occult aspect of the store and see if we could move some of the "haunted tours" to using our shop as a base for their sales.

Labor costs go way down. I have Sil, Pffif, and Shey working shifts. They all appear to enjoy it for their own reasons. Shey enjoys meeting people. Pffif enjoys catching shoplifters. And Sil - God knows what she enjoys, but sales are always strongest by far during her shift.

Today is an important day. Today we meet with the city about our changes. After hearing how things are done here in the Big Easy, I thought it best to meet these people before engaging architects and contractors. Sort of pre-greasing the gears so to speak; or more likely their palms.

Robert has experience with these folks. I'm going to follow his lead. I'll play the role of the young man following the older man's sage advice. That is until bullshit needs to be called.

We're meeting at the shop to discuss the plans for expansion. So, of course, I must load the deck by having both Sil and Shey there. I prep both of them that they must co-exist for the greater good. I emphasize it. Sil asks me if she'll have to play with any of the city guys.

I tell her honestly, "No." She seems very disappointed. Shey seems very disgusted. I very much wish this was over and we can just move on.

We get there, and the girls take their positions: Shey at the register and Sil at the floor. Chanika, Robert, and I are going over the pitch. The crux of the pitch is simple: new and local with enough sizzle for the tourist trade.

The city guys finally arrive, and Sil greets them. She walks them through the store, guiding them back to the garage where we are set up along with the catering and the presentation boards we've made up.

City guy, Charlie, obviously enjoys Sil's attention. Obviously, Sil knows this too. City guy Carl, I think, is gay. That generally poses little problem for Sil, or so she claims; lust is lust after all. However, it does mean that she is not paying the same attention to him.

I think it's the law of low-lying fruit: easiest always gets picked first.

I ask Sil to leave us and introduce myself to some raised eyebrows. Probably, because I look about nineteen years old. I go through my ownership credentials on the block and then touch on Robert and Chanika's long-standing retail experience in the quarter.

Robert takes over, and first thing points out the catering. After everybody serves themselves, he starts into the pitch. Chanika steps in to talk about the local tie-ins - bringing in the bakers and other retail. Robert takes it from there and begins to talk about what we need for build out, permits, etc.

This is happening. The city guys are engaged, I can tell. Then my phone rings – it's Jerry. I'll have to call him back. I won't be long. I click the call to voicemail. A few moments later, my phone lets me know he left a message.

I know he'll understand I couldn't get right to him.

Robert works through the questions of permits and inspections masterfully; setting the stage for what I hope is an easy renovation. Charlie and Carl seem sold.

Then it goes downhill.

Charlie takes me aside and lets me know, "I'd sure like to get to know that brunette hot-thing better."

"I'm not a matchmaker for my employees."

Robert, picking up on the conversation interjects himself.

"Hey, she just works here, but we may be able to arrange something. Maybe we can have her act as coordinator with your office."

Dang it, all but the wink-wink, nudge-nudge, say no more.

"Well, it don't look like I'll be needing a matchmaker, son," Charlie says.

I just smile and say, "Be careful, she's a man-eater."

He laughs. I laugh too. But I really want to throw up. He doesn't know what he's asking for.

Hands are shaken. Promises made. Goodbyes said. And I don't believe any of it. But that's business in the Big Easy. I just need to be flexible and not stress over it.

Robert, Chanika, and I post-mortem the meeting. They both feel it went great.

"You, know it would be good if you'd suggest to Sil that she take some time with Charlie," Robert says.

"Talk to her about it yourself."

That seems to placate him. I know she won't do a thing unless I allow her to. That buys some time, but the implications still weigh on me.

We all concur that it's all good and I'm free to call the architects and begin on the plans. So, on to phase two – and the spending of real money.

Then I remember that Jerry called. I pull up voicemail and listen to his message, but it's not him. Instead, it's some person with a decidedly Italian accent.

"Necromancer, you who consorts with devils, know that we have your blood kin. And know that we will spill that blood and end your family line unless you submit immediately to judgment. The abomination of your acts must be atoned for. Come to the home of your first born, alone. Prepare to be judged and punished for your sins."

I do the only logical thing I can think to do and call back. The same Italian voice answers the phone: "Necromancer, your time is waning."

"What is this about?" I ask.

I hear my son Jerry in the background spit out "Bastards!"

The Italian voice comes back on the line. "You will be here before the sunrise of the next day or the first line of your blood dies, followed by the next – call the police, and they will find your kin dead. Your actions in New Mexico were not unnoticed by the Church."

I start to reply but hear the click of the line hanging up. I try to call back, but it goes immediately to voicemail. The bastard turned off Jerry's phone.

New Mexico could only mean the fiasco at Hondo's. But how was that tracked to me? My head is reeling. The Church? I've got to book a flight. It sounds like they're going to kill me.

But better me than Jerry and Marge.

Chapter 8

I rush upstairs to see what flights can get me to Charlotte, fastest.

Shey and Sil are hot on my heels. All my summonlings converge on me. They know something is wrong as they are very sensitive to me. Being in the state of total panic and shock I am in, it must ring out like a school bell.

Shey is first to pipe up, "What happened?"

"Someone's taken Jerry hostage. They know about the Hondo thing."

I play the voicemail. Hjuul growls. Sil gasps.

"I need to book a flight and get there immediately."

"Who's the damn church," Pffif asks.

"No way to know, sir."

I sit down in front of the computer and prepare to search for airfare. A stark white hand with pointed black nails sets atop my hand, stopping me. It's Arix, all glamour dropped, looking very serious.

"My wielder, did it occur to you that they could have someone waiting for you at the airport? You will be without us, vulnerable. Even with proper wardings, multiple gunshots might prove fatal."

I spin that scenario through my mind amidst all the other swirling thoughts. It makes sense. These are obviously ruthless people with no concerns about harming the innocent. So I make plans to fly into Asheville versus Charlotte/Douglas airport. I arrange a rental van. It adds three hours' drive time, but arriving in advance of sunrise would not be an issue at all.

We work out a very simple plan; arrive at the airport, get a van. Summon everyone and get to Jerry's. Shey will go Tinkerbelle size and provide reconnaissance before approaching Jerry's block. Inside the block, Pffif will scout up close, as he's the innately sneaky one of the group. Pffif will report back, and we improvise from there.

I remind my merry band of summonlings that this is a rescue mission – not an assault.

"We'll be getting 'em out safe, Master Arthur – ye can count on it," Pffif says.

Arix, of course, has to add his two cents.

"The Clurichaun is correct, we will ensure no harm comes to your family, and if needed, we will bring woe to our enemies. Now, dismiss us and call us when you are ready. Time is passing."

I dismiss them one by one, making promises of a quick return. I bolt downstairs and tell Robert the bad news that a family emergency has come up and we'll be without staff. He protests. It's not up for discussion. He can close the store if he wants until I return.

I'm sure he thinks I'm crazy. I don't care.

I go to the car, then to the airport and finally off to the gate for Asheville. If only they allowed firearms in your carry-ons, I would feel much more secure. I have worries that someone is waiting for me here. Nothing happens – thank goodness.

While waiting for departure, I dial up Jerry's cell number to let the captors know I am coming. No answer – "This phone is not in service at this time." I try again – same. I feel my blood pressure exploding. I call Jerry's landline. I get voicemail and leave a nondescript message

"I will be there, please confirm you got this message."

The flight up is hell. I am nothing but nerves. I am nervous for Jerry and Marge. I am also kicking myself for putting them in this situation. Why did they disconnect Jerry's cell? I pray for Jerry's and Marge's well being. I pray for strength. I pray that Dory and God will look over us all.

Too many thoughts, too much time to do nothing...

Getting off the plane at 11:05 p.m. is a relief, I can take some action. I make straight for the after-hours rental pick up. An eternity later at 11:30, I have the keys and the van. At this point, I am ahead of sunrise by at least five hours. I pull out of the lot and head in the direction of Charlotte.

After a while, I pull off at what appears to be a rural exit and move over to the shoulder - no eyes, no cameras. Getting out, I open the rear doors to the panel van and begin to summon my troops one by one, ushering them inside. Each asks me for news; I tell each there is no news.

Arix wolf-sizes Hjuul after asking, "why can't the beast wait in the white?"

I remind him that summoning anyone in the middle of a neighborhood is asking for attention.

I put myself behind the wheel and set us back on the highway. I make sure to obey speed limits though my heart wants my foot to put more lead into it. Being pulled over will only create delay, not to mention potentially raising some questions about the folk in the back. Caution is good; we have time.

During the ride, my mouth is engaged continually, going over what ifs.

"What if they have guns? What if there are explosives? What kind of traps could they set? Do they understand the nature of summonlings or do they think I'm a true necromancer?"

Everyone shares in nervous conversation. Everyone except Arix and Sil. Arix because he doesn't seem or sound nervous at all; in fact, he sounds supremely confident and in a way that is reassuring. I'm sure that's what he intends. Sil, though, is silent. Not a peep the entire time. So I bend the mirror to survey what's going on.

Sil is in the very back. Her eyes are closed, and she's intent on something. Then I notice that her hand is inside her skirt and she appears to be rubbing away slowly. I'm sure none of the others said anything because she does that all the time without regard.

"For the love of Christ, Sil!" I bark back.

She jumps to awareness, startled. "Oh, sorry!"

"What the hell– Sil - is this getting in the way of your personal time? Should we have left you home?"

I am totally pissed and judging by her reaction, that anger is leaching through my every word and smacking her with an almost physical response. I learned a while back that when I get very, very angry with them, it causes them real, almost physical discomfort. And the opposite holds, when I am very pleased with them, it's like euphoria.

"I'm sorry, it's a nervous habit… There's something about this situation that feels more wrong than I can explain." She looks over from me in the mirror to Arix. "I am very uncomfortable."

Arix immediately jumps her case; his glowing purple eye opening in all its horrific glory.

"What is it that bothers you temptress other than our wielder's very life and legacy has been threatened? What do you have to say?"

In the mirror, I see her blanch away from Arix's glaze, the soft purplish glow of his open third eye adding more light to the back. She turns her eyes to me in the mirror, but only for a moment as Arix barks, "Well?" Her eyes return downward.

Shey, in tiny Tinkerbelle mode, has my ear.

"Do you think she'll fight?"

Sil animates immediately.

"Of course I will, Pixie! How dare you! You are not the only one who has watched Arthur's family grow… bitch."

Sil turns away toward the rear doors - scowling, pouting, sullen and just maybe, scared.

Damn it. We don't need to be fighting among ourselves. Before I can pipe up, Arix booms, "This will stop now!" in the voice of doom.

I swerve the van because a foghorn just went off in the back. Shey falls off my shoulder into the crevice between my seat and the door.

In a lower more controlled tone, Arix continues. "We can all return to our petty differences after we rescue our wielder's family."

There is a silent pause.

"I be agreein' with ye on that, demon, gods help me," Pffif adds leaning back from the front seat.

Hjuul barks.

Vets adds, "Indeed."

Shey flits back on my shoulder and says nothing; which is good.

Sil, motionless and not looking at anyone, says, "Let's just get this done."

"Oh, it shall be done, temptress," Arix says.

The purplish light goes away. Arix has closed that eye of his.

The next hour goes by quickly and is relatively quiet. Shey sits on the dashboard, and I go over what we need in aerial reconnaissance. She is very engaged; this isn't her first dance.

We pull into Myer's Park, and I park us two blocks down the street from Jerry's house.

I tell Shey, "We have a little over three and a half hours until sunrise, so be thorough, but don't take too long."

I roll the window down. Shey kisses me lightly on the cheek and buzzes out the window, shrinking even more.

Now we wait. I think I'm going to be sick.

Shey returns after fifteen minutes and I manage to not have puked from the tension. Her report is to the point: "I see nobody in any of the cars around the house. I did not see where anyone was spying from other houses. There is nobody in any of the little forests around the houses. The lights are on at Jerry's, but I saw no movement. I believe it is safe to approach."

"Thanks, Shey. Are you sure you didn't miss anything?"

She looks at me hurt.

"This is serious, Shey, I have to ask, and you have to consider it."

She nods and closes her eyes. I assume she's reviewing her sortie. She opens her eyes, "I am sure."

I look over to Pffif in the seat next to me, "You're up."

He nods and begins to do a quick inventory inside of his red lined jacket: lock picks, daggers, climbing cord, and flask. I ask for the flask.

"Me flask?"

"Yes, not the time for liquid courage. We need the real thing."

"Aye," he says, and hands it over.

I twist the key in the ignition, and slowly move the van down the block, stopping two houses before Jerry's.

"I'll be vera sneaky, figurin' at least one of 'em has true sight," Pffif tells us. "Donna you have a worry," then he winks, opens the door and slips outside.

Time to wait again. Hello, butterflies… Let me introduce you to my stomach. At least we still have hours before sunrise.

Twenty-seven minutes later the door opens, and Pffif jumps into the car. He is trembling, and tears are streaming from his eyes.

He looks over to me and in a low quivering voice says, "Master Arthur, they been killed, most badly… Jerry and Marge… They be dead."

Chapter 9

My heart stops. I can't breathe. Like a shock from two electric paddles in the emergency room comes a blood-curdling screech of "No!" from the back of the van.

Sil.

I spin around to see two eyes blazing luminescent green. In what feels like slow motion, she tears from the back of the van toward us. Vets tries to stand in the way and is cast aside like a paper doll. There is a purplish light, and I hear a word of power. Sil flies backward, crashing through the rear van doors, spilling out onto the street head over heels, and landing sprawled out on the pavement.

Arix.

He looks back to me and hisses, "We don't have time for this foolery!" and stalks out of the van toward Sil.

I look to Pffif, who is outright crying. Shey, making him look like a giant in comparison, is looking up at him, saying "Please… no."

Hjuul is hyperventilating. Vets raises herself up from the back of the van. I hear Arix tell Sil "Compose yourself."

The light on the top of the post away from us blinks on and off. The insects swarming around it don't seem to care about any of it.

There is a sick clarity to this moment. The clarity of knowing my only son and his wife are no more. There are sounds around me now, but none of them breaks through this wall of clarity. My world implodes. There is nothing but me and pain: Dory, Jerry, Marge - all gone.

How? Why? I was early. I called. I did everything asked of me. Why? My pain begins to turn to rage.

I feel a hand on my arm that brings me back – Arix.

"We all need to calm ourselves and evaluate the next moves."

I don't want to hear that. He looks at me, the third eye still open.

"You can be sure they are."

I look over to Pffiferil who is trying to compose himself.

"Are those bastards still there?"

He nods no. "Bests I be tellin', they done the deed hours ago."

Arix interjects, squeezing my arm again, "My wielder, they may have left something. If they did, we might scry their location."

The van tips lightly and all attention shifts. Sil climbs back in. She looks at me and then looks away, shaking her head.

"Close the damn doors," I say. "We're heading to Jerry's."

The rear doors close and we slowly make our way up to Jerry's pulling into the driveway.

"I left the back-door open. But what you see in there, you don't want to be seein'.

I know he's right, but what I don't want to see comes second.

What I must see comes first.

We leave the van and enter the house, except for Hjuul, who I ask to cover our backs. Pffif warns me not to touch anything – all those episodes of CSI must have left a mark. I walk into the kitchen and look at the landline phone. There are no voicemails. They must have listened to my message; they knew I was coming.

Pffif takes me by the forearm, and we go upstairs. He stops us before Jerry and Marge's bedroom.

"Ye step through that door and ye cannot unsee what is there."

I tell him with my eyes that I understand. He lets go of my arm and opens the door.

The carpet is blood-soaked. Jerry, my only son, lies curled on the floor, his neck cut wide open. His eyes look upward, and his face is in a grimace. Marge is suspended by one leg hanging from the ceiling fan. She has been violated with a curling iron. Her belly is splayed, and her entrails dangle from her. Her eyes are open too, and her face in agony.

It is horror. More than anything I saw in world war two.

And I saw horror there.

I take a deep breath. I hear Shey gasp, cry, and then run back down the stairs. I hear Pffif take a deep breath and feel his hand on my back. I hear a dull thud and turn around. Sil has fallen to her knees and is staring blankly in the doorway.

Arix pushes her aside and enters. Sil's head bounces off the door jamb. She doesn't seem to notice, she just stares blankly at Jerry and Marge. I try to make eye contact with her, but nobody's home.

Arix immediately assesses the room. "I only see evidence of one assailant, there is one set of footprints in the carpet. Based on the size of his foot I would say just under six feet tall, wearing dress shoes." He opens his monstrous third eye and scans the room. After a moment, he walks toward Marge and looks about. He reaches into the blood-soaked bedding under her and produces a golden-hilted dagger.

"This we can use to scry their location."

In my mind, the words police evidence scream out.

"Police evidence," I say absently.

Arix looks at me with all three eyes and says, "The human police? Perhaps they find these beasts in a few months, maybe a few weeks? What damage to your family could they do in that time? We find them now and put them down."

He closes the third eye and holds up the dagger with two fingers. He's right. I ask him to let me see the dagger. The hilt is ornate. On it is a symbol of a crown with two keys in a cross mounted on the round pommel. I've seen it before, but can't focus to think where.

Then it comes to me: the Church. It's the Roman Catholic Church. The insignia is definitely papal. Damn, this is a witch-hunt. Torquemada all over again.

But when did the Inquisition take to killing the families of the accused? This evening apparently …

I look around at the horror. I want to hug Jerry. I want to take Marge down from the fan. I want all of this to never have happened.

Pffif snaps me out of my thoughts.

"Time to be a-goin' Master Arthur – or time to be calling the police."

The choice is there. Find these bastards, or hope the police can.

"Let's go," is my answer.

I turn to head out and go downstairs, Sil is gone – just as well. We make our way downstairs, and I go over to the phone in the kitchen where the message machine is. I take a paper towel out and take the phone off the hook.

"Get in the van and get ready to go," I tell everyone. They head out. I punch in 9-1-1. No way am I leaving Jerry and Marge like that. No way. I let the phone fall to the ground and leave.

We make our way to interstate seventy-seven, and I'm desperate to find a hotel. I have to think, have to plan. I need to find these bastards. The van is silent. All are waiting to hear from me. Except for Arix.

"Get a map of the town, we will find them," he says.

I pull off at an exit that has a Carriage Motor House Motel and a Shell. I send Pffif in for a map at the Shell. I get us a room at the Carriage.

We all pile into the room. Arix takes the map and tears a strip off of one of the towels. He tears the strip again to make it even thinner and attaches it to the end of the dagger. He stretches the map across the table and suspends the dagger by the ragged cloth. He closes his eyes and silently mutters unintelligible words while spinning the dagger around the map. His body sways, and he releases the dagger. It embeds in the map and the table beneath.

He comes out of his trance and looks down. "They are found."

Vets pulls her sword and says, "I am ready."

My head is swimming with thoughts of revenge. Then for whatever reason, another thought enters to muddy the water further. Revenge won't bring Jerry and Marge back but will put blood on my hands. Is that how I want my great-greats to remember me? Or if I do nothing, then they might get away with it. Or come after other family members. He said they would…

I come back to the moment, as Arix sets his hand upon my shoulder. "I feel your conflict, my wielder, as I am sure we all do. These vermin have committed an act that must be responded to." His eyes pan from me to around the room. "If this was a slap to the face we must respond with a closed fist. To do anything less is to encourage and embolden them. If these cowards even for a moment feel that they can cause us harm without retribution, they will certainly bring more death upon our wielder's family. They have said as much. This is war upon you and ours - you must act. Or other generations will pay."

He is right. What I saw was beyond atrocity. It was a message to me. It is war. I look at the map and ask, "what say you all?"

Shey doesn't hesitate – "The fuckers need to die."

Vets agrees with a fist thump to her chest armor.

Pffif nods gravely and says, "aye."

And Sil is silent. Again, she is in her own world, touching herself, leg raised over the wooden chair onto the a/c unit with one hand disappearing under her leather skirt and the other slowly running through her hair. Her eyes are open this time and gazing out the window. My anger registered with her before my words even had a chance to come out, as she sits up straight in the chair and looks at me.

"I told you, it's a nervous habit!" She takes a deep breath and looks around. "Nothing good can come from this. But I will stand with you if that is what you choose." She looks back outside, and I see a tear run down her cheek.

What a manipulator. Go bring on the waterworks. Next up, she has to console me. Right…

The real truth is we are going to bring it to those bastards.

I turn to Arix, "So where are they?"

Arix examines the map where the dagger stabbed into it. "It appears they are around the streets of Buchannon and Dilworth."

I enter those streets into mapping software on my phone. The most likely culprit is The Cathedral of Saint Patrick.

I think it's time to visit the church. But I won't be the one paying penance today.

Chapter 10

Midway to the Cathedral, I stop us and grab my phone. I am besieged with questions of "Are we there?" and "What are we doing?" A quick browse of the internet and I have what I need.

"We need weapons. We're heading to Fat Daddy's and Pffif – you're going to get them for me. Get your lockpicks ready."

"Aye, Master Arthur," he says, and immediately fishes them out.

"We have more than enough magical firepower," Arix says.

"It's not up for discussion. We can get you a gun too."

Arix sneers.

"I'll take one," Sil says.

Pffif turns around to her pointing a finger, "Consider it done, demoness."

"Anyone else," I ask.

Vets of course pipes up, "twelve-gauge shotgun or large caliber semi-automatic rifle."

I look to Shey, who reaches into one of the folds of her dress and pulls out the small cylinder that expands into her bow. I've seen that thing in action back in the war – she doesn't need a gun. It contracts in her hand, and she puts it away. There is a full arsenal, knives, short-swords, the bow, an unlimited quiver - all locked away in that light flowing dress; it's some kind of fae dimensional magic I could never understand.

All needs discussed, I take us to Fat Daddy's. I park us across the street. "Get going Pffif."

He climbs out the front door, and away he goes. I wait a bit, knowing that he's scouting. Then, poof, he appears at the front door. He clambers up the security grate a bit, jumps down, and looks back at us. He puts his hands over his eyes telling me to look away. He can't go invisible if someone is looking at him. So we do.

I keep looking out for police and listening for alarms. Eventually, the door opens, and Pffif hurls his thief bag onto the seat. The thief bag is an amazing item. It's a dimensional pocket and can hold an enormous amount of stuff – assuming it can fit in the top. I have no idea how it works; more fae magic.

"We best be a-goin' now."

Hint taken, I put us back on track to the Cathedral. As I drive to our destination, Pffif pulls what appears to be a Remington shotgun out of the bag and hands it backward.

I hear Vets' approval, "Six in the magazine, one in the chamber – this will do." Pffif digs into the bag some more and pulls out a box of shells and tosses them back.

"Birdshot?" comes Vets' deep and disappointed sounding voice.

"Ach!" is Pffif's reply and he digs back in the bag, head first. Pffif's head comes out of the bag with another box in hand that he tosses back.

"Much better – Bandolier?" asks Vets.

"Ach! It be a pawn shop, warrior."

Another round of digging and he produces a smaller handgun, I presume a nine millimeter. He reaches around the seat, "Here ya go, wench," and tosses it back to Sil.

I hear a very demure, "Thank you, Mister Pffiferil." Another round of search the bag and toss the ammo back occurs. We are all quiet, except for the clicking sound of loading ammunition.

I see the distinct architecture of the Cathedral and my stomach drops a bit. I pull into the parking lot nestled in the rear of the complex and turn off the van.

I look to Pffif, "Weapons, please."

In goes his head and upper body into the bag again. He comes out bearing two weapons, one appears to be a Smith & Wesson .357 snub nose revolver; excellent in close quarters. The other appears to be a Sig nine millimeter. Ammo, extra clips and holster follow.

I arm myself and give the next command.

"Arix, wards up, me last."

The purple glow of his eye washes over the van, and with soft mutterings, he begins to cover us in invisible armor. After a few moments, I feel the ward wash over me. Better than Kevlar, but not as durable. I'd rather have both, but that's not happening – except for Vets who is fully armor-clad. She is now officially the tank of our group.

"Arix, make sure they're here," is my next command. He makes his way to the front of the van and sticks his arm through the front seats, palm extended. He places the dagger in his palm and orients the tip of the blade away from the buildings. There is a pulse of brighter purple light from his eye, and he says, "Where." The dagger spins ninety degrees.

The rectory - thank goodness. I do not cherish the thought of laying waste to the Cathedral itself. At one time I considered myself a good Catholic but somewhat drifted away in my explorations of better understanding what had been given to me. I close my eyes and pray, calling to Jesus in apology for what I am about to do and wishing that he get his house in order.

I open my eyes and say, "Amen."

Arix scoffs.

"So, stealth or assault?" I ask. "We have two floors to contend with. Arix, which floor is our target on?"

"One moment, my wielder." Arix turns toward the rectory and holds the dagger point down in between his palms so it can swivel up and down. "Where," he whispers again. The dagger pivots upward – the second floor.

"Stealth, then," comes Vets' deep voice from the rear. "Better to have high ground fighting out than fight against high ground going in."

We all nod in agreement.

I give the orders. "Pffif, scout ahead – take out security. Shey – you're with him above. Take out any interference quietly. Return when it's safe to enter." The front door opens, and Pffif jumps out, Shey buzzing out the door after him.

I lean back over the front seat, "Assuming we can get in quietly, I need you to point us in the right direction, Arix." He nods in acknowledgment. "We use hand signals, like in the old days. We get in, we whack the bastard good, and we get out."

"What about information, Master Arthur?" Arix asks quietly, "Surely these thugs did not work without orders. We need to know from where, as we may have to take the head off the snake. May I suggest, that we incapacitate him and take him to interrogate – or allow me the time at least to rip through his mind?"

Damn, if he isn't right again. "Okay," I reply, "No taking him with us unless he can resist you Arix. Just leave me enough, so he knows who finishes him."

I am going to finish this monster, and it will not be pretty, or too terribly quick. Images of Jerry and Marge flash through my mind and my fists clench. Payback will be a bitch.

Minutes later the front door opens and Pffif reports. "Security ana phones be down. All be quiet scepts' for one in the kitchen. Locks be picked ana doors be open." Shey expands to her more normal size. I brief them on stealth approach – they remember the drill. Pffif asks everyone to look away.

We all pile out of the van; I have Arix restore Hjuul to his regular form. I whisper to him that he is to take the rear and remind him of our stealthy ambitions. He nods his massive head in understanding.

Good dog.

We make our way quickly to the open front door and enter. I am on point, gun drawn. Arix is behind me with the dagger. Shey is behind us, followed by Sil and Hjuul. Who knows where Pffif is. I would guess ahead.

I make it about six stairs up when the person from the kitchen appears. Shocked at the sight of this other than human crew, he drops his coffee mug on the hardwood floor. Hjuul whips toward him as if to lunge. The man's eyes bulge in fear. Sil's hand quickly grabs Hjuul by the scruff, stopping him, and then she releases him with a pet as if to say, "I have this." She makes eye contact with the man and puts a finger to her lips as to say, "Shhh." He is fixated on her and caught in a paralysis of fear, confusion, and seduction. Sil walks over to him, locking in on his eyes, whispering quietly, "It's okay."

My eyes dart upstairs, partly because I don't want to be surprised and partly because I just don't want to watch her devour his soul, but like a train wreck, my eyes can't stay away.

Sil is right next to him now. She smiles. He smiles. She brushes her hand across his cheek, then rests it behind his head. Her lips brush against his in a gentle passing kiss. Her eyes close. His eyes close. Her other hand reaches up to take him by the chin.

I look back upstairs because I can't watch her eat his spirit; there are multiple wrongnesses to it. Then, there's a wet cracking sound, which causes me to look back down again. The man's head is turned ninety degrees, and Sil has him suspended in the air by it. No soul sucks deluxe, and that's okay with me. With a quick heave, he's now over her shoulder. She turns, looks at me, and signs me to go up with a pointing finger.

At the top of the stairs, I take a quick look in both directions, and all is clear. Quietly I move into the hall, putting my back against the wall facing the stairs and beckon Arix for a reading. He lays the dagger in his hand and with a whisper, it spins to the right. I sign him to figure out what room, followed by instructing Shey to cover the opposite hallway from the stairs.

Vets and Hjuul are given orders to stay. I indicate to Sil to come up and take my place. If we do get a roamer, she can hopefully take care of it silently again. I move down the hall watching Arix and the dagger. Four doors down, he points.

We have the bastard.

I signal Vets to come up and cover the hall where Arix is, and I will be. Hjuul is directed to hold the stairs and cover our flanks from below. I check the time: 5:17a.m. I'm still well early for sunrise.

Good, I think – I hate to be late.

I make my way to the door, revolver in hand. I let Arix know to be ready. I check the knob silently – not locked. I look back to Vets, and then to Arix. I signal "on three" – I count it down, swiftly open the door, and enter.

A golden-hilted dagger bounces off of my chest, thanks to the wards. Another flies in my direction, and I jump to the right.

Our target cries out "Necromancer!" in that Italian accent, and I know for a fact he's our guy. He is a skinny, greasy looking man with a receding hairline and pencil-thin mustache. He looks at me and spits out, "Prepararsi alla morte!" I fire my gun, and he flies back against the wall, leaving a reddish-brown spatter behind him from the wound to his shoulder.

All stealth is officially gone.

The murderer bounces back up again, and I put another round into his right leg, hobbling him. Arix strides into the room eye ablaze, gestures at the man and issues a black bolt of energy into him, which elicits a groan from the bastard as he crumbles to the ground.

I look at Arix, "Take him and leave something for me."

Arix quickly makes his way to the murderous motherfucker and hoists him up by the good arm.

Quick as a hiccup, using his injured arm, the Italian jabs Arix in his third eye. Arix is startled and releases him, stumbling back. Then our target jumps out the second story window six feet away. I fire reflexively.

I believe I got another round into him on his way out. I hear the thunder of Vet's shotgun in the hall, with repetitive fire.

I rush to the window and look out. The Italian is sprawled on the ground face down, not moving. I hear pistol fire; Sil is engaging the enemy now. We'll visit the Italian on the way out – he's not going anywhere

I turn from the window and Arix is wading into battle in the hallway. I follow quickly. There is one body in the hallway. There appear to be two combatants on Sil's end of the hall that are armed. On our side Vets is nowhere to be seen, so I presume she's gone into one of the rooms to flush someone out.

A door down and across the hall from me opens, and a shot is fired, missing me by about a foot. I immediately jump across the hallway to force him to exit if he wants to get a shot at me. Instead, he slams the door shut. Another volley of bullets whistles down the hall from the other side. I hear Arix respond with a spell and smell sulfurous fire.

I step out in front of the door, and well up the hate inside of me as Arix taught me. I holster the pistol and use both hands to pull that black, hateful power out and shape it. I name it mentally and call it – "Tznok!" casting it forward in a powerful wave. The door splinters, the jamb caves in, and the wave continues into the room.

I hear, "Damn!" coming from inside the room along with the windows breaking.

I follow the wave in and see the thug getting up; he gets off a shot before I do. It crashes into my shoulder, and I feel the ward shatter and deep radiating pain screams from my pectoral muscle. I get off the next shot, and it hits him in the mid-section pushing him back against the wall and creating red spatter at the exit.

I feel myself moving toward him, fast. I hear myself screaming, "Why! Why! Why!" while unloading another shot that hits him in the hip and third in the chest area. "Click. Click. Click," is the sound of my empty weapon.

I stand atop of him and smack the gun from his hand.

"You bastards killed my son." I snarl at him. "Have a taste of hell."

I drop my gun and look him in the eyes.

"What?" he gasps.

I reach back into the deep well of hate, creating a mass of sickening dark energy that I extend to my hand. Then I jam my hand into his stomach and release it into him as a coil, feeling it connect with his life force. There is a sense of confusion about him that I feel strongly. Then, envisioning that black vortex, I speak the word, "Vnaam" and pull the black coil back to me – along with his life force attached to it.

It's a rush, his very life flowing into me. He grimaces and tries to shout out – but he can't grasp a breath. I am getting stronger. He is getting weaker. I see an image of Jerry and Marge in my mind and pull hard on the black coil with my desire as Arix showed me. There is a wheezing sound, and the thug turns into a desiccated mummified shell of a man. His life is mine.

I feel like a superman! Power courses through me. I know I will kill them all! I will burn down this false church and send a message that cannot be mistaken for those who would harm me and mine.

But my moment of exaltation is interrupted by the combat in the hall.

Vets' voice calls out – "Paladin!"

Chapter 11

I run to the hallway door quickly scanning toward the stairs. Shey is sending volleys of arrows toward a doorway. Sil is looking down the hall in my direction, wide-eyed. I duck back in and then stick my head out again to look the other way.

In the hall, there is a large man with wet hair and wearing only a towel. He is holding a great sword. Directly in front of him, a pile of ectoplasmic goo steams away to nothing that must have been Vets

Arix says, "Essha Tornu," followed by, "Curses Paladin!"

That spell must not have gone as planned.

I step into the hall and call out, "Hjuul, here – now!"

That gets me the full attention of the towel-clad man. That attention shifts when he sees the four hundred pound wolf-monster barreling off the stairs and down the hall toward him. He shifts backward and takes the sword back in both hands, awaiting the onslaught. I notice a glow emanating from the weapon.

Figuring him to be occupied, I reach down to my arm and summon back Vets to the battlefield.

I hear Hjuul's mighty roar as he goes into an airborne lunge at the towel-clad man. The man, intent on Hjuul, steps to the side and with one strike cleaves Hjuul's head clean off. Hjuul's body continues in momentum all the while liquefying and beginning to steam away.

Damn. Curses indeed, Paladin.

But Vets is back, and she wades into battle immediately. Sword versus sword, Vets, takes a mighty downwards strike, no doubt intending to bring the big man to his knees. The swords meet, and Vets' sword shatters. Undaunted, she holds on to the hilt and lands a crushing forearm blow to the man's head. He reels back from the impact, and she drives into him with the broken hilt which he barely manages to turn with his sword. With a mighty "Rawr!" Vets pushes on, letting go of the hilt completely and grabbing the man's sword hand.

He collides with the wall, and Vets pummels him with her free arm. The plaster breaks in behind him from the force of the blows.

I pull the 9-mm and take aim. No clear shot.

Then in a tactically brilliant move, the Paladin peels the towel from his waist and throws it over Vets' helmet while kicking her away. I pull the gun back up and take a shot, but he's already ducked into a roll putting him behind Vets.

Vets spins around to meet him. But the big man is ready first. With a cleaving blow, his sword now glowing again, he splits her in half through the midsection. Through the armor. Through her. Like a hot knife through table-warm butter.

I am awed. So much so that I haven't taken the shot, which gives our now naked adversary, time to grab one of the hall tables and flip it up as an ad-hoc wooden tower shield. Arix approaches the man, his fingers nimbly forming some magical attack.

"Turn unclean beast!" the Paladin shouts, keeping the table toward me, but holding out one hand toward Arix. Arix recoils and then runs into the Italian's room. I put a round into the table just to see what happens.

Gun still fixed on him; I see Sil has joined the hunt. She stalks forward, eyes locked toward his. She does the shush thing. I hear her say, "It's okay." I hear him say, "Yes," and the table drops slightly. She closes the gap with him.

Then, like a roaring lion exploding from the bushes – sixty pounds of the oak table comes flying at me, knocking me to the ground.

I look up to see the expression on Sil's face as one of shock and fear as it tumbles freely to the ground from her shoulders, beginning to liquefy along with her falling body.

I am the next target. We make eye contact, and he stalks toward me. But Arix's return stalls him; I flip the oak table off of me. He pounces toward Arix and with a driving blow, shoves the sword through his third eye; finishing Arix off by pulling it out through the top of his head.

He's two steps from me now. I lunge for the nine millimeter and turn toward him.

He's stopped in his tracks. He has silver arrows protruding from his body. Pffif appears behind him, dagger in hand. With what can only be a sixth sense, the naked Paladin mule kicks little Pffif into the wall, leaving him a crumpled mess.

Another arrow embeds itself in him – then another. What is this guy made of? I think to myself as Shey's arrows usually go totally through people.

So, it's time to find out if he's lead resistant. I take aim and fire. Leg. Leg. Shoulder. Stomach.

He's not lead resistant and falls to the ground. I spring up from my crouch, run over to him, and kick that vile sword away.

He looks up to me, and in a strange Nordic accent says, "You will pay for this evil."

So I stomp on his sternum about where his liver should be.

"You first, asshole." I toss my gun down and look into his agonized, but defiant eyes, "This is for murdering my son."

His eyes turn quizzical, and he attempts to squeeze out some excuse I don't want to hear, "Your son?"

A quick kick to the groin shuts that up. I concentrate, again reaching down into my ever-bubbling cauldron of hate and begin to pull the coil of sickening dark energy to my hand again.

I smile at him, "Let me give you a hand."

And then two gunshots go off rocking his head sideways followed by a crimson and grey splatter.

Shey. She is standing to his side, my 9-mm in hand, glowering at me.

"No! Not like that!" She is furious at me. "That is foul, unclean magic and I will not have you tarnish your soul like that!"

The black coil in the meantime has nowhere to go and is growing inside me, calling me to release it to hurt and destroy.

"Damn it, Shey, he was mine!" I scream at her in absolute rage. She grabs onto her head and falls to her knees from the concussion of my magically enhanced anger and malice.

The black coil is inside me, twisting and hungry, calling for release. So I put my hand on the nearest wall and release it. The wall immediately sprouts mold and begins weeping a foul-smelling substance.

I stare at the wall for a moment, realizing that was in me. Shey slowly picks herself up, shaking. She continues admonishing me.

"You'll be no better than demon scum if you go down that road. What would Dory think, you sucking the life out of people like a vampire? It's nasty, addictive magic, and you know better!"

I nod to her, not wanting to discuss it or to tell her what I just did moments ago. I give her instructions to tend to Pffif and begin re-summoning my wiped out troops. Once all together, I instruct Hjuul to clear the first floor and howl if another Paladin shows up.

Shey says, very lightly, "I don't understand. A Paladin should have never allowed what happened at Jerry's."

Pffif chimes in weakly with an "Aye."

Arix, of course, had the answer: "No doubt this corruption has stretched to all elements of that organization. How many good people have died in the name of holiness, after all? They are zealots, and we are obviously at a new age of inquisition."

It makes sense to me.

Pffif shakes his head, "Naa, it don't make sense."

"We need to go now," Sil says.

Arix agrees, "We can sort this out later."

We make our way downstairs and Hjuul greets us, meaning downstairs is clear. I look over to Arix and give him the orders: "Burn it down. No witnesses. No evidence."

The rest of us go to the van. A moment later Arix returns. Black smoke is beginning to billow out the upstairs window. That leaves only one more detail – the Italian. I pull the van around to the back, where he should be laying or trying to crawl away.

But he's not there. What in the name of Dante's Inferno is going on? I jump out of the van and see bloodied tracks leading to the six-foot tall wooden fence. Blood is on the fence. How the heck did this guy climb that fence after two or three gunshot wounds and a two-story pancake fall?

Shey calls out, "We have to go!" She's right. I tear off a piece of my shirt and dab it in the dark brown blood, finding it hard to believe it's turning that color already. I get back in the van and head down the alley, turning onto Dilworth Street, slowly.

We drive away like nothing's going on. After a few blocks, a fire truck passes us – sirens and lights engaged. I hear other vehicles joining.

I hand Arix the bloody swatch and say, "Find the bastard."

Chapter 12

We pull back into the Carriage House without incident. I dismiss everyone and exit the van alone. Once inside the room, I call back my team, touching one glyph at a time.

I turn on the TV and switch to the local news. Coverage of the inferno at St. Patrick's Cathedral is on. Firefighters struggle with the blaze… No apparent survivors. The rectory housed three full-time staff including the beloved Father Melvin Ploughman. His photo graces the screen – it's the man from downstairs that Sil took out. They begin to go through his accomplishments.

Next up for sure will be people crying and speaking of him in reverence. I turn off the TV, feeling more than a little uneasy. Was that man in league with the brutal murderers of my son? They were staying in his house, eating his bread, enjoying his hospitality; the rationalization makes me feel a little better.

"We got lucky with the Paladin," Shey says. "If he were wearing his armor, we'd have been done for."

"Aye," Pffif agrees. "Ana, it don't make no sense at all that one of 'em would be mixed up in any of this. Foul deeds ana the Paladin order donna mix."

Arix scoffs, "The evidence speaks for itself."

"Enough already," I say.

I'm becoming quite agitated. I know the Italian was behind this and an armed contingent only points to complicity. At least that's how I continue to rationalize it to myself.

"Arix, use the damn swatch and find the bastard."

Arix goes over to the table where the city map is still laid out.

"Pffiferil, give me one of your lockpicks," he says.

He begins to fashion his dousing rod.

While Arix is making preparations, Shey walks over to Sil. She is sitting in a corner on the floor, her arms and tail around her legs and chin resting on her knees.

"You know this isn't right."

Sil looks up at Shey.

"I've already said that."

Shey puts her hands on her hips and sticks her head down at Sil.

"There's something you're not telling us, I can tell! You are not acting normal. Spill it... right now."

"Shut up, little bitch.".

"I can't concentrate with this female babble," Arix says. "Perhaps good Silithes, if there is something so terrible you wish the master to know, you can whisper it in my ear and I can share it on your behalf."

Shey turns to me. "She'd probably just be a big liar-liar anyways." She turns back to Sil and sticks her tongue out at her.

Sil stands up. Shey steps back and bows up ready for a scrap. Sil points a finger at Shey.

"Fuck you." Then she points it at Arix – "And fuck you more. Do your job sorcerer and stay out of my affairs."

Arix bristles and opens his third eye.

"Something you wish the master to know?"

"No, nothing I wish our wielder to know, but yes, something I will share!" She looks at him coldly, then over to me – "Bind me to speak only the truth."

"How do I do that?" I ask.

We both look over to Arix, who has now closed his eye and appears very uncomfortable.

"Yes Arixtumin," Sil purrs, "wouldn't that be one of the first things a good teacher would share with a new wielder?"

Arix stammers.

"Never mind," Sil continues, "I swear what I am to speak is the truth by all my essence and all my power. Now you command me to tell the truth of this with feeling and authority and do so using my full name, Arthur. We will be done with this."

Her head cocks and her eyes go steely on Shey.

This is awkward and not the least bit untimely. The Italian is digging in somewhere.

"Fine, but let's get back on track… Silithes, I command you to tell the truth."

Shey rolls her eyes. I must have done it wrong.

"I have made an oath and been bid to the truth by my master."

Sil's eyes turn to Arix, boring a hole in him, causing him to uncharacteristically turn away, and then her eyes turn back to me.

"Arthur, I… I have care for your family. Jerry, I felt a particular kinship with."

"Yes, that weakness might be considered embarrassing in Helterezen," Arix quickly interjects. "May I get back to work? You can be embarrassed at your weakness later."

Shey looks at Sil curiously and puts her hands back on her hips.

"Enough already," I say gently to interrupt Shey before she gets started. "Let's stay focused on the Italian. Sil, I understand that particular emotion is in conflict with your moral upbringing and laws. But in this case, it is much appreciated."

I turn back to Arix.

"Now find that fucking Italian."

Moments pass while Arix waves the lockpick over the map. He finally looks up.

"He's not in the city."

"He be dead?" asks Pffif.

"No, he is not, I feel a spell link has been made; he is just not in the area of this map."

"You sure he's alive?" I ask.

"I am positive, my wielder."

I realize we need another map. I go to the nightstand and pull out the phone book and tear out the page with the U.S. map.

"Use this – now," I say and hand the map to Arix.

Arix repeats the procedure and begins to hum continuously. The lockpick begins moving upward at a very slow pace. He stops, and the lockpick returns to its normal gravity.

Arix closes his third eye and turns to me "The Italian is moving quickly, I would venture a guess by air. I will not know his destination until he arrives there. He appears to be moving due North."

My heart stops.

How did he get on a plane? How did he get up after the abuse we dealt him? I don't even know where he's going. Will my family be safe? What if he leaves the country? What will I do?

I bury my face in my trembling hands and begin to sob.

I feel a small arm around me and a strong hug. Shey's voice breaks through my implosion.

"Bad things happen to bad people. We'll make sure of it."

She plants a light kiss on my forehead.

"For once, the Pixie and I agree on things," is Sil's hushed response from her huddled position in the corner.

Arix, looking and sounding disgusted, scolds me.

"This is no time for weakness and no time to waver. This Italian will stop somewhere, and you will end him. More than likely he goes to his superior. The snake needs beheading. Do you agree?"

I look up from my hands, still teary-eyed, and scan the room. "Of course I agree." I take a deep breath, "Who here wants to go on a snake hunt with me?"

Everyone is in.

"Group, I need time alone."

And I do. One by one, I dismiss them, Arix last.

"Three hours and I'll have back for another reading."

He nods and leaves me with a parting thought.

"Do not be afraid to be angry; do not feel shame for your hatred. Let it stoke the fire of your power. I am proud of your performance today; you have learned well and performed magnificently."

"Thanks, Arix."

I send him to the white.

Is it good when a demonic sorcerer is proud of your actions? I don't know, but we were at least effective. I set the alarm on my phone for three hours and stretch out on the bed, exhausted.

I fall asleep immediately, but horrific dreams of Jerry's and Marge's death jolt me awake. I try to rest again. I jolt awake again. The alarm goes off. I reach down to Arix's sigil and call him back.

Not moving from my prone position on the bed or even looking at him I tell him, "Read it."

A small while later, Arix tells me "He is in Massachusetts."

I bolt up from the bed and look to where the lockpick is – Boston. I say it aloud. Quickly I summon everyone back and let them know what we have discovered and what the plan is. I will get on a plane, go to Boston, get another van, and call them back.

"Get a better room next time," Pffif says.

I just shake my head.

I dismiss everyone – except Pffif. I need him with me, covering my back because I am that exhausted.

"Don' ye have a worry, I'll be with ye the whole way. No-one'll be seein' me." Then he adds, "I donna know why the demon sorcerer didn't teach ye the true sight spell, it be an easy one, I hear. Sure'n be nice for ye to see me at yer side. I could be mockin' people unawares for yer entertainment."

"Yeah, that would be keen."

Truth is I don't care.

I only need to care about four things right now: dumping the weapons, returning the van, flying to Boston, and killing that bastard Italian.

Chapter 13

The only time the nerves set in is while I'm waiting to purchase my flight to Boston – what if I'm a person of interest? I imagine the lady at the counter looking up at me from the screen and saying something like… "Please wait a moment Mr. MacInerny."

Nothing happens. Thank goodness.

I make my time productive waiting for my flight. We are going to have needs again, so I research military surplus stores and the various locations of churches. And for Pffif's sake – better hotel accommodations. I know he's watching.

Unlike the first flight, my complete exhaustion doesn't allow me to stay awake. But my active imagination doesn't let me stay asleep. I jar awake shortly before the crew calls to turn off electronic devices for landing.

After landing, I take a seat in the gate area and turn my phone back on. A beep tells me I have voicemail. It has to be family. I open it up, and all my grands have called, Helen, Bobby and Jerry Jr. They have called multiple times.

I know why.

I take a moment to compose myself and say aloud for Pffif's sake, "I can't call them all back."

But knowing I must at least let them know I'm aware of what's going on, I make an executive decision to call Helen, the oldest, so she can be the point of contact. I don't even listen to the message, I can't. I just take a deep breath and hit call-back.

The phone rings; once… twice… three times…

"Grandpa?" There is crying, and I try not to join in. "Thank god, we were worried about you too when you didn't answer, it's so terrible."

"I know," I try to say calmly and in control, but my voice is cracking.

"Oh, god," she says, and more pain comes through the phone.

If only I were there to console her. Steve, her husband, comes on the phone as, apparently he felt Helen didn't need to deal with this anymore.

Good man, good call.

"Arthur? You need to get here. I can't begin to tell you how bad it is. They…"

I cut him off.

"I know what's going on. The people that killed Jerry were trying to get to me. I'm on their trail. You damn sure make sure to circle the wagons. I may not be coming back, as this situation is beyond serious. Just let everyone know I love them and I wish I could be there for them. But the truth is I have deal with these bastards. Get me?"

"Yes."

"Nobody should call me. Bad stuff is getting ready to go down. Maybe even worse than the church burning."

"What?"

"Circle the wagons."

I hang up. I feel a hand on my leg and see Pffif standing next to me with a tear in his eye. He reaches into his coat, pulls out his flask and hands it to me.

"Don ye worry, no one's noticed me appearin'."

I look at the flask and remember myself before I was gifted with my merry band of summonlings: a drunkard, a man of little character, moral value or ambition. I hand the flask back to him.

"Later, maybe."

We rent a van, and I make sure to pick up every free map they offer. I brief Pffif on plans while making our way to a Residence Inn. Once checked in, I roll up my sleeves and summon the rest of the team.

Then the phone rings. So much for the family not calling. I pull out the phone and see "Number blocked." I make the universal "hush" sign. I answer the call.

"Hello."

"Well played, necromancer," says the greasy Italian voice. "Your little display changes nothing; you will submit to The Church for judgment. Only now, your crimes are more."

I want to scream. I want to jump through the phone and strangle him. I want so many bad things. But cool heads prevail, so I take a deep breath and say nothing.

"Necromancer?"

"I was there well before sunrise. I left you a message I was coming," I say calmly as I can.

"We know of your kind, you would think to use your powers to defeat us. Your kind always needs to be taught respect."

His words ooze confidence.

I take another deep breath.

"So you brutalize and butcher innocents? That must be new to church doctrine."

"Their blood was tainted of your evil, as is the remainder of your family. Now, submit yourself for judgment."

He just threatened my family again. My fists clench. My heart pounds. I close my eyes and know this is the reaction he wants.

"Necromancer?"

"I am here. Let me share something with you. I know two things. There are only so many Catholic churches and organizations here in Charlotte and that you are badly hurt. So, you need medical attention which is why I am canvassing hospitals. If that doesn't work, then I'll just have to burn each church to the ground then, won't I? You're threatening my family – I'm threatening yours. By the time I am done, the Pope himself will be handing you over to me, you evil bastard."

I hear his laughter.

"Just tell me where you are, and we can get this over with quickly," I say.

"You keep searching necromancer, we will meet at the place and time of my choosing. And you should know that even if you find me and are able to dispatch me, The Church will send another in my place." He laughs, "Shouldn't you be with your family? We know where you are and you should stop your futile search. Drive instead to say goodbye to your grandchildren, since they are so close by. Either you will be leaving this world, or they will. Would you like their addresses?"

That puts a smile on my face. So, with as much venom as I can muster, I spit out "I know where they live!" into the phone and hang up.

My smile returns.

Arix looks at me knowingly, "The Italian I presume?"

I nod yes, then fish out the cloth with the Italian's blood on it.

"We need his location, right now."

Pffif hands him a lockpick and the maps.

Shey tugs on my sleeve, "That's not a happy smile."

I look down at her and smile even bigger.

"But it is happy, because they have no idea where we really are."

She digests that for a moment. A very mischievous look comes over her face, and she says, in her singsong voice, "Somebody's going to be surpriiised."

Chapter 14

After a few moments, Arix peers down at the map and lets us know that the Italian is currently near the intersection of Shawmut and East Berkeley. I plug that address into the mapping software on my phone and figure that he is taking a meal. I expand the area and see that three blocks away is the Cathedral of the Holy Cross.

That just happens to be the seat of the Catholic Archdiocese of Boston. And home to Archbishop Callon O'Dale. That's at least one snake-head on the hydra.

I share the plan with them. First, we weaponize, and then we repeat the St. Patrick raid: late night, take security down, and stealthy entry.

First things first, I direct Arix, Sil and Pffif to take the van to General Surplus – supposedly a purveyor of fine weapons and military surplus items to secure the armaments on my list or best they can. Sil is to put the whammy on the manager, and Pffif will stuff his thief bag with all the things he hopefully gives us willingly. If it breaks down, Arix will stun whoever he has to.

Shey protests, "We're stealing from innocent people again?"

Dang her conscience.

"Yes. They'll have insurance if they figure it out." I look over to Sil, "Leave him really happy if he goes along with the plan."

Sil, who was sullen and off to herself, perks up.

"Really? And I can have a little taste too?"

Now, look what I've done.

"Fine, as long as there's no permanent harm and it's good for him. We are, after all, trying to make up for stealing."

You'd have thought I bought a sixteen-year-old a Porsche for her birthday. I guess it's the little things…

"Everyone human-up before heading out. There are cameras out there."

I throw Arix the car keys. Shey gets some money and a card to our room.

"Shey, get a ski mask something to disguise my face."

She really needs something to do other than tell me we're acting like bad people and I don't want to show my face more than I already have.

"Is all this going to make our family safe," Shey asks.

I like that she thinks it's her family too.

"I can promise they aren't safe if we do nothing."

She understands and leaves.

Hjuul gets up and brings his bulk over to me, dropping his head in my lap with a light whining sound. I scratch his head and say, "Me too. I miss them too." He looks up at me, gives a light chuff and settles at my feet.

There's no telling what's going on with Vets behind that death's head helmet. She just sits there still, tail occasionally twitching.

I put one of the throw pillows from the sofa behind my head and stretch out.

*
**

I jump to alertness when the door opens – I must have fallen asleep. It's Shey with bags in hand.

"I got your disguise and something for you to eat." She cocks her head at me and wags her free finger. "Silly-willy, you have to keep your strength up."

She's right. I look over to the dining table and see that neither Vets nor her chair is there. I feel a large hand on my shoulder.

"Here," Vets says.

She moved her chair next to the sofa to guard over me while I slept. Wow. I step around Hjuul and head over to the dining room table to eat my sandwich. I check the time; I've been out for three hours. Good. I'll need to be crisp tonight.

I grab the remote, click on the TV, turning it to one of the continuous news channels. After several cycles of news, punctuated by "Charlotte under attack?" there is a knock on the door. I signal to Vets to check it out.

The crew is back. Pffif has his bag. Arix looks non-plussed, but he always does. Sil is all smiles and throws me a wink.

"Apologies, my wielder, for our delay, but one of us felt that both the manager and the owner needed special attention," Arix says.

Sil saunters over toward the dining room table where I'm seated.

"The owner got curious, and I handled it. You said to leave a happy impression. I did." She turns to Arix. "And there was no drama."

"Well then, good job," I tell Sil.

She takes that opportunity to sit across the table from me and look at me in that way she does that leaves no doubts about her desire.

"I can do a better job for y..." She stops, and her eyes go from come hither to something else. She looks away from me, then back, then away again and finally back. "Sorry," she says. "Not the right time for that."

"Angel's mercy!" cries Pffif, "The wench be thinkin' of something other than her appetites. The devil's sure to be cold!"

That brings a round of well-needed laughter.

Everyone arms up. Arix takes a reading, and the Italian is at the Cathedral of the Holy Cross. We wait, taking time with the news.

Chapter 15

Ten o'clock – it's late enough. We pile into the van. Two blocks out from the Cathedral, I stop so Shey can do aerial reconnaissance. She goes tiny and out the window.

My stomach's new friends the butterflies return. I wish I never introduced them.

Half an hour goes by and Shey returns to report.

"It looks clear. There are two persons in the upper Cathedral. The Italian guy is meeting with some people in a basement room, they seem very intense."

I punch up a picture of Archbishop O'Dale on the phone.

"Is he there?"

I show her the picture.

"Yes, yes," She tells me nodding emphatically.

"We go now."

The key goes in the ignition, and we move. I'm going to get the head and the tail of this snake.

"Arix get wards up. Pffif, we'll need that security down ASAP."

I park on Union. Pffif exits with a wink.

"How many in the meeting, Shey?"

She pauses a moment to reflect. "Two robed guys, three guys with priest collars, and the Italian."

"Tiny up, and make sure they aren't going anywhere. If they move, we need to know. I'll call you back when Pffif returns."

I'll be damned if I'll let them slip through my hands. I am literally bouncing in my seat with anxiousness. Ten minutes pass. The passenger door opens, and Pffif enters.

"Tis done, alarms be down – lucky it wasn't one of the fancy ones."

I dismiss Shey and summon her back immediately – it's the fastest way to get her here.

"Everyone to human form. No need to draw attention until we get inside. Here's the plan. We go in, go downstairs. I take the Italian, and Arix knocks the clergy on their ass with a mild wave. You get that Arix … mild. No fatalities, I can't negotiate with dead men."

"Negotiate… Bah," Arix says.

We pile out and make our way to the door Pffif opened for us. We step inside, and I put on the ski mask.

"Hjuul, do not to let anyone leave."

With a shake of his head, the wolf form disappears; he is large and in charge. I see the stairs to the downstairs across the sanctuary. We head that way but are stopped by the voice of a man.

"What is this?"

I draw my weapon and say, "freeze."

"This is a house of God!"

Arix closes on the man and touches him on the forehead saying, "quiet." The priest falls out. I hand signal to Vets to get him. He goes over the shoulder like a sack of potatoes. Quickly, we make our way downstairs. I signal for all to restore their normal forms. I want shock value. Vets sets the priest on the stairs. I can hear them. I can hear the Italian – saying something about how he uses his own family's blood for foul magics.

That's enough for me. We assault. I swing around the corner with the .45 drawn. No words, no warning.

The Italian stands, his eyes wide open, points at me and says, "Necro…"

The gun's blast is deafening as I put a slug into the same shoulder I did last time. He recoils from the shot. Arix steps in front of me, saying, "Tznok!" and the collection of clergy go flying pell-mell across the room into the wall.

I stalk over to the Italian and put a slug in both legs, causing him to fall to the ground. Then for good measure, I put boot to face.

Now, it's time to negotiate. I walk over to the discombobulated pile of clergy and grab the good cardinal by the cloak, dragging him up and putting my .45 to his forehead. His eyes come to focus on me, then to the Italian. He points at the bastard.

"Tainted! Benitio…" That earns him a backhand, and he sprawls to the ground.

"You're the tainted one asshole! Tainted with the blood of my family, you murderer!" I scream.

I hear the thrum of Shey's bow and see she's just put an arrow through the Italian's leg as he was trying to rise. I shoot him in the other shoulder.

Then I feel it. Someone's back in the white. It must be Hjuul.

"We have company!" I announce.

Everyone takes to formation. Vets is on point with her shotgun in hand. Next thing I know her head is falling to the ground, and there is a man clad in what appears to be black Kevlar body armor, wearing something like a Darth Vader mask holding a Katana standing off to her side.

Arix starts to gesture a spell, then spastically twitches as his head rolls off his shoulders. I feel the point of the Katana at my throat and see the man in black in front of me. I drop the .45. In the reflection of his face mask, I see the Italian standing again. Then the man in black is gone. Just gone. I hear a commotion behind me. I turn and see the man in black has staked the Italian to the wooden paneling of the wall with a very large knife.

"Stay, we'll get to you," the man in the mask says.

The Italian rages something to him in Italian. The man in black waggles a finger at him – no, no, no.

I turn and see that the man in black has been joined by others: a stern young woman in red, two large men in armor carrying swords like the Paladin's at St. Patrick's, and a man in a trench coat wearing a bowler hat.

The man in black somehow appears in front of them – he just appears. He casually sheathes his sword in the scabbard behind him.

His voice reverberates from behind the grill of his mask.

"Arthur MacInerny, this is where you stand down or die."

Chapter 16

Shey steps in front of me, dropping her bow. "He's standing down!" She turns around to me, pleading, "You can't fight them. You can't."

I hear Sil to my side mutter something in a Germanic sounding language sounding like "Schwert des Gleichgewichtes." She whispers, "Scary demon killer – the sword of balance. Let me handle this."

Sil steps forward and purrs in her signature way, "It's such an honor to meet a legend."

She begins to take another step toward the man in black.

"Sil, no," I say.

She does stop, scanning and smiling at the group of five in front of us.

"Enough, succubus!" spits out the woman in red. She brandishes what appears to be a small metal shaft and exclaims, "Tintreach!" which is followed by a blinding bolt of lightning that hurls Sil across the room, leaving her in a crumpled liquefying pile. The ensuing thunder is deafening, more so than even the gun-shots and causes me to lose balance.

The man in black turns to the woman in red, his hands to his helmet like he's trying to clear out his ears.

"Overkill a bit?" he says, "He told it to stop."

Their group seems to agree the sonic boom was overkill.

She pays him no heed and her eyes are totally on me.

"What part of or die did you not understand? Stand down your minions and get on your knees."

"Do it, Arthur, they aren't kidding around," Shey says.

The man in the bowler extends his hands toward the wall, and a blue bolt of energy releases from his rings toward the wall. Pffiferil appears limned by the blue energy, twitching and grimacing. The man in the hat looks at him and says, "We see you sneaky little… leprechaun? And is that a… Pixie?" he asks, looking back over to Shey.

"Yes," I say.

I very slowly pull up my sleeve where Pffif's and Shey's glyphs are, and dismiss them. The woman in red cocks an eyebrow at me. I get on my knees, slowly. The man in the bowler pulls a gun out of his trench coat and shoots me in the arm with a small dart.

Crap. My world goes very dim.

Chapter 17

I come to, surrounded by total blackness. I feel movement, acceleration. Perhaps I'm on an airplane? We're lifting off – yes, an airplane. My hands won't move; they feel like they're encased in a concrete block that is chained down. I am bound to my seat. I slowly realize that the blackness is from a hood over my head. Panic sets in – I feel like I'm suffocating. I start to try to thrash around to loosen myself. I scream that I can't breathe – over and over.

I feel a hand on my arm. Someone's there. There's another hand on my opposite shoulder. The hands squeeze lightly; telling me to calm down. I try to relax. The hands release me, and the hood is pulled off, revealing the stern young lady in red.

I get a good look at her. She's young, I'd say mid-twenties. Her hair is long, curly, and red. Her eyes are a light reddish brown and her skin very fair – she's no fan of tanning. Her features are those of a classic beauty except for her broken nose. We make eye contact, and for a moment I get a chill like I've been looked through.

"You need to calm down, Arthur," She holds up the hood. "This is a hood of silence. You can't hear or see anything, and more importantly, we can't hear you. We use this with dangerous magic users who might try some form of mental manipulation or curse. You will not suffocate, that's just your brain tricking you."

"Why haven't you killed me?"

I see we're not alone. The man in black is there without the Darth Vader face mask, the man in the bowler hat is there too, and there's someone next to me I can't quite recognize.

"You may ask questions later when we reach cruising altitude."

She puts the hood goes back on me.

I take a deep breath. The blackness is all-encompassing. Nobody can hear me. I am totally isolated. I think to my merry band of summonlings in the "white." This must be what that's like for them. That makes me feel better about not keeping them there.

So, I am captured by the church and on a plane, going who knows where. Perhaps I can talk them into keeping my family out of it? This group didn't seem too pleased with the Italian. Maybe these are reasonable inquisitors? Images of Jerry and Marge fill my mind. My body tenses and rage fills me. I struggle for some self-control. Thoughts of being able to assure my family's safety run wild. Thoughts of being reunited with Dory, Jerry, and Marge in the afterlife soothe me.

Then the image of Father Melvin Ploughman on the news comes crashing through. What if I've killed an innocent? I remember the man I sucked the life out of; I remember the visceral feeling of his confusion and pain. The realization washes over me that I have committed heinous acts. I've hurt others with no regard, leaving pain and sorrow for their families and friends in my wake. I became the evil I thought I was fighting.

Oh, God. I'm not seeing Dory or Jerry in the afterlife. They're not going to be where I'm going. What have I done?

Confusion sets in with a healthy helping of panic. What should I have done? The Italian killed my Jerry, I know this. I begin sobbing from frustration, loss, and shame.

The hood comes off.

"Are you crying under there?" Ms. Red asks in that accent that rings of British.

Bowler hat guy looks over at the man in black.

"I told you he wasn't laughing."

Man in black shrugs and continues playing with a butterfly knife.

Embarrassed, I try to compose myself.

"Okay, the church can judge me however they like – but there's no reason to involve my family anymore. They're…"

"Be quiet and listen," says Ms. Red. "We know what happened, we are not with any Church, but you are in deep shit. You appear to have been set up. The man who killed your son, I think he was your son, really wasn't a man – he is one of the tainted."

I am stunned and confused. My face must show it.

The man in black says, "The tainted are human shells with demon spirits in them – there's a spirit transfer they pull off somehow: demon in the man – man in the demon. Eventually, the man's body conforms to the dark spirit – did you notice the off-color of the blood? That's a newly turned one. Eventually, it turns black. We interrogated it and then put it down." He spins the butterfly knife again. "Your interrogation is next."

I remember the Archbishop pointing and saying, "Tainted." He wasn't talking about me. He was talking about the Italian. I realize that I struck him for no good reason; I heard only what I wanted to.

"So, all those people I harmed were… innocent? Oh, god…"

I begin to tremble.

Ms. Red takes me by the chin and refocuses me.

"You are going to have to atone for quite a bit, Mr. MacInerny. We are going to ask you questions, and you will answer them honestly. You have no choice, trust me on that. Once you have answered our questions, we will see about your questions and your fate. Understand?"

"Uh-huh."

The guy in black undoes his seatbelt and leans forward.

"I'm confused Red, does that make me the good cop or the bad cop?"

She turns to him with an exasperated look, "Damn it, Greg, would you grow up?"

I realize the person next to me is one of the two Paladins I saw at the Cathedral. He reaches into a bag, pulls out a small ornate wooden box and hands it to Ms. Red while shooting me a look to kill. She pulls a brooch with a large blue gem or glass piece in the middle from the box and hangs it around my neck.

"That's a truth stone," she says. "Blue is true, you get the idea, right?"

Greg steps over and slaps my knee, "You're having some fun, right?"

"Oh, sure I am."

"See," he points to the brooch which is now red. "We have established you are lying about having fun here. He's all yours, Red."

Bowler Hat chuckles.

Ms. Red looks exasperated again and rolls her eyes.

"Arthur, this is very serious, and any attempts to deceive us will go badly for you. We know you are ninety-four years old. We do not know how you have maintained your youth and suspect some form of vampirism."

"It's not vampirism."

She looks at the brooch, which is blue, and then back up at me. "Okay. We'll come back to that. First things first, we must know who taught you the ritual magic to summon these creatures from the outer dimensions."

Her gaze is intense. She's thinking I'm performing a ritual summoning with sacrifice, invocation and all; icky, black stuff. I take a deep breath and consider my answer.

"I do not use a ritual summoning; these beings are attached to me. They were given to me as a gift. There are sigils on my forearm that I use to call them and dismiss them. I would show you, but my hands are sort of locked down in this box contraption."

My answer is not what they expected to hear. They all look at each other with questioning eyes.

Finally, Greg breaks the ice with, "Well, that's not something you hear every day. So, who gave you these gifts of yours?"

"He said his name was Maldgorath."

The name gets everyone's attention.

Ms. Red turns to me, "Are you sure?"

"I am."

"We need a moment, Arthur," and with that said she puts the hood on my head again.

My world goes black. It seems appropriate.

Chapter 18

I have no idea how much time has passed, but it feels like quite a while. My focus is on keeping my mind still and blank. That's much better than the flood of self-incrimination and worry that fill it up otherwise.

The hood comes off, and the light of the cabin burns my eyes. Red is in front of me again, with the same steely gaze.

"We need to talk about your friend."

She must mean Maldgorath.

"Okay, I'll tell you what little I know. But there is something I must know first."

"You are in no position to negotiate, sir."

"Please?"

I must have looked or sounded pretty pathetic because her posture lightens. She looks over to the man in black, Greg.

He peers up from some kind of handheld video game and says, "What's our hurry? We're stuck in this plane for at least another six hours."

"Okay, Arthur, what do you need to know?" she asks.

"Is my family safe? The Italian said they would be targets. "

She smiles. It's a very nice smile; though I have a feeling, it doesn't see the light of day much.

"To the best of our knowledge, Arthur, your family is safe. As Greg told you, the tainted one you call the Italian has been interrogated and put down. The Church harbors no grudge against you. In fact, the Archbishop asked for mercy on your behalf.

She turns to the man in the bowler hat.

"Kevin, be a dear and see if the Techno-mage guild will look over Arthur's family for the next week or so."

Kevin agrees and heads to a forward cabin.

"Thank you."

It feels insufficient.

"Anything else Arthur?" says Ms. Red.

"Toilet facilities?"

"You're wearing them dude," Greg says.

Great.

"So tell me how you met Maldgorath," Ms. Red says.

"I was coming home drunk and heard a cry for help off the road in the woods. I went to check it out and found this small… being… inside of a glowing circle. He told me he was trapped and that he would die a grisly death at the hand of witches or burn to nothingness in the light of the sun. He said he would make it worth my while to release him and would be most grateful. I was skeptical because he was well, obviously not human. But eventually, I guess his sob story and promises of power got to me, so I let him go. Remember, I was very drunk at the time, so details are sketchy. I remember him opening his shirt, and his skin looked like it was swirling in the moonlight. He pulled off one of the swirls and put it on my forearm, which about knocked me over. He told me he just gave me a lover who would pleasure me in any way at any time I wanted. He explained how to summon her by touching her mark and calling her name. Then he did that five more times to me. It was all too much, and I passed out. When I awoke, I had the sigils on my forearm, and he was nowhere to be seen."

Greg seems amused for some reason. "So you've got a pocket succubus? That's got to be some kind of intense action there. How often do you tap that thing?"

The question bothers me, so I shoot him a look to go with his answer, "I've never laid with it… err, her."

All eyes went to the truth stone. The Paladin took note especially. His blue eyes meet mine. In what sounds like a Nordic accent he asks, "Why would you not lay with it?"

"I love my wife. Loved, I guess, she's passed on."

His eyes leave mine to the truth stone, then return. He turns to Ms. Red.

"This changes much in my report to The Order."

I have no idea what he means.

Kevin returns from the front. Greg taps him on the leg.

"Check this Kev, our boy here has a pocket succubus – and he's never tapped it."

"Seriously?" Kevin says. He looks at me incredulously. "You know kings have given away untold riches and parts of their kingdom for just one safe summoned night with one of those things?"

I shrug. The Paladin sneers.

Karen says, "We need to get back on track. When is the last time you saw Maldgorath?"

"About twenty years ago in a grocery store. He came out of nowhere, looking like a normal person. He wanted to know how I've enjoyed my gifts. He wished me well, and that was that."

There was a litany of questions following. Do I spell cast? What spells do I know? Who taught me? Have I killed? There was a discussion of the circumstance at Hondo's. I answer everything directly and honestly.

But things become very uncomfortable. Not because of the questions, but because I have to pee; real bad.

"Just a warning that things may get smelly here in a bit, but I'll try to hold it."

The Paladin clears his throat.

"Do you give your word to bring no harm to anyone if allowed to go to the restroom?"

"Of course. Yes.".

The Paladin looks to Ms. Red.

"Release him, Karen."

Greg pulls his katana from under his seat. Karen looks back at the Paladin.

"Are you sure about this, Gunter?"

"I am."

Karen fishes out a set of keys and inserts one into the block containing my hands. It unlocks, and she opens it, freeing my hands.

I slowly remove them and say, "Thanks."

Gunter's eyes have not left me.

"Do not thank me yet," he says. "There are two things you must know. First is that my brother in arms you killed was named Herrmann Mueller, and we were very close. Second, you have left Herrmann's wife a widow and their four children without a father."

A violent tremor shakes through my body. My eyes well up, but I can't look away from Gunter. He will not release his gaze. My stomach churns, and I throw up in my mouth. I stand up, and I look furtively for somewhere to release it. I am heaving and hyperventilating. Gunter deftly unbuckles my seatbelt, takes my arm and hurries me back to the restroom.

I make a mess. I do my best to clean up the bathroom all the while thinking of the monster I've become. The people I hurt; the families of those people. I get sick again. I try to compose myself. I take a few deep breaths and return to the cabin.

Gunter steps over to me and puts his large arm around me.

"That is how I would expect a good soul to respond."

He guides me back to my seat. Karen is nowhere to be seen – she must be in the forward cabin. I set the block in my lap and put my hands in it.

"We'll do that when we land," says, Greg. "Now you need to know what to expect. You will be on trial for the harmful and inappropriate use of magic resulting in death. You will be brought before the council of The Protectorate. So you know, we all work for The Protectorate and make up sort of a police and enforcement unit."

He then explains to me that the Protectorate is made up of varying organizations. The Magerium is made up of wizard types, like Karen. Kevin is part of the Techno-mage guild, which uses technology to amplify magical abilities in the gifted and less gifted. Gunter's organization is called the Order of Light, and they are holy warriors; Paladins.

"And as for me," Greg says, "I'm a freak of nature that the earth conjures up when the balance of good and evil needs to tip back toward good. Now, you'll be in front of the head honchos of each organization which make up the Protectorate. They will hear evidence from us and ask our recommendation. They may ask you questions. Answer them honestly. At the conclusion, you will either live or be put down."

"Oh yeah, you'll probably be bagged and blocked through most of it," Kevin says.

All I can say is, "okay."

I will be tried and not hear or see most of it. Funny enough, it doesn't bother me a bit.

Chapter 19

The remainder of the flight is fairly benign. I show off the glyphs on my arm and explain who is behind each one. I answer general questions. Karen lets me know that she will be reporting on behalf of the team. They seemed very curious as to how I kept off their radar for over seventy years.

My only answer to them is good friends and a great wife. The truth stone stays blue.

We talk briefly about my service in World War Two. I speak with reverence of my squadmates who kept my secret until their end. God bless, so many people I have loved I have also watched pass on.

The pilot's voice comes on announcing our descent. We all buckle up.

The landing is smooth and we taxi to somewhere. Karen unbuckles and looks at me knowingly.

"Arthur, we have to bind your hands again. We will need to need bag you too. "

There's nothing to say. I pick up the hand-block, place it on my lap and put my hands in it and let it close. She locks it down. Then I realize there is something to say.

"Thanks for making sure my family will be okay, whatever happens to me doesn't matter – they do. I'm most appreciative for your looking over them."

Without any fanfare, Karen bags me, and my world goes black and silent.

After a while, I'm guided from the plane to what I think must be a car. We travel for what seems a long time. When we stop, I am walked a great distance, being helped through turns and some stairs. Eventually, I am backed into a chair and directed to sit.

I must be there.

The bag comes off.

Karen is facing me. "Arthur, say nothing. We have permission to remove the bag of silence, but you must remain silent unless spoken to. We're a little early. You may be bagged again. Do you understand?"

"Yeah."

"Good."

I take in the scene. I am in a stone semi-circle with glyphs cut into the stone; protective wards I assume. There is a large stage with eight ornate chairs in the back and one forward. There are stands to my right, and people are populating them. I see Greg sitting there; I get a wink from him. Gunter is in the stands too, talking with others who may be of his order. People are filtering in.

My trial is a much bigger deal than I thought. There are at least fifty people in the stands. People start to make their way across the stage to take their chairs. No one gives me notice. I don't care. A man with a long braided salt and pepper beard takes what seems to be the lead chair.

A hush falls across the area. I look over and see a well-dressed man with long grey hair in a ponytail enter, flanked by a huge beast. The man is thin, standing about six feet and appears somewhat aristocratic. The beast I guess is closer to eight foot with a barrel chest, leathery wings folded back, and purple, almost black skin. Its head is adorned with horns like those of a ram, pointed ears, and flowing black shoulder-length hair which frame a fairly handsome face. Its eyes, I can't fully make out, but I sense intelligence about it. It is wearing a fairly swanky black silk two-piece outfit with oriental dragon ornamentation that reminds me briefly of Jimmy Page's get up in the seventies.

The man with the braided beard in the lead chair stands immediately.

"Grey Lightbringer! You will remove that abomination from this hall immediately!"

That brings a big smile to the beast's face.

The well-dressed man with the beast in tow smiles and bows to the man on the stage and replies: "High Magister Alistair Burningwood, it has been some time, and it appears that time has been good to you. First, I think you will find that there is a precedent for Ahtsag Znuul's attendance by the allowance of familiars within council meetings. He is, after all, bound thoroughly to my will."

The beast nods his head and makes a face as if to say, "He's right."

"Second," Grey continues, "Given the peculiarities of the accused and his apparent benefactor, Ahtsag Znuul may bring some insights which could prove helpful to the council."

Alistair looks back to the other seated people, one of which has a cat in her lap. He looks back to the well-dressed man.

"Fine, Grey, this time only because of the peculiarities."

The man, Grey, gestures to the stage says, "thank you," and makes his way to the stands near Greg, appearing to stop and share a pleasantry with him. They sit, and the beast reaches his massive fist backward over his shoulder toward Greg, who gives the thing a knuckle bump. Karen comes over and embraces this "Grey" in a warm hug. They talk for a bit. Then she makes her way over to me.

"Sorry, but we have to get started," she tells me. She holds the hood up. I bend my head down so she can apply it. Things get dark and quiet.

I can't judge time properly, and I'm not concerned about it anyway. I do think of my summonlings who have been in their sensory deprivation areas for what is probably a day, at least. I wonder about my trial – the evidence is damning, and I won't deny any of it. The bite of Gunter's disclosure of his friend's family tears at me. How do you make that right? I'm not sure that you can. I try to console myself with thoughts of my family's safety and say prayers for their well being. I say a prayer for Dory to forgive me for not being able to join her in heaven. I say a prayer of thanks to God for taking her into his kingdom.

I feel a hand on my arm, and the hood comes off. Karen is facing me.

"Please give me your hands so I can remove the block," she says

"Is it over?"

She shakes her head "no," turns back to the stage and proclaims loudly, "The prisoner is ready for examination."

The beast, Ahtsag Znuul as they called it, rises and walks toward me. I get a good look at its eyes now – they are serpentine, like a rattlesnake's – only deep red. Its expression is inscrutable, which when added to its formidable size, makes for an aura of menace. It walks around my little stone seat area, just looking. Finally, it stops in front of me, raising an eyebrow. I feel like it's looking right through me.

"Okay then, let's see them," it says, gesturing for me to move along. "Come on."

I undo my cuffs and roll my sleeves back and extend my arms. It grasps each arm in its huge hands. The touch is warm and firm, but not rough. He releases one arm and runs his fingers along the sigils of the arm he's holding.

"Arixtumin, really?" it asks, looking at me with a mixture of curiosity and amusement.

"Yes."

"Pale white sorcerer with an ugly purple eye in his forehead?"

"Yes."

The creature laughs and releases my arm. It beams a smile at me.

"That makes my day." It leans down next to my ear and whispers, "By the way, you need a shower." It bends back up, winks at me then turns to the stage.

"The answer to the first question is yes, they can be removed if he so allows it," the creature says, in a booming voice. "The answer to the second question is broccoli."

Alistair is not amused by that answer and lets everyone know it. "Demon, spare us your riddles and speak plainly!"

"You're never any fun," the creature replies with a wry smile. "You had asked to what effect their removal would have on him and plainly he would be a vegetable afterward. I think closer to broccoli, but some may feel lettuce more apropos. Their spirits are deeply intertwined, especially the fairy and the hound. If you remove the bound spirit, which by the way would also effectively kill it - it would also take out chunks of this man's spirit along with it. Think of it as they have roots and he is their earth. Messy, nasty thing pulling them out."

"So how may we prevent him from calling these minions of his," asks the lady with the cat.

Znuul considers the question then answers "Killing him would be the humane way. Unless you have no regard for the spirits bound to him, trapped alone in a nothing dimension going silently mad. If that is the case, then I would suggest some form of a permanent sleeve to prevent his touching the glyphs. Eventually, though, a way will present itself. Maldgorath himself only has to will his summonlings forward as do most Garrigan."

Not good. I pipe up.

"I would prefer death to knowing that my friends are locked in a prison, going mad from isolation. That's just wrong and selfish."

"Silence prisoner!" Alistair says.

I make with the quiet.

"And we have heard enough from you, infernal beast," Alistair says.

The monster makes his way back to the stands, plopping down next to Mr. Grey. It gives me the thumbs up and a funky fake smile.

Alistair announces that the council will now take up deliberation. That could be good. Deliberation at least implies some potential for an outcome other than death. Karen walks toward me with the hood in hand. It's time for lights out.

But stopping her is a general disturbance in the air. To the left of the stage, is a glowing orb appears that begins to grow. The orb begins to open, like the petals of a blooming flower. Two armed pixies fly through, wings aflutter. They are followed by two non-winged foot soldiers. An older pixie woman walks through, her hair gray, her eyes solid gray, and skin pale and somewhat translucent. A leprechaun walks through next to her.

The guards take position, and one bellows out. "Bow your heads before the beauty of Ambassador Balmaen of T'uel Faeden!" A leonine female walks through, with no wings, like the foot soldiers and slightly taller than the old pixie woman. She has shockingly red hair twisted in an upward do and solid green eyes. Her silky dress shimmers green with hints of red. She stops, and the portal closes behind her.

In a beautiful, almost musical sounding voice, she addresses the council.

"I have come for that which belongs to the fae."

Chapter 20

The man in the bosses' chair stands and bows.

"Ambassador Balmaen, we are honored."

She smiles demurely and acknowledges him. Suddenly, she turns sharply to me. Her face becomes enraged. She points at me and in a voice that no longer resembles anything pleasant or musical and demands, "The names of our kin now, human. The ones that you hold against their will!"

The weight of her glare and the force of her words slam into me. My heart beats faster, and I feel a cold sweat beginning.

"Uh, do you mean Sheyliene and Pffiferil?"

The older pixie cries out in anguish, "My Sheyliene!"

The leprechaun has little reaction other than a brief nodding of his head at the ambassador, followed by fishing out a pipe he begins packing.

The ambassador's banshee voice cries out again.

"Unacceptable! The Fae will have what is theirs!"

Things go bad.

She reaches out to me with both hands and a look of ferocity. Immediately, I fall in crippling pain. My bones feel like they are being pulled through my muscles and skin. I am being torn into pieces. My vision goes white, and the pain is not suppressible. I think I scream. I feel something akin to my eyeballs being pulled out by a vacuum cleaner. My brain feels like it's following them through the sockets.

At the very edge of what little consciousness I have left, I hear a deep voice.

"This is neutral accorded ground."

And just like that, the pain stops. I collapse, noting after a moment that my eyes, brain, and bones all appear in place.

The voice strikes again, booming in deep tones. "You would bring harm to one of this realm and in here of all places. Truly, the Fae have no concerns for mankind or the binding of their agreements. Your arrogance astounds even me, Ambassador!"

I look up to see the ambassador's hateful glare directed to the stands. I hear her say coolly in her more musical tone of voice, "Dearest Grey Lightbringer, please control your dog."

I look over my shoulder to see the booming voice apparently belongs to the creature Ahtsag Znuul, who is standing, meeting the ambassador's glare with a wide grin and what appears to be a total absence of fear.

The beast turns from her and to the council, his smile like the proverbial cat that ate the canary.

"Perhaps those in this good man's care would rather live than be torn from him to dissipate into nothingness?"

The ambassador hisses at him.

"I do not hear anyone asking them for their opinion," Znuul continues. "The ambassador claims they are held against their will. Do they indeed prefer a true death?" His gaze fixes upon the older pixie, "Would not mother prefer to enjoy her daughter's company over her most final death?"

Alistair apparently has heard enough too.

"Grey, silence that abomination, now – or leave. That thing has no voice for this council to hear."

Grey begins to stand, and Ahtsag Znuul turns to him. There is a silent communication between the two, and it takes a seat, smiling. It throws a wink at the ambassador, who bares her teeth back at the beast.

Grey holds his hand up, looking at Alistair.

"Would the council hear me?"

Alistair rolls his eyes and gestures him to go on.

"Most beautiful ambassador, we all know the long-standing history between those of the T'uel Faeden and the vile denizens of Helterezen. And we know your mission here is one of mercy in the eyes of the Fae and we feel your passion for the well being of your people. However, Ahtsag Znuul makes a valid point. The concerns and well being of those who are bound have not been addressed, much less those of Arthur MacInerny, who would, without question, suffer greatly."

He turns from the ambassador to the council. "Would the council not agree?"

Grey sits. I guess there's nothing else to say.

Alistair turns to the council members, whom all nod in the affirmative to him. He turns to the Ambassador, and before he can say a word, she makes a dismissive stroke of her hand, and in a lilting musical tone says, "Yes, yes, we may have acted prematurely. Let us hear from the prisoners."

She turns to me and gestures dismissively.

"Bring forth the warrior Sheyliene."

I look over to Alistair, as he's the man in charge. He gives me the nod, so I roll up my right sleeve again and call Shey from the white. The air ripples and there she is. Her face brightens when she sees me. Then she looks around and comes to the realization that we're not in a happy place.

She sees the older pixie and the T'uel Faeden contingent.

"Mother mine?"

Immediately her face becomes one of elation. Then, almost as quickly she turns her eyes downward and takes a deep breath.

"Oh, Sheyliene," I hear mother fairy say. She takes flight from the stage, light wings fluttering, landing in front of Shey. Mother looks at her curiously. Shey's eyes never come up, her feet and wings move nervously.

Mother takes Shey by the chin in both hands and makes her look up.

"Is it really you?"

Shey begins trembling, with small moist trails evident on her cheeks.

"I am me." Shey tries to force a smile now having to regard her mother in full, then blurts out, "I was weak mother and tricked. I should have taken a true death. Instead, I am disgraced."

She tries to look away, but Mother is not having any of that.

"Little fierce Sheyliene, hear your mother now. You are loved."

Shey explodes through the hands holding her chin into a full-on hug. Mother gives her a few pats on the back, then with a hand on each shoulder pushes her to arm's length and regards her with a serious face.

"Sheyliene, would you want to be free of this... human master?"

She punctuates the last part by looking over at me with a sneer.

"Free means a true death, pixie," comes Znuul's deep voice.

Mother's eyes shoot from me to the beast seated comfortably in the first row. Shey's face turns to complete shock. I meet Shey's eyes for the briefest moment, and I sense there's some recognition. Breaking from her mother's hold, Shey whips around pulling that bow from nowhere in the folds of her dress and reaches back for one of her deadly silver arrows.

"No, Sheyliene!" I cry out before she can let loose.

After a moment of what I can only presume was deliberation, Shey drops the arrow, and the bow collapses in her hand to its tiny hide-able form. She points at the lounging beast.

"What is General Znuul doing here?"

She turns to me in a panic, "You are in great danger!" She looks around at everyone like the building is on fire and shouts out, "You are all in danger – the Destroyer is here!"

Mother quickly collects her attention, "Sheyliene, he is bound as a slave to that human wizard, the beast you knew of is now no more than a dog on a leash. He has only his bark."

She shoots a sarcastic smile to Znuul, who shrugs in recognition as if to say, "Yeah, you're right."

"Now," mother continues, "We need to speak of things important – do you wish to no longer be a slave to this human? We can separate you from this... man and allow you a true death. Is that not what you wish for?"

Shey looks over to me. She looks back to mother.

"That will harm Arthur greatly."

Mother takes a breath in what might be exasperation.

"The consequence to the human means little."

Shey takes a second, and then cocks her head to the side, "But it means much to me, mother. He is a good man and my bondage to him has not been like slavery at all. I wish him no harm. I have so much love for him. Besides, if I die truly, will we not be able to visit anymore?"

"You would rather be a slave to the whims of a filthy human animal, than free in spirit," Mother says with venom.

That statement gets the attention of the humans in attendance, creating a stir. The ambassador, picking up on the change in the room interjects herself.

"Gowaille, it appears your daughter would prefer to exist with this human and that he treats her well. Is this so, shade of Sheyliene?"

The shade remark rankles Shey. I can tell. It bothers me too.

Shey turns to the ambassador, putting her fists on her hip. Oh goodness, this is not the time for one of Shey's signature rants. She looks to her mother, she looks to me, and back to the Ambassador. I can see it beginning to bubble up to her mouth like verbal lava moving to the top of the volcano.

So, knowing I'm not supposed to speak unless spoken to, I do the next best thing and clear my throat very loudly.

Shey looks over to me and after a brief moment bares her teeth, letting me know how she feels about it. I ask her with my eyes not to make a scene. She closes one eye, like she's wincing, then readdresses the Ambassador.

"It is so, good lady. I only have one complaint of Arthur, and that is, he will not lay with me. Despite permission of his Dorothy and that his forever young body cries for it. But such is the bond of true love. It blinds one to the needs of others and yourself."

Oh goodness, she went there. Again. Sil wants freaky, and Shey wants lovey. All I want is my Dory – and my Jerry.

"True love?" asks the ambassador with real curiosity melding with her musical tone.

"Uh-huh," replies Shey her head nodding emphatically. "Her name was Dorothy, and I loved her too. They were magical together. I know it to be true love without question – no question at all."

"Fascinating and good," chimes the ambassador with a wry smile directed to me. "Then our business with Sheyliene is done."

I can tell she wants to get this over with after Mom's "animal" comment turned the room against them.

But Mom has other ideas.

"No! I have two more questions that must be addressed."

The lady ambassador is not pleased but waves her on all the same.

Mom flutters over to me and hits me with the mother-in-law glare. That glare that lets you know you are in no way worthy.

"Why will you not give my daughter the attention she wishes? Is she not worthy, is she not beautiful? Do you prefer the attention of males or farm animals? Tell me now."

Shey is chuckling. I'm getting pissed off.

"I'm mourning the loss of my wife and son. You'll have to excuse me if I can't exactly bring the mood on. Do you remember what it's like to lose a loved one?"

I raise her mother-in-law glare with one of contempt.

"Yes, I remember it well," she says and takes a few steps away toward Shey. She turns back to me, "You will give my daughter everything she wants and devote your life to her never-ending happiness."

I expect to hear "or else," but she turns back to Shey. I guess some things can just go unsaid.

"Now for my second question – daughter mine, what of your sister Neiliene? I must know. Is she still in the possession of the Collector? Does she still live in captivity? Was she killed on the field of battle? Tell me true, by your family's blood I bid you, tell me all true."

While my summonlings are very sensitive to my emotional state, I am not as much to theirs. But at that question, I felt sheer panic course through her. That is a lot of panic.

Voice quivering, Shey looks to her mother,

"She died a true death."

"How?"

Shey looks to me, then back to Mom.

"Please don't make me. Please, Mother… it's too much. I don't want to remember. I can't…"

Now shaking like a leaf, Shey looks over to me to protect her.

But mom is a hard ass, "Tell me all, true. It is a mother's right to know." She looks over to me. "Compel her! Now!"

So much for assuring her daughter's never-ending happiness.

"Shey," I say quietly, "you need to do this."

Shey falls to her knees and buries her face in her hands.

Mother's face is stern and unmoving.

"When did you become so weak, child? Tell the story."

Shey appears to collect herself and looks up from her hands.

"As you wish, Mother."

Shey stands and begins her tale. "We were captured by General Znuul's forces while scouting the Billowing Hills. Neiliene fought magnificently, and we inflicted many casualties before being overrun. After several rounds of torture and humiliations we were brought before that beast over there." Shey moves her head to indicate Znuul. "He attempted to torture, seduce, and corrupt us to become one of his, as was his way. He failed. We were punished and traded to Maldgorath the collector in exchange for what I cannot know. I was tortured and brought to near death many times over and over again, only to be healed and endure it again. I was told lies. Lies that my sister had given in and that I should join her. I knew she never would. I do not know how long this continued. Eventually, we were brought together, and the collector began inflicting torment upon Neiliene, horrible, unspeakable tortures. The entire time, telling me what he was going to do, like it was nothing to him, with each torture he asked her to give herself to him."

She stops and closes her eyes.

"Mother, must I continue?"

Ball-buster Mom, of course, says, "You must."

"She was taken from the room, and I was left with The Collector. I told him, she would not give in to him, despite how much he may torture me, for she was my bigger, stronger sister. I knew it was my time to endure the horrors. He told me he knew that, and I would not be next. He told me that if she resisted through this round of questioning, he was going to kill her and feed upon her flesh. Then, he would focus on me. He also told me that if I gave myself to him willingly, he would grant her release. I know the word trickery of these devils, so I was extra careful to make sure by release, he did not mean that he would kill her. I remember his exact words: I will not harm her. I will not release her to death. Nobody under my control, now, will harm her. Her hands will remain bound, but she will be made free and allowed to leave. But, she will see you collected unto me. It is better to have one than none."

Mother shouts, "You did not!"

I find that response idiotic because obviously, she did.

Shey continues looking away from her mother to the ground. "They brought her back, mostly healed and chained her to the wall across from me. The Collector asked me how we should continue. I asked him to take me and release my sister. I gave myself willingly to him with Neiliene protesting and imploring me not to. My next memory is being summoned from the nothingness of his keep. Neiliene was crying, and one of his minions unchained her. He told her she was now free. He looked at me and told me that his word was unbroken."

Shey looks up from the ground, tears beginning to stream in her eyes. She meets her mother's unwavering stare.

"Then he put a knife in my hand and compelled me to kill her."

She falls back to her knees, her face totally blank. "He made me enjoy it. He made me taste her blood. Oh, by all divine… He restored me to myself, to know and live with what I have done and become."

Mom recoils from her with her hand over her mouth. Shey turns to a quivering mess. I can see why Shey is all screwed up. Only a true monster would do something like that. And I freed that damned thing. Shey… I had no idea.

Distracting me from the sight of Shey is her mother exclaiming, "You are no daughter of mine!"

I can't take anymore. Shey is hurting so much that it bleeds into me. It tastes of emptiness, guilt wrapped in sorrow topped with feelings of failure and unworthiness. I cannot stand my little fairy feeling this anymore. I leave my little area of the accused and go to her, causing the council to stand, the Fae warriors to draw weapons and a gasp from the crowd.

I run over and pull Shey's crying heaving form into me in an enveloping hug. I say nothing, just holding her tight and rocking her. Her arms wrap around me in an anaconda grip that is way out of place to her size.

I hear Mother say, "Send it away," and look up to only see her back and a dismissive hand gesture as she flutters back to the ambassador. My attention goes back to Shey, where it belongs. I stroke her blond hair as she cries, her head buried in my chest, her body shaking and heaving.

How messed up is this? I'm supposed to be the one being punished.

Chapter 21

My rocking with Shey comes to a premature end. I see out of the corner of my eyes a pair of black dock martins peeking out from under a long red dress. I look upward, and Karen stands there looking down at me, carved wooden rod in hand. At least her demeanor hints at some sympathy, but the message is still clear; listen up.

"You need to get back in the prisoner's stand, now."

I get the message. I've pushed the rules consoling Shey. It's time to get back in line. I try to extricate myself from Shey, and she does not want that.

I whisper to her that I have to go. She looks at me with tearful eyes and a wistful look and releases me from the bear hug. I get up and return to the stone ring. Karen gives me a nod.

The damn ambassador voices up in her musical tones, "Now that we have restored some order to these matters, please have your prisoner remove that shade and bring forth the shade of the luchorpean Pffiferil."

The Ambassador smiles to Alistair like they are best of friends.

"Please don't send me away," Shey says.

"I have to."

So I do. I compose myself and call Pffif. The air ripples and he arrives.

He gives me a nod, and then looks around, catching the T'uel Faeden contingent on the stage.

"Begorrah!" he says startled, then composes himself, straightening his jacket. He sees Znuul and does a double take, looking at me with concern.

The ambassador nods to the other leprechaun. He walks forward to the edge of the stage, removes the pipe from his mouth and then jumps down. He puts the pipe back in his mouth, takes a puff and lets it expel. He walks to Pffif, looks him in the eye and spits next to his foot.

"Ye gave yerself up."

Pffif looks him in the eye, then spits next the other leprechaun's foot

"He called the tradition, I didn't forsake me or me clan's honor."

The other leprechaun nods to him, "Good ye didn't, aye. But bad luck for ye all the same. Called tradition? Ach. So, ye kill any of ours in the scum's service?"

Pffif shakes his head. "Nah. I was only spying and thieving for him."

The other leprechaun takes a deep pull from his pipe and fixes Pffif with a serious look.

"So ye be wanting the true death or be servin' that human there?"

Pffif cocks his head and looks at the other leprechaun with a face of disbelief. "Ye be daft? I still be drinkin', breathin' the air, ana see'n pretty women! 'Sides he's not be making me do anything I don' wanna."

Pffif throws me a wink.

"Makin' sense to me," the other leprechaun says. He looks to the ambassador and says, "That be enough for us." Then he makes his way back to the stage.

Pffif stops him with a word – "Brother."

The other leprechaun turns to him.

"Do me a favor, there be no proper pipeweed here. Can ye spare a pouch for one who'll never grace the blessed green grass of T'uel Faeden again?"

The other leprechaun reaches into his jacket and tosses Pffif a pouch.

"Don't let yer human be smokin' on it, or ye'll be havin' to fetch him down from a tree."

They grin at each other and share a laugh. Then, with an inhuman jump belying his small size, the leprechaun joins the others on the stage.

The ambassador nods to the leprechaun.

"We are almost done," The Ambassador says. She reaches into a pocket of her dress and pulls out an envelope. "Magister Grey, this is for you from the Queen herself."

She holds it out in front of her, making no effort to move toward him.

The man, Grey, gets up and walks to the stage in front of her. She bends down and hands him the envelope.

"You know the game that the beast plays and you know you cannot win," she says. "His is a game of patience. You will either fail and release him or face being his slave for eternity. You lose either way."

"That is the conventional view of the situation, Ambassador Balmaen.".

She smiles. "Enjoy your years, Grey Lightbringer. I hope you use this invitation the queen has given you to come join us in T'uel Faeden again."

He touches the envelope to his forehead in salute.

"Again?" says Alistair.

The flower of light blossoms open again, and the T'uel Faeden contingent begins to walk back through. But before making her exit, the ambassador turns and looks over to the lounging Znuul. Their eyes make contact, and she says in her lilting, singsong way, "Ahtsag Znuul, you should come back to T'uel Faeden with Grey and visit. We have pikes that would fit your head perfectly."

Smiles are exchanged between the two, and she steps into the light, which folds up behind her.

The man, Grey, turns to me and says. "Your friend has to return, deliberations are called for."

"Hold this for me," Pffif says tossing me the pouch. "Don't ya lose it."

I dismiss Pffif. The man looks at me in the eyes. Gray is more than his hair; his eyes are gray too. He picks up the hood from the side of the stone semicircle around me and opens it. Time for things to go dark again. I bend to allow him to put the hood of silence over my head. My world goes black. I feel a reassuring pat on the arm and feel for my hard stone seat.

I guess at this point they are deliberating my fate. It occurs to me that it's not just my fate; it's the fate of those I carry with me too. My thoughts turn to Shey and what that monster Maldgorath did to her. How long did she serve in his clutches? What other scars does she bear?

If I had only left that monster to burn in the sun…

But then I wouldn't be who I am now either. I wasn't a good person back before my group came to me. I was a drunk and a letch with a moral compass that only pointed down.

It was that healing power from the summonlings that sobered me up and let me look at the world with clear eyes. Clear eyes that saw how I had hurt Dorothy and that she was actually afraid of me. Clear eyes that showed me all I ever needed was right in front of me – with her.

Funny how such an unholy creature could change me so wholly – for good.

After other various ponderings for who knows how long, I jump from a small pat on my arm. The hood comes off. Grey is standing before me, hood in hand.

"Stand, please, and face the council," he says.

I do. Alistair stands also.

"Arthur MacInerny, you have been found guilty of abuse of magic resulting in death," Alistair says. "We understand your actions were provoked and questions remain of who or what was behind it. This council remands into the custody of Grey Lightbringer for a minimum period of two years. It is our hope you will be assessed, rehabilitated, and hopefully integrated into the community.

Oh, goodie.

Grey turns back to me and dangles the hood.

"Lights out until we are away from here, Arthur," he says in his French accent.

My world goes black again, only this time I am being guided somewhere. I guess that would be to Grey's Lightbringer's dungeon for magical miscreants.

Chapter 22

I feel a hand on my head and a tap on my shoulder telling me to duck down. I'm being put in a car. Once in the car, the hands gently push me across a soft seat. I feel a seatbelt being buckled around me.

Moments pass, and we start moving. I imagine myself in the back of a paddy-wagon with soft leather seats. The hood comes off, and I can see it's not a paddy wagon, but a well-appointed limousine. Across the seat from me is Grey, next to him a huge man in black silk. It must be that Znuul thing in some kind of glamour or shapeshift. Next to me is Karen, legs curled up under her, dock martins off and on the floor.

"Welcome back, Arthur," says a cheery Grey. "We have about a three hours' drive before we get to the vineyard. There's much to discuss. I'm sure you have questions too."

Znuul groans and rolls his head back over the seat.

"Don't mind him," Karen says. "He just dislikes small places, and we have the windows blacked."

Znuul rolls his head toward Grey. "Can we at least roll down the driver's privacy window?"

Grey smiles back at him. "Let's get a little distance from the council."

Znuul grumbles and tries to stretch his legs, knocking into Karen's boots. Karen takes notice, and a mischievous smile crosses her face.

"Grey, heeee's on my side."

Grey rolls his eyes and takes a deep breath. Znuul's head lolls forward, and he looks at Karen. He puts his foot on the seat Karen, and I are sharing. She flicks his foot with her index finger.

Znuul pulls his leg back quickly like he was lashed with a whip.

"She hit me."

Grey looks at me with some desperation and says, "You at least act like an adult, right?"

"I'll try for the sake of our budding relationship."

"Well then, formal introductions are in order, even though you have met everyone. I am Grey Lightbringer, mage and child of the light in my one hundred and sixty-fourth season and former member of the protectorate council. To your left is Karen Redditch, mage also, and my star pupil. We won't discuss her age."

With a warm smile, she says, "my twenty-eighth season."

Grey returns the smile and continues "To my right is Ahtsag Znuul, Destroyer of Hope and Devourer of Souls. We are not sure of his age, other than he predates man's civilization, was deeply involved in the T'uel Faeden invasion and the cleaving of our dimensions."

Znuul sighs. "And I can't get a senior citizen discount at the buffet. Are we there yet?"

"Obviously, Mr. Znuul chooses not to always act his age." Grey leans in toward me. "Don't ever forget who and what he really is."

"Grrrr… Rawr," Znuul deadpans, his head still bent backward looking toward the blacked out rear window above him.

Karen takes my arm, which startles me, "Znuul's being scary again, make him stop!"

Noting that she startled me, she releases me, pats my arm and smiles warmly. This is not the same stern lady that brought me into custody.

"Do they always act like this?"

"Karen is normally much more reserved," Grey says, "but they feed off one another, so yes, this is fairly normal – for them. Now, there are things I would like to be more informed of too. Let's start with the beings you keep within you. How often do you release them? Will we need to make accommodations for any special needs?"

"Well sir, it's not a matter of how often I release them because I don't send them away unless they either ask for it or need healing. I feel like the nature of their captivity is punishing. They reside in an endless white nothingness. It's kind of like being in that silence bag thing. You are isolated and alone."

"I see. It sounds like we will have to make accommodations. So you know, the binding of Znuul's will is much different. He is not summoned. He is flesh and blood, one of the eight Greater that walk this world still, brought over long ago by dark blood-fueled magics."

"How did you end up binding him?"

"I was in a prison of my own, and he drives a hard bargain," Znuul says.

We discuss the general needs of each member of my party, and I impart a warning about Sil being a succubus which perks Znuul up.

He leans in and takes Grey by the leg, shaking it. "Hey, Dad, can I make a play date?"

Grey is not amused.

Karen chimes in with, "Is that all you ever think of?"

I look over at this enormous man that isn't really a man. He raises both his eyebrows at me twice with a look that says, "come on."

"Do you have any idea what she is capable of? She consumes peoples' lives."

He turns his head and shares a lurid smile.

"In Helterezen, I kept a stable of over a dozen of them. And… I am not a man."

His comment reminds me of Shey. In the trial, she said, "He attempted to torture, seduce and corrupt us to become one of his, as is his way." I remember she said they were punished for refusing him. I remember the shock and fear when she realized he was in the room. Pffif was shaken too. I try to suck back my anger at this creature for doing what he did. But it's not working, the feelings of hurt from Shey are still fresh.

"Good memories for you, I'm sure. Speaking of memories, big man, you hurt my Sheyliene and sent her to that other monster, Maldgorath, messing her up permanently. Why should I do you any favors?"

Grey tries to step in, but Znuul stops him.

"I have this."

Znuul's demeanor changes. His face now appears devoid of all emotion. He leans in and meets my eyes. I feel the very real weight of his presence – a menace. Just like that, he looks away as if the still darkened side windows were clear.

"I deny nothing. Nor is it in my power to change that which has already come to pass." He looks back at me, that gaze stopping me from saying a word. "I will not apologize for behaving in accordance with the rules of conquest." His face softens, and he closes his eyes. "I do understand your anger though, and will not begrudge you your feelings." His eyes open again and he leans back. "Much time has passed since then, and even I change."

His face explodes into an over the top smile and he holds his arms out.

"See, I didn't threaten to utterly destroy him, even once!"

Karen gives him a pitty-patty of applause with a disapproving look.

Grey rolls down the black security windows and the driver's privacy window.

"Thank you," Znuul says.

"All right, let's get back to matters," Grey says, pulling a notebook from a bag at his feet. "You discussed your spell inventory with Karen. Let's give that a look over." He flips to a page and studies it, asking questions of me for each spell.

"Well, almost all of these are vile, addictive, hate-based spells and you're going to have to forget them. We'll show you a better shock wave type spell. One question though – did you ever use what you call the coil of death. Please tell me no."

Damn. I'm sure my face gave it away. "Well..."

There is no pause on Grey's part, and his eyes are intent upon me. "How many times have you consumed human life?"

"Twice."

Znuul seizes the moment. "Maybe we aren't so different, no?"

Crap, he is right. I have done terrible things. The thought of Gunter's friend and his family washes over me, and I am sickened at myself.

Karen bolts up, smacks Znuul on the leg, and points at him.

"This is serious, at least to us. Cut out the alpha male bullshit now and apologize."

This isn't playful banter; this is the stern woman I met in the cathedral.

Znuul looks over to me, then to her.

"I do not apologize for truthful observations. In fact, generally, I do not apologize at all."

Ever so quietly Grey says, "Enough already."

Karen sits back in her seat, re-folding her legs back under her and then turns back to me, her expression softening.

"Well, I am sorry, Arthur," she says and goes back to topic. "I think you had said you used that spell twice - when were those times?"

I take a deep breath and prepare to let them know how far I descended into madness.

"Once in world war two and once during the attack on St. Patrick's."

Grey nods and says. "That's good, it doesn't seem habitual. That's the real trap. I guess you realized the foul nature of that hex in the war."

I nod in the affirmative.

"I had someone tell me also – Shey, the fairy. She said that spell puts dark marks on my soul."

That brings a smile to Grey's face.

"I look forward very much to meeting your little one. And speaking of that, I would like to address the elephant in the room."

"I'm more like a Tyrannosaurus Rex," Znuul quips, not looking away from the window.

"Fine Ahtsag, if that makes you feel better," Grey says without losing a beat. "But the real issue is that we must all coexist. Arthur, I will not stand for you or yours creating disturbances. And I speak most plainly of the tension that will exist between the leprechaun and the fairy with the dinosaur over there."

He punctuates that with a wink to me.

Znuul smiles, looking into the window.

"Please remember that Ahtsag was brought into my house well before you. He has lived with me for over sixty years. He has known Karen since she was eight years old and put in my charge. You and your friends are our guests. Please strive to be good guests."

Karen puts her hand on my shoulder, which takes my attention.

"That does not mean that you have to take any attitude from Ahtsag. Right, Father?"

"Yes, we encourage putting Ahtsag in his place." Grey lightly raps Znuul on the leg with his knuckles.

Znuul acts like he's been wounded and rubs his leg where he was rapped: a strange sight in contrast with his huge size. He looks over at me, to Karen, to Grey, then back to me.

"Two on one is not fair." A small smile follows, but not that car dealer smile this time; it feels genuine. "I'll not antagonize the pixy, Arthur, but know I won't tolerate physical attack," Znuul says as his smile melts away. "She can say what she wants; I have become accustomed to such disrespect from my little sister there."

Karen scrunches her face and says, "Little sister? Eww."

Grey laughs, "See, you have been sentenced to at least two years of having to be around our little dysfunctional family."

"Yeah … two years."

That brings out a belly laugh from Znuul that reverberates in our limousine space, followed by the booming voice I heard during my trial, "Give me the thousand deaths! Please! Anything but Grey's house of horrors! Anything!"

Karen tries to muffle a laugh, and even Grey seems a little amused. The driver hits the intercom and says, something in French that is probably "Don't startle me like that!"

I look back from the driver to see a seven foot plus, four hundred pound man curled in a ball as a smaller redheaded woman smacks him about the arms, shoulder, and head while laughingly ranting at him. "Anything… really? How about this? You want a thousand deaths… I've got thousands for you."

Grey taps me on the knee, taking my attention from the spectacle unfolding next to him. He whispers "It's not always like this, they have not seen each other in some time – Karen's work is quite demanding of late."

I kind of doubt that. I bet they act like that all the time.

Karen flops back in the seat and takes me by the arm, encircling hers around mine. "What kind of nonsense are you telling him, Grey?"

"Nothing but the truth."

"Arthur," she says, tugging on my arm slightly. "Two years will fly by."

"But not all of it will be easy," comes a somber sounding Znuul, now uncurled. "We need to broach the subject of Karen's investigation and what the things she doesn't know could mean."

Karen removes her arm from mine, and sits up properly, looking to the big man, then to Grey.

Grey nods to her, then looks back to me and says, "Well, it can't be all fun and cupcakes can it?"

He's right.

"Let's not talk in code here. Someone or something had my only son killed. Someone or something had me kill innocent people for reasons I can't even comprehend. So, if there are questions I can answer to bring some clarity to this matter, please don't hold back thinking I'm too fragile. I'm already broken, I can't be broken anymore."

"Well Karen, spell it out to him," Grey says

"Alright Arthur, here's what is bothering me. Local paper clippings and a note naming you as a practitioner of the black arts were mailed to the Catholic Church anonymously from New Mexico. The Roman Catholic Church advised The Protectorate, and I was dispatched along with their own investigator, separately. We now know the church's investigator was a plant. I went to the scene at the bar, and while my trained eyes can piece together some of what happened, there was no direct evidence to link to you, You did well covering your tracks. Nobody remembered anything, and all security evidence was gone. So the big question is, who would know the name of a man just passing through?"

Grey leans into me. "You see the quandary, no?"

Just when I think things can't get worse, Znuul proves me wrong with four simple words.

"We smell a rat."

Chapter 23

The conversation that took place up until turning into the driveway was very serious. I agree to an interrogation of my summonlings – one by one. Znuul insisted that Arix be first. Those two have a history, and from what I can tell, Znuul does not care for Arix at all.

Apparently, Arix once assisted Maldgorath in an attempt to collect him.

Their plan for interrogation is for me to compel them to tell the truth and stand back. Except for the compelling, that I apparently am no good at, it sounds easy enough.

I take in my new home - a sprawling mansion set in beautiful hills. Grey tells me his little slice of Dordogne sits on sixteen square kilometers of land hosting vineyards and a walnut grove. The driveway, I am guessing, is at least a mile long.

We pull up to the mansion, chateau, castle, or whatever you'd call it. Znuul is first out of the car. Much to my surprise, he is greeted at the front door by five children of varying age. The younger ones hug his leg, the others also seem happy to see him. Grey gets out of the opposite door, and the mob runs over to him.

Karen looks over at me and says, "I was one of those kids once."

She exits the limo.

I'm in no hurry. There's no happy greeting for me, just the knowledge that I am to watch an interrogation of my friends and that there is a real possibility that one of them has betrayed me. I get out of the limousine, following Karen. I am stiff. I am tired too; exhausted is more like it. Other than my dart induced coma, rest has been nonexistent.

Grey comes around to me, kids in tow. "I will introduce you to your new friends later, now we have business to attend to."

He takes me by the arm and leads me into the chateau. We walk down a hall, take a left and go down another hall, finally entering a dark room.

"Wait here, do nothing. I will fetch chairs and some refreshment as you must be exhausted. Summon no one, please."

Grey leaves, and I am alone. The room has no windows. There are runes or glyphs carved into the crown molding at the ceiling and at the baseboard that are filled with gold. I turn and notice the markings are carved into the door jamb and casings as well. I look down and see there is a metal ring embedded in the marble of the floor. Bronze braziers with polished metal backs sit in each corner. The room is lit by a glowing orb in a metal stand. There are no cords to it. There are no outlets in the room.

Damn. This is a scary room. So, I take Grey's direction and do nothing but walk around it and wonder what's going to happen. After a while, the door opens, and Karen enters carrying some folding chairs and a folding table.

She greets me and then looks around the room. With a measured eye, she walks to its rear and begins to set up the chairs and table.

"Arthur, come sit. You are exhausted."

By the time I sit down, Grey enters the room with a decanter and some glasses. He pours me a glass of dark liquid and hands it to me. Then he turns to consider the room.

Karen leans over and says, "Grape juice."

Grey makes a gesture and the two braziers at the rear of the room converge to the middle of the room just outside the brass ring. He mutters a word, and they begin to blaze. He points to the orb, and it goes dark.

After standing back up, he looks over at me and says, "There, we should be ready now. You stand next to the ring, summon your companions, compel them to tell the whole truth, and sit down."

It's time to address my limitations.

"Uh, I seem to lack ability in the whole compelling thing."

Grey looks at me with curious eyes and says, "Gather your will and apply it to your command using their true name."

I see he realizes I don't have a clue.

"Oh dear, you've only worked in hate and rage. Right, well, we don't have time, so we'll work with rage then. Pool your rage like you do with that shockwave spell. Only instead of shaping it into a wave and releasing it with your trigger word, link it to your command and release it with the verbalization. It may overwhelm them at first, but it's all we have to work with for now."

It makes sense. So I nod like a bobble-head in agreement, though the whole overwhelming thing bothers me.

The door opens again, and Znuul bends down to come through it, clad in a black kilt and tunic. He's back in his more normal bestial form and upon entering stretches his leathery wings. He has something in one of his massive hands and strides to the back of the room and unfolds it; a stool. He plants it at the very rear of the room and takes a seat behind me in the shadows.

"Ready here, bring on the first victim."

Not what I want to hear.

Grey gestures to me to come.

"Arthur, follow the plan: summon, compel and question. Now, let me sit down and bring forth your Arixtumin," he says.

He sits. I'm up. I touch Arix's glyph and call him forth. The air ripples and he stands before me in the circle.

He immediately opens his third eye, I presume to scan the room. His posture stiffens.

Znuul's voice comes calm and cool from the shadows, "You will close that or I will remove it from your skull and feed it to you."

"Ahtsag Znuul?" Arix shuts the eye and looks to me in confusion. "Master Arthur, my wielder, what is this? Are we in danger?"

"Now compel," Grey says.

Arix's two eyes widen.

I do as Grey instructed me earlier, using my memory of my rage at Jerry's death as the focus. I feel it, shape it and link it, then I release it with four simple words; "Arixtumin, speak only truth."

He screams, grabs his head, falling to his knees and convulses. I guess it worked. I hate that I hurt him like that, but I know no other way to "compel."

"I'm sorry Arix," I say, then go behind the braziers and sit down like I was told.

Grey stands and says, "Well..."

Znuul's voice again comes from the back of the room, "Master Lightbringer, please allow me to conduct this interview. You know I have a history with this one, and that may prove… helpful."

Grey looks over to me. "What do you think, Arthur? I am inclined to let Ahtsag question him."

"My master Arthur, I would prefer that you question me. But I confess I don't understand why any of this is necessary."

"All will be explained in time, for now, be patient," Grey says. He walks inside the area offset by the burning braziers and regards Arix.

"You must be the human master of Ahtsag Znuul, greetings to you. It is unfortunate that one who was as powerful as he has fallen so low to be easily led like a collared lap dog. By a human no less – no offense to you, fellow sorcerer."

I cringe in my chair, expecting to hear a bellow of rage from the back of the room and all hell to break loose. But there's nothing: silence.

Grey must have expected that too; he turns to the shadows in the back of the room and cocks an eyebrow. He turns back to Arix

"No offense taken. Good to make your acquaintance, fellow practitioner." He walks back behind the braziers and sits back down next to me and says, "I am of a mind to let my easily-led lap dog continue this interview. In fact, Ahtsag, please do." He puts a hand on my leg, "Let's not forget, Arthur, it is, after all, my decision to make."

"Thank you," is Znuul's resonant but controlled response.

His massive frame passes us and enters the more lit area. Arix is dwarfed by Znuul. They say nothing. Arix has his superior face on. Znuul just appears to be analyzing him.

Finally, I recognize the game. He who speaks first loses.

Arix loses. "Ahtsag Znuul, you look good. Captivity becomes you."

Znuul nods to him. "Thank you."

Silence ensues, and Arix is the one uncomfortable with it.

"I see your Master has taught you some restraint Znuul."

"Reminded me, would be more correct."

Znuul begins circling Arix again as if he is looking for something. My guess is he just wants to make him uncomfortable.

Arix bristles, "Arthur, this is disrespectful! Have this gargoyle ask his questions or end this game."

Grey's hand immediately pops up in front of me. Translation: Stop.

Znuul finishes his circling facing Arix, with a knowing smile. "Arixtumin… Very clever. Incite the stupid beast to rage, and hopefully, we forget about all this nonsense in the ensuing chaos. But you forget; I am not stupid. Quite far from it."

"Get on with it," Arix says, folding his arms over his chest.

Znuul turns around to us and makes that goofy car dealer smile of his and throws us both thumbs up, emphatically nodding, "Yea!"

Karen and Grey shake their heads then smile at each other as if to say that it had to happen.

"You seek their approval before you even ask a question? Weakling! You perform for them like a trained dog."

Znuul turns back to Arix, smiling, then stretches and wiggles his arms followed by a brief flexing of his wings. "Alright then, question number one… How did you come into Maldgorath's collection?"

Arix looks at him and then toward us.

"You should know, of all people, that Maldgorath is capable of turning on anyone."

Znuul nods to him, stroking his chin.

"Yes, you are right Arixtumin – I remember clearly when you assisted him in his failed attempt to add me to his collection."

Znuul turns to us.

"Note please that he has given us a response that implies he fell to Maldy under foul circumstances. But note more importantly, that he evaded the question of how he came into Maldy's possession."

Znuul turns back to Arix.

"You are compelled to tell the truth. Now, please share with us the details of how you came to Maldy's collection."

"Master Arthur, please do not make me re-live these events! The stress it will cause me will be unbearable."

I remember how traumatic it was for Shey. Those memories destroyed her. I can't do that again; to me, it's akin to torture.

"Can we just move on to the next question, please," I say.

"Thank you, kind master," Arix says, with a sigh of relief.

Znuul turns and walks back to us. He goes down to a knee in front of the three of us; making things more eye to eye.

"He is hiding something. Arthur, I do not believe that one will feel emotional trauma like the pixie did. I must insist he answer the question."

Grey nods in the affirmative. Karen does too.

"I think you just want to see him break down."

Znuul looks at me with a smile and says, "That would be a fine bonus indeed, but I do not believe that is going to happen."

He turns the red snake eyes to Grey and Karen. There is a silent communication.

"He answers," says Grey. "If he tries not to answer, you will compel him to, Arthur."

"Bullshit."

Znuul closes his eyes and begins to rub his temples, making a displeased face.

Grey, without looking at me, says, "Minimum of two years could mean a maximum of your lifetime. I need to get to the bottom of this matter. So do you and so does your family." He turns to face me. "Don't mistake my pleasant nature for weakness, you are my prisoner, and I am your warden. I am not asking you – I am telling you."

There it is. My opinion is not needed.

"Fine," I say. "Arix, answer the damn question so we can move on," I say in a loud voice.

Arix is wide-eyed – at least his two regular ones. Znuul looks at Grey and mouths "Thank you." Then the great big beast gets up and stalks back to Arix.

Znuul is looming over Arix. "Your master tells you to answer, and you disobey? Obey your master, Arixtumin, and answer the question."

Arix is shaking at this point. I recognize that shake. He is resisting my direction. What the hell?

Grey says ever so quietly, "Compel him to answer the question now, please."

So I reach for that God-forsaken memory of rage and repeat the compelling process by saying, "Arixtumin, you will answer the question – how did you come into Maldgorath's collection?"

Arix lets out a blood-curdling scream and collapses into a pile on the ground, clutching his head.

Znuul laughs at Arix, turns around and begins clapping at me. He turns back around and kicks Arix lightly.

"Get up and obey your master."

Arix stands slowly, his face is nothing but vile hatred.

"I allowed myself to be collected."

"We all know that collection and binding cannot occur without consent." Znuul cocks his head at Arix. "Tell us why or I will have Arthur compel you for every question I wish answered."

Arix hisses at Znuul and then lunges at him. Znuul catches him by the throat and lifts him into the air the effortlessly. Arix opens his third eye, and I see him, gesturing and mouthing a spell. Like a striking viper, the index finger of Znuul's other hand plunges into Arix's third eye, causing gouts of glowing purple liquid to spray out. I think Arix would have screamed, but the vise grip around his neck wasn't letting any sound out.

I see pain, lots of pain.

Znuul drops him.

Arix clutches his forehead and spits out what I think is a curse in a language I've never heard.

"Stand and deliver, Arixtumin," Znuul says.

Arix looks up at Znuul and does stand.

"The truth is I came to Maldgorath's collection in a bargain. He would give me to a human pawn, and I would train him and guide him to create chaos and conflict once we have blackened his soul with lust and greed. In return, when he was done with the human and has reacquired me, he would make me whole in this realm. I would be as a god. Like you would be if you were not stupid enough to be bound to that human wizard!"

I'm out of my chair before I know that I'm out of it.

"You son of a bitch!"

Karen intercepts me and says, "Wait!"

Grey hasn't moved an inch.

Znuul's steps over and his large frame blots out Arix from my field of view.

"Let me handle this, Arthur," the beast says.

I try to relax, but am still trembling in rage.

I close my eyes and decide to put that rage to use, I touch it, shape it, connect it to the words and scream "Arixtumin you will answer all questions from Ahtsag Znuul honestly and promptly you fucking piece of shit."

Arix doesn't scream this time; it was more like a gurgle. No smile from Znuul at this compelling, just a nod. Karen guides me back to my chair and whispers for me to "be strong."

Grey has not moved the entire time, his eyes riveted on Arix.

The next while is like an out of body experience. Znuul revives Arix and peppers him with questions. Arix tells us he has a small coin that he can use to contact Maldgorath. Arix has been in contact with Maldgorath regularly and told him of the incident at Hondo's. Arix knew that Jerry was going to be taken.

At that, I snap.

"You bastard!"

I lunge from the chair. This time, Znuul steps out of my way. The force of my words and emotions already buckled Arix, but that's not enough. I swing a wild right hand and knock him to the floor. I mount him. I am pummeling and screaming and pummeling and screaming. My vision is white with rage.

I feel two enormous hands under my arms around my rib cage pulling me off of him. I flail about trying to escape, but the grip won't budge.

I come to realize that Znuul is holding me out at arm's length like a small child having a tantrum. He shakes me once rather violently, and that takes my attention away from my rage. I take a deep breath and relax. He sets me down. I turn around to face him, tears streaming from my eyes, my breathing still very heavy. The light of the flames bouncing from the braziers adds to how surreal this moment is: a giant black winged beast with burning red eyes looks down at me, as two shadowy figures sit in the shadows.

The sorcerer I thought was my friend and mentor just confessed I was nothing more than an evil job he had to do.

Grey's voice breaks the moment. "Arthur, come sit down. You have a lifetime to punish him. But we need more information now."

Chapter 24

I sit in my chair, my head in my hands. Betrayal hurts. Grey, Karen and that thing Znuul are conferencing off to the side. Arix lies on the ground moaning, purple ooze seeping from his third eye and dark purple blood coming from his mouth and nose.

I put my head back in my hands and let the room know how I feel.

"Can we get this over, please? I am tired of looking at Arix."

The three break their conference. Znuul walks over to Arix. Grey comes and sits back down next to me and puts his hand on my shoulder. I shrug it off because it irritates me. Karen walks to the opposite side of Arix from Znuul.

"Arthur, you had to know, and we will continue," Grey says putting his hand back on my shoulder. "This is a great deal to take in over such a short period. And the truth is that more bad news may be coming. We don't know how deep this runs in your contingent."

That gets my attention. Damn, what if all of them have been playing me? Sil, I can see. Vets may be one of them too. Shey, never. Hjuul, never. Pffif? I look up out of my hands at the man with his hand on my shoulder.

"You're the warden…"

"Yes, I am."

He gives me a thoughtful look then beckons Znuul to continue.

Znuul holds his hand over the prone Arix and mutters something unintelligible. Arix bolts up from the ground, screaming. That is one alarm clock from hell. Arix looks at Znuul and scowls at him through a grimaced mask of pain. Znuul smiles back at him.

"Well, Arixtumin, shall we get going again?"

My last compelling did the trick. There is no hesitation in any of Arix's responses. The only other member of my party involved was Sil. He describes her as a miserable failure. He is not sure of why Maldgorath had me target the Roman Catholic Church. He was not told. He guesses it has to do with manipulating the "balance."

Someone will have to explain that to me.

"Show us the implement you use to communicate with Maldgorath," Znuul says.

Arixtumin produces what appears to be a wooden coin from his robe.

Znuul examines it and says, "It can be rendered useless."

"We shouldn't," I blurt out. "We can use it for misinformation and maybe to call him to a trap. I can compel Arix not to use it without permission."

"I like the way you think," Znuul says.

Nods of agreement follow around the room.

"Please do so immediately," is Grey's response. Arix looks at me in fear, knowing that one of my sledgehammer compellings is on the way. I don't hold back and hit him with all my rage and feelings of betrayal focused on it.

"Arixtumin you will not communicate with Maldgorath without my permission."

That must have been a little much because he doesn't scream. He just convulses, coughs up purple blood, and falls backward.

"Wow," says Znuul. He looks over to Grey. "Don't even think about trying to do that me."

Without even a flinch, Grey responds, "Don't give me a reason."

Touché. But I've had my fill of their banter.

"If you two are through I have some questions for the son of a bitch."

I stand and look at Grey.

"He's all yours, have some restraint for our sakes, though," says Grey.

I approach Arix's prone form and look at Znuul and Karen. They give me the go-ahead.

"Arixtumin, you vile son of a bitch. Wake up and answer my questions, now!"

That gets him up, spitting purple blood from his mouth, and coughing. His two good eyes look up to me and he re-arranges himself to sit more comfortably.

"So, you get up the nerve to face me yourself?"

I remind him of the beat down I put on him with a smack to the face. His eyes roll back in his head, and he falls over.

I didn't think I hit him that hard. My confusion must have shown.

"Summonlings are overly sensitive to both physical and emotional abuse from their wielder," Znuul says. "That's why you were able to kick his ass, Arthur. He would have laughed off any other human."

Good to know. So I force Arix to attention. Once he is sitting up, I start again.

"First question, scumbag: why did you let that bastard kill Jerry and Marge? You could have warned me."

Arix scowls at me.

"As for letting them be killed, I had no say or knowledge that it would happen. I just thought it was a ploy to bring you before the master so you might be reaped. Their death surprised me as much as you. As for warning you, that would defeat the purpose of an ambush, wouldn't it?"

I let my feelings of rage toward Arix wash over me. His face twitches in response. It makes me happy to see him in discomfort.

"So, it's okay to feed me to that beast? What did you think would happen to Jerry and Marge after I was, as you say… reaped?"

Arix's eyes meet mine with impunity.

"Your fate was always to be reaped; from the first day. You would serve your purpose and then the master would collect you. And us back with you. You are a fool if you think you can stand before the power that is Maldgorath. You think you freed him? He chose you and tricked you. But obviously, he did not choose wisely. You fool, you think you are special? You are less than a pawn on the chessboard and no more than a soul to be collected at his will. You are nothing."

My rage begins to take over, but a belly laugh from Znuul interrupts it. I shoot him daggers with my eyes. He holds his hands up, laughing still, as if to say, "Wait."

Karen looks at him and says, "Ahtsag, that is rude."

The beast composes himself, still chuckling. "Let me grab my stool, and I'll explain. Arthur, I'm not laughing at you. I'm laughing at that sorry sack of excrement."

He goes back to the shadows, grabs his extra sturdy folding stool and plops it down next to me, in front of Arix. He takes his seat, looks at me and starts to chuckle again.

"He called you a fool, Arthur. You did, didn't you Arixtumin?" Znuul reaches out and flicks Arixtumin with his middle finger on the forehead, just above his injured third eye. Arix bares his teeth in response. "Here's the thing, how smart do you have to be to give up your spirit, your very essence – your free will - so you can have a chance at buying the Brooklyn bridge?"

Znuul snickers again and looks at me eye to eye, only this time I don't feel the weight of his presence; I feel a kinship of sorts.

God help me.

"He calls you the fool, Arthur, but he's the puppet." He regards Arix with false compassion. "Oh yes, I am sure he can make you whole and release you as a God unto this world. You are smart to take that deal. I am so sure he can do that – and that he would. "Muahahahaha!" Znuul's laugh echoes through the room.

Karen starts to snicker too.

"That's a good trade there, Arixtumin, your very essence for… nothing."

Znuul continues to laugh.

I can't laugh. I do get the joke, and it should be funny. But the price of that joke was a little high. I look at Arix and shake my head.

"I did not realize until this moment how truly stupid you are."

I see Arix gets the joke too. He's not laughing either, though I suspect for different reasons. He tries to stammer something out but fails.

"Goodbye Arix," I say looking him in the eyes. "It will be a long, long while before we speak again. Enjoy the décor. I hear it's very white."

Then I reach to his glyph and dismiss him.

"Very well done," says the beast Znuul, smiling at me.

From the back, Grey says, "Succubus next. Let us take a break, do what we must, and collect back here."

The orb begins glowing again, and the room is now filled with light other than the ominous braziers.

I don't need to wait. I am ready now. That bitch is finally going to get a piece of me, only I don't think it's going to be the piece she wants.

Chapter 25

We depart the room and Grey is kind enough to show me where the facilities are. We are all to return to the interrogation room in five minutes or so after tending to our personal needs. I stand in these old, well-appointed halls and wonder what kind of prison I've been assigned to.

Thoughts of Jerry and Marge's violation fill my mind. Visions of finding Dory's body follow. I sink down into a ball next to the door of the interrogation room and cry. I remember Arix telling me about their culture; that love and compassion are seen as weakness, and that predation and deception are exalted. It never registered to me, after all that time he was still a soulless monster.

Stupidity on my part. Arix is a soulless monster.

Silithes is up next. And she is no surprise to me. We will be done with her quickly. I think of her pretending to proclaim feelings for Jerry and my family. I am going to bust her ass for lying to me… and more.

The first to return is Karen. She says nothing, she just sits down on the floor next to me. Grey is next and ushers us all in. Last back is Znuul who gracefully ducks under the door in his well-practiced way.

The light globe goes out, and the braziers come up again at Grey's command.

He looks over at me and asks, "Are you ready?"

"Hell yeah."

"Good. Arthur, you summon her, compel her, and then we will have Znuul conduct the interrogation."

My plan is different.

"No Grey. I summon. I interrogate. I kick her ass."

Surprising me, Grey agrees.

"But I have three conditions, Arthur. I must determine if she knows where Maldgorath is, what his intentions are, and if she has any idea of what his future plans are."

"Not a problem."

Znuul takes his heavy-duty fold up stool and returns to the shadows.

"We're here if you need us," Karen says.

"Proceed when you are ready," Grey says.

I am ready. I touch Silithes' sigil and call her. The air ripples and there she is. She looks around the room and back at me.

"This isn't a friendly room, is it, Arthur?" she asks.

I don't reply. Instead, I reach down and touch that ball of rage and let her know what kind of room this is with my words, "Silithes you will answer me truthfully and fully in all questions I pose – you fucking bitch."

The words don't just make her buckle; with a scream, she is literally cast across the room, slamming into the wall, head over heels.

"Glorious power of the black!" I hear Znuul exclaim from the back of the room. "Did you see that, old man?"

"How could I not," Grey says.

Sil lays crumpled on the ground. I see her beginning to pick herself up.

I figure I'll let her know what is up.

"Sil, Arix told us almost everything. About Maldgorath, about you. About using me as some kind of pawn. We have questions, and you are going to answer them. Now get your slut ass up."

She looks up at me with her alligator-like eyes, hikes up her corset and stands.

"It's about time all this was in the open," she says, then walks back toward me. She sits down in the middle of the circle on the floor, curling her tail around her legs. She looks down, not seeking to meet my eyes like she usually does.

"Ask me whatever you will. I will answer."

"Where is Maldgorath?"

"I cannot know."

"What are his plans, why did he have me attack the Roman Catholic Church?"

She looks up at me. "I cannot know - the whole matter was a surprise to me." She returns her eyes to the floor.

I continue. "Do you have any knowledge of his future plans?

"No, not specifically though I am generally sure what he seeks is a tip in the balance of good and evil in this realm, to make the opening of portals to Helterezen easier."

I look back to Grey and Karen. "Anything else you want to know?"

Karen's voice responds, "Are there any other in Arthur's possession with direction from the Collector."

"Not that I know of," Sil replies.

"That takes care of us, ask what you need to," Grey says.

Damn. Their questions are much easier. There's much less emotion to them. But I have to put this bitch in her place before I put her in a very quiet, lonely place – forever.

"Silithes, you told me and the others that you had feelings for my family and for Jerry in particular. I know now that's a lie, so what do you have to say, bitch?"

The last syllable causes her to flinch in response to my anger. That makes me happy. Her response doesn't.

"I didn't lie then, and I am not lying now. You know this, Arthur, as you have so thoroughly compelled me to speak only truth."

She turns her alligator eyes up to me. I turn away because I don't want to see them.

"I was a coward, Arthur," she says, "I should have said something when I first heard Jerry was taken. But I did not for fear of my own future well being."

My fists ball up. My heart begins to race.

"Arix told me in confidence that he thought this was a ruse to bring in you for reaping. I now know it was not. The truth is, if that one wished to reap you, he simply would."

I meet her eyes again. I think I see sadness there, but remind myself she is a seductress and put up my wall of stoic coldness.

"I assume I am going away for a very long time," she says quietly.

"You are, bitch."

The venom in my words make her wince as they bounce off her.

"There are things I need to tell you so that the truth about me can be out in the open. I wish no more hiding or deception. Would you allow me that, Arthur, before sending me away?"

"Little late for that now, you soulless monster, don't you think?"

She looks back down at the ground and daintily straightens the leather skirt barely covering her knees. "I've earned your hate and disgust, yes." She looks back up at me, "But you have earned the right to some truth, no?"

I look away from her. I want to send her away right now. I don't want to hear from this monster whose sole purpose is to corrupt me and turn me into a monster too. I know the truth of her.

But, then for a moment, I wonder if I do.

Sil was acting strangely throughout this ordeal. I remember her rage when Pffif told us of Jerry's fate; was she attacking Arix? I remember her falling to her knees and that blank stare of hers. I remember her head bouncing off the door from Arix pushing her aside. I remember her saying, "nothing good can come of this," on attacking the church and the tears in her eyes.

I look back at her. "In the hotel, you tried to warn me – didn't you?"

"It was too little, too late."

"That's a fucking understatement," I spit back. There must have been more venom in my words than I thought. She jumps.

"Okay, I'll let you get what you need to off your chest. Don't think for a moment, though it will change anything. You are going away to a very white place for a very long time."

"Thank you."

She looks down and nervously straightens her skirt again. "Before I begin, though, I need your word you will let me finish. Parts of what I must share will anger you - maybe enrage you. Some you will not wish to hear. But, all will be true as I am so compelled." She looks back up at me with sad green eyes. "Your word, please."

Who is this, I think to myself. There's none of the come hither. None of the self-assured yes, you may worship me attitude that I know her by. All I see is a broken down thing.

"All right, Sil, but don't take all year."

Znuul's voice booms from the back of the room, "I should have brought popcorn."

I see Grey shaking his head in the shadows.

Karen says, "Ahtsag, hush yourself."

I note recognition in Sil when Karen says his name.

"So you know him too Silithes," Karen says.

"Only of him – if that is Ahtsag Znuul, that is. He was thought dead, at least before Maldgorath took me." She pauses for a moment and looks around. "Shall we begin, Arthur? Did Arixtumin ever tell you of the one true law?"

"No."

"That figures. Great one, would you please share with Arthur the one true law," she asks, looking back to where Znuul sits in the shadows.

"The one true law is self before all," he booms across the room.

"Thank you," she says. "This law is ingrained into all of the more powerful races. It is why I did not speak out. To be one of the Collector's possessions and to have his ire is to endure horrors you cannot imagine. This is an excuse, no question about it. But an eternity of torture and degradation is unacceptable. This is also why I worked to seduce and corrupt you. It was not for my gain, it was only to avoid the collector's punishment. Because Arthur, you cannot hope to stand against all that his him."

She looks away again. "I don't say that to belittle you, Arthur. He is legion."

She claps her hands together, looks at me and a small smile appears on her face.

"Now to share some memories that I cherish and will probably enrage you. Please try to remember your promise to me. I have wanted to speak of these things for ever so long, but the one true law comes to play again. You would send me away forever, and I could not allow that. Since I am going away anyhow, it doesn't matter now, does it?"

"I guess not."

I am nervous. I feel myself begin to sweat. What could it be? What could be so horrific?

Then she drops the bomb…
"Arthur, Jerry laid down with me."

Chapter 26

I blink a few times. Did I just hear what I thought I heard? I start to say something and stop.

Sil is looking at me, expecting a tidal wave of something painful. I'm just stunned. That boy… I furrow my brows, and Sil looks away, bracing herself. Then the words come.

"Oh my God, Sil did you eat his soul?"

Thoughts of Jerry being denied entry to heaven start to swirl.

Sil giggles and puts one of her deadly looking hands over her mouth. Somehow she still manages to make that almost taloned, muscular hand look dainty.

"No, Arthur, there was no soul eating. We both know how Jerry died. He was so much like you. What you said, it's so funny. I will have to share of that." She takes a deep breath and appears to compose herself. "Please know, I did not seek him out. He was young. That age where they are going through changes and always running around with a bulge in the pants. I have so many fond memories, but I will share only three of my favorite memories of Jerry."

"Our first encounter occurred in the room I shared with Vets when he was about fourteen."

Oh, dear God.

"I was alone, hungry, looking out the window touching myself as I tend to when hungry, bored, stressed or just... Anyway, the little sneak was watching. I wouldn't have known he was there, being somewhat preoccupied and all, but he was just so aroused. I can sense these things, you know? So I called him into the room. I will spare you the details, Arthur, but let's just say I didn't have the opportunity to unwrap the gift. Just a touch… and poof. He was so cute, standing there all shocked out of his mind and apologizing like nobody's business. Such an innocent. He wanted so bad to run away, but I didn't let him. I made sure he understood that what happened was okay by me and that I was not judging him."

My head is swimming.

"What the heck, Sil. Do I really need these details?"

She smiles at me, "Arthur, the point isn't the mess he made in his pants. The point is he was a sweet, innocent young man. And for whatever reason, I made the decision not to let him feel guilt or shame for what happened - or to use that emotion for my gain."

"Aww," Znuul says.

Sil rolls her eyes and sighs.

"Okay, second memory – and a very fond one. It was the first time he was actually with me, in me."

"That's enough! Sil, are you just trying to torment me, you want me to remember Jerry like this?"

Sil winces slightly.

"Please let me finish, you promised. This memory you will appreciate, I know it."

"What's the point, Sil? Is there a point?"

"Yes, there is. You see that too was a brief encounter. And after he had… you know, he looked at me with this frightened look and asked me if I just ate his soul. If I ate his soul! We had such a good laugh. You just asked me the very thing he did. He was so your boy through and through. It is rather amazing. You see?"

I'm not sure what to think.

"Anyway, I was his personal playboy magazine until he went off to college. I showed him how to pleasure a woman, how to woo them, how to seduce them. But always, he came to me. I never sought him out because that would have been in violation of your direction."

I am stunned speechless. Maybe it's the exhaustion; maybe it's just too much. What the heck direction did I give her anyway? Then I remember -- she was never to "hunt" without my express permission.

"The last memory of Jerry I want to share with you is when he came home to tell everyone about Marge. It was very sweet. He managed to break away from everyone else and took me out to the Gazebo to tell me all about her in private. I was proud of him, but jealous too. I made up my mind that I would have to show him who's really the better one."

Sensing I'm about to say something she holds a finger up to me and gives me a stern look.

"I will finish. My plan was deliciously simple, I would ask for a kiss goodbye, and once I had his mouth, I would have him. So I asked for my kiss goodbye. He takes my face in his hands and gives me the softest, most delicate kiss on the lips. No lust, no desire, just a kiss with so much feeling. And I was so shocked that I didn't get to put any influence on him. We stood, he hugged me tightly, and said, "Thank you. It wasn't the old toss the whore a dollar and tell her thanks. It wasn't thanks for the wink-wink good time. I felt genuinely appreciated for who and what I was, not for what I was doing to him or would do to him. I realized right then, that if I manipulated this tremendous young man, I would never get another feeling like that from him again."

She looks away, her eyes becoming somewhat misty. After a moment, she looks back at me defiantly.

"And as it turns out I got many of those hugs throughout the years. He even told Marge about us. He kept no secrets from her. It's that MacInerny true love thing, I think. Marge and I became quite close too. All the children, the grandchildren – they're Jerry's. So in a way, I feel like they're mine too."

My jaw drops open.

"This is not easy to say because where I come from it is considered sin, weakness and an invitation for abuse. But I will say it. I loved your Jerry."

"I cannot believe you committed that feeling to words," Znuul says.

I look at this thing, this succubus, confessing all this crap. But is it crap? There's the compelling. I am confused. But one question comes to me amidst the confusion.

"Sil, if you felt that way why did you let them take him?"

"I learned of his capture when you told us. By then, it was too late." She looks down again. "I tried to contact the collector to beg for their release, once. He did not respond to my beckoning. My failure with you has me out of his favor."

"Show us the means of your communication, succubus," Grey says.

She reaches under her dress and pulls out two halves of a broken disc, almost identical to the one Arix has.

"I broke it in my rage after finding I was powerless over Jerry's fate. I have no desire to speak or be spoken to by that one ever again." .

Grey steps forward and holds out his hand. Sil drops the pieces into his hand, and he examines them.

"Useless," he proclaims and offers them back to her.

Grey looks over to me, "What now, Arthur?"

"I will finish, and he will banish me," she says.

Grey cocks an eyebrow at me, "Plucky thing, isn't she? But aren't they always?" He turns to her. "Finish quickly, please. This is not a family counseling session."

I have to wonder what else she has in store.

"The last thing I wish to address is our relationship, Arthur."

"We don't have a relationship, Sil."

She uncoils her tail from around her legs and stands to look at me in the eyes.

"But we do. For over seventy years, you have rejected me. For over seventy years, you have looked at me with disgust and dread. For over seventy years, I have lived with the constant humiliation of failure. You see me as untrustworthy and manipulative; which are titles I know I've earned. But, at the same time, you have not kept me prisoner in the white and allowed me my little hunting expeditions. Oh … yes, the shopping too, I loved the shopping. You should know I gave up on corrupting you after I discovered my feelings for Jerry."

The old Sil peeks back through. The aura of desire just oozes off of her. She takes a step toward me. I take one back.

She points a finger with one of those sharp black pointed nails on it at me.

"But I will never, ever, ever, stop trying to seduce you. I don't wish to corrupt you - that would hurt our family. But I do, so very, very, much want you to want me. You see the pain you inflict on us with your anger and hate? Imagine what you would do to me in that moment of ultimate pleasure. I tingle at the thought. And if you knew what I could do for you, you'd tingle too. So if you ever bring me back, you know what to expect. You own a succubus."

Then her face breaks out into a smile. Not a come hither; just a smile.

"Besides, what's life without a challenge?"

She begins to sit down, then stops and stands back up.

"Just one other thing; if your new friends figure out a way to bring the collector to an end, I would very much appreciate it if you would let me participate. Or at least let me watch." She sits back down, curls her tail around her legs and turns her head away. "Now, send me away forever."

So I do.

I lie down on the floor and say, "What the heck was that?"

"That's the corruptor becoming the corrupted," says Znuul. "You should bed that, she would follow you through fire and ice if you did."

I am beyond exhausted and don't even bother to respond. Too much information, too much drama, too much confusion. Jerry and Sil? In my house? Marge knew? Sil is capable of love? Our family? What the heck is that?

The light changes from brazier to globe. It hurts my eyes.

I see Grey standing over me. He holds out a hand to help me up. I take it and get up.

"Well, Arthur, that was much more than I wished to know."

"You're telling me. Can we be done for the day, Mr. Warden?"

"Yes, trying times these are. We will continue with the others tomorrow after we show you how to gather will instead of rage. It doesn't sound like the remaining deserve to be compelled with such force."

Karen walks over.

"I'll take you to your cell now," she says winking at Grey. "Come on, Arthur."

I follow her out the hall and back to the main entry. We go up to the third floor and down a hall. She stops in front of a door.

"Your dungeon, Arthur. Rest up, clean up. Someone will come for you in a few hours. It goes without saying; summon no one." She opens the door and walks back to the stairs.

I step into my cell. It's actually a fairly pleasant room with a large bed and furniture in the empire style. I walk to the window and have an excellent view of the rear yard. It is unreal. Palatial is the word; stone stairs, reflecting pool with fountain, and landscaping to die for. In addition to this nice view, my cell also has a tiny bathroom with a huge tub.

I stumble back out to the bedroom.

"Our family" that's something I would expect Shey to say.

Crap, family. They have to be worried witless. The funeral. Crap! I don't even know what day it is. I look around for a phone. There isn't one. Maybe they'll let me call tomorrow. I recall the family is being looked over and that gives me some peace.

I fall onto the bed. It feels right. I think I'll just lay here a while until they come for me.

Chapter 27

Loud knocking on the door startles me awake. The sunlight is very diffused coming through the sheer drapes. It must be almost evening.

"Come in," I say, as I groggily pull myself up off the bed.

Znuul ducks under the door jamb bearing a small tray; at least it looks tiny in his huge mitts.

"Wakey-wakey, prisoner." He wrinkles his face at me. "You still smell." He hands me a tray with a coffee service on it.

I probably do smell. How many days has it been? I tell him "thanks" and accept the tray.

"When's dinner?"

My stomach is beyond empty.

"You mean breakfast. We let you sleep through the night. You passed out. It's six am, here in beautiful Dordogne. What day is it again, Arthur?"

He knows that I have no clue at all.

"Up yours."

I pour some cream into what appears to be a double espresso.

"Ooo, the mouth on you." He cocks his head at me with a wry smile. "I'll get you some clean clothes, we need to burn these." He eyes me for a moment, I think judging my size. "Get cleaned up, I'll let the others know you are acting belligerent and what is that expression … Yes, dragging ass."

"You do that, big guy."

His smile grows, and he leaves without saying a word.

I savor my cup, it's European flavor brings back memories of world war two. Good ones, followed by memories of funerals of my friends – not good ones.

I draw a bath and disrobe. The water is hot, and the soap smells like lavender. I clean up and begin to soak, trying to prepare myself for the day. I am due a lesson in using my will instead of rage and hate. We have to interrogate Shey, Pffif, and Vets. I chuckle at the thought of Vets' interview; it will go something like: "Yes. No. I will die for my wielder."

I come outside to find clothes on my bed. I hear Znuul's voice from the hall, "Out here when you are done."

I conclude dressing and adjust as needed because the fit is a bit loose, but that's what belts are for. I step out into the hall

"Grab the tray and follow me," he says.

We head downstairs and turn the opposite way from the interrogation room, into a large kitchen. There is a short, older woman tending to something on a stove.

"Arthur, this is Marthe, she is the queen of all things kitchen," Znuul says, "Marthe, this is Arthur; Grey's newest charge."

The woman puts her utensil down, wipes her hands on a towel, and turns to face me. She puts both fists on her hips and looks at me sternly.

"Dis is my keetchin, you will clean up after yourself."

She turns back around to her stove.

Znuul directs me to the sink and looks at the tray. I get it. I hand wash everything and put it in the dishwasher.

"Well done, Arthur," Znuul says, slapping me hard on the back. He bends down and whispers in my ear, "Don't ever get that one mad at you."

He beckons me to follow. We go through a set of double doors leading out the beautiful rear of the mansion. With the sun having just risen and dew showing on the landscape still, it's a remarkable sight.

"It is beautiful, no?" says Grey. "Come, sit with us."

At the table is Grey, Karen and a man who has seen a whole lot of sun in his day. The creases on his face are deep and his skin leathery. I sit down and eye the bread, butter, cheeses and sliced fruits. My stomach rumbles.

"Please help yourself," Karen says.

So I do. Bread and butter never tasted so good. The cheese is to die for.

"Arthur, please allow me to introduce Reginald Blackmon. He is the head groundskeeper for the Chateau," Grey says. "Reginald, this Arthur."

"Good to meet you, Arthur. Remember, it is Reginald, not Reg, not Reggie," Reginald says in a rough voice, with a thick English accent.

He excuses himself and leaves the table, walking over toward Znuul sitting on the stone wall gazing out over the grounds, apparently lost in whatever thoughts that thing has. Reginald stops and says something to him, and Znuul's posture deflates.

Reginald pats Znuul on the back and moves on. Znuul spins around on the stone rail coming back onto the patio. He waves goodbye to Grey who waves back. Then with a small flex of the legs and an expanse of wing, takes to the air like a shot.

Frickin' amazing and yet kind of scary how easily and quickly that mass takes to the air.

"Ahtsag will be assisting with the grounds today," Grey says. "I thought it best to help ease the fairy and leprechaun into their new relationship."

"That's good thinking, sir. And while we are talking about them, do we have to do the whole compelling thing? I know them, and Arix said it was only him and Sil."

"You thought you knew Arix too. It may be he is just not aware of their complicity. A sleeper cell, so to speak. We must be diligent."

"Better safe, Arthur," Karen says.

Grey takes a sip of his coffee and offers me a smile.

"We will teach you today how to feel your will and use that for a compelling that is not so… harsh. I take it your quarters are satisfactory?"

Nice change of topic.

"I have no complaints. It is a much better jail cell than I expected," I say, going with the flow. "I do have a question, though; will I be able to contact my family anytime? My grand-daughter is probably thinking the worst."

That question takes Grey off guard; it is the first time I have seen him off-balance.

"Oh my, Arthur, I have completely overlooked your family. I do apologize, that should have been the first thing we tended to. This is all just such serious business. There is a time difference to take into account, let us call them at two in the morning. That should be after their supper and allow us to conclude the day's business."

I really want to call now. But I know I shouldn't push the warden. I thank him and turn my attention back to the food. A small commotion of voices comes from behind the closed doors to the kitchen that gets the table's attention.

"You will excuse me, Arthur," Grey says. "I have promised some very special children I would take breakfast with them." He looks to Karen. "Please tutor good Arthur here how to use his will to bind a compelling. Time is of the essence, but do not fail to explain to him the how and why of it, Karen."

He turns to me, "That is the boring part, but important as a learning base for you."

He heads to the kitchen, leaving us at the table. Karen seems much smaller now than when I met her in the Cathedral's basement room. Or maybe it was just that she seemed so much larger then.

"It's a good morning for this exercise, so please eat up. It will make the day easier," she says.

I take that as the doctor telling me, "You may feel a little prick."

We make some small talk, she asks of my family. I ask of hers, which apparently is Grey and some people she doesn't really know in Birmingham, England.

I take a final drink of coffee and say, "I am all yours."

"Right then, onto the teaching," she says as she stands and pulls her chair over to me. "First thing, let's talk about will. The term can be somewhat misleading. What we are delving into here is the core of your personal power; that force which is innately you. When you tap into your rage or hate as you've been taught, you are tapping into that force but through a particular prism or focus. Kind of like how a laser is light, but a particular frequency of light. Do you follow so far?"

"Yes, ma'am."

"Okay, here's the thing: rage, hate, love, happiness, etc. are all very identifiable, tangible emotions and therefore, somewhat easier to tap into. We all know what it feels like to be right pissed off, yes? What we are going to try to do today is to introduce you to that innate current of energy that runs through you that most people are oblivious to. It's that very current which allows us to tap into and manipulate the greater pools of positive and negative forces that weave together this realm we exist in."

I understand.

"It's the force? Use the force, Luke? Like Star Wars."

She laughs.

"Yes, in a way the greater forces are exactly that. But what we are going to focus on is you, the force that belongs to you anywhere, anytime. So, we'll be doing a cheat course for you. Normally it's much better to find it for yourself organically. I am going to let you feel my energy, my will – if you would. Then I will touch yours. Once you have felt your own energy, you should be able to find it again."

She asks me to move my chair closer, so we are just about knee to knee.

"Okay, when I tell you to, close your eyes and try to be open to the sensations I give to you. I will take your face in my hands and project my energy to you. Not my thoughts. Feel for the general vibration and texture of it."

"Vulcan mind meld?"

"Don't be an ass. Just prepare yourself as you know how."

I try to use what Arix taught me when preparing for access of my hate and rage. I try to put myself in a state of blankness. I close my eyes. I feel her hands on my face. I try to feel beyond the physical sensation. I sense an electricity, without the pain. The thrum of Karen pours through my head from one of her hands to the other, forming this arcing circuit. There is a pulse to it. A flavor too… A sound of sorts. No, it's just a feeling, a tingling - a connection. Her hand runs down from my face and rests over my heart. Then I feel her touch something, but it's not a touch. I sense my own energy and feel Karen's energy passing deeper into my own.

I jump back from the intrusion, and our connection is broken.

"So you felt it," she says smiling. "Good. Now find it on your own."

I close my eyes and feel for the second energy she connected to. I relax and just try to feel my own vibration. I do. There's a big difference between knowing something and feeling something. I feel it throughout my entire being.

"Damn!"

"Good show. Now Arthur, remember, your will is their will so, connect with yourself, your will, your energy, and tell them gently, by name, what you expect of them. It's like saying… finger bend and then… the finger bends."

I get it. This is heady stuff. These are real-life wizard-types, and they are teaching me about my innate abilities. Arix never did that. I was just told what I could not do because humans are limited in ability.

Grey joins us after the work is done.

"Karen would you help Bernard with his studies?" he asks.

"Of course father."

She leaves us, putting an arm around the young man.

So, do you think you can compel your summonlings to the truth now without harming them," Grey asks.

"I think so."

"Well, let's find out. Why don't you summon the fairy, she will like the rear lawn."

So I do,

I touch my new-found will and say, "Sheyliene, please speak only the truth.

Other than her saying, "Was that really necessary?" which Grey takes the blame for, there are no issues: no Shey flying across the porch or lying on the ground convulsing.

She looks at me with sad eyes.

"You don't think I'm terrible. Do you, Arthur?"

"No, Shey," I say and hold my arms out for a hug. She slowly walks over, hugs me and rests her head against my chest. I feel her start to cry.

"He made me do so many bad things."

"Well, those days are over now," Grey says. "You are Arthur's now. Not so bad – no?"

She turns around to face Grey and wipes away a tear from her golden pupil-less eyes. She looks back up at me.

"Who is that, Arthur?"

"That is Grey Lightbringer. He is in charge of us for the time."

Grey stands and takes a deep bow flourishing bow to her.

"You have courtly manners," She says.

"Why thank you, good lady Sheyliene," Grey answers. "But we have need to ask questions of you, and we mean no offense by them. It is merely a precaution. You see we found out that Arixtumin and Silithes were in league with Maldgorath."

Shey goes thermonuclear.

"Demon scum! I told you that you can't trust them! Let's kill them over and over again! Summon them right now so we can kill them! Damn demon scum!" She screams and begins jumping up and down, the next thing I know, she has a dagger in each hand.

Grey shoots a look at me that reads, "Get her under control."

I touch my will and say, "Shey."

She stops and looks at me.

"Please put the knives away, you are scaring my warden. We will not be killing anyone today."

"Oh… Sorry," she says, and the daggers disappear into that light gossamer dress of hers. "What do you mean by Warden, Arthur?"

"Sheyliene, Arthur was found guilty of several crimes. But because of the circumstances, he has been put under my charge instead of death."

Sheyliene's eyes go wide.

"Yes, rather serious business," Grey says. "Also serious is whether or not you had or have any knowledge of Maldgorath or what his plans are?"

"No. No way I'd help that walking pile of troll shit. But if you find him, I can fill him with arrows."

My little fairy is coming back to normal.

I'd rather see her cussing, ranting, and raving than crying.

"Sheyliene," Grey says, "There is something else we have to address now. It would be best for you to sit."

She looks at him with those yellow orb-like eyes and then to me.

"Am I in trouble?"

"Not exactly," Grey says "But please take a seat."

She does.

I know what's coming and brace myself.

Grey sits down in front of her and puts his hand on her shoulder.

"Sheyliene, Ahtsag Znuul lives here with me. He is bound to my will and poses no threat to you or Arthur. It is very important, to me, that you not fight with him."

Shey's face goes blank. Her mouth opens, but no rant comes out. She looks up at me stunned.

"Arthur, we are not safe." She looks at Grey. "You cannot control General Znuul; he has faced the queen herself and lived to destroy again."

"Sheyliene, may I call you Shey? Ahtsag has been in my charge for over sixty years. He is not as he was then. He does not fight the yoke."

"He is still demon scum. Demon scum, really bad demon scum. The kind that will eat us all if he has a chance."

"We hear you, Shey," I say. "But can you just try not to attack him? You don't have to be nice."

"Okay. As long as I don't have to be nice to him."

That's my fairy.

She stands and looks around. "Wow," she says, looking out over the lawn and woods.

Grey smiles and says, "These are very old woods. We have vineyards and walnut groves too. I bet you would like to go explore them."

"I would. Arthur, can I? They are so pretty."

"Of course."

She reaches up to her hair, and a cascade of silver dust comes down. She becomes very, very tiny and buzzes away making a circle around my head twice before disappearing to the lawn.

Grey smiles and gets up from sitting on the ground. "I do think I will enjoy the company of that one. Well, shall we address the leprechaun now?"

I have a different idea.

"Can we summon Hjuul next? He would love to run the grounds, too."

"Certainly Arthur."

I touch Hjuul's glyph and call him. He appears and lets forth a mournful howl. Head down, he walks over and plops down next to me, sprawling out on his side. I bend down and scratch him behind the ears.

"You want to go for a run?" I ask. "Great grounds here."

No response. Hjuul is sad, and I know why.

"It's Jerry, isn't it?"

Hjuul makes a whining sound.

"Me too, big boy."

"Oh dear," Grey says. "Not only did I overlook your family but I have not allowed you to grieve your loss." Grey takes my arm and looks me in the eyes. "Once we are done today I insist you take time to grieve."

We move on to summon Pffif. He is not in cahoots with Maldgorath. He too wants to exact revenge on Arix and Sil. He is also uncomfortable with Znuul's presence - but won't be picking any fights.

"Ye'd have to be a fool pickin' a fight with that one," he says. "And I'm no fool."

Then Pffif moves on to important matters.

"Might I be havin' the pouch of pipeweed me clansman gave me? I'm thinking a taste of home would be right nice."

Shock. My clothes are being washed or burnt. My face gives it away before I can say a word.

"Oh no! Master Arthur, ye lost it? Already?"

"Not lost, it's in my jacket. Which is being cleaned."

"Begorrah! Sweet mother of the hills! We need to be rescuin' it, now!"

Grey immediately leaves us to make sure the pipeweed isn't washed. After about ten minutes he returns with the pouch intact, stuffs Pffif's pipe and offers him a light. I get the feeling Grey is enjoying this time. Based on Pffif's, "Oooh's and Aaah's," I know Pffif certainly is.

Karen returns to us and immediately sees the huge beast lounging at my feet.

"I remember him," she says. "He seems much less… animated now."

Hjuul whines in response but doesn't move. Pffif looks up at me from his pipe.

"The doggie be sad, I think I'm bein' sad now too."

"Karen, this is Pffiferil," Grey says. "He's one of Arthur's. Would you mind helping find him a room?"

"Of course."

They leave us in search of a room

"On to the Vetisghar," Grey says. "Ahtsag wishes to be here for that. He has both questions and information for you, Arthur."

Grey pulls a phone from his pocket and dials up someone.

"Reginald, please send Ahtsag back to me when he is at a good breaking point. No. Thank you, Reginald. He'll be on his way. Now, Arthur, I have a question for you. Please think about it carefully. At the end our time together, whenever that may be – what would you like to have gained from the experience?"

I don't have to think hard about that question at all.

"Mr. Warden, I would like to be able to exact revenge on Maldgorath."

Chapter 28

"That is a most unfortunate desire, Mr. MacInerny," Grey says.

I am looking at this man, Grey Lightbringer, obviously unhappy with my answer. But I answered honestly, and I know he knows that.

"Revenge is never a meal that leaves you satisfied," he says.

Grey's right and I don't care. I care less for overdone analogies. I look into his eyes to let him know how serious I am.

"Fair enough," he says. "Your revenge won't happen here, or today, so please release those feelings for the time, so we may move on. Come now."

I follow him back to the interrogation room.

"Summon the Vetisghar."

I do, and there is Vets.

"Please be at ease Vetisghar," he says.

Like that would work.

"Vets, it's okay. Stand down, we're among friends," I say.

She relaxes – a little.

"Please, might you remove that helmet so I could better see you?"

She doesn't. Instead, she looks to me.

"Take it off, Vets."

She takes off the helmet, bares her teeth at Grey and growls.

"Vets, he's a friend."

She looks at me confused and back at him with a pensive look. So there it is - Vets as best as she gets.

I compel her to tell the truth and Grey questions her. Vets had no knowledge of anything either.

The door opens, and Znuul glides in. He unfolds his wings and walks toward us. Then he looks at Vets and says some guttural phrases that I cannot understand. Vets recoils and takes to her knees in front of him.

"Is this Vetisghar yours?" he booms.

"That's a stupid question – of course she is."

"Let me see your arm." He takes my arm and looks at the glyphs on my arm. "This is Vetisghar," he proclaims.

I try to pull away from him but fail, Znuul's grip is like a vise embedded in concrete. He looks at me with those red snake eyes, totally devoid of what I perceive as any emotion.

"You call it Vets," Znuul says. You mean that as a contraction of Vetisghar, obviously."

He bends over me.

"Dismiss it. Now!"

I look at Grey who affirms. So I do.

Znuul smiles and his demeanor changes once Vets is gone.

"Do you even know what a Vetisghar is," he asks.

"It's a warrior thing."

Znuul looks at me as if to say, "Well, what else?"

No idea. So I shrug.

Znuul fixes me in his gaze.

"It is a breed of servant. It either fights for us, cleans after us, or is eaten. It is a conquered race which we have subjugated and is nothing but cannon fodder or whatever else we wish it to be. They are not allowed a name, for to do that gives them individuality. But, once named they are considered beings in their own right."

Saying Vetisghar do this, is akin to ordering Human do this. Heck, this whole time I thought it was her name. The whole time it was like saying, "Cat."

Znuul looks at me and asks, "So you call it Vets?"

"Damn right I do."

"Do you care for this beast?"

Znuul asks me if I care for my Vetisghar. I do, I care for all of my summonlings. Or least I used to. Now there are two that can just rot away.

"Of course I care for Vets."

"Then you need to stand up for it. Call it forward now and stand in its defense. Don't waiver. I will take the role of the antagonist as our tradition calls. Try not to be too scared."

I run my finger along her sigil and call, "Vetisghar."

She appears.

Znuul's voice booms, "Vetisghar! You are nothing. Kneel before those who are your superior."

She takes a knee immediately and bows.

I don't like that.

"Vets, you don't have to kneel before him."

Znuul steps in front of me, his eyes literally glowing from some internal power.

"Do you name this creature? Do you call it Vets?"

He is somewhat intimidating, but I remember what Znuul said. So I bow back up to him.

"I do name this creature, and I do name her Vets! I did that long ago… What about it?"

Znuul smiles at me and then smiles at Vets whose eyes have not left the floor.

My arm feels ablaze where her glyph is. I look at my arm, and her Glyph now reads "Vets" instead of "Vetisghar" in that strange glyphic spelling that I intuitively understand. Znuul takes my arm roughly and looks at the Glyph. He throws me a wink and stalks over to Vets.

"It seems you are now a being of worth. You are named and recognized. Thank your wielder that he made you someone."

Vets is in shock. She looks at me with something I have never seen before – emotion.

"You have named me?"

Crap, I did long ago.

"I have, and you are Vets."

I show her the changed Glyph.

She bolts up immediately from her kneeling position and pulls her sword from its sheath on her back, thumping it on the heavy chest plate armor.

"Vets will die for her wielder!" She proclaims, taking to a knee before me.

Znuul asks Vets, "How does it feel to be a being of worth?"

She recoils defensively, bares her teeth and hisses at him.

Znuul takes no mind of this display. He puts his hand on her shoulder.

"No one other than your wielder can take this from you. You are now and forever Vets. Congratulations on becoming a being of worth. Serve your wielder well."

She falters a little under his hand and looks at him.

"How can you take pleasure in this? I do not understand."

"Good," Znuul says.

He turns and leaves the room.

Grey steps up to Vets and offers his hand to her.

"I would be pleased to meet you formally Vets, I am Grey Lightbringer and look over your Arthur. Welcome to my home."

She takes his hand and with a far-away look meets his eyes. I can see her search for words. Vets off handily takes notice of her sword and sheathes it.

I wonder how many years Vets lived as a slave. And then, with sadness, I realize she still is one.

But she is more now than she was then and that knowledge makes me happy. And she is happy too. I can tell because for the first time ever in over seventy years I hear a deep purring sound as she steps next to me.

Heck, I had no idea she could even do that.

She says, quietly, "I will die for you, my wielder."

"Naa," I say turning to better face her. "Try living, it's a lot more fun."

Chapter 29

It's hard for me to believe that more than a month has gone by. Grey, true to his word, offered me this time for mourning. As I'm not going anywhere or dying anytime soon, I thought it best to take the time. My family knows I'm okay and that I am serving time after being arrested by the "magic police."

I have to wonder if Grey is short for gracious. He insisted on a small service for Jerry and Marge, here at the chateau. There is a small stonework to the back offside rear lawn inscribed "Jerry and Marge MacInerny. In their loving memory."

Grey tells me that I am now part of his family and this will mark it forever. He has the service attended by a druid priestess, Carmella Morningdew and to my shock Archbishop Callon O'Dale. The service itself was beautiful and intimate; just me and what is left of my summonling gang after the banishments. Again, I couldn't get the words out. Hjuul did howl in mourning for all us, and Pffif emptied his flask on the marker afterward.

After the service, the Archbishop and I spent some time together; it was very emotional. There was much sorrow was expressed by the both of us, and I joined him in prayers for those who have fallen by my hand. For the first time in I don't know how many years, I confessed my sins and proclaimed my faith.

I am now feeling more familiar with the workings and faces of the house. Karen, who officially lives here, is never here. I presume she's busy taking down bad guys like me. There is a contingent of four younger children who are staying here for a "camp" of sorts; Aryun, Bernard, Kaitlin, and Luna – all sons and daughters of families "registered" with The Protectorate. There is an older fifth boy, Roger, who apparently is a permanent guest like me; an orphan.

It didn't take the kids long to discover Hjuul, or for him to discover them. It makes me smile to remember Kaitlin asking if the "bear" is friendly. I think the kids have been good therapy for Hjuul too - heck I know it has.

I have come to like Marthe a great deal. She cooks with love but rules the kitchen with an iron fist. I learned first-hand that you do not get that one mad at you. I left a glass out after a midnight milk run once. That morning for breakfast I was given, without notice, a ghost pepper muffin – the muffin of shame. She made me eat the whole thing, taking away my juice, in front of the kids, Pffif, Grey, and Znuul – who all just thought it was so funny.

Lesson learned.

Speaking of lessons, I have also learned that the mighty Ahtsag Znuul, Destroyer of Hope and Devourer of Souls, answers to a second master – Hunter, his large maine coon cat. Grey tells me he started "animal therapy" with Znuul about forty years ago. Hunter is his third cat. I was told by the big guy to keep my hound in check, which I have. Seeing Znuul with that huge cat in his lap makes me think of those villains in the movies, telling the hero how he's going to die, all the while petting their kitty.

Remarkably enough there has not been an explosion between Shey and the Destroyer. Words for sure, but for the most part, they stay clear of one another. On those times when they are near, it's always been Shey being less than verbally kind to Znuul. We get to hear the much used "Demon Scum," and newer ones like, "Abomination," "Hell monkey," and "Ahtsag Fool."

Most times he just deflects Shey's digs with an, "isn't that precious?" or a comment of the like.

The only time I think I've ever seen her get to him was the other night when she said, "Grey loves me more than you." That time he did not respond verbally. There was that stare – devoid of anything you could attribute to emotion. My little fairy is playing with fire; I told her as much.

She let me know, "It deserves torment, and you can always summon me back."

I was informed yesterday, that today officially begins my training, so I am up early in anticipation. I am not sure what to expect. I was told there would be some general assessments and, following that, we would discuss some possible courses of work to help me in my poorly chosen goal of revenge.

I come down to the kitchen to take breakfast with everyone at the huge center island. I offer my services to Marthe in setting everything out. It's better to be in the good graces of the queen. We set out the usual spread of bread, porridge, cheeses, and fruits. We are joined by the kids, Reginald, Pffif, Shey and Grey. We take in our meal and the banter of the day's activities.

"You may wish to eat lightly, as the assessments can be taxing on the constitution," Grey says patting me on the shoulder.

Roger looks at Grey and asks, "Is this his first assessment?"

"Yes."

Roger looks at me like he knows something, laughs a little, and says "Good luck."

Great. They're going to have me run laps around the Chateau until I puke.

Vets comes in through the double doors to the rear yard, in human form thanks to a charm Grey gifted her. Her skin is glistening with sweat from her morning workout of various katas using the sword strapped to her back. Hot on her heels is Hunter, who apparently has taken to her. Vets examines the spread and scrunches her blunt-featured face, looks at Marthe and says, "Meat, please."

"Oui, oui, eggs, and meats for Madame Vets," and Marthe makes way to the refrigerator. Even Vets apparently knows to say "please" to Marthe.

"I have been admiring your mastery of the sword and arts martial, good Vets," says Grey.

She looks at him but says nothing.

"You are quite accomplished, you know" he continues.

She looks at me for affirmation, then back to him.

"Thank you."

"We are not often graced with one of your skills, and I thought since you will be here for a while perhaps you would be kind enough to teach the children, and Roger, some of the basics of hand to hand and sword fighting."

That takes the big girl by surprise. She looks over at me and then back to Grey.

"I will do as my wielder instructs me."

Grey smiles at her and me. "I did not ask him, I asked you. Arthur, I am sure, will let you do that which you want to. Would you want to instruct the children?"

That, of course, causes choruses of "Do it! Do it!" to erupt from the island and she is mobbed. Not fair.

Vets looks at me, genuinely confused.

"Whatever you want to do," I say.

She takes in the kids tugging on her and imploring her to "come on." She turns to Grey and says, "I will."

"Wonderful!" Grey says. "I will confer with Arthur on my expectations after his trials today."

My assessment has just turned into a trial. I look at Grey and ask, "Trial?"

He waves at me dismissively, "trial... assessment – no matter."

We all clean up after ourselves except Vets, who is busy licking her plate clean. Grey takes me aside.

"Please meet Ahtsag in the interrogation room for your first assessment. I will catch up you with shortly after. Oh, by the way, please dismiss everyone – now."

Well, that explains where Znuul is. So, I dismiss everyone making apologies to those around me.

I make my way down the halls and to the room. From the outside, it looks like any other room, but on the inside it is intimidating. I collect myself for a moment and then enter. The room is lit by the globe. All the braziers are tucked away to the corners of the room. Znuul is sitting on his heavy-duty folding stool reading a copy of the Economist.

I greet him with a smile and say, "Howdy! I'm here for my assessment."

He smiles back at me, stands up and puts the magazine on the stool. "I don't know why the old man insists on using this room of all places for this. Come here and we'll get this going."

I walk up to him and look up, as he is basically towering over me. Something is not right.

Znuul's smile turns sinister. His eyes appear to be glowing. The room gets very, very small. I hear him muttering something in that guttural language of his.

Then I know what's happening. He's going to kill me. He's casting a spell. I feel the pressure of it on me. Spiders! He's summoning spiders! I see them starting to appear from the woodwork. I feel my stomach twitch. He is making them come from inside me! I see myself lying on the floor, torn apart with them crawling from inside me, and Znuul holding my beating heart.

I have to get out of here now! I scream and fall backward, Znuul comes forward to loom over me eyes ablaze. I pop up and charge headlong for the door. It opens. I must get away, or I know I will die horribly. I am running down the hall, and hands grab me. I throw a punch immediately which Grey calmly blocks, so I follow with a spinning kick that lands right in the bread basket, pushing him back into the foyer.

I run. Run like hell…

That is until my feet are brushed out from under me by an unseen force, and I spill hard on the floor. Grey is back in the hall looking down at me. I am screwed. I look to my arms and reach for Vets' sigil.

Then with a tingling thud, everything goes black.

I come to, my ears ringing. I'm still in the hallway where I was. I hear Grey's voice telling me to calm down. I roll over, and he has his hands out in the universal, "it's okay" gesture.

"Your first assessment."

He walks over to me and sits down against the wall on the floor near me.

"You are both flight and fight," he says. "And you recover quickly too. Reaching for your friends showed rational thought coming through the veil of fear. It is the ones that curl up in a ball we can do nothing with."

"Dang," is all I can say.

"I do apologize for the use of force on you, but I did not care to contend with whomever you were reaching for. But we have learned much – no?"

Grey stands and offers me his hand, and I get up.

"Now you understand why I had you send your friends away?"

We walk back to the foyer, and he points to a chair indicating I should sit.

"Describe the encounter to me."

"I felt something wrong … then his eyes started glowing and all the spiders started coming."

"Now focus on the very beginning of the encounter, before your terror set in," he says. "You should have felt something… wrong."

I search back and remember it.

"Yes, for sure. Something felt, not right."

"Good," he says. "Memorize that feeling; it may save your life someday. Now, one of the primary defenses against an enchantment or mental intrusion is recognizing it for what it is. Ahtsag is using a fear casting on you. Knowing that he is doing that offers you a basis for a defense against it. Now, are you ready to go back in there?"

The look on my face must have given the answer away. It brings a bout of laughter from Grey, who afterward tells me, "Take a moment and prepare yourself, Arthur, but you will be going back there."

I sit there for a moment and get my dander up. If I can survive World War II, I can survive this. I know what's coming and he's not going to get the best of me. I stand up and say, "I'm ready."

And by God, I am. I storm down the hall to the door and fling it open.

"Come on! Bring your worst!"

Znuul responds by standing up, throwing his magazine down to the ground.

He says, "Okay, human."

He towers over and makes an angry face at me. He turns away then does it again.

"I got nothing… good job," he says. "Go tell Grey."

I turn around to head to the door and begin to feel that sick feeling. That rat bastard Znuul...

Feelings of my doom start to grow; torture, spiders, and failure begin to monopolize my thoughts. I reach down to my will and can feel the intrusions pushing into me like tendrils. More panic follows as I realize they are eating my spirit to leave me a soulless monster. But I don't let go of my will.

Instead, I tell myself "No," and turn to face Znuul. I feel the panic, I feel the fear, but I know it's not mine. I look him in his red eyes and say, "Is that all you got?"

The feelings lift immediately.

Znuul smiles.

"Not bad, still had my hooks in you though. We'll have to work on that. Let's go find the old man."

He makes way to the door, ducks under the jamb in his usual manner, and leaves.

If this is the easy introductory course, I am so screwed.

Chapter 30

I stand here in this ominous room waiting for the next shoe to drop.

Znuul's voice booms from down the hall, "Come!"

I leave the interrogation room, close the door and head to the foyer where I hear Grey and Znuul conversing.

Grey greets me with, "Well done, Arthur!" He looks over to Znuul.

"Professor, would you give the student his grade?"

Znuul looks me up and down. He puts his hand to his chin in consideration and then crosses his arms across that barrel chest of his.

"A minus, or B plus," he proclaims.

"Quite a good performance, Arthur," Grey says. "Most do not succeed until their fourth or fifth try, but of course the majority of those are also about 13 years old. How hard did you hit him, professor?"

"Quite hard. Not with my full fury, but enough. I wouldn't want to break him, you know."

Break me, great.

"Are you two having fun?" I ask.

Grey walks over and puts his arm around me.

"We always enjoy success. And I enjoy not having to chase you and calm you down afterward even more."

"I can hardly wait for the limits of pain test," Znuul says.

My face gives it away immediately.

Grey's arm around my shoulder pulls me in closer.

"He does that every time. There is no such test that I will allow in this house."

I feel relief. Znuul begins laughing.

"Hey!" I shout at him and step forward. I have his attention. I smile at him and put my fingers to my temples.

"Tell me what I'm thinking, big guy."

His only reaction is that poo-eating grin of his.

"Pardon us Ahtsag," Grey says. "Arthur, with me please."

We walk down that same corridor toward the interrogation room passing it to the plush corner office. Grey takes a seat behind his desk and directs me to sit down. Crap, I feel like I'm in the principal's office. But then again, I sort of am.

"Arthur, let's talk first about your desire for revenge."

"Well, Grey, it's like this, that thing not only had my son killed but tried to turn me into a monster no better than itself. I have blood on my hands, and the only thing that will wash it off is his."

Grey sighs. "You are a smart man, Arthur and more than old enough that I will not lecture you, or bother you with overused sayings which you already know. Your age is what troubles me. You are well established in your pattern of thought and view of the world. The disciplines you need would require a fundamental change in them."

Damn, I get it.

"Old dogs, new tricks, eh?"

"Yes. I hope I can give you the tools to survive an encounter with one as ancient as Maldgorath. And that even may be a far-fetched wish on my part."

I can't accept that statement. I know I'm capable of more,.

"Hey, I just stood up to your boy. I did take his almost best shot there with no practice."

Grey considers me for a moment.

"Arthur, you did very well, yes. I am pleased with that, and you should be too. But there are several things you need to take into account. Not the least of which is in the time it took you to come to grips with what he was doing to you, he could have crushed your head like a ripe fruit."

Crap, that's a reality I hadn't considered. Again, I'm pretty sure my face gave that one away.

Silence. It's the he who speaks first game again. I'm in no mood for games anymore, so I throw in the towel immediately.

"You're right Grey, but that doesn't stop me from wanting what I want. So you propose we focus on defense?"

Grey shakes his head and says, "No." He pauses and steeples his fingers. "It's not that one dimensional. In some cases, offensive tactics make the best defense, and in some, a good defense allows the opportunity for a killing offense. But you are six at most versus legions."

"Grey, a wise man once said in conflict, straightforward actions generally lead to engagement, surprising actions generally lead to victory."

I knew he'd get the quote. His smile proves it to me.

"Now are you testing me Arthur?" he says. "A student of war? Sun Tzu? There may yet be hope for your survival." He laughs, then turns very serious leaning across his desk. "Know this, for centuries the protectorate has tried to trap, capture, or otherwise lay hands on that one; the Fae for much, much longer. We fail miserably, and it costs us in lives and pain. Your chosen prey is strong, smart, and as you know by now - without conscience or pity."

I have to look away from him. He is right, and I don't want to hear it. Silence. Again, it's the he who speaks first game. I'm not winning.

"Master Lightbringer will you help me?"

"As much as I can Arthur, but what you seek may be beyond the both of us."

We sit in silence again; this time, no games. Just the as-of-now mutual realization that the task in front of us is probably impossible.

Grey breaks the silence.

"Here's something positive; he can't take your spirit unless you give it to him. It is the law of free will. If you can withstand what torture or lies he sets upon you to try to make you give yourself up, he'll have no choice but to kill you or set you free. Much better than being his slave."

"Oh, good, there's a chance he'll set me free."

We both get a good laugh out of that.

"Let us change the topic, Arthur. I think we have hit an impasse. Your Silithes."

That hits me in the pit of my stomach. Her confessions have haunted me since the day I heard them. So I deflect.

"You want her?"

"No …It is quite unusual for one from her realm to admit what she did. Would it not be a shame to let hate and pain take back over what good may have grown within her? Imagine the pain and horror Maldgorath would inflict on a summonling that betrayed him. You recall that she never called him by name? A sure sign of fear - as names do carry power and spoken properly can call attention. If you're worried about being seduced, we have given you means to negate that with a simple compelling. Arthur, consider showing mercy and summon her now."

"I can't."

Grey sighs and stands from behind his desk. "It is your decision, Arthur - I respect that."

He beckons me to stand too, then comes around the desk and puts his arm around me, now guiding me to the door.

"We will work on ways to enhance your chance of survival. And I will see what information we can find on Maldgorath so you may better know your enemy."

"Thank you, sir."

Standing in the hallway, I realize it's time to re-summon my crew. I also realize I am facing an impossible foe. I remember Sil's words: "If that one wished to reap you, he simply would."

Those words take on a new dimension now. What would I do if faced with Maldgorath right now?

What could I do?

Chapter 31

After summoning my lighter crew back, I take Shey aside. I share with her what Grey had asked me about Sil.

"She is demon scum, and you cannot trust demon scum," Shey says.

Shey doesn't have the benefit of Sil's confessions because honestly, I just did not want to deal with it. So, I lay it all out to her.

"She's still demon scum and will turn on you.".

"So, do you think we stand a chance against Maldgorath?"

She looks at me with those golden eyes of hers, kisses me on the cheek, and says, "I wish we could."

Crap, even Shey thinks it's an impossible challenge. And she'll charge headlong into anything.

We hug and part ways.

I am left with my thoughts. I go to the sitting room and sit on the sofa. My head is spinning. What if I gave into Sil before all this? Would Jerry still be alive? Would that have been enough for that bastard Maldgorath to have thought he had me and leave my family alone? Was it my arrogance that caused these events? I come to realize I am beating myself up for nothing.

You can't change the past.

Grey's suggestion echoes with my own thoughts. Sil can't change her past either. But she can't change her nature either - or can she? She tried to plead for Jerry and Marge. She broke communication with Maldgorath after failing to be able to help Jerry. But the truth of her "one true law" rings with me; I can never know if she will stand by me when that time comes. Will she fold and leave me to be reaped?

Given such an insurmountable foe, would it matter?

Dammit. There is no easy answer. I stretch out on the sofa and drift off to sleep.

I startle awake to a wet feeling on my face. Hunter, Znuul's cat, jumps back also and looks at me like I need to behave myself. He sits down and examines me. I tell him, "sorry." No idea why, but I do. He leaves the room, tail in the air.

I look at my watch and see it's quarter till five. I decide to distract myself productively and head to the kitchen to see if I can help with dinner preparations. Marthe is happy to have my help, and I'm happy to have Marthe happy.

Dinner goes by with little drama, except for Shey's constant digs at Znuul which he deflects offhandedly, as usual. I help with clean-up. Being busy is a very good distraction. But like all things, distraction comes to an end.

"Join me on the patio, when you can," Grey says.

After helping with dishes, I come out to the patio and say, "I can't summon her."

He just looks at me inquisitively and says, "We need to talk about Vets' teaching of the youngsters."

I'm such an ass.

I sit down next to him and say, "Sorry to assume. It's been on my mind."

"So it has. I would appreciate it if you might speak with Lady Vets. She is pushing the children harder than they need to be pushed. I understand she comes from a harsh environment, but …"

"We need to tone her down."

"Yes, and I am glad you are at least considering my suggestion regarding the succubus."

"It's complicated."

He stands, puts his hand on my shoulder and says, "Those kinds of decisions always are."

He leaves, and I am alone again with my thoughts. I figure it's best to sleep on it. I head back upstairs to the sanctity of my room.

I get there and stretch out on the bed. After some time, I realize sleep is not happening. I also know what I must do. So I sit up on the edge of the bed, touch Sil's sigil and call.

The air ripples and there she is – Silithes, in all her horned, voluptuous, woman-demon-thing glory. I point to the loveseat in my room.

"Sit."

She does without a word, her head bowed downwards.

There is silence. I search for the words and can't find them. Finally, they come to me.

"Silithes, please stand," I say, feeling silly having just asked her to sit.

She stands, her head still down, not attempting to make eye contact.

I walk over to her, take a deep breath and hug her.

"Thank you for loving my Jerry."

The words hit her like a gunshot. She buckles under my arms and begins to sob, clinging to me. She lets out a mournful "Ahab" and trembles, holding on to me tighter. I expected nothing like that. I rub her back between her wings to console her. It seems to comfort her, and it feels kind of nice to me too.

Then I feel something warm, followed by something wet and very nice on my neck. It's Sil's mouth. My body goes electric, and my mind is in panic. Her mouth goes from my neck to my ear caressing it with her tongue. Arousal courses through my body like an out of control chemical reaction. She pulls back and looks at me with those beautiful alligator eyes. When did they become so beautiful? I am lost in them. She kisses my lips ever so softy. It tingles. Then she kisses me again parting my lips and exploring my mouth fully. It is sumptuous. It is rapturous.

I feel a tug at my waist followed by something even more glorious. My arousal is in her hand. I want more. Her hand is soft and moving gently, tenderly. This is so very good.

Just as quickly as she came on to me, she pushes me away, causing me to stumble backward and fall on my ass. She plops down on the sofa and leans her head back in exasperation. She sighs and puts her hands on her face as if to say, "What have I done?"

"By the dark well, Arthur, I am so sorry."

At that moment, I am half tempted to say, "don't be sorry," spread her ever-so-eager legs and enjoy the bounties of her talents. She wouldn't mind. She'd love it. I'm stunned speechless and beyond jazzed up.

She sits up and looks at me with a very serious expression.

"You better zip up your britches or I will take that as an open invitation." She buries her face back in her hands. "I'm going away again, aren't I?"

Crap. My better senses return, and I realize I just lost it. I just gave in to her. Dory would shun me. So I zip up and button down fast. And then the reality of it hits me – she didn't take me. And the other part kicks in, I wanted her to.

"What the hell, Sil?" is all I can think to say while trying to muster up my mental defenses to some approximation of normal.

She looks back up at me, tears in her eyes.

"You have no idea how hard that was for me to push you away."

I think I do.

"You gave me love. Not lust, not want, not conquest. Your hug… your words… Jerry… I can't just ambush you like that. I won't repay your feelings with… But I do want you so badly. It could be so good."

I stand there for a moment looking into her eyes, saying nothing. They are sad, conflicted, confused - I think.

"You're my wielder, and I do want you, Arthur MacInerny. Just not like that. Not now, not after your words and your love."

Her face goes back to her hands, and she is hyperventilating. She mutters something like, "I can't go back there. I can't go back there."

I am freaking stunned; this is just totally surreal. I take a seat on the edge of the bed and look at this creature that just a moment ago had me in the palm of her hands after so many years - literally.

"There's something I want to share with you, Sil."

She looks up at me.

"Am I going away again?"

I stand and head to the door.

"Not right now, follow me."

I take her downstairs and through the kitchen. Pffif sees her, and his pipe drops out of his mouth. We head out through the doors to the rear lawn. We walk wordlessly across the vast rear lawn to a far corner. I stop.

We are at Jerry's and Marge's memorial stone. I point to it. She looks at it, then back at me.

"Grey allowed us a funeral, here. He orchestrated this memorial. A druidess and the Archbishop we attacked were there. It was some closure for us. Now, it's your turn."

She takes it in silently. Eventually, she takes a seat in front of the stone, caressing it lightly, her wings billowing slightly in the night breeze.

"Thank you, Arthur."

I move away to give her time. The time I give her carries on and on with her being totally motionless except for occasionally caressing the stone and the wind in her wings, but mostly just still; creepy still. So I wait, sitting off to the side. At least two hours pass. When she stands, I do too. She walks over to me and takes my arm in hers, grasping my hand. She feels so warm and nice; it tingles through me.

That is succubus stuff. I ignore it.

"It's just an aura we put off, I'm not doing anything. Besides, you have your walls back up."

The tingly feeling expands, and I feel something across my shoulders. One of her wings wraps around me. She leans her head on my shoulder as we make our way back to the chateau.

"Thank you, Arthur. I don't have words."

"Words aren't needed."

We approach the stairs to the chateau, Shey buzzes out in front of us, expands to size in a burst of fairy dust.

"Arthur, she's touching you! You know what they can do with just a touch!"

Sil releases my arm reflexively and pulls her wing back.

Shey starts in immediately, "Demon scum…"

I cut her off right there.

"Shey There's more going on here than you see."

"By the autumn breeze," Shey says with wide eyes, "She's had you."

Sil steps in front of me and says, "No, I have not, you little bitch. And if I did, I would make sure you were the first to know it."

Shey looks at us with a mystified expression

"Oh."

Sil steps up to her, hands on her waist, tail twitching and says, "Yeah... Oh."

Shey looks at me with welling eyes. "Don't let her take you, Arthur. Don't let her change you. They can't be trusted."

"I'll do my best Shey, try to trust me."

Shey reaches up to her hair and brings on the fairy dust; making herself tiny again and then flits away. I think I saw a little tear in her eye. Damn. I watch her disappear into the grounds.

Sil breaks the silence.

"Can you imagine how she'd flip out if we told her what happened?"

Sil's mischievous smile is back.

"I appreciate you not going there, Sil."

She walks back over to me, takes my arm again and looks me in the eye.

"So, back to my bright white cell?"

"No."

We head back upstairs to my room.

"You sleep on the love seat Sil."

"Of course."

I give her the comforter from the bed and a pillow.

"Thank you, Arthur."

"No creeping, just sleeping, Sil."

I turn the lights out.

After a while, she interrupts my drifting to sleep.

"I had you. You can't ever tell me you don't want me. You did... you do. I'm not just a disgusting, vile creature to you... Am I?"

What the hell do you say to that after what happened? So I say the least I can.

"Geez, Sil."

"You kissed me back. I can tell a lot by a kiss, you know."

I take a deep, exasperated breath. She is right, damn it. I try not to think of the kiss in too much detail for fear of arousal. Part of me did want her; badly. But that must be the part of me I left behind long ago. That must be the part of me that used to be a crazy drunk and letch - or just the force of her powers.

"I know you can tell a lot, Sil."

"That was an incredible kiss, Arthur, you'll be great. I can tell. It will be like fireworks when we come together. No... Dynamite. I can hardly wait."

Her declaration is followed by a few "mmm's" and the sound of the comforter shifting around. I have a pretty good idea what's going on under there and refuse to acknowledge it.

"I'm glad I didn't take you. Our first time should be special, you should really want me."

I continue saying nothing. Another round of "mmm's" follow.

"Goodnight Sil."

Time passes. I finally start to drift off again, only to be woken again.

"Arthur? Is this what grieving feels like?" Sil asks out of nowhere. "I hurt all the time. I feel bad. I feel guilty. I don't like it."

"Yes, Sil," I tell her. "The pain reminds you that you care."

"When does it stop, Arthur?"

I think on that; I remember my friends that have passed, my Dory, my Jerry, my Marge. Sil's answer comes to me.

Never, Sil, if you're lucky. It just becomes more manageable. Why would you ever want to forget those you loved?"

The silence hangs.

"Goodnight, Silithes."

Chapter 32

I like routine. There's a comfort in things being predictable. After a bit over a year at the Chateau, I find there's a rhythm here, despite the incoming and outgoing of various dignitaries, merchants, campers, and Karen. Karen's arrival always throws the house into a tizzy of anticipation. The kids, regardless of who they are, love her.

We got Sil her own room, thank goodness. My issue with Sil's advances was solved immediately by Grey's simple advice: "Compel her not to." I was surprised at the lack of protest when I did it.

She just said something to the effect of, "That's okay, you'll come around eventually, now that you have a feel for me."

That's fine; she can think whatever makes her feel good.

The truth is I have a demon to hunt and kill.

Grey has been true to his word in training and information. I've learned much about Maldgorath and the denizens of Helterezen as a whole. We discovered that my strengths are in the healing arts more than the ones that blow things up. I would prefer to be able to reign down fire upon my foe, but your strengths are what they are. While my abilities are far from the abilities of some of the extraordinary people he has introduced me to in the healing arts, my ability to heal my summonlings is off the charts. The energy and time it takes me to close a small superficial knife wound on anyone else translate to virtually bringing one of my summonlings back from the brink of death.

I've also been the subject of study by what they call the Techno-Mage guild – the bowler hat guys. I've been scanned, poked, and prodded along with my summonlings. But they've also been a great source of information on my adversary. I have learned that Znuul, Maldgorath, and the other eight full flesh and blood denizens of Helterezen that walk amongst us do not have a cellular composition – they are more akin to viral. Many of the nastier strains of viral-based diseases can be traced back to them.

I have been told they suspect Znuul to be responsible for the original Ebola virus.

Speaking of the big, black winged one, over the course of the last year I feel we've bonded a bit. I still remember Grey's warning "Don't ever forget who and what he really is." I have no questions about what he is. The who is sometimes a question for me. There is a part of him, without question, he guards against being seen. I can't tell if it's the beast of legend or something else. There are times where I think sensitivity shows, but as I learned with Arix, they are adept at appearances. His smile certainly feels genuine, and my time with him I have come to enjoy. I think he does too.

Vets has blossomed since becoming a being of worth. Grey's making her the combat master of the household has brought her out of her shell considerably. I know now it was a calculated move on his part. We did have to rein her in at first as he imagined. But she has made her workouts for the kids, something they look forward to, while still being fundamentally sound. She is even learning to read.

I will never, ever, forget how proud she was to read "Go Dogs Go!" to me.

Routine finds a break today as Grey tells me that the Order of Light - the Paladins - are coming to check on my progress and to give their input on the length of my sentence. This visit, of course, has me a bit nervous. Logically I know there's no reason for nerves; anything decided is well beyond my control. Emotionally though, I feel this can't be an easy visit – after all, one of theirs is dead because of me.

That anticipation has me up a little earlier than normal. I say good morning to Marthe, prepare myself some coffee, and watch the sunrise come up from the front lawn, sitting on the stairs leading into the Chateau. I come back and take in the routine. Pffif flirts harmlessly with Marthe. Roger and the set of new campers come for their breakfast. Vets and Znuul always show at the tail end of breakfast, as Znuul has taken to performing the various sword Katas with her.

She tells me he has even taught her some new ones.

Sil is not a breakfast person, and Shey is hit or miss; most of the time she is flitting about the grounds and nearby woods.

Today we are graced with her fairyness. The kids adore her. There is happy, pleasant banter all around as she flits from person to person with hugs and kind words. Talk of the day's activities. Talk of future greatness. Talk of Marthe's yummy cooking.

I take it in and enjoy as a voyeur, letting the scene unfold. This is the best damn country club prison ever.

I hear Hjuul's cry and know that he's tearing toward the driveway. We have visitors, and I know who they are. I take another coffee and make my way in the opposite direction - the rear lawn. I need to allow Grey and the Order of Light's representatives time to discuss my progress.

They'll find me when it's time. No need to rush.

After an hour or so, Roger comes around.

"Grey would like to see you in the office, Arthur."

Off to the principal's office I go, again.

I enter the room and find it's just Grey and Gunter, the Paladin from the airplane. Gunter rises with a smile on his face and says, "You look well, Arthur. Please, take a seat."

I do, and he wastes no time starting in.

"Arthur, we know that your net worth is approximately sixty-seven million dollars thanks to your smart investing and the windfall of your uncle's estate. Most of that is not liquid, tied in various real estate, leaseholds, and trusts." Gunter leans into me. "We will require twenty million dollars, American. This money is to replenish our funds in ensuring the well being of Herrmann Sorenson's family. His wife will not accept anything directly from you, so we have been and will continue to ensure the family's well being through our resources. She believes it is a pension. But…"

"But the debt needs to be paid," I say. "I can begin arrangements immediately."

"No haggling? No bargaining?" Gunter smiles at me. "You are indeed a child of the light, as Grey says. It is just a shame the both of you are bound to such foul things. Our needs are only anticipated at nine million. They shall not want."

"Money is easy," I tell him. "Living with what I've done is the hard part."

Gunter smiles and says, "True, but facing Svea, Hermann's wife will be hard too. And she arrives shortly, to look into the eyes of the man who murdered her husband."

The butterflies are back. My stomach thinks they brought friends.

Chapter 33

The look on my face gives me away, again. I do not have a career on the poker circuit. Gunter's laugh shakes the room. I check my pants to make sure I didn't wet myself.

"You didn't think this would be easy, did you? She has been briefed and knows of your manipulation. She knows everything we do; she is family to the Order. All the same, know she is a hard, but good woman. She has assured me that she will not kill you. Short of that…"

He shrugs.

I can handle a beat down, that's okay. But I'm not sure if I can sit there while she shows me pictures of the kids and tells me how much they miss their daddy. I remember the feeling of sickness that overcame me in the airplane. It's back with a vengeance.

Gunter gets up and hands me a wastebasket. Damn my poker face.

Grey must have sensed the tension also and changes the topic, "Gunter, Ahtsag would love to see you."

That comment brings no apparent joy to Gunter.

"I do not consort with dark beasts, and normally I do not give company to those who do."

"Indeed, good Paladin," Grey says. "But if we do not share the light with them how can we expect it to take root in their dark souls?"

Gunter smiles again and even laughs.

"I bring them the holy light through the edge of my sword, spell slinger."

All this pithy banter is grating my nerves. I just want to know when Svea is coming to lay waste to me.

"And when exactly is Mrs. Sorenson arriving?"

They both look at me like I am a rude young man busting in on a robust discussion of politics or religion. I guess I am. Grey looks over to Gunter who in turn looks over to me.

"I would guess in about two hours, Arthur," Gunter says.

That seems like an eternity.

"Am I needed until them?"

"I can get what I need from Master Lightbringer," Gunter says. "Make your preparations Arthur. By the way, are you still resisting the demon whore?"

I give him the abbreviated version – "yeah" and leave. I'd just as soon forget being in the palm of Sil's hand.

I make it to the foyer and am greeted by Pffif. Hjuul is putting nose stains on the door to the rear yard. Sil is coming down the stairs, still in her nightwear with a stolen pair of my boxers. I just know Shey is buzzing her way over to us. Vets would be here too if it weren't for training time with the kids. Then Vets comes stalking around the corner from the kitchen anyway.

"Hills and away, Master Arthur, what happened!" Pffif asks.

I remember how very sensitive they are to me. I gesture for them to follow me out to the rear lawn porch. Fresh air is called for. I head to the patio tables and sit down.

"The wife of the paladin I killed is coming to look me in the eyes."

I feel a pair of hands on my shoulder and a delicate kiss on my cheek; it's Shey – I knew she had to be on the way.

"That be some stout medicine, Master Arthur – but it may be the healin' ye both need," Pffif says, stepping up to me. "It will be a foul goin' down but in the long run, might be makin' ye both better."

I am looking at this motley crew of assorted supernatural figures and feel pretty lucky. Hjuul's head is in my lap, Shey's hands on my shoulders and Pffif is standing in front of me telling me to take my medicine. Vets stands there, I know willing to give her life for her wielder, and Sil is sitting crossed legged on the ground surely willing to take my mind off matters if that is what I wanted.

But I don't want to avoid Svea. I just don't want to wait for hours.

"No sense hanging out here guys. I do appreciate y'all, but this is a solo mission. Thanks again."

Vets nods to me, pounds her fist into her chest, and leaves to go back to the kids.

Nobody else apparently has anything to do.

Shey leans over my shoulder and says, "You don't need space, but if that's what you want."

Sil joins in. "I don't normally agree with the Pixie, but there it is."

She smiles at Shey who in turn sticks her tongue out at her. Pffif pats me on the knee and leaves too.

Eventually, I have my space, except for Hjuul. And the truth is I want him here. He is plopped down at my feet. He's not asking me anything or trying to tell me anything; he's just there. That tells me enough.

My big wolf beast buddy.

We sit for a long while, then Hjuul gets up because he hears something. I'm betting it's a car coming down the long drive. He looks at me and plops back down. That's nice; he'd rather be with me than chasing the car down the drive.

I begin to collect myself and wait. After a short while, Gunter comes out to the rear porch.

"It is time."

I scratch Hjuul on the top of the head and join Gunter on the walk to Grey's office.

We enter, and I see a solid woman with light brown hair sitting in the chair I was in just earlier. She stands and approaches me. Standing in front of me, she says nothing and looks me over. Anger is in her eyes as she takes me in.

She slaps my face. And again. And again. She shoves me backward. She steps up and slaps me in the face one more time.

She takes a step back away from me and looks me dead in the eyes.

"I do not care if you are a good man, or if you were made to do what you did," she says, her eyes not wavering from mine.

I dare not look away.

"Both our families have been hurt deeply." She turns and walks back to sit down. "That thing killed your son, and because of that, you killed my husband. You owe both our families vengeance. Vengeance against that the evil one who destroyed our lives and those whom we love. I will have your promise. You will kill it. Your sworn oath to its death or yours trying; I will have that now."

Her eyes bore a hole in me. But the answer is a no-brainer. I've already sworn that oath. I get down on my knee in front of her.

"My death or it's. I will not rest until our vengeance is had. That is my oath."

Grey is shaking his head that this is bad. Gunter is shaking his head that this is good.

I stand. "My sworn oath, Svea, both our families will be avenged, or I will die in the effort trying."

With that said, she stands and looks at Gunter.

"He has sworn an oath of vengeance, I no longer need to be here or see him."

She turns to me, her expression not cracking, and says, "Do not disappoint our families."

Svea and Gunter waste no time leaving the room.

I look over at Grey who also stands in respect of her. I know his concerns. But there is a singular truth.

"Revenge, Grey. However impossible it may be, there must be revenge. I am now oath-sworn to her."

"So it seems, Arthur. Please leave me to reflect for now."

I know to listen to what the warden says. I go.

Chapter 34

After becoming oath sworn to vengeance, my training shifts into a different gear. At the suggestion of the order, I am to take up sword training. Grey explains to me that the knights of the order can channel divine energy through their specially made and blessed swords. I remember how Herrmann's sword glowed and how it cut through Vet's sword, armor, and her like a hot knife through butter.

That is something that could come in handy. He also tells me that swords are very good for decapitation – the preferred method for dispatching dark foes.

I am sold.

My days became very full, very fast. Early AM is sword Kata with Znuul and Vets. After breakfast is study and exercise of the healing and protective arts - then more sword and martial arts training with Znuul. Study of general magic history follows. Then work on my poor evocation skills – the boom and bang magic. More study after that on my foe, Maldgorath, and dark entities as a whole. Then my evening concludes with study and practice of potions, herbs, and alchemy.

After months of this routine, seven days a week, I find myself just a little on the tired and grumpy side. Noting the change in my attitude, almost everyone has a suggestion.

Sil suggests release therapy – "but not as a seduction."

Shey suggests the same, not disguised as "therapy."

Pffif thinks that I should drink with him as "a wee bit O' the spirits cures many an ill."

Znuul mostly makes fun of me, which makes me grumpier. But he does tell me that the idea of drinking with Pffif followed by having our way with the women could be a good break in the routine.

I should have never confided all that with him.

Hjuul though seems to get it. But then he always does. No suggestions, he just makes it a point to be there.

Today begins another grind. I make my way down the rear lawn and meet with Vets. We wait for Znuul, who this morning is a no-show. We embark upon a complex form that is intended to mimic combat against six foes. She has been working with me on this for the last two weeks.

"Well done, my Wielder you have the movements down," Vets says. "Now we will work on your speed."

Great.

We head to the kitchen for breakfast, and I am famished. I see why Znuul did not join us: Karen is home, and he is at her side. She greets me with a big smile and a hug.

"Somebody needs a shower," she says.

She's right – heaving a practice sword around is hard work.

Grey comes over to us after putting his dishes away; I guess even he fears Marthe's wrath. I'm wolfing down my breakfast and in between bites talking chit chat with Karen.

"You didn't spoil my surprise, Karen, did you?" Grey says patting me on the back. "Change in the routine today, Arthur. Take your time, get cleaned up and visit us in my office when you're ready."

"Yes sir," I say after a sip of coffee.

My mind immediately wonders what kind of diabolical test may lay in wait for me.

"And relax," he says, parting ways. "This time I think you'll like it."

Karen gives me a wink.

"See you there," she says.

She heads off following them after taking a moment with Vets. And a moment it is too, because the big girl doesn't talk a lot while she's eating and protecting her food.

I clean up, make my way down to Grey's corner office, and knock on the door. After hearing, "Please come," I enter the room and find Grey, Karen, and Znuul sitting as they almost always do: Grey behind the desk, Znuul in his huge leather lounging chair, and Karen in the chair in front of the desk. Grey makes a motion to me to take the other chair opposite Karen with a smile on his face. Something is up.

"Well, tell me what I'm going to like," I ask.

"You get to leave the Chateau," Karen says.

They have my attention.

"A recruitment cell for the Gratia Potentia has been discovered near Rio de Janeiro," Grey says.

The Gratia Potentia, or "Grace of Power," is basically a cabal of dark entities and dark magic practitioners who wish to rule the world from the shadows. They are basically the polar opposite of The Protectorate.

"The Protectorate advises that cell appeared quite normal with a compliment of rogue vampires, tainteds, and defiled servitors leading recruitment efforts," Grey says. "But a sudden and unexpected surge in its numbers has caught their attention. Further, making up these numbers are creatures that would require summoning, and these creatures persist beyond the normal rules of summoned entities." Grey leans over his desk. "We suspect Maldgorath was hired for the use of his collection and has deposited re-enforcements there."

Involuntarily, I straighten in my chair.

"I think you got his attention, old man," Znuul says, not even looking up from filing his pointed nails.

"We have no evidence of his presence at the compound," Karen says. "This kind of reinforcement is not unheard of as I hope you should know by your studies. He comes, deposits some helpers, and leaves."

But I have been paying attention to my studies, so I know what else that means.

"But it means that Maldgorath is here, somewhere in our realm. If he wasn't, they would dissolve, and their spirits would return to him, in whatever other realm of the multiverse he may be in."

"I told you he wasn't just looking at the pictures," Znuul says.

"You are coming with us to Nova Iguacu, Arthur," Karen continues. "We are going to raid this compound, clean it out, and track down what we can of their recruits. You and your group will be assisting in the raid. Think of it as a training exercise."

"One that can leave you quite dead," Grey adds, punctuated by his serious implacable gaze.

"I won't let that happen," Znuul says offhandedly, still intent on his nails.

Grey swivels his chair to face Znuul, who doesn't stop with the nail grooming but does look up to note him.

"You won't be going," Grey says. "Orders of the council."

Now Big Z is pissed. I can tell, even though he's trying to put a calm face on it. He puts down the nail file and sits up properly in his chair, looking at us all.

"There is a chance Maldy may be there, and if that is the case, I will be needed. Furthermore, if he is there, I would like to be there for personal reasons. The council is plainly in error."

"It is not your or our decision," Grey tells him. "You will abide."

Znuul bares his teeth in a sneer. He points at Grey with his pinkie and Karen with his index finger.

"This reeks of a plan. You both know that."

"I suspect as much, the information comes too easy, and their actions are brazen," Karen says. "It's damn near a dare. But we can't ignore it. We do not need to watch the numbers of dark-bent Paleros swell. Or rogue vampires. Or… must I continue?"

Znuul gives a dismissive gesture and looks away from her out the window.

Karen reaches to an attaché by her side and pulls out a sealed file pocket.

"This is your mission brief, Arthur. You'll have time to read it on the flight. Pull together what you need to. We'll be leaving within the hour."

I take the folder and say, "Thank you."

Grey looks to Znuul who is looking out the window, his version of a pout I think.

"Ahtsag, Karen is running this operation in total communication silence. The council will have no idea of her plans. And Greg will be there."

Znuul looks away from the window and back at Grey.

"Greg ... At least that is good news. Make sure The Protectorate Council knows this. That way if there is a leak from within, it may cause Maldy some pause to come visit personally."

Znuul obviously is dubious of the council. After all the time here, this is news to me. And based on the glance between Grey and Znuul he may not be alone in that feeling.

"Okay, Arthur," Grey says deftly changing the topic, "You go enjoy your vacation, but please come back to us alive."

We all stand. Znuul stalks out the room without a word. Karen and I look at each other and shrug.

"He is still unaccustomed to not having his will be done," Grey says with a wink.

We leave the office, and the plan is to meet at the front drive in about an hour. I have to let my team know what is going on and have them provide a list of any special needs. I figure the fastest way to get everyone together is to dismiss them and re-summon them. The best place to do that is from my room. I head that way and get to the top of the stairs only to find myself accosted by Znuul, who takes my arm brusquely as I round the corner.

"What the heck, Z?"

I know better than to try to break free of his grip. Regardless of how much buddy- buddy time we have had together, there is something very disturbing about being snatched up by an eight foot, winged, red-eyed, purple-skinned, man-gargoyle thing. He knows that, which is why he says nothing for a moment.

I relax in his grip, take a deep breath, and look at his hand on my arm; translation: "cut the drama."

He releases me and says, "If you see that bastard Maldy – you run. You do not become a hero. You get what you can of the team out. And if he does get his hands on you, put a bullet in your brain if you can – it's better than the alternative."

Not giving me an opportunity to respond, he steps away then bounds over the third story balustrade; gliding into the foyer with an easy "poof" of his wings. What a drama queen, geez.

I get to the room and bring the team together.

"We have news, team. We're going to be part of a para-military effort. Please pull together a quick list of needs – guns, body armor, whatever. We don't have time for questions and answers as we're heading out in less than an hour. Pffif, help Vets with her list. Let's meet up at the driveway in half an hour. Now, get. All of you. I have work on my list."

I sit down at my desk and jot down a quick list of firearms, bladed weapons, body armor, and explosives that I feel would be helpful. I grab a duffel bag, throw in some clothes, toiletries, foci and a box of various potions that I've brewed during my training.

Good enough.

I sling the bag over my back heading for the stairs. I have time, so I figure I'll grab a quick snack and say "au revoir" to Marthe. Marthe offers to slice me some hard salami and cheese. In return, I offer to take over washing the potatoes for her.

She tells me, "You are a sweet boy," and tweaks my cheek.

I am damn near twice her age, but one does not correct Marthe.

I start the water running and grab a brush and a potato. Through the kitchen window, I see Karen and Znuul having a very intense conversation. No doubt he's pulling the same routine on her that he did to me. I begin to clean the potatoes but can't help myself from keeping an eye on them. Karen is jabbing her finger into Znuul's barrel chest. That's asking for trouble. The big guy looks up and away, but doesn't move an inch. They stand there in silence. She's looking at him, and he is looking away.

She steps right up to him and wraps him in a hug. He hugs her back, setting his chin on the top of her head. Then he engulfs her in a second hug from his wings, and I see Karen no more, except for her calves and feet. Znuul unfurls the wings, and they part toward the foyer entrance, her arm around his waist and his giant mitt on her shoulder.

Big brother is worried about little sister. We must be walking into serious flack. I best not let anything happen to her.

I notice Marthe standing next to me. The potatoes aren't washed. I better get busy.

Chapter 35

I make sure to be at the drive early. Znuul and Karen are there. Karen sits on the bumper of the limousine, Znuul stands with arms folded on his chest. I gesture to Znuul to come over. He gives me an exasperated look and he plods over to me. I make another gesture for him to bend down. He does.

"Don't worry, I'll make sure she's okay," I whisper.

He stands up straight and lets out a huge bellowing laugh.

"Karen, you're going to be okay now – Arthur's going to look over you!"

Znuul is giggling at me now. Karen shakes her head and mouths, "sorry" at me.

Znuul's hand is shaking my shoulder, gently for him - like an earthquake for me.

"You would do well to grab hold of whatever robe she wears and follow behind her," he says.

Great. I just offended the leader of my team.

Grey, Shey, Vets, and Pffif approach with Hjuul trailing behind.

Znuul bellows out, "Old man! Arthur thinks he's going to protect the Red Witch!"

Znuul looks down at me with his patented shit-eating grin.

"Isn't that so sweet," Znuul says, piling it on more.

Grey approaches me with a smile and an outreached arm.

"That is an admirable sentiment, Arthur. Don't let Ahtsag's ridicule stop you from thinking that way. I would very much appreciate you protecting her." His voice steps up a notch. "Of course I would like her to make sure she protects you too."

"All good leaders look out for their teams," Karen says getting up from the bumper.

Grey walks over to her, hugs her, and whispers something to her that I presume is something along the lines of, "come back alive, please."

Last joining us is Sil, no luggage, thank goodness; just a scrap of paper. At least she addressed the list. She hands it to me and takes my arm, making me a little uncomfortable, as her touch carries that warm tingly little vibration with it.

"Okay," says Karen, "Only so much room in the limo."

Translation: time to send some folks to the white.

"Send me to the holding. I will meditate in preparation," Vets says.

Off she goes.

I look at Hjuul who folds his ears back and makes a whining sound.

"Sorry guy," I tell him with a scratch on his head and a look to the eye. "Back as soon as we can, hey how about you just stay here until we arrive?"

Shey immediately reaches up to hair and in a shimmering silvery downfall makes herself tiny.

Pffif looks at Karen and says, "I don take up no space either."

"Okay, let's go," Sil says, leading me by the arm. Karen's look at me is plain enough – send the skanky bitch away.

I extract myself from Sil's warm, inviting touch to walk over to Karen.

"If that is an order from my team leader to dismiss her, I won't hesitate. But if it's just a personal issue, I hope we can work through it, God knows I had to."

"Fine," she says. "All in, we go now."

With that, we get in and leave.

Three hours of drive feels like three days. To one side of me is Shey. The other Sil. That's enough tension. Pffif sits next to Karen, and I keep thinking he is going to put his hand on her leg and say something like, "fetch me a drink ye fair wench."

Luckily no such drama occurs. Shey doesn't call Sil demon scum once, and Sil doesn't touch herself. Pffif sticks to his flask, lightly, and doesn't try to light his pipe. We get to Air Lightbringer with minimal drama.

I try to sleep through as much of the flight as possible. I hear that helps with the lag. The mission brief is very complete: full diagrams of the compound, estimates of numbers and types of combatants. We are walking into a shit storm with multiple choke points. Major firepower will be required, with a heaping helping of good luck.

We arrive and pile into a large Humvee that takes us whizzing away to a safe house. Or more like a warehouse. We enter, and I am greeted by, "Arthur, the many! You tapped that succubus yet?"

It's Greg, the sword of balance, sitting on the hood of a large armored vehicle.

Before I can get a word out, Sil responds for us.

"Hell no!" She swaggers over to Greg "But you make sure he gets out alive, and I'll give you a night you'll never forget – ever."

That brings the usual male, "Hell Yeah!" and such from what appear to be the mercenaries around us.

Sil's offer takes Greg aback a little; he knows her for what she is.

"You mean safe, no eating on me - I'll never forget such a good thing, right? …Succubus."

That brings a little hush from the mercenary types.

"Keep my Arthur safe, and you get whatever you want."

More raucous comments follow.

I feel like a total weenie now. First thing out, a girl is saying I can't handle my own business.

Crap.

So I do what needs to be done to recover some of my mojo and go full-on testosterone.

"Sil, shut it! We are kicking ass and leaving bodies behind. You want to roll with her, Greg? No problem, I'll tell her to love you a long time."

Daggers sprout from Sil's eyes.

"You'll tell me?"

"Why not, since you see fit to offer yourself to someone without as much as asking your wielder."

She backs down and quick, thank goodness.

"Woo," is the general consent from Greg and mercenaries.

I just stride up to Greg and say, "Gimme some love, you fast bastard."

He jumps down and gives me a man-hug.

I feel a bit like less of a weenie now.

Shortly after, the doors to the warehouse slide open, and we are joined by Gunter, one other person I would assume is of the Order of Light as well, along with Christophe LeBlanc who has been an exceptional teacher to me in the healing arts.

Gunter looks around the room and bellows, "Who is ready to smite some evil!?"

Cheers come from all around.

So much better than my introduction…

Gunter strides over to me and takes me by the shoulder to the foldout tables in the middle of the room.

"Come, Arthur we have something for you," he says, in that Germanic voice of his.

Having no choice but to follow, so I do. We get to the table, and he pulls one of the boxes off his shoulder and sets it on the table. He unlatches the fasteners on it and flips the lip open. Before me lays a blessed sword of the Order of Light.

"Take it in hand and call forth the divine!" he says.

I take it up and feel its hum coursing through me.

"Call to it, Arthur. Bring forth the light!" He says clutching my shoulder harder.

I remember my training and connect with its hum, it is powerful and reassuring, but it does not call to me; I must call to it. I do and step back into a defensive stance.

Gunter cheers. I hear cheers from those around me. I realize that the blade in my hand is glowing.

"Down with your blade now, brother," says, Gunter. "I knew you were of the light, even with demon spawn in your keep."

I relax, and the glow leaves the blade. I look at this blade, its hum still vibrating through my whole body, and set it back in the box.

A gift too precious.

"I am not worthy my friend."

He laughs, then turns serious.

"The sword says you are. Besides, each blade from a fallen warrior must be passed down to a new champion. This was Herrmann's blade. You did not think Hellfire could touch such an instrument?"

I am in shock.

Gunter takes my face in his large hands.

"The sword has chosen you, and it is a most fitting tool for vengeance, is it not?"

He gently slaps my cheeks.

"Yes, sir … No question."

He releases my face, smiles and gives me a hard pat on the back.

"Normally I would welcome you to the order, but you keep foul company, so instead I tell you I look forward to battle by your side."

He turns to the assembled crowd around us and shouts, "Evil will cower before us!"

A roar responds from the room.

Man, that guy knows how to work a crowd.

Chapter 36

The briefing of our plan is simple and to the point. Over the course of the next two days, we will deploy vehicles pretending to keep an on eye the enemy's compound. But in reality, those vehicles will be quietly picking up decoy persons. After we have enough to mimic our true force, we will stage a false exit of the country by sending the decoys away.

Once our exit has been reported, Pffif and Shey will make sure any of their spies are silenced quietly, so as not to announce the presence of the true attack force, still in place.

With their attention elsewhere and no way to be warned, we'll drop the hammer on them. Disinformation, military sleight of hand – Karen knows what she's doing. I am impressed.

Two days is a long time to live in a warehouse with very little running water. Except for Vets physically abusing one of the mercenaries, who for whatever reason decided he couldn't keep his hands off her, the time is mostly uneventful. If nothing else, the mercenaries think to take her very seriously after that incident.

I am just glad she didn't kill him. Things can happen fast with Vets; scary fast.

After what seems an eternity, the day comes, and two military transport vehicles arrive. The decoys plus my summonlings pile into separate Humvees. Hjuul is changed into a human form, and I can tell he is not comfortable with it.

For the first time, I get to hear him speak to me: "Not leave you."

That is worth a hug and reassurance to him that he will be back as soon as possible.

I knew he was smart.

Shey provides aerial reconnaissance to let us know if there are any cars or activity that follow the feigned exit. After the vehicles leave, she comes back letting us know that, yes, we are being watched and some cars are following our bait. One van stays to keep an eye on the compound.

Shey and Pffif are dispatched to make sure whatever report they send in will be their last.

After Pffif and Shey return, the real team makes its exit, and we converge on the compound in our appointed positions.

"Karen, how about we arm Pffif with explosives to set around the place? He can become invisible and is super sneaky," I ask.

"Would save some wear and tear on me," Greg says.

"Right. Give the charges to Mr. Pffiferil," Karen says.

A mercenary brings four devices. Pffiferil takes off with them. I hope there is nothing with true sight in there, or at least that he is sneaky enough to get by them.

Almost half an hour passes, and he returns.

"Yer special deliveries been a made, ana where ye asked em' to be."

"Thank you Mr. Pffiferil," Karen says followed by pulling out a large box with several switches. She flips two switches, and we hear the eruptions.

That's the signal for the first team. I know they are entering the compound now; that's Greg and the mercenaries. We are to wait. I hear the gunfire and know the battle is on. After what seems like forever, but is probably only a couple minutes, she flips two more switches; booms follow, and she says those fateful words, "We're up."

I call together the my crew. I take a moment to let Karen ward them, and open the trunk of the vehicle for weapons. We wade into battle. I realize immediately what Znuul meant. Karen, with her wands/foci in either hand, is standing in the middle of the yard casting a storm of fire and lightning before her. The paladins are wading in, armor and swords aglow in the dim light cutting down all in front of them of dark origin.

We take the flank as we are supposed to. Vets wades in with Hjuul on her heels. We are met by at least twelve adversaries of inhuman origin. Vets' sword lashes out like a buzzing chainsaw. Hjuul, back to normal, bites, claws, and pounces. But the numbers are too much.

So I reach into my will and project out healing care to Vets, followed by the same for Hjuul. They rebound, and the tide turns as Hjuul and Vets become as strong as when they first engaged.

Silver arrows poke out from many adversaries. Shey's bow is thrumming from behind the metal drum she's using for cover.

My attention on them, I am knocked to the ground. A frog-like creature bellows, "The master will be pleased!" and makes a face like he's going to vomit.

I don't want to be barfed on, so I roll frantically out of the way.

It coughs up a ball of acid that eats its way through the concrete where I was laying. I stumble to my feet and look to face my foe. A pair of hands grabs it by the mouth from behind, jarring it open and most likely dislocating its jaws. Black fingernails rake across its neck splitting it open, releasing gouts of blackish ichor like blood; Sil.

A silver arrow blows through its head, and it falls to dissolve into ectoplasmic nothingness. I know Maldgorath felt that summonling return.

I look over my crew, my focus on following them, keeping them healed and standing in the face of our foes. It feels like we have met the most of the enemy. Those that are left are falling back and running. We are not. I see major fireworks coming from inside the main compound that we blew with the first salvo of explosives. I direct the group that way to provide support.

We get inside to find Karen and Greg standing amidst piles of steaming ectoplasm, headless bodies and one being, half-charred, begging for mercy and promising information. Just like that his head rolls and Greg is standing over him.

I was going to protect them… right.

Karen looks over at me with eyes of a woman possessed.

"Assist the others!"

I listen for the sound of conflict and head my group in that direction. I signal to Vets to take point, and she busts through the door out to the courtyard, Hjuul is hot on her heels followed by the rest of us. There is a fire-fight taking place, and I note Christophe attempting to heal a very injured mercenary.

Using my sidearm, I lay down suppressive fire in the direction of our enemies who are using a truck as cover and make for protection of our own.

Vets, apparently thinking I can heal anything, sheathes her sword, charges toward the truck, now brandishing a shotgun. She takes major flack, but between her armor and my healing, she chugs ahead like a freight train. Making it behind the truck and running out of shells, I see her swing the shotgun at one of our adversaries as a makeshift club.

More shots ring out, and I am struggling to keep Vets in line of sight for healing.

A voice yells, "Kill the healer!"

A wallop to my chest knocks me to the ground.

Thank god for Kevlar.

But Vets' distraction is more than enough to allow the Paladins to overwhelm them from the opposite flank. Things become very quiet behind the truck.

I sit up to see a concerned Pffif, Shey, and Sil hovering over me. Shey is running her hands over me to make sure I'm okay. Sil's attention is between me and our surroundings; her eyes searching like a predator for enemies or signs of danger. I stand and see one of the mercenaries helping a very wounded Vets away from the truck. Without hesitation, I send healing her way as strongly as I can, and she rebounds almost instantly.

The mercenary takes notice of Vets miraculous recovery and excitedly yells, "Follow me!"

I follow him to where Christophe is trying to heal the seriously wounded man.

The mercenary says, "Do that thing to him you just did to the were-cat."

I try, but it just doesn't work the same way on people as it does on my summonlings. Christophe stands and puts a hand on my arm.

"It's too much," he says, "he's gone."
Christophe gives an apologetic look to the standing mercenary.
"Damn," says the mercenary.
The yard is quiet now. I think that means we won.
I look down at the dead mercenary and don't feel like a winner at all.

Chapter 37

It was an almost complete rout. We did suffer three casualties; three of the mercenaries. Christophe says words and pronounces blessings over their bodies. All join in.

I am brought back to air Lightbringer and sent back to the Chateau on my own. Well, with my team anyways. Hjuul gets to ride this time because I say so.

I try to absorb what has just happened because I know Grey is going to ask me what I learned. I learned that Karen is a devastating force in and of herself. I learned I could wield a Paladin's sword. I learned that keeping my team standing in the face of insurmountable odds takes a hardy effort of focus and will.

Oh yeah, I learned not to let frog-faced demon things barf on you either.

We are quiet all the way back. There is a general feeling of defeat that pervades the air, even though we won. It isn't a celebration by any stretch.

Vets addresses it, coming over to sit down in front of me, declaring, "It is hard to celebrate victory when you know many of your foes can just be raised again."

There is no reaction from the jet's chamber. I think we all understand the truth of her statement.

"But you kept us standing, and they fell," she says. "And if we do fall, we can rise again too - if you call us. We all fought well. We always do because of you, Arthur MacInerny, and for you too."

That gets a, "Here, here!" from Pffif. Vets leaves me to my contemplation and an attempt at sleep.

After landing, the limo ride back is solemn too. Until Pffif starts handing around that never-ending flask of his. Vets, Sil, and Shey tear in. And eventually, on Pffif's instance, I do too -- despite my former tendencies to excess. It doesn't bring me any happiness; just a numbness. But that's okay; I'll take numb for now.

I note that Pffif's magic flask seems to help Shey and Sil coexist a bit. I think it is the first time I ever see them hug and girl banter. If Vets is affected at all I sure can't tell; she's just stoic. Pffif is having a great time though, singing bawdy songs and encouraging everyone to join in.

I take a pull from the flask, look out the window, and pass it on. I lean my head against the window. What would Dory think of all this? I am vengeance-sworn. I face impossible odds. I have two mythical beings that want to bed me for radically different reasons. I'm friends with a demon that may be just as awful as the one I am sworn to kill. I'm drinking with a leprechaun. I go from leaning my head into the window to thumping it against the window.

It feels good.

I hear Shey say, "He's thinking of Dorothy."

"Yeah," Silithes says.

I feel a small hand on my leg and realize it's Pffif.

"Ye be all right there, Master Arthur?"

I lean back in the limo's comfy leather seat and say "Gimme that damn flask."

It instantly appears in my hand. I take a big pull, hand it back to Pffif, and say, "I am as all right as I can be for now."

Shey and Sil are analyzing me with much concern from the facing seat. It's time to change the tone and have a little fun with them. I bend forward in my seat and put my head in my hands and begin shaking slightly, mimicking distress. I sense them leaning in to comfort me.

"Blah!" I yell at the top of my voice jumping out toward them.

They fall back over each other in surprise.

Sil shouts, "Damn!"

Shey says, "That wasn't nice!" and smacks at my knee, mostly missing it.

Pffif is literally rolling on the floor of the limo, laughing.

Vets is smiling - which is a thing in and of itself. She sees me looking at her and says, "Do it again."

Maybe the flask was doing something to her after all.

We pull up at the Chateau in what seems like no time at all for a three-hour drive. Grey, Znuul in human form, and young Roger are waiting for us. We stumble out of the limo.

Pffif gives Grey a salute with the flask and says, "Greetin's to ye, Master Lightbringer!"

Roger says, "They're waaa-sted."

"We wasted nothing!" Vets says.

Then she puts her hands in her face and after a second or two yells, "Blah!" mimicking my little joke, thinking it's still very funny.

I am starting to feel a little self-conscious. Grey and Znuul look at one another.

"We survived!" I say, thinking that will explain everything.

Znuul snickers and cocks an eyebrow.

"The battle, yes. The return trip is questionable."

"Welcome home, Arthur," Grey says. "Please take the evening for yourself and tomorrow morning we will talk about what was learned. Mr. Pffiferil, might I have a sample of the contents of your magical flask?"

Pffiferil hands him the flask. Grey takes a sip.

"Positively vile, Mr. Pffiferil," he says with a look of disgust.

Pffif smiles, takes the flask back, and says, "Bet if ye be taking a few more sips, ye not be noticing."

"Walk with me Mr. Pffiferil," Grey says. "I will share with you liquors worthy of drinking."

And like that, they are gone. There goes the flask. Damn.

"Aww," says Znuul reading my expression. He looks over at Shey and Sil, still acting like best buds. "Hey, girls, Arthur's drunk… Easy pickings."

He even adds the over the top bouncing eyebrows.

Sil screams, "Ow, damn it!" and I realize the compelling against seducing me just hit her upside the head. Bless her heart for thinking to try.

Shey weaves over to me, takes my arm and looks at Znuul.

"I would never take advantage, Demon shcum!"

"Oh pu-lease," Sil sighs.

"Thanks buddy. By the way, you are an asshole."

"Shmelly unwiped ashshole," Shey adds.

I realize she is using my arm to stand straight.

The driver plops down my duffel next to me.

Shey breaks away from my arm and stumbles a little. She reaches up to her hair and the cascade of pixie dust falls. Shey is a tiny pixie fairy again, her wings buzzing her mid-air. She flies up to my face, kisses my cheek and says, "Catch me if you want me!" Then she takes off in a loopy, careening flight into the dark.

I'm not running through the dark now. Nuh-uh.

Sil sashays up to Znuul, takes his arm and says, "You want to get lucky?"

The disappointment shows on his face.

"I'll have to get Grey's permission; I'm sort of on a short leash there, due to past transgressions."

Sil shoulders sag. She looks at me and says, "I can't catch a break, can I?"

She basically drags Znuul up the stairs toward the house. Good luck there, indeed.

I am alone. I am drunk, but probably not for long given my spirit fueled metabolism. I take a deep breath and look at the stars in the clear night sky. I reach down for my duffel and realize that I am not alone.

Vets. She's just quietly standing there, looking at the stars also.

"Pretty aren't they?" I ask her.

"Pretty? It is vast."

I grab the duffel and ask her if she's coming up. She nods, and we make our way up the stairs to the foyer, where I drop the bag. The sofa in the sitting room looks inviting, and best of all it doesn't involve standing or stairs. I head over and plop down. Vets follows, not sitting on the sofa, but against it on the floor next to me.

"We fought well," she says.

"Yeah."

It occurs to me she's making small talk in her way. In my seventy plus years with Vets, I can't recall us ever chit-chatting. I know. I've tried and met the wall of mono-syllabic responses. And never, ever, has Vets started a conversation unless it was related to instruction for a task.

Hunter comes trotting up. He rubs up against Vets, who returns the attention with a scratch under the chin.

"Znuul named this one well. Have you noticed how much prey he leaves at the rear doors for his master?"

"No, I hadn't."

My speaking gets Hunter's attention who jumps up on the sofa, now demanding my attention.

"What do you think Hunter did to deserve his name?" and with that question, she turns the ring Grey gave her and says its trigger word, "T'shigar."

She returns to her native Vetisghar form. She stretches her legs and arms in a lazy catlike way.

This question of hers bothers me, mostly because I can't answer it in any good way.

"Well, Vets, here on earth things are different," I say, figuring that's better than "I dunno."

"Indeed," she says. "Much different."

"You know, Vets, all this time together and I actually know very little about you. I'd really like to know more."

She turns to me, looking confused. "You do not know me? I am loyal, I am fierce. I will die for you."

"No, no Vets. I know you; the essence of you. I mean stuff about you, like your family. Tell me about your family."

"I am not sure what I can tell you. We do not have families like humans do."

She pulls off her shirt. For Vets, being without clothes is more natural than wearing them. She scoots from my side to sit in front me, in between my legs with her back to me, showing me her broad shoulders. She reaches her left hand over her shoulder to her right, showing me where her back was branded with a series of glyphs.

"The first is my mother's number, second my father, third mine, and last the compound of my birth. This way they follow the line of successful breedings."

"When did they brand you?"

"We all are branded when they remove us from our mother's care, basically when we can walk and feed ourselves."

"Do you remember your mother at all?"

"I have few memories of my mother, given the young age of separation. I know nothing of my father. I do have memories of my young. I have been successfully bred three times."

Damn, Vets is a mom; three times over.

"What were they like?"

She adjusts herself so she can look at me, "They were all most beautiful. They were happy. They were, as you humans say, loving. But the culling would cure them of those problems."

She must have read my confusion as to what she meant by that.

"The culling begins when the young are separated from the mother," she says. "The young are assembled with others of their age and not given enough food, so the weak perish as they cannot take for themselves. It is like your school, there are six seasons, and all kept to the same age as new young arrive. At the end of the culling, the strong are brought into a group where they are instructed and stay until of breeding and selling age."

I am horrified. That is nothing like our school system, despite what the kids may tell you.

"Vets, I am so sorry you had to endure that. It's barbaric."

"That is the life of Vetisghar."

"What about the fathers of your children?"

"All I know is they are all strong."

My poker face gives it away again, she begins to explain.

"When the females deemed of value approach season, males of similar value are given the opportunity to fight for their choice. When the breeding pairs have been determined, the female is beaten to submission, tied to a breeding block, and seeded."

She says it so offhandedly; beaten and raped. That is normal for her. But not me; it is nothing less than evil to treat sentient, feeling beings in such a way.

"This is not your way, I know. But if the Dzemond of Helterezen find a way to your world, it will be. It is their way. They conquer, destroy, and defile. I would prefer this not to happen. This realm is rather pleasant. I think ours was too, before."

She smiles at me. "Here, even simple beasts like Hunter can be beings of worth. I like being of worth."

With that, she turns, lays her head on my thigh and closes her eyes. The thrumming purr sound begins to come from her. I reach over to stroke her hair, and she starts back wide-eyed and baring teeth.

"Sorry," I say recoiling.

Realizing it's me she relaxes immediately and smiles. Then she crawls away from the sofa and sprawls out on the floor, stretching from finger to toe.

"I am tired, this is comfortable."

"I'll leave you to your rest, Vets," I say getting up from the sofa. "I hope we can talk more, I do enjoy your company. I hope you know that."

"I will not forget," she says. She kips up suddenly and grabs me in a purring bare-chested bear hug. She must have sensed my surprise because she takes a quick step back and holds her head down submissively.

"That was not my place, Master; I thought that was the human way of showing kinship."

"It is Vets, my apologies to you, please. It's just that we've been together so long and you have never done that."

I step into the big, scary cat-girl-warrior and give her a hug of my own to make things right.

The purr is back. She licks my face. Eww.

"That is how we show kinship," she says with a smile while gently breaking away from the hug. She settles back down to the floor and lazily stretches.

"Good night, my wielder."

"Night Vets."

I grab my duffel, and attack the stairs; thankfully much more sober due to the combination of what I just heard and my spirit-reinforced constitution. I think to what Vets said about what would happen to Earth if Helterezen finds its way here and begin to understand the Protectorate a little more.

It also gives me more insight into the mind of my prey. We, mankind, are far beneath Maldgorath; no better than beasts of burden or food stock. But even the most highly-trained beast master can be surprised. Finally, I see what may be a weakness; arrogance.

Maybe my quest isn't so impossible after all.

Chapter 38

The alarm wakes me up this morning, which is a surprise. Normally, I wake before it has a chance to go noisy. Luckily because of my enhanced metabolism, there's no real hangover. I look over to the box with the blessed sword in it and think better of it. Instead, I grab the leather scabbard with my practice sword.

It's a return to routine.

Vets and Znuul are waiting for me. Znuul is looking large and human. We must be expecting visitors today.

"About time," he says.

Vets has not bothered to use her ring so is still very Vetisghar. She leads us in the six combatant Kata, moving at a much brisker pace. I make many mistakes trying to keep up.

I blame the pace, not last night.

After a review of my shortcomings, we join everyone for the tail end of breakfast. Food sounds real good.

Grey and Roger are still lingering around the island. Pffif is at the corner of the island with his head down, looking like crap.

Grey greets us and asks, "And how are you this fine morning?

"Never better, sir."

"Find me after your meal, and when you've freshened up. Oh, you may wish to tend to the Clurichaun."

That would be Pffif.

I grab one of Marthe's delicious croissants, some butter, fruit and then make my way toward Pffif's end of the island. I set my plate down next to him and grab his little shoulders and rub vigorously.

"Ach! Locusts and toads! Canna ye not see I be in pain?" he says.

I sit down on the stool next to him, smile and start in on my breakfast.

"Do'n you have to eat so loud? Take mercy on me, Master Arthur, ana send me away to heal." He plops his head back on the island.

"That must have been some booze Grey shared with you."

"T'was a glorious golden whiskey from the hills of Scotland. Ana a beautiful amber Brandy from France. Ana some disgustin' spirits from the Mexico that's I hadda drink a few of to make sure. There was a…"

"You two drank one of everything?"

"Naaa… Master Grey was only drinkin' the whiskey. But a great host he is. Though, he took me flask. Mercies on me head, Arthur, send me away."

Hilarious. I take mercy on him and send him to the white, where he'll be as right as rain. I finish my breakfast, rinse my dishes and put them in the dishwasher. Vets has just been served her "Meat, please" and is beginning to dig in. Since Pffif isn't here and we had such a good bonding experience the night before, I head to Vets.

"How're you doing?

As she looks at me to answer, I swipe a slice of bacon and give her a big smile. She looks at me sadly with her cat-like eyes, and for a moment I think she channels that puss in boots from those ogre movies. Quick as lightning, she grabs the wrist of my hand holding the bacon and twists it. My wrist and arm are locked as she pulls me over to her and chomps the bacon slice up to where I was holding. All without inflicting any pain that would come back on her.

"You may have the rest," she says releasing my wrist and turning her attention back to wolfing down her food.

I very carefully lay the remaining nub of bacon next to her arm that is around her plate. She scarfs it up immediately and throws me a look that I can't interpret. So I smile and move on.

I head to Grey's office, stopping to call Pffif back in the foyer. He's very happy. I think that's because he has his flask back.

I move down the hall to Grey's office. The door is open, but it's better to ask before entering.

"Are you ready for me?"

"Of course," Grey beckons me in, gestures to a chair in front of the desk, and walks around to take the one next to me. This is an informal meeting, obviously.

"Visitors today?"

"Why yes, Arthur. A Greek contingent inquiring of a walnut order."

"Your bar sure made an impression on Pffif."

Grey laughs.

"I saw that impression this morning. And truthfully, I haven't drunk that much in some time. Can you believe Mr. Pffiferil needed six pours of the Patron just to be sure he didn't like it."

"That's my leprechaun."

"Indeed. Now, to business. Share with me your impressions of the mission."

"Well, mission accomplished, casualties were relatively light. But still... casualties. It's part of any operation that size, I know. Karen, she's impressive. Her planning was top notch, and honestly, on the battlefield, she was a little scary. Greg too, they literally don't see him coming. Umm, I can wield a holy sword now."

Grey's eyes are intent on me. He wants more.

"Battlefield tactics are a little different. Spells are being slung around, healing, and heavy weapons to boot. But it's still about surprise, position, and force. Maldgorath's minions were there. He wasn't. I think that's part of the issue The Protectorate has had cornering him. He drops off his trouble-makers and then goes on vacation. Now, what's the verdict on my performance? I know I'm being graded, right?"

"Indeed. You performed as I hoped you would, as a healer to your group. I will not lie, there were concerns you would put yourself at the point, or act in a damage dealing role. I understand you took direction well and acted as a team player. None of this surprises me, or Karen, but there are those who needed to see how you behave in a team setting."

"Who?"

"That's not important," he says. "What is important, is that you are being invited to be a part of the Protectorate's very special operations team. You have proven that you can wield a Paladin's blade - which is no small thing. You bring your own disciplined team of experts. You have maturity, despite last evening's follies. And lastly, these teams and the Protectorate can offer you the extra protection, intelligence, and firepower you will need in your quest for vengeance. I think it's a perfect marriage and I pray you consider it."

That's a pitch. But there's a problem with it; those teams have never even gotten close to Maldgorath. Not in hundreds of years, by their own accounts. I measure my response.

"I do like the idea of being of assistance to the Protectorate, Grey. However, the perfect marriage it isn't. To think that Maldgorath is going to all of a sudden become a viable target for any Protectorate team is flying in the face of experience."

Grey gives me a raised eyebrow.

"So what happens if I say no?"

"This is not a demand or blackmail. I fully plan to release you on the first day after your second year here. You are no threat to mankind; maybe to yourself. Do not think the invitation comes with strings. I know the Protectorate needs you more than you need them. People with your talents are few. People with your gifts and attitude don't really exist. There have been those with your gifts when Maldgorath chooses to create them. Usually, they have to be put down."

That is no lie. I am not the first to be given such gifts. But all before me became monsters in their own right and have either been put down quickly or just mysteriously disappeared. More than likely "reaped" as Arix put it.

I take a deep breath. Again, Grey has been more than fair with me. I have to be fair with him and fair starts with the truth.

"I can't put anything in front of my quest, Grey. I just can't. But we both know Maldgorath is elusive and not always even in this realm of ours. How about an independent contractor? There will be times I can assist, there will be times I can't. I need the flexibility."

A smile appears on my warden's face.

"Fairly and honestly answered, Arthur. It's not my place to say what the Protectorate will accept or won't. I am a bit of an outsider myself, given that I cannot be trusted except to take orders because of the evil influence constantly pushing me." He rolls his eyes. "Personally I would think them fools not to snap at your offer."

He stands, meaning our time is done. We shake hands.

"Your intensive preparations resume in two days. Please, enjoy the downtime.

"I will."

I make my exit and my mind races with things to do. Phone calls to home. Naps are good too.

I head up to my room because that's where my pillow is. Kick some of Maldgorath's minions around and get a nice vacation. I'm feeling Pavlov's influence; that sneaky bastard. I'll get him and his little dogs too. But now it's time for lights out. I head to my window to pull the curtains. I take a gaze out in the yard, and something is out of kilter. It's not Vets with this batch of campers - it's Znuul and Shey sitting out on the rear lawn. And they appear to be getting along. It's not because he's in human form because she still manages to lay a "demon scum" on him in human form regardless. There they are, chatting away about something in a perfectly civil manner. Shey is cross-legged and looks relaxed. Znuul is lounging on his side. Dang next thing I know I'll find Sil wearing a Nun's habit.

Wait, she's strange enough to do that for all the wrong reasons.

I close the curtains deciding not to give it another thought. Off to nappy-land I go. The bed is comfy, the pillow is right. But routine is hard to shake, even semi-jetlagged, and I drift in and out, but after an hour and a half, I figure I am meant to be awake. It's a good time to make a phone call or two, I figure, and really nothing could make me happier. So, I roll out of bed, put on some shoes, and go to open the curtain.

Shey and Znuul have vacated the lawn. That would have been creepy if they were still there talking. I think about what I heard from Shey almost two years ago; about her captivity in Znuul's camp and his "treatment" of her. I would have never imagined what I saw today.

As my eye roves over the yard, I spy the patio table and around it is Znuul, Pffif, Shey, Sil, and Vets. Hjuul is even sitting near them. The conversation is more robust, in fact, Vets seems rather agitated. She bangs on the table, points at everyone and stands up. Pffif stands up on his chair and says something to her. It's hard to tell her exact reaction, but overall - not happy. She stalks off, leaving them.

I figure I'll make a cup of coffee and join in the conversation.

I make my way to the kitchen and pass Vets.

"What was that about around the patio table?"

She gives me a stern look.

"I disagree with them. Know that. Talk to them first. That is what they want."

I say, "okay" and let her stalk off.

At the kitchen, I grind and pour a double espresso, making sure to leave everything as I found it. Then I head out the doors to the rear patio.

And I am alone. The party has broken up. So, I figure I'll at least take in my cup of coffee there, enjoying the view and the afternoon sky. The coffee is dark and rich. I ponder the remainder of my afternoon. Doing nothing does not come easy when you're used to being busy every moment.

I settle on going to the library for more learning, stopping by the kitchen to rinse my mug and get it in the dishwasher -- no more muffins of shame for me. I'm putting the mug away when I feel a tug on my trousers. It's Pffif.

"Master Arthur, we'd be likin' to have a team meetin' with ye, if ye be agreeable."

"Sure."

I follow him into the sitting room off the foyer, where Shey, Sil, and Hjuul are. I survey the room. Hjuul is lying on the floor and making no attempt to come to me. Shey is sitting very properly in one of the wing-back chairs. Pffif is moving from foot to foot and also scanning the room. Sil is on the sofa in her summoned clothing of corset and black pleated leather skirt looking away. She has one hand under the skirt on her thigh, though not apparently going there, yet. They are all nervous.

"What's up guys?"

Pffif steps up. "Well, there's bein' somethin' we's need to talk about an…" He shuffles his feet a little more, looking around. "Ana, Sheyliene's gonna tell ye bout it."

Based on the look that comes over Shey's face, that wasn't the plan. She sticks her tongue out at Pffif who rushes over to a chair.

"We need to talk to you about chasing the Collector," Shey says. "We think it's best to stay as far away from that one as possible unless we can bring forces with us. The truth is, Arthur, we can't hope to stand against an ancient one like that. He would either kill you or take you. We don't think either of those are good outcomes."

"What are you all thinking? You cannot be serious. All of you have been abused by that monster in one way or the other. You cannot tell me you don't want revenge."

Everybody winces at my outburst.

Shey holds her hands out as if to say calm down.

"Arthur, we would all like to see him perish but we just don't have the strength. You don't know him. We do. You don't know the depth of his sick mind. Can you imagine if he took you, we'd all be back where we started, and he'd probably send you after your own family just to enjoy your torment afterward – sound familiar?"

I stand up. They just don't see it like I do.

"First, I would never give in to that bastard. Second, we finally have a weapon; have you forgotten? We have the sword. We can take his head and never have to worry about that piece of garbage again."

"You're thinkin' ye be gettin' close enough ta use that slicer?" Pffif says. "Tell ye what, count ye' out a minute ana there's sixty foes in the room as fast as he be thinkin' their names. Ana while we be messin' with them, he'll be castin' foul and dark magics, or that damn dragon of his be spittin' silver fire. We love ye, Arthur, ana donnae wanna see ye dead or worse."

"I can't believe this! Is Vets' the only one that believes in me…? Believes in us? We can do this. I will do this! Hjuul?"

His response is to whine and fold his ears back. Traitor.

I look over at Sil, and she must be full on nervous now, based on her damned habit.

"Really, Sil, I thought you wanted that bastard dead as much as I did. One true law, eh? Jerry doesn't need vengeance, does he? Answer me, bitch."

She stops what she is doing and spins around on the sofa to get up. When she gets up, the glamour drops, and it's Sil the monster. She looks at me, virtually trembling in what appears to be rage.

"Maybe I just don't want you to die too. Bitch, hag, succubus monster – can you degrade me anymore? Nobody in this room wants that parasite dead more than me!"

She looks around the room at the others, and she stiffens with her hands out to her side like she is grabbing two pillars. Her hair begins to stick out like she just put her hands on a Van De Graf generator. Her eyes roll up in her head. "I want to taste his blood! I want to look down as his eyes become milky white, while his life leaves him in my loins!"

Her eyes roll back down, and she is boring holes in me. She closes her eyes and lets out a deafening banshee scream. The windows break. Hjuul yelps and runs from the room claws scrabbling on the marble. Pretty vases on end tables fall and break. The scream goes on and on. Finally, it stops, and she relaxes, trembling.

The glare returns.

"I think we want him dead about the same," Shey says, pulling her hands from her ears and turning to Sil. Sil's glare shoots over to her and relaxes a wee bit, into more a look of recognition.

This whole thing is completely out of control.

Grey comes running into the foyer, takes note of the windows and says, "Someone better have a very good explanation for this, I have guests in my office."

He sees Sil and points at her. "You will make yourself presentable now. This is unacceptable behavior. All of you are to separate and calm down. You will explain this to me later when my guests have left."

"Yes sir," is all I can think to say.

Grey stalks off to resurrect his meeting. I turn back to the group.

"How long have you all felt this way?"

Shey steps forward. "We all had talks with Ahtsag Drool today, he made sense. Apparently, he doesn't want you to die or worse either."

Chapter 39

We all go to our respective rooms, except for Hjuul whom I assume went outside to clear his sensitive ears. After a little time to myself, I realize that I handled the situation very poorly. The matter of revenge affects us all. But, so does hiding away forever, living in constant fear of being found.

I figure I owe all of them an apology. Especially Sil. I was quite out of line with her, though her response was out of line also. If anyone deserves a piece of my mind, it's that damn Znuul.

He's playing demon mind games with my team and me: creating doubt, causing strife. I am absolutely going to call him out on it. I don't care if he is an ancient bringer of death and destruction. I'm so past all of it. Grey is going to have to deal with it and leash his dog.

There is a knock on the door. I brace myself to either rip into Znuul or apologize to one of my own.

I open the door, and Reginald is standing there with an envelope.

"This is for you, from Grey." Nothing else; just that and he walks off.

Anyone else might think he was a prick. But Reginald is just very no-nonsense. I thank him as he's walking away and he raises his hand in acknowledgment.

I open the letter, and it reads:

> *Arthur,*
> *The Greeks will require some entertaining, and I have someone to pick up from the airfield. Please use my office phone to call a glazier and have the windows tended to. If they cannot attend today, Reginald has plywood boards, and you should secure the windows with them until they can be properly addressed. Please avoid any further conflict resulting in the destruction of my property.*
> *-G*
> *Ps:*
> *You may use my office phone to call your family after you have made arrangements for the window repairs.*

I stop by Shey's and Pffif's room and give a very brief apology, letting them know we will still need to convene with Grey after he returns. Then the apology I dread -- Sil.

I knock on the door and pray she doesn't answer.

"Come in, Arthur."

Damn, so much for quick and easy. I open the door and there she is, with her back to me and sitting in a chair pulled onto her balcony, one foot on the rail and apparently doing that thing she does. She neither stops nor turns around.

"What?" she says.

"I'm here to apologize; I was out of line in my tone and words."

She leans her head back over the chair now to regard me in an upside down way.

"Yes, you were."

"Grey will be late, we will all convene with him when he arrives. I'll see you then."

"Thank you, Arthur... Come sit with me."

"Sorry, more apologies to deliver, maybe next time."

Got to give the girl credit, she is always trying to try to find ways to tempt me without actually overtly seducing me.

It turns out the glazier knows the Chateau well and offers to send somebody after hours to tend to it today. That's one thing gone well. I distract myself with calls to Helen, Bobby, and Jerry, Jr. It's good to hear their voices and get the updates. Helen tells me that my great, great grandson Matthew starts Pee-Wee baseball next month. I'm excited that I might be free in time to catch a season.

That is unless I have penalty time from this window thing.

I brief Reginald on the glazier, and he will be there for them. He'd rather supervise it anyway. This is his house and grounds, after all.

Sitting around the dinner table with everyone is not something I want to do. I grab a quick sandwich while Marthe prepares dinner. I let her know I won't be attending tonight. I'm going to review my files on Maldgorath for anything I might have overlooked.

Know your enemy.

While on the way to my room for study, I stop by Vets' room and luckily, she is there.

"Just wanted to say thanks for standing by me. Please try not to hold the others' feelings against them."

"Yes, my wielder."

We share a hug -- no face lick this time.

When I get back to my room, I get out my book of notes and my laptop. I begin to look over my information and notes, hoping to find something I may have missed; a pattern, a commonality - something. It drags on going nowhere. I'm on the verge of laying my head on the desk I hear Shey's voice from our meeting: "You don't know him, we do."

I pop up. All this time… The biggest font of information on my foe has been right in front of me! I lay my head on the desk; rest is deserved for noticing what I should have almost two years ago.

Chapter 40

I snap to wakefulness by the rapping of knuckles on the door, and by the tune, it should be Roger. I look down at the little puddle of drool on my desk and realize I must have needed the short rest more than I knew. I greet Roger at the door.

"Grey requests your presence in his office. His words."

"Sure, I'll collect everyone and be right there."

It's one forty-five AM. Wow, he must still be pissed. Not even waiting for the morning.

I collect everyone, then touch my will and compel Hjuul to the foyer.

We converge on the foyer and Vets lets Hjuul in. We make our way to the office, and I knock on the door.

We are told, "Enter, please."

We enter. Grey sits at his desk, Znuul in his large corner chair, and Karen has returned - that explains the airport pickup.

Over steepled fingers, Grey says, "One by one, I will hear what went on today, that resulted in the damage to my home. Not to mention scaring the crap out of my valued customers."

He cussed! He never curses. We are so screwed. I try to grab my composure.

"Sir, let me start," I say, "as I think it was my emotional response that triggered everything. You see, your goddamn demon pet has been telling my summonlings that I'm crazy to even think about following through on my oath-sworn duty." I look over to Znuul. "If you had a backbone, you'd have come to me and share your thoughts rather than trying to manipulate my friends here."

He looks at me dismissively.

"I knew what you'd say."

"Oh good. Well, you get to hear it anyway, I will get that bastard – he will fall, I will celebrate. You are wrong."

Znuul stands and cocks his head at me.

"Arthur, your arrogance is going to land you dead or enslaved. You face a foe you can't possibly comprehend or prevail against, by yourself."

I meet his stare and say, "I'm never alone."

He takes a stride toward me, his eyes narrowing on me.

"What I say is fact, and one easily proven."

I take a step forward too.

"So says, you."

His face goes from serious to contemptuous, and he moves in front of Grey's desk.

"I'll prove it now. If you cannot best me, you cannot best him."

Immediately I feel the pressure of Znuul's will. I put up my mental barriers. He takes on a dark steaming aura and begins muttering something in his guttural home language.

Grey bolts up from his desk.

"Ahtsag, you will stand down now," Grey commands.

Znuul's face scrunches, I've seen that look before; he is resisting.

"He is not enough," Znuul says through clenched teeth. Znuul's eyes lock back on me. "Prepare yourself human, this is going to hurt. But not as much as if Maldgorath himself has you."

Hjuul growls. Vets' eyes dart around, looking for weapons. Sil grabs my shoulder and yells, "Arthur, wards!"

I can't breathe, it's like a coil that's wound itself around my chest. Hjuul reacts immediately, lunging at Znuul and the distraction must have broken Znuul's concentration as my breath returns. Vets goes into action behind the great hound.

Znuul's tail lashes out like a whip, striking Hjuul with what appears to be a poison stinger appearing at the end of it. Hjuul's body crashes into Znuul and flops to the floor, dissolving.

"Ahtsag, stop," Grey cries out again.

Again, Znuul's face winces. Karen screams at him to back off also.

That gives Vets time to land a blow on his chin; she follows with blows to his body. None of which seem to have any effect upon him at all. His hand shoots out, and he palms her face. Holding her fighting body at arm's length, he looks me in the eye. A silver arrow appears in his chest, then another. Billowing black smoke appears from the strikes.

In response, he crushes Vets head like a ripe fruit and releases her dissolving body to the ground.

Grey is screams, "Znuul you will sit!"

His legs begin to bend, but he straightens immediately.

"He is not able to withstand Maldgorath!" Znuul bellows and turns his attention to the little fairy shooting him full of arrows. His eyes burn bright red, and a pulse of red light crashes into my archer, and she crumples.

Pffif throws his dagger, and it is caught without effort, then returned to him – through the chest pinning him to the wall. Pffif dissolves away.

Grey skids across the desk. He grabs Znuul by the arm attempting to spin him around, but Znuul is going nowhere.

Grey says in a determined tone, "Ahtsag Znuul, by the force of the bond to my will, I command you to cease!"

Znuul's whole body spasms under the command.

He turns on Grey, "Human, your will is no match for that which is Ahtsag Znuul. This one must learn the truth!"

Znuul turns his back to Grey and flexes his wings, which causes both Grey and Karen to stagger back from an unseen force.

Sil pushes me to the side and screams, "Run!" She posture ups in front of Znuul yelling, "Come on!" He does - closing in on her with a blur of a step. He backhands her, which crushes her head, snaps her neck, and sends her spinning head over heels crashing into the wall.

Grey picks himself up and says, "Ahtsag, stop!"

Znuul again shrugs it off.

There is a huge boom, and I realize that Karen just did the lightning thing to him. That does make him wince and arch his back where he was struck. But damn, he's shrugging that off too.

Again the wings flash out and Grey and Karen this time are flung back even more violently from an unseen force. His grimace becomes a smile, and his eyes lock on me. Again, I can't breathe. I reach for my will, for anything. I feel my ribs bending.

"No one to hide behind now, Arthur. You think you are so strong. Stand and face your pain. You will submit."

But I can't stand. I can't breathe. I can't defend. The fear sets in; I am going to die – horribly. The damn spiders return.

There is a great wash of light. I can breathe again. The spiders are gone. And floating in front of me is some ethereal being clad in armor. It says six words in the most beautiful voice I have ever heard.

"Dark one, you shall not pass."

The voice is beautiful because it is Dorothy's.

Znuul's face changes to dumbfounded. He immediately takes to one knee and bows his head.

"He thinks he is strong enough. He is not," Znuul says.

Dorothy's voice says, "He is not alone."

The ethereal Dorothy slowly spins around to face me, as if on a lazy Susan. I see her eyes through the helm she is wearing.

"You are much loved, Arthur MacInerny," she says.

I reach for my Dory, and she just evaporates like a puff of steam in front of a fan.

"No!" I scream, "Don't go! Don't leave me again."

I'm crying. I've lost her again.

I hear Grey tell Znuul to sit. I see him sit this time, out of the corner of my eye that isn't still searching for Dory.

Karen is in a panic. She yells, "He disobeyed you," and other things I can't make out through my sobbing.

Grey says something back to her urgently. Nobody is saying anything about my Dory. Then I stop crying. She was here. She's looking over me. She loves me, still. Now I'm elated.

This must be what being bi-polar is like.

"That was my Dorothy!" I yell out.

All eyes are on me now except for Znuul's, whose are straight down to the floor with a blank expression.

"That was my Dorothy, she's an angel, and she still loves me."

Grey and Karen acknowledge me with, "yes."

But I can tell their minds are on other matters.

Grey says quietly, "Ahtsag."

Znuul rises. He walks over to Grey and Karen his head down, not making eye contact with either of them.

"I am to go to the small room?" Znuul says in a hushed tone.

Grey tries to make eye contact with him, but Znuul does not look back up from the floor.

"Well, it appears I may have trouble making you go there. Leave us to speak privately. Wait for me in the rear yard that is unless you have other ideas."

"No more ideas, master," Znuul's says. He exits the room.

Karen says to Grey, "The council must know about this."

"Yes, they must," he says.

"You mean that my Dory is looking over me?" I ask.

"No," says Karen, "That Ahtsag Znuul the Destroyer of Hope and Devourer of Souls may soon be loosed upon this world."

Chapter 41

I leave Karen and Grey to their serious discussion and head to the foyer. I want to summon Hjuul, heck I want to summon all of them. They all need to know about the miracle that just occurred. I start for the rear yard and then remember that *he* would be out there.

I count my blessings. That son of bitch Znuul just cut through all of my team and had me cowed on my knees in what felt like a breath's time. It was too damn fast; too damn brutal. I start to see Znuul's point of view, then kick myself in the butt for that.

The encounter was on his terms, his timing, his turf. I did not have my blessed sword. I had no preparation.

I shake off those thoughts and step out to the front lawn. I run my finger across Hjuul's glyph, say "Hjuul come," and he appears.

He immediately takes up a defensive posture and scans for danger. My hulking hound, upon coming to the opinion we were safe, walks to me and presses his head against my legs. I give him a deep scratch and kneel down to hug him.

"Thanks, Hjuul. You'll never guess who saved us – Dorothy; she's an angel."

That gets a quick turn of his massive head and a "rooo?" from him.

"Yeah. She's looking over us."

Hjuul leaps and lets loose with the happy chuff-barks.

"Hey guy, I'm excited too. I need to tell the others. Run tomorrow?"

He doesn't have to say a word. I know he's all in.

Back inside, as I'm heading up the stairs, I can't help but smile at Hjuul's reaction to my news. He's probably still chasing his tail in puppy-like excitement. He loved Dorothy. She's the one that brought him out of his shell.

I get to my room and know who's getting called back first; Shey. It saddens me that she didn't get to see Dory. They were so very close. I know the news will mean most to her. I trace my finger across her Glyph and call "Sheyliene." My fairy warrior appears; bow appearing in hand almost instantly and an arrow is drawn.

"We're in your room," she says. "Did you defeat him?"

"Not exactly, Dorothy appeared as an angel and stopped him."

The bow drops to the ground followed by her jaw.

"A real angel? Dorothy? She saved you?"

"Yes."

I am tackled in a crushing hug. The little fairy is very strong.

"What did she look like? Was she beautiful? Did she ask about me? Did you get a hug? Will she come back? Did she destroy General Znuul? Did she ask about me?"

Shey is literally bouncing around. She takes my hands before I can even begin to reply and dances us in a circle.

We stop, and she looks at me seriously with those golden eyes of hers.

"Now I know we can beat that stinky Maldgorath. You hear that, Collector? Arthur and Dory are coming for you, and they're bringing us with them!"

She is seriously worked up and so happy. I'm not going to ruin that with the thought of what would have a happened Znuul opted to kill me first instead of them.

"Hey, let me get the others. They need to know too."

I bring Pffif first, then Vets, then Sil. All of them are ready for battle until they realize where we are. Before I can tell them what happened, Shey spills the beans.

"Dorothy is a beautiful angel! She stepped right in and stopped that demon scum right in his tracks!"

"By the pearly gates," Pffif says

Vets gives a nod and adds, "This bodes well."

Sil's just pulls the chair away from my desk, sits, and transforms herself human.

Shey jumps her case immediately for not sharing in the collective excitement.

"I should have known that demon scum wouldn't appreciate Arthur having an angel on his shoulder! It's Dory, too. That's double better, except to you. Skanky succubus slut."

Sil's reaction is demure. With a roll of the eyes and a sigh, she looks from Shey to me.

"Arthur, you are positively aglow with joy. I have not felt you this happy in a long, long, while and you so deserve this. I would never, ever wish to take it from you. But you know, that woman absolutely despised me." She stands casually and smiles at Sheyliene, "I understand how you feel too, Sheyliene; it's okay."

Without warning, Silithes slaps Shey across the face with such force she goes crashing into the nightstand.

"Now you know how I feel, Fairy." Without missing a beat, she looks over at me casually and says, "Control her please, now is not the time for fighting."

Silithes sits back down.

Shey, dazed, picks herself up and immediately goes for the daggers. I touch my will and say her name, just to get her attention.

"Shey - time for celebration, not that."

The daggers in her hands are put away, but the ones coming out of her eyes are still there.

"I hate to bust up all this feel-good, but let's not forget something," Sil says. "Ahtsag Znuul laid waste to all of us in the blink of an eye, and I know he was taking his time for the show. That was done even with one of this realm's most powerful wizards pulling on his will to cease. The Collector will have no such encumbrance upon him."

Silence

"It be true, what she says," Pffif mutters.

Sil smiles to Pffif and then at me.

"Good, I'm glad we recognize that," she says changing to a perky, happy voice. "Now that being said – we have an angel, a holy sword, and more than enough desire to see the job done. I think we stand a chance."

"More than a chance," I say. "Especially if we control the terms of the engagement."

Sil is beaming and clapping lightly. She turns to Shey.

"That right there is one reason why we love our Arthur so."

To Shey's credit, she doesn't rip into her for using the words "love," "our," and "Arthur" in the same sentence.

Instead, Shey just looks over to me and says, "Yeah."

Vets beats the chest plate of her armor with her armored fist.

"Death to the Collector!" she roars.

Following Vets' lead, we all join in a hearty collective, "Death to the Collector!"

This is good. We are all back on the same page. We share in a little more group cheer, and I ask if I can get some sleep since it's almost three AM. My desk nap just isn't going to cut it, especially after the stress of the day.

Besides, I have a whole other day of vacation ahead of me.

Everyone exits and I head over to close my curtains. I plan a sleep party, and Mr. Sunshine is not allowed to crash it. But before I can close them, I see Znuul sitting on the rear lawn past the steps silhouetted in the moon's light. Grey is standing in front of him, and they are speaking. Znuul's posture is slumped. Grey walks to his side and puts his hand on his shoulder. Znuul's head lolls over to the side atop of Grey's hand.

Grey walks away, up the stairs toward the Chateau.

Znuul rolls his head forward, and I see the heave of a heavy breath. Then he goes still; deathly still.

I close the curtains and walk toward the bed. Almost to the bed, I am stopped in my tracks by a loud mournful keening from the rear lawn that sends shivers up my spine. I run back to the curtain and fling them open.

Nothing is there but the moonlight over the lawn.

Chapter 42

A light rapping on my door wakes me that I don't recognize. I look over at the clock and see it reads ten-twenty AM. That's late for me.

"One moment," I say and roll out of bed.

Jeepers, I slept in my clothes.

I walk over to the door and open it to find Grey standing there with a breakfast tray.

"May I come in? I brought gifts."

"Of course."

What the heck is going on? I've been here just short of two years, and he has not once come to my room. I am always summoned to him. He comes in, sets the tray on my dresser and walks over to open the draperies. The sunlight pours into the room and tears at my sleepy eyes.

"Much better," he says and gestures to the tray. "You have croissants, fresh goat cheese, tomato, and a pot of coffee from the press. Marthe sends her love. You start in, I will get another seat. We have much to discuss."

He leaves the room, and I take the tray over to my desk, plopping down in my seat. He returns with a chair from the hall, brings it over to the desk and sits down facing me.

"In the excitement and surprise of last night's activities, I failed to give you proper acknowledgment for what must be a most heartfelt reunion. Your Dorothy certainly does light up a room."

"Thank you for that. I wish I could have spent more time with her."

"Yes. I wish we all could have." We pause on that thought. "But we must talk about less pleasant affairs."

"Znuul."

"Yes, among other things. First, you need to know I have sent the children to their homes. I cannot have them in the jeopardy of wicked influence. I have sent Roger to stay with the LeBlanc's as well. Obviously, I just can't shut down the vineyard or grove totally, but I will give those who work here, and understand our secrets, the opportunity to leave. I must admit, Ahtsag's display last night has me most concerned."

That's a big wow. He must be pretty concerned.

"Have you regained control over him, Grey?"

He laughs.

"Oh my, the question isn't if I have control now, but when did it slip away from me? I've searched myself relentlessly and do not see where I've fallen prey to dark suggestion. Of course, this will just be another reason for Alistair and some of the council to further distance me from the community… I could use some sleep, Arthur."

He rolls his eyes.

"On a positive note, Karen has agreed not to advise the council of anything until she and I have thoroughly assessed the situation and can advise on a proper course of action. I fear Alistair's solution without such input would be to kill Ahtsag, which most likely means killing me because I would be the easier target. That is the nature of our bond; if one dies, so does the other."

Again, my poker face gives me away.

"I know it sounds cold."

It doesn't just sound cold to me, I know it is.

"Surely there must be some other way. Wasn't he locked away for like a billion years by the guy before you?"

Grey shakes his head. "Well, first I doubt we'll be able to trick him into containment so easily. Second, and I know this - that incarceration left him scarred terribly. You remember the limousine, how he didn't care for the small space? You should try to get him in an elevator. Knowing the pain it would cause him, I don't know if I could. But that is our weakness as children of the light, no? We care."

"That's what makes us better than them, not weaker. So maybe we use that fear to keep him in line?"

"Maybe. I had hoped that maybe my time with him had influence. He showed promise. I've used very little control over him for the last twenty-five years. But what is twenty-five years to one so ancient, yes? I must admit some confusion on my part. I must be cautious not to see what I want to see, as opposed to what is really there. Like with your Arixtumin."

He sits back in his chair, and his eyes search me for an answer.

"What do you think, Arthur? Your succubus admitted openly to having love for your son and family. Do you think they can change? Or is it just because she's leashed to you?"

This is a man conflicted. Znuul is more than just a burden to bear for him. I think to how I felt when Arixtumin's betrayal came to light. I remember the anger. I remember the hurt. I would not wish that on anyone. He doesn't need doubt and negativity now. He'll find the truth if that's what he wants.

"Grey, I can't say. In my belief, anyone – anything – can change for good or for worse. I would have never imagined last night happening, not just Dory's appearance, but Znuul's rebellion if that's what we want to call it. If he's using you, he's fooled me too."

A smile comes to the gracious one's face.

"Arthur, you're going to have to self-train for a while until we get this situation better understood. I suggest you keep up what mental defenses you have, particularly when you visit with Ahtsag later this afternoon."

"When I visit with him? This afternoon? So he can try to prove his point again?"

"That's not what he indicated. He asked me if he could apologize to you. He said he could make it worth your while. Whatever that may mean."

"I'm on vacation today, remember? He can wait until tomorrow. I'm really in no hurry to see him after what was done to me and mine."

Grey nods and stands.

"Enjoy your day off, Arthur, I will let him know, and he will have to wait."

Chapter 43

After cleaning up a bit and putting on some fresh clothes, I make my way downstairs to return my breakfast tray, making sure everything is put away in the dishwasher. Marthe is working on lunch preparations. I stroll over to the queen of the kitchen and put my arm around her.

She looks up at me from slicing hard salami into paper thin slices and points the knife at me.

"Monsieur Arthur, you must wait for lunch like everyone else."

"Marthe, you hurt me implying such a thing."

"Young men should not trifle weeth the emotions of older women."

It's all in jest, we share a good chuckle.

"But seriously, Marthe, it's my day off, and I want to share. I'd like to cook dinner tonight, and I know what I'd like to prepare – American Hamburgers with fries. If you'll get the ingredients, I would love to cook for you and our little skeleton crew here."

"Yees," she says, "It ees an interesting time with zhat one meesbehaving." She sets the knife down on the counter. "Sweet boy you are, write your list down and I weel shop for you."

She tweaks my cheek again.

"Marthe, you know I'm about twice your age."

She turns around, picking up the knife.

"Eef I call you a sweet boy, you are a sweet boy, no?"

"Yes, ma'am." There's nothing else to say. I am a sweet boy.

"So how many am I cooking for?"

"You will need to prepare for nine. But zee big one that is meesbehaving usually eats more than one portion. Zat one eats way too much. Do you theenk Znuul ees really a danger to us? He deed attack you, no?"

"Yes. He did. But Grey seems to have everything under control."

She gives me her stern queen-of-the-kitchen look.

"Nothing to worry about, zat one knows to respect me, or else."

I make out my list and hand it to her.

"We have potatoes and eggs. They are over there." She fishes out several loaves of French bread. "Here. Don't be a lazy boy, make your own breadcrumbs.

I am a lazy boy now. She looks up from the list and sneers, "Ketchup?"

We get a good laugh out of that and part ways. I head out to the rear lawn and call out for Hjuul. I promised him a run, and I plan to make good on it. He comes bounding around from the side of the chateau. Shey buzzes down and joins us. We head out toward the vineyard for an afternoon romp.

After that, I return to the kitchen and begin my preparations for dinner. Chopping potatoes, crumbling loaves and toasting them in the oven. All this is very therapeutic, it smacks of the fourth of July for me. I fantasize I am with family; it's a nice distraction.

Karen enters, bringing her plate and cup back for the wash.

"I can't believe you talked Marthe into letting you prepare dinner tonight – American Hamburgers, eh?"

"Not just hamburgers, Arthur's special holiday hamburgers."

She approaches and puts her hand on my shoulder.

"Are you okay, Arthur? Last night was bad."

I stop with the dicing of onions.

"Yes. Yeah, I got abused a little, but I saw my Dory. I heard her beautiful voice too – how can you say that was bad? Damn Znuul could have flayed the skin off me, and I'd still say it was good in the final equation."

"Sorry. I'm just so focused. The council will take this matter very seriously – as they should. It's just that... Your Dorothy sure made an entrance. I am so happy for you, Arthur. That's just so unheard of nowadays for an angel to present itself."

I'm not going to ask her to finish that first thought and go back to the chopping.

"Thanks. Have you spoken with Mr. Big and Purple about it?".

"I have," she says. "He seems contrite, but what if that's a deception? It concerns me that he not only disregarded Grey's command but took action against him. If he can do that, what's to stop him from lying to us? Arthur, do you have any idea the amount of destruction and chaos he could bring, unbound?"

I stop chopping and look her in the eyes.

"Think I got the flavor for that last night, Karen."

"Sorry. I'm still a bit jet lagged, and lack of sleep doesn't help either."

"Yeah, welcome home, right? Hey, a favor, please? Can you make sure he doesn't attend dinner tonight? Our nerves are still a bit raw."

"I'll pass the message along. It's about all I can do. I am looking forward to a good burger."

So am I.

*
**

Dinner service goes off without a hitch. We eat in the kitchen, at the island instead of the dining room. Grey takes a plate for Znuul, who thankfully is not joining us. I made two burgers for Hjuul, rare of course, and I enjoy serving him almost as much as he enjoys gulping them down. Shey, who does not eat meat, gets special treatment with sautéed mushrooms, onions and cheese on a bun – she's a happy camper.

Dinner is a good time. The chef gets kind words from everyone – even Reginald, who told Marthe, "Add this to the menu," in his crusty way.

Brave man.

Once all is cleaned up, I excuse myself and go up to retire for the evening. Tomorrow I have to deal with Znuul's apology and begin quizzing my crew on Maldgorath. It's early to bed, but I don't care. The bed feels comfy, and the pillow is inviting.

Nature's call wakes me a little after one AM. After addressing what I must, the thought of a midnight milk run sounds good. Especially since Marthe always leaves a tray of cookies, or "biscuits" as she calls them. After making my way downstairs, I round the corner to the kitchen to see Znuul, in human form, wearing his torn-up AC/DC tee-shirt and cut off jeans.

He's washing his dishes from the night's dinner.

I actually pause for a moment, then decide I won't give him the satisfaction by waiting for him to leave.

True to form, a platter of goodies waits on the island. I begin to stride over to where the cups are, near the sink. Before I can arrive, Znuul opens the cabinet, grabs a cup and turns back around to hand it to me.

Well, here we are. I take the cup and give him a nod. I turn to go to the refrigerator for milk.

"It's tomorrow you know," he says, attempting to break the ice.

I go over to the island without saying a word and take one of the oatmeal raisin delicacies. Znuul walks over to the refrigerator and pulls out a bottle of beer, pulling the cap off without the help of an opener.

"Bring your snack outside."

I turn around, cookie in hand.

"You're telling me to?"

He takes a pausing breath.

"Sorry. Would you please consider joining me outside? There's much to discuss."

I just glare at him and take another bite of cookie.

"I owe you an apology. Please."

He turns and goes through the double French doors to the rear lawn's porch area.

Chapter 44

Damn. He who never apologizes has apologized twice now and has even said 'please' to boot. I figure it's either now or later, so why not now?

I top off my milk, grab a paper napkin and another cookie along with a bottle of beer. I take my time walking to the table where Znuul sits. I plop the beer down in front of him and take my seat next to him, setting my snack down. I scoot the chair around to face him.

"Okay, me first," he says, taking a sip of his beer. "Truth to start, then excuses – fair enough?"

"Sure."

He sets the beer down and leans in.

"The truth is my actions were inappropriate by human standards." He stops, probably reading me. "My actions were inappropriate for…" He sits back in his chair and looks away then looks back at me. "My actions last night were wrong. One does not treat a friend in such a way, I see this plainly now. This is the truth; I have come to enjoy your company. You are quite… unique and somewhat infectious."

Like that's going to get it…

"You kill my friends, abuse me, and now I'm sorry is supposed to make everything okay? What's with this calling me a disease? And oh yeah, I didn't think your kind has friends, just victims being made comfortable before the strike."

He closes his eyes, and I see his jaw clench. He opens them back up, gives me a half smile, then reaches for his beer, and downs it.

"Good foresight on the other beer. We are still on truth, excuses will come. First, I cannot undo that which is done. I do regret my actions, and I am coming to learn that an apology is not enough. But an apology is only where I know to start. I did not mean to infer you are a disease. What I meant is that you leave an impression on those you take time with; you have left an impression on me. Lastly, what you say about friends and my kind is very true as a stereotype. But I am an individual, and quite a flawed one, at that. I do think of us as friends - by the human standard."

"Funny way to treat a friend," I say back.

"Yes, I suppose it is." He reaches over and pops the cap of the second bottle of beer with his thumb. "At this rate, I will need more. Okay, onto excuses. I did not want to see you get yourself killed or worse by challenging a being that can destroy you quite easily. You are stubborn, and words don't seem to work as well with you. I thought the first-hand experience might make you understand how outmatched you truly are. This is much how we teach our young; to teach of fire we burn them and laugh at their pain."

Sweet Christ O mighty that is a seriously demented culture. I don't say anything, I just look at this creature now masquerading as a person as if to say, "so what." The game is on, he-who-speaks-first loses.

Znuul loses in no time flat.

"As I said, this is an excuse. It was what I thought. I know now I was wrong."

He bends backward and puts his face into his hands. He pulls himself back up and looks off across the yard.

"I have few friends and only one that may live as long as I." His eyes return to me, "I enjoy your stubborn, do-gooding company, Arthur, and was being selfish in letting my wish for your survival overtake your need for closure."

He sits back and grabs the beer, taking a quick swig then sets it back down.

"This really isn't easy for me, you know that?"

"Tough shit, big guy. Someone I thought was my friend kicked my ass and killed my buddies– you think that's easy? Do you even know the first thing about what being a friend means?"

I can tell a smart ass reply is coming. I can see it percolating around in his head. But instead, Znuul reaches over, takes the remaining beer and downs the rest of it.

"I am going to need more powerful intoxicants." He stands and takes the two bottles. "Being a good friend is not something that was beaten into me as a youngling. I am trying and must admit I could use some help to better grasp the nuances. Would you wait for me? I have things to share with you that may help you in your quest. You don't have to give me forgiveness. The knowledge is yours, freely – no strings."

He strides off to the kitchen.

To err is human I think. Then I wonder if I'm being played. But if I am, what in the heck is he going to get out of it? Not much that I see. What is this stuff that he has to share with me? I'm confused and look to my cookies and milk for inspiration.

A while into my cookies and milk the rear door from the foyer opens, and Znuul comes through carrying two bottles of Stoli. He holds them out like a prize and takes his seat.

"Size and metabolism work against me for alcohol to have any effect," he says.

"Poor baby."

That brings a smile to his face. He cracks open the bottle and takes a big swig.

"All right," he says, "Here's some information to help you..."

I hold my hand up to stop him.

"Let's finish with the asking for forgiveness part. Big Z, I will accept your apology, and we can start fresh if, and only when, you apologize to each and every one of mine that you hurt."

He did not expect that. I can tell there's some, "what the heck," going on in his head.

"They are only summonlings," he says with some disdain.

"And I'm only a lowly human being, quite possibly lesser than even a Vetisghar. They are my friends and sort of family."

Znuul actually winces at my statement. He takes a huge gulp off the bottle.

"Point for you," he says. "Tell you what; I will apologize to each and every one of them – even the hound." He regards the bottle for a moment. "I'll even apologize to the Pixie for what I did to her in the war, though she will not accept." Another big swig follows. "Arthur, I erred badly and am on the verge of losing everything I hold dear."

He's looking at me dead on, and I detect some welling in the eyes. Then, just like that, he breaks eye contact and takes another swallow.

"Let me tell you what I know," he says, changing the topic.

"Shoot."

He offers me the bottle, and I decline.

"Here's the thing, you've read all the files, and you know a little about him. You know about the planar dragon that can take him basically anywhere. I was in the Fae invasion with him. I know the son of shit – for who and what he is. He is a coward and a bully."

Znuul's whole demeanor changes, he is very much in touch with his strength.

"Listen to me, Arthur. I do not think you will kill Maldgorath by yourself. I do not think you can. But, you can bloody his nose. If you hit him hard enough, he will run. His dragon will whoosh him away at the first sign of trouble because he's willed it so. I know this. He wields great power, but he also knows that if he does perish all the spirits in his possession will then own him. Why do you think he avoids direct conflict and uses pawns?"

He takes another swig and settles into his chair.

"Coward and bully, Arthur. You are neither and, therefore, maybe with some luck and planning, you might survive an encounter with him - especially if your wife shows again. Though, I would not expect him to take a knee to her. Hit him hard, hit him fast. Make him run away and not want to bother with you again."

Not what I wanted to hear; but still very valuable intelligence. I want to react to the, "You can't." I am so tired of hearing that over and over again. But after having my ass handed to me so completely, only arrogance would have me disregard it.

Crap.

"Gimme the bottle, you friggin' flying monkey."

Znuul hands over the bottle and I take a shot. It burns going down but still feels good. I hand it back.

We sit there in silence for a while. The bottle passes a few times.

Znuul breaks the silence.

"If I could stand with you, Arthur, when that time comes, I would be pleased to do so. You and I together, I promise you would have your revenge. I bet we could get Karen and Greg too. Heck, even the old man; he'd love to stick it to Alistair by acting without his permission."

"Yea, that's probably not going to happen though, is it?" I ask, more of an observation, really.

The big guy just shrugs. "I'm giving up on absolutisms."

We share some more silence and the passing of the bottle.

"I need advice, Arthur. Grey and Karen have shut me out. I've explained everything to them almost as I have to you. I have apologized. Now when they speak to me, it's behind thick walls of mental defense. Grey is important to me. He's been… fatherly; only without beating me, raping me, and degrading me in front of others like my real one did. He never treated me as a slave, even though I've been bound to him. Now, I can't sense him at all. He wouldn't do that except for fear of me."

"Crap sticks, Znuul." The offhanded comment about his father's treatment of him just bothers me, "Your dad did what?"

He waves his hand dismissively at me.

"It is our way. I did the same with my young. Eventually, they grow strong and kill or dominate the parent. Except for me of course, no child of mine has succeeded in that endeavor."

He closes his eyes and reaches for the bottle.

"Arthur, that was then. I don't know what do to or what I can do, now. I have explained everything as rationally as I can. They are very important to me."

"Okay, they are important, like family. Have you told them how you feel?"

"Ah, that is so degrading," he says, scrunching his face.

"You had no problem telling me," I counter.

Znuul's laugh crashes through the night. "You see what I mean about you being infectious? I can't believe I…" More laughter bellows out from him.

Then his face goes serious again. He leans into me. "What exactly are you, Arthur MacInerny?"

"I'm the guy telling you that you love them and you need to tell them that; at least for your own sake. Rational explanations rarely address emotional situations that well."

I sense a moment of protest and rebuttal in him, but nothing comes of it.

"Thank you for the advice, Arthur."

We both know that means he probably won't take it. Pride's a bitch.

Chapter 45

True to his word, Znuul made apologies to each and every member of my team. Shey confided in me that he even made an attempt to apologize for trading her to Maldgorath, though saying something to the effect of, "I should have tried harder to dominate you," does fall a little flat.

I take time with all my summonlings, quizzing them and taking notes on Maldgorath's behavior's, quirks, and potential weaknesses. Putting aside my feelings, I even quiz Arixtumin who foolishly thought he would be released from his very white prison. Close to two years in the white have taken a toll on him; he actually groveled for mercy. Makes me wonder how well he'd hold up after five thousand.

I distill my learning into a top ten list:

1. Maldgorath is awesomely strong; he carries his own power augmented by at least two thousand spirits. The real count is unknown.

2. He heals miraculously fast thanks to the power of his legion; any damage dealt has to be catastrophic to be of any concern. I heal fast, he heals at light speed.

3. The baby planar dragon is his greatest asset. The dragon allows him to jump to other planes of existence at a whim. It is his escape tool. Should he become seriously harmed, the dragon is compelled to get him out of danger immediately.

4. He is a coward and a bully; he runs away.

5. He does not fight his own fights - that is what summonlings are for.

6. He has delusions of grandeur.

7. He craves status and recognition.

8. He is a mercenary and holds no status in the hierarchy of Helterezen; primarily because he will not fight one on one for his status. His kind rarely do.

9. He is a liar; nothing that comes out of his mouth can be trusted.

10. He is a sick son of a bitch —a depraved sadist extraordinaire.

I share my list with everyone. It seems like I did well. I may have a job as an FBI profiler.

After a few weeks, things seem to be coming back to normal. Znuul is showing his face at meals. Roger and staff have returned. The only thing that is strange is that Karen hasn't left. She's usually only around a day or two at the most. I am assuming that has to do with her report to The Protectorate council on Znuul's disobedience. The thought of the council sending orders for Grey's death, just to kill Znuul bother me to no end.

Today, I'm a bookworm. With less than two months left on my sentence, I need to take advantage of what is here, and here only. I hear the locks to the library door click open. Roger enters, beaming a smile.

"What are you reading?" he asks.

I hold up the book; the translated treatise on the weaving and binding of protective wards.

"Oh, yeah, I remember that," Roger says nonchalantly, "If you want I can show some cool shortcuts I worked out."

Damn know it all kids. And to think Arix had me convinced humans could not perceive the intricacy of that kind of magic.

"Grey is looking for you," he says.

"His Office? Of course..."

We are now back to the usual, officially. Here comes the training grind...

I go to the office, knock on the door, and am invited in with an, "Arthur!"

Grey puts down the spray bottle he's using on the plants and greets me warmly in a hug.

"I have the most wonderful news for you – early release. As of this moment, you are free to come and go as you please."

I see genuine happiness in his eyes at the news.

"Please take a seat. Let us talk about your plans."

I take my seat, and he does too. This is not a sit before the warden's desk moment. I am stunned at the news, speechless.

"I pulled a few strings. So, visit family first?"

I get the feeling he may be as happy with this news as I am.

"Geez, Grey, I have no idea – that would seem the thing to do."

"Yes, yes, I imagine this news is overwhelming. Take some time and consider what you wish to do. All my resources are at your disposal; after all, you have become a part of this family."

"Thanks. Who else knows?"

"Just Karen and the council as of now. That will change as soon as you leave."

He pins those all-knowing eyes on me.

"Arthur, nobody says you have to leave or that you can't come back. Once in my fold, always in. Of course, if you choose to stay, I will have to put you to work somewhere."

I smile. Grey does too.

"If I stay, can I be the lead grape stomper? I bring extra sets of feet with me."

I think he appreciates the humor.

I stand and say, "Once I know my plans you'll be the second to know." I sit back down. "You and Znuul got everything patched up? Did you ever figure out how he was able to disobey you?"

Grey sits back down too, a more serious look on his face.

"Yes. We had a very uncharacteristically emotional moment with him and I, unfortunately, discovered how he was able to apply himself as he did. All is known now."

"Unfortunately?"

He smiles and holds his hands out in defeat.

"I am a simple country mage and was tricked by one much older than I. Without getting into detail, the binding he agreed to was for all he was – at that moment. And at that moment, he was a shell of himself; weak and emaciated. As you can see he is no longer a shell and I have no dominion over the strength and will he has regained since that moment. I should have known better, I should have scrutinized the agreement, but time was pressing. I was younger. However, he is still very bound to me and I to him."

That means the nuclear solution is still there. Znuul can be stopped by killing Grey. A cold chill runs down my spine.

"So, do you have control over him? I mean, now that everything is on the table, he has no reason to not… not be Ahtsag Znuul at least to some degree?"

He stands, meaning time for me to go. I must have touched a nerve. When I arise, he takes me by the arm gently guiding me out.

"I think he is held by an even stronger bond now – trust."

I stop. He looks at me as if to say 'yes, that's what I said.'

"And how does Karen feel about this… Trust?" What of her report to the council?"

"She desperately wishes to trust him. The depth of their bond at times disturbs me, but I must trust her perception and ability to be dispassionate." He winks at me. "She is not a weak one, you know. As for her report to the council, they are aware of his disobedience and that all, for now, appears under control."

My poker face gives me away, yet again.

"At this point, there are no plans I'm aware of to kill either of us."

I step out of his office. The hallway seems so wide and long now. I think my world just got bigger. I go out to the rear lawn porch and plop down at the table. I feel my will and call out to each of my troop. They all convene wanting to know what is going on. Once they are all there, I share the news.

"Early release; we can go home."

There is an explosion of celebration. Even dour Sil is clapping and celebrating.

"No plans yet guys, but they'll be coming soon. I'd suggest you get to packing."

We break on that direction. I head upstairs to begin my packing and also to figure out what the plan is. This is a curveball, but a good one.

I plop down at my desk and try to clear my head. Despite my desire to see family, I have an oath-sworn mission, and in all honesty, none of them are safe until that mission is complete. The door opens, and Sil enters, still clad in her frumpy warm-up pants and flannel shirt – not exactly dressed to impress.

"Knock knock," she says, as she walks over to my bed, falls on it, and stretches. "You need to bed me before you fling us headlong into almost certain death. I know that's what you're thinking. Right?"

There was no come hither with that statement. She might as well have been asking me if I wanted fries and a drink with that. She sits up and looks at me

"I'm not asking for your sake, I'd just like to have experienced you before we go to wherever it is we go when we truly die. You've seen how you can hurt us with your anger and disapproval – I want to experience the opposite of that. I am being selfish and admit it."

Well, there's no seduction there for her to be compelled against.

"What happened to, we stand a chance, Sil?"

She falls backward on the bed again.

"We still have a chance, but that's a far cry from a sure bet. Come on, throw your succubus a bone – she wants to be overwhelmed in pleasure by her wielder before wading into battle against impossible odds."

"Sorry, can't."

"Why not, Arthur? What could possibly be the reason?"

She's not even looking at me, as she's still on her back on the bed.

"Dory's watching."

Sil sits up immediately and snarls at me.

"Well, then I guess we're never going to do it because she's always going to be watching over you!" She jumps off the bed and glares at me. "I am desirable! I am not a disgusting thing! I am a prize befitting a king! I could… Fine, Arthur. Whatever."

She makes a bee-line for the still-open door.

"Sil, just stop, damn it."

She turns and says, "It's okay. I don't want you anymore."

Like I believe that.

"Alright Sil, but hear me out. When we kill him, I promise you one night. But only one night. And only after that bastard is dead and cold."

I have her full attention.

"What about Dorothy?"

She looks at me skeptically.

"Well, you and I will just have to hope that Jerry's able to convince her that avenging him makes it all okay, won't we?"

With a little swagger back to her, she crosses her arms over her chest, cocks her head and says, "I know he can… and Marge will help convince her too."

She saunters happily out of my room leaving me alone again.

I know I did the right thing. I need all of my team motivated. Because we will only have one shot at surviving what I have in mind.

Chapter 46

I go to Grey first thing and let him know my plans. Go to Charlotte to visit with family for a day. Then we head straight to New Orleans to deal with my quest.

"And how are you going to deal with your quest, Arthur?"

"I am going call a meeting with Maldgorath and whack him with the blessed sword. All other details will be on the fly. Surprise is my only advantage."

The completely blank look on his face tells me what he thinks before he does.

"That has to be the poorest excuse of a plan I have heard in all my years. You need a strategy. You need to plan for an emergency exit. I taught you better than that."

"Yes, you did. And he'll see right through it all."

Arms across his chest, Grey relents.

"You are an adult. And a rather old one. I can't tell you what to do. I can offer use of my private jet, assuming you pay for the fuel and the pilot's time."

That, I didn't see coming.

"Of course, sir. Thank you. Thank you very much."

I inform the team and say my goodbyes to the good people of the Chateau. Marthe is emotional, shedding a tear.

"You must come back," she says.

Reginald tells me, "Good luck, then."

Roger insists I write and send New Orleans stuff.

He has no idea of all the touristy crap that will be coming his way.

As we are converging on the downstairs with duffel bags in hand, Grey takes me aside.

"You'll be flying with another passenger: Ahtsag. Now, please know this has nothing to do with my lack of faith in your plan if I can even call it that. How do I best put this? He has been … complaining about your leaving. I think he may miss you."

Destroyer and Devourer my ass. I acquiesce, realizing it's not going to hurt anyone having panty boy tag along. I can just play it off to family that the freakishly large professional wrestler looking man with me is really an assigned bodyguard.

At the time to leave, all are there to wish us goodbye. Hugs are exchanged. We pile into the car… and wait. Znuul eventually comes down looking human and dressed in a blazer and slacks, small roller bag in tow. He stops with Grey; they share a hug and a moment.

Destroyer and Devourer – sure, right.

We get our bags in the trunk and leave for a three-hour trek to the airfield. The drive to the plane is uneventful. Pffif thinks it's flasky fun time for us, given the festivities before. I pass on the drink; so does Shey and Vets. That meant Pffif and Sil got hammered. Znuul just holds his own like he tends to and pokes fun at the drunks.

The flight is as long as it has to be. I wanted to sleep through most of it, but a certain large someone was feeling chatty and full of questions. Asking of my family; what they're like. Asking what it's like to have a loving family. Asking how he should behave. Asking how I feel about being united with them.

After a while, it becomes a bit of blah, freaking blah. I do my best not to let on to those feelings. Not out of fear, but because Znuul seems so genuine about it. It's like he's trying to understand how we feel - or at least understand how better to mimic it.

We land at Charlotte Douglass airport and taxi in. I make a call to Helen, who's going to be picking us up. It's very late, and after an emotional reunion, we make our way back to her and Steve's place. Sleep is on the docket.

The next morning is a family reunion, and I am as happy as I can be. Not all can join in the gathering as some of the great-great-grandchildren don't really know the truth of who I am, and there is some drive time involved. But there's more than a good enough turn out to make me smile; along with Pffif, Shey, and Sil.

And if Hjuul could smile he would be smiling too. Surprisingly, Znuul ingratiates himself with everyone, especially my great-great Matthew who at three years old thinks he is a giant.

Despite the years, it's all still a bit foreign for Vets, but I sense she is at least trying.

Steve takes me, Shey, Pffif, and Sil to Jerry and Marge's real gravesite. That visitation is more than a little overwhelming. I'm glad Helen stayed behind, she would just feed off of my pain; he knows that too. It is emotional. Sil loses it. Pffif repeats the emptying of the flask. Shey is silent; mourning in her own way.

This visit has to be short; just a day. Grey needs his jet, and I have to get my plans in order. They drive us back to the airport, and we have a heartfelt parting of the ways.

Helen cries and hugs us all.

"Don't do anything too crazy," Steve says.

If he only knew – I'm going to poke my finger in the eye of an ancient, powerful entity and try to lop its head off.

The flight to New Orleans is pretty somber, despite the excitement of having seen everyone. Znuul professes interest in "seeing how you live." That, and he's never been to New Orleans. He does mention to me that New Orleans is quite a nexus of practitioners and home to the South's preeminent vampire clan holding to the accords of the vampire war.

That means "good" vampires. Based on my reading that means they don't kill except in self-defense and only procreate after petitioning the protectorate for permission. Outside of that, they are still blood sucking vampires that can spread like a disease.

The jet comes to a landing and arrives at the private terminal. There is only so much room in a taxi, so Vets, Hjuul, and Sil go bye-bye. Shey reaches up to her hair and goes tiny in the cascade of fairy dust. Znuul takes a moment to talk with the pilot, confirming plans for the return to France. We collect our bags, trolley them out and make our way to hail a taxi.

But we don't have to. Grey has made arrangements for us. There's a limo driver there, holding a sign, "MacInerny."

That Grey, he thinks of everything.

Chapter 47

Znuul and I follow our driver, and he piles our bags in the trunk.

"My place is on Decatur, sir."

"Yes Sir!" he says and pulls out from the terminal. "I'm supposed to bring you to meet somebody first, but we'll be goin' where you need ta."

Znuul and I look at each other.

"Maybe the Techno's or The Order wants to open official channels," Znuul says.

"So, where are you taking us," I ask.

"Just a bit past the city, not far."

"So who are we meeting with?"

"I's just the driver, sir."

"Hmm," Znuul says.

We cruise along I-10 and turn on 510, then turn onto 90. It doesn't feel right to me. We're heading for the bayou. I bend over to Znuul, who leans down to me.

"Meetings in the swamp generally aren't a good thing."

He gives me a look of recognition.

"How much farther?" Znuul says.

"Not much farther, sir, not much at all."

We cut up to highway eleven, and I know there's nothing there but bayou. Damn. I concentrate and try to cast a shield discreetly on myself, then on Shey. Znuul reaches into his blazer and puts on a pair of dark sunglasses. Guess he just wants to look the part.

The limo suddenly pulls over off the road. The driver leaps out and runs away.

That is never, ever, a good sign.

A blue Chevy Tahoe comes tearing down from the opposite direction toward us. It skids to a stop in front of us, and the doors fly open. Out of the rear, three persons unload - two to my left, one to my right. All are very armed. The one to the right is armed with an AA-12 assault shotgun, the two to my left have a nice mix of arms; an AK in the hands of the one at the rear and the man at point sporting a Glock.

The front doors open and the men are joined by the driver also holding a handgun. Out of the passenger side, a man in a well-tailored suit emerges, no weapons in hand.

"Caster type there most likely," Znuul says, indicating the well-tailored one. "Follow my lead. Pixie, cover Arthur. Arthur – don't get killed."

Znuul opens the door to face the two on the right.

I hear him say something to the effect of, "Good afternoon, what's all this…"

The shotgun goes off, and I see Z topple downward. The second man with the pistol rushes over, and they both drag Znuul's large frame to the front of the Tahoe. I see the pistol holding man let go of Znuul, grab his eye and fall out.

There is the end of a silver arrow poking out from under his hand. I see the well-tailored man look upwards, mutter something and gesture outwards.

Shey's burning form comes falling from the sky, her voice screaming in pain through the flames. I immediately reach for her sigil and send her away – it's the fastest way to stop the pain. The window next to me explodes thanks to a warning shot from the AK. I hit the floor in case further ordinance is incoming.

Pffif, who despite being sneaky, is spied by this well-tailored bastard and gets set aflame as well. I send Pffif away as quickly as I can.

I hear someone, most likely the well-tailored man, call out to me.

"Arthur… Arthur MacInerny, please exit the car with your hands well in sight, or we will have to kill your rather large bodyguard, here.

"Do as they say, Arthur," Znuul says.

What the heck, this is our world crushing demon-thing?

I crawl toward the door Znuul went out of, away from the two on my left and stand behind the door because that still offers some cover. The man with the AK is trained on me from the other side. The other man with a pistol runs over to Znuul and puts it against his head. Now that damned assault shotgun is on me too.

What the hell did they shoot Znuul with? Destroyer my sweaty ass…

I can't tell what's going on with Z, as the sunglasses cover his eyes. But, I see him reach up to the pistol guy's belt. Then in one sudden motion, he stands and flings the pistol carrying man into well-dressed man with extreme prejudice, basically pancaking the sorcerer on the front end of the car.

I dive for the rear of the car and call Vets. I hear a series of booms from the shotgun and cracks from the AK. Vets appears, and she goes after Mr. AK-47. She bounds after him, sword in hand. He wheels on her and lets loose a volley of shots.

Thank goodness for plate armor. She is taking some harm, so I look up and send healing to her. Then I look over in Znuul's direction. Shotgun man was apparently flung far away and is now picking himself up. Znuul has the sorcerer by the arm and is twisting it while pinning him down with a foot. I hear a "splort" and realize that the sorcerer's arm has been totally twisted out of the socket.

My eye flashes back to Vets who has closed the gap with Mr. AK-47. A downward strike of her sword disarms him. An elbow to the face downs him.

"Boom! Boom! Boom!" Echoes from the shotgun make me take cover. That sound is swiftly replaced by a wet thumping sound. I stand from the rear of the car and see Znuul beating the snot out of shotgun man with the well-dressed sorcerer's dismembered arm.

Damn, that's not an image I'm not going to forget anytime soon.

I turn away and see Vets has finished Mr. AK. I summon Hjuul immediately and walk toward Znuul. He is dragging the bloody and beaten shotgun man back to the front of the Tahoe.

"Can you believe this insect shot me in the knee with that thing?" he fumes. He flings the man like a rag doll into the limo. "That's for my glasses and blazer."

Sorcerer guy is moaning and bleeding out.

Znuul smiles and says, "Waste not want not."

His fingers turn their more natural form, and he jams them into the sorcerer's rib cage. Znuul's eyes roll, and his face is one of unnatural pleasure. Sorcerer looks up at me and tries to gasp something, but nothing comes out. His eyes turn milky white, and he shrivels into a dry, mummified carcass.

Znuul pulls out his fingers and stands tall.

"He was as good as dead anyway, seems a shame to waste. The devouring never gets old - you remember how it feels, don't you, Arthur?"

Znuul is all smiles now.

I do - I remember my victim at the rectory. I remember the feeling of superiority, the power. The desire for more. Shit, Z's off the rails.

All thoughts stop when I hear, "Nobody moves!"

The other pistol-wielding man has come to after being flung into well-dressed man and has his gun trained on me.

Znuul cocks his head, looks at the man and says, "Sir, you do not want to do that."

The next instant both his hands are lying on the ground in front of him, thanks to Vet's blade. He holds his bloody stumps up to his face in disbelief. Znuul pushes me aside and grabs one of the man's arms.

"You are not eating him too!"

Znuul turns, looks at me with that shit eating grin of his and shows me his palm, which is glowing red. Just like that he grabs the end of the stump and it hisses and steams. Pistol man is screaming and shaking. Znuul grabs the other wrist and repeats. Pistol man passes out.

"Cauterizing the wound," Znuul says. "Can't interrogate a dead man."

Znuul takes off his blazer, looks at it, mutters, "Fuck," then takes his shirt off.

"We need to get the limo driver - you try to find out what all this is about," Znuul says.

His body expands, wings unfold, and he transforms into regular bestial Znuul. With a whoosh, he is in flight after the driver.

Of the five in the car, two are alive to interrogate. I call Hjuul over to watch the shotgun man as I liberate him of his weapon. I've always wanted one of these bad boys; the AA-12 is one fine combat weapon, I hear. Shotgun man moans and begins to come awake. He jerks backward and is plastered against the car in fear, as he comes face to face with a snarling, four hundred pound-plus Hjuul.

"Behave," I say and then clarify, "That means you, whatever your name is."

He looks at me wide-eyed and then back at Hjuul.

"Yes, he will tear you into kibble."

Mr. No Hands is lying on the ground twitching. I'll guess we'll have to question him next.

I wave Vets on to join me, and we take our place next to Hjuul in front of Mr. Shotgun. I signal her to take her helmet off. Shotgun's eyes get even wider beholding Vet's fierce feline-like face: the desired effect.

"We're going to ask you some simple questions, and you're going to give truthful, simple answers, or, the body count goes up. Understand?"

"Yes sir."

Now that we have that understanding, we begin.

"Who sent you?"

"He did," Shotgun man says, pointing toward the well-dressed mummy in front of the car.

That's not helpful, so I must clarify, and impart some urgency.

"Real funny, damn it. How about you tell me who he works for, who you work for, and what in the fuck this is all about."

I grab him by the shirt and drag him around to the front of the car so he can get a better look at No Hands and Well Dressed.

"The Potentia!" he says, "The Grace!"

That's a start.

"Okay, keep going… What? Where? When?

"I'm just a damn merc," he pleads. "I was to assist Bartholomew there in acquiring… you and bringing…"

We are interrupted by the sound of a man's screaming. Znuul releases the driver from about twenty feet in the air, and he falls to the ground, landing feet first on the pavement and crumbling into a mass.

"My legs! Goddamn, my legs is broken!" he screams.

Znuul touches down lightly next to him and drags him unmercifully to us, the driver screaming all the way. I shoot Znuul a look of displeasure.

"He won't be running away anymore," Znuul says.

In between Vets pretty Vetisghar face and Znuul's handsome winged visage, we have just totally rocked Mr. Shotgun's world. Taxi driver seems to be more worried about his legs.

I tap Mr. Shotgun with the business end of the AA and say, "Continue."

"All I know is we were to pick you up, sedate you, and bring you to the bar."

Hjuul growls and snaps - good doggie.

"He wants to know what bar, where exactly."

Sometimes you have to translate for Hjuul.

"The Happy Place, man. It's a bar Marigny and Royal. We were supposed to bring you to the boss, some guy named Jean. I don't know nothing else man, please – it's just a job for me."

"Alright, Mr. Znuul, please confirm this information with his friend there – and no devouring, please."

That gets a nonchalant shrug from the big guy, who hoists handless up and begins lightly slapping him into consciousness. Once conscious, Znuul's tail flicks to one of the guy's hands still on the ground. Znuul stabs it with some stinger thing in his tail, and takes the poor guy around the side of the Tahoe, away from us.

I turn to the driver.

"You don't seem so surprised by all these colorful characters."

"Listen, Mister, I drive a cab in New Orleans… I's seen some shit. Not quite all this… but vamps and zombies and crazy magician types like…" He looks over at well-dressed mummy "Damn." He looks back at me, "Y'all don't mess around now, do ya? I's just the driver. I don't know nuthin' - don't want to know nuthin.' I just work for the cash money - got a family to support. Hey, once my legs get healed, I'll drive y'all for free. I specialize in transporting strange folks. Why don't you just drop me off at a hospital…"

He is interrupted by the sight of Znuul coming back around the Tahoe. He plops down handless mercenary on the ground.

"Story checks," he says. "We waste them now?"

Znuul has everyone's attention, certainly mine. I turn and look at him with all seriousness.

"I figure they're going to be helpful getting us into the bar. We need to have a heart to heart with this Jean guy."

Znuul's laugh fills the bayou.

"I knew I was going to like New Orleans," he says. "Let the good times roll."

Chapter 48

"Which vehicle are we taking?" Znuul asks. "We'll ride one and burn all the evidence in the other."

"Man, that ain't no vehicle – that's my livelihood there," the driver says.

"You got insurance," I ask.

He looks at me sadly.

"Damn, that's just cold."

"We take the limo, Znuul."

Znuul nods and goes about moving the bodies into the backseat of the Tahoe. I tell Vets to pat down everyone for weapons and help get them into the limo. Mr. Shotgun man doesn't wait; he just starts unloading knives, a small pistol, taser, and other items as fast as he can.

I think we made an impression on the gentleman. I collect them all, as they may be useful later.

Znuul throws well-dressed mummy in last and looks over at me with that over the top smile.

"Kindling."

Znuul takes in a great breath and blows bright blue fire inside the car. He shuts the door and calmly walks around to the front of the Tahoe.

"Off we go," he says, with a wink, taking hold of the front bumper, apparently measuring the vehicle for something. Then he lifts it up by the bumper. With a twist and a step, he hurls the burning Tahoe about a hundred feet into the bayou.

Now everyone is staring at him: me, Hjuul, the mercs, and the driver being assisted to the limo by Vets are all slack-jawed.

The driver sums it up: "Damn."

I will never, ever, arm wrestle Znuul.

Znuul dusts off his hands, gives us a look that says, "What?" and kneels down. There are sounds of bones popping, and he grimaces as he begins to transform into human appearance again. After what appears to be a less than pleasant experience, he collects his shirt and blazer and puts them on.

He walks over to me and clasps my shoulder.

"Not fun changing human, but it feels so fine changing back ... We going now? You're driving – I call shotgun!"

"Shotgun?" You sure you're thousands and thousands of years old?"

"Older."

"Vets you watch over our guests," I say.

She piles into the back. Once in, I hear her give a growl just to set the tone for them. I call Hjuul over and give him a good pet.

"Sorry, back to the white just for a bit."

I dismiss him and get in the limo. Key's still in the ignition – good.

I drive us to our first destination - the LSU Medical Center.

"What's your name, driver," I ask.

"Carl, sir, Carl Turner."

"Okay, Carl Turner, you are at a hospital. Your limo will be parked in the public lot at Jeff Square. You owe me. In fact, for all this, I think you are now my bitch – got it?"

"Yes sir, thank you, thank you, sir!"

"Vets, please help him from the vehicle."

She literally throws him to the pavement.

I take off, no time to waste. I have a bar to be at. I'm sure it's close to five o'clock somewhere.

I cruise by "The Happy Place" once, just to set eyes upon it. It's a dump. There are no signs of guards, henchmen, mercenaries or anything. I park us a block away and pump Mr. Shotgun for information.

"Jean's office is in the back, down a long hall and that he will most likely have bodyguards with him," he says.

"Here's the plan," I say to the group. "Znuul, you Pffif and Sil will arrive before us, find a seat near the hall and deal with anyone coming from the bar after the commotion starts."

"By your command," Znuul says. "Hey, if I buy her a drink does that mean she has to do something for me too?"

I just shake my head in disbelief and turn to the two mercenaries.

"You two will escort me to the office. I suggest you keep your… stumps in your pockets to avoid attention." That one was not looking good at all. "Once we get to the office, you would both be best served to run away and forget you ever crossed paths with me."

Mr. Shotgun nods emphatically, Stumps basically blinks and lolls his head. He's looking worse by the second.

"Vets you are back to the white. I'll have you and Hjuul back as soon as we are at the door."

I dismiss Vets. Znuul gets out of the car as do I. I walk around to the back of the limo and get in. I immediately summon Sil and Pffif, quickly briefing them on the situation. Sil transforms herself human and exits the vehicle, taking Znuul by the arm as they walk down the street.

Pffif is nowhere to be seen. This is good. He is in super sneaky mode.

"What in the hell are you," Mr. Shotgun asks.

"Someone you never want angry at you, and if you have any thoughts about turning on me in the bar, there are worse things than death."

"Loud and clear, sir."

I summon Shey, and she goes teeny-tiny to be able to follow us stealthily after making sure to point her finger at both of the Mercs faces. Enough time has passed.

"Showtime boys," I say. "You are almost free from all this crap."

We get out of the car and Stumps falters. I put my hand on his exposed neck and concentrate on connecting to the world around me, closing my eyes. I say a prayer of healing, focusing that energy into an image and word. I open my eyes and say "vitae" releasing the word and energy through my hand to him.

Stumps jerks and blinks a little at me. "Thanks," he says, "How did you…"

"Just know I can do that in reverse too. Let's go."

With a grimace, he stuffs his wrists into the pockets of his cargo pants, and we proceed. We enter the bar, and Mr. Shotgun nods to the bartender. I play groggy. Sil and Znuul are staged near a corridor enjoying beers. Nobody notices the little glowing firefly buzzing above.

We shuffle into the hall and Shotgun indicates the door on the end. I scan for cameras and see none. I look at them both and say, "Scram."

Noting the size of the hall and reconsider summoning Hjuul. I summon Vets.

"Kick the door in."

She pulls her sword and with a kick takes the door off the hinges. Shey buzzes in after her, and I take up the rear.

"You must be Jean!" I say to the fairly skinny, well pierced and inked man. I would peg him to be in his late thirties. He's flanked by two large tattooed gentlemen sitting in chairs to either side of his desk with their heads down. "I'm Arthur, I think you wanted to meet me!"

I expected some surprise. Instead, he just scoots his chair back up to his desk and steeples his hands.

"Yes, thank you for coming." He moves his hands, pointing each one to the men in the chairs. "Get him, now!"

Both men look up simultaneously. Both men have very dead, gray eyes. They stand immediately and lunge forward with unnerving speed.

Zombies.

Vets intercepts the first, skewering him straight through the chest. That gets her a series of clubbing blows that knock her to the floor. The second zombie is met by a volley of arrows from the now regular sized Shey. The arrows don't slow it down at all. I have to roll to evade, only to stand and see a zombie with a sword in its chest barreling right for me.

Vets dives and tackles it by the legs at the last second, allowing me to jump away. Pincushion zombie now realizes it missed me and turns. Out of the corner of my eye, I see Jean smiling as he pulls a wand out of the desk drawer – that can't be good.

Pffif appears next to him and nails his hand to the desk with his dagger. The little guy jumps back, whips out his flask and takes a big gulp. Jean starts to say something, but Pffif jumps back toward him and spits the contents of his cheeks into Jean's eyes, blinding him with that very potent liquid.

The zombies react to their master's trouble, and attention turns from me. Vets wrestles her sword out of the zombie in a gory spray, followed by a head-lopping strike. My attention shifts to the familiar voice coming from the door.

"Oh, flesh golems."

It's Znuul. He casually strides over to pincushion zombie and turns its head one hundred eighty degrees.

"This must be Jean," Znuul says.

"Yes, our host," I say.

Vets pushes me to the side and puts herself in front of me. I hear the "crack crack crack" of a gun and the pinging of the rounds against her armor. A man bounces off Jean's desk. I see Sil's bare feet standing in the doorway.

"Good girl," I mutter.

"Shoot me in the back? You have to be kidding," Znuul bellows.

I pick myself up and see Znuul lifting the man with the gun up by his belt and slamming him on the desk in front of Jean. He releases the belt and shoves his hand deep into the man's lower back which elicits screams of agony.

With one deft and powerful move, he tears the man's spine out, silencing him forever. With a shake, he tears it from the body and then tosses the body across the room, setting the spine on the desk in front of Jean.

"Damn it, Znuul! That was not necessary. You are leaving me one hell of a trail to clean up."

Jeans eyes widen, and he looks over at me.

"Ahtsag Znuul?" His eyes turn back to Znuul, then to the door where the bartender is now standing with a sawed-off shotgun in hand.

"No problems here, Bull," he says to the bartender who is surveying the gory scene around him and noting Jean's hand, still daggered to the desk.

Sil smiles at the bartender and says, "You go on now before someone gets really hurt."

Nobody has to tell him twice.

"You keep impressive company, Mr. MacInerny," Jean says. He turns his attention to Znuul. "I am honored to meet you great one, we look forward to your liberty from the wizard Lightbringer."

"Thank you," Znuul says.

Znuul reaches for the dagger stuck in Jean's hand and removes it with a painful back and forth motion. Znuul wipes the dagger off on Jean's shirt and hands it back to Pffif.

"We need to be done here," Znuul says.

"Agreed." I walk over to Jean. "What is all this about?"

He looks over at me while attempting to staunch the flow of blood from his hand. "I was instructed to offer you an invitation to join our fine network of practitioners. I thought that it might be helpful to illustrate that we can protect you from certain incidents."

"Can we just off him now," Znuul says. "He's just going to come after you."

Jean realizes his life is fleeting.

"You have my assurances nothing else will happen – on my word, my bonded oath on my power," Jean stammers out. He is trying not to look nervous and failing.

"Good enough for me," I say. "Please don't make me come back; we won't be as subtle next time."

"I will tell the inner circle that you respectfully decline their offer," Jean says.

Znuul turns back to Jean and touches the spine laying across his desk, which rears up like a snake. The spine snake sways a bit, then strikes him on the nose, causing a spout of blood to appear. Jean jumps. Znuul takes his finger away, and the spine falls.

The message is pretty clear.

We get out to the hall, and I dismiss Vets. Shey reaches up to her hair and in a cascade of fairy dust changes to human. Pffif just tags along. We all make our way to the Limo calmly, and I drive us home. Once in the garage, I look around and summon Hjuul and Vets. I hand Vets her ring and attach the collar with the talisman around Hjuul's neck. All are presentable again.

We empty the trunk of bags, and I toss Sil the keys along with a twenty.

"Park the car in the Jefferson Square lot, please. Wipe it down for prints, etc. You know the drill."

"I do," she says, sharing a curtsy in her pleated leather skirt. She gets in the limo and backs out.

We head upstairs, and I lift the gate. We all pile out of the lift except for Znuul, who hesitates.

"I would prefer a formal invite, just in case. Your home's threshold is pretty stout," he says.

All homes have a form of energy that acts as insulation from outside influences. It can interfere with magical activities and psionic activity unless bidden to enter. Most people don't even notice it.

"Enter and be welcome to our happy home, Ahtsag Znuul," I say with an inviting flourish.

I unlock the door to our quarters, and we all enter. I give Znuul the dime tour, and we settle down in the living area.

"I want to see Bourbon Street at night," Znuul says, "I hear it is a true exhibition of human excess and debauchery."

"Aye," says Pffif, "'tis truly embarrassing. Most of 'em need more practice holdin' their liquor."

Then a start of fear takes me. Pffif, Hjuul, and Shey note it immediately. Znuul notices the change in the room.

"Oh, you're not thinking about that whole devouring thing earlier," he says. "That guy was going to die regardless, it would have been a waste…"

"Thanks for the reminder Z, Grey is going to blow a gasket. You can't just treat people like a quick snack. We generally don't want to be friends with things that make a habit of eating us."

Shey goes up in arms.

"He did what?"

Znuul is definitely uncomfortable now.

"Arthur, there is no reason to involve the old man. Things happened. It's not like I'm out hunting or harvesting. He was going to die anyway. Hey you…" He stops there, which is a good thing. He turns to Shey. "That asshole burned you to the ground, remember?"

"Oh, yeah – I guess he deserved it," Shey says.

"Aye, we were due a bit of the revenge," Pffif says.

Not fair, that's three on one.

"Well, that's settled then," I say with a sigh. "But we have a bigger problem – it's been two years since the refrigerator has been opened."

"Oh, dear," says Pffif.

"Guess we're dining out," Znuul's says.

I hear the gate to the elevator open and know it must be Sil. She makes her characteristically flamboyant entrance and plops down at my feet, making my knees her armrest.

"What's the plan for tonight?" she asks.

Shey is up in arms.

"Get your hands off him, demon slut! Don't let her touch you, Arthur."

I don't even have to see Sil's face to know she's rolling her eyes. I gently guide Sil's arms off my knees and step up and around her.

"Dinner out it is, we can draw straws for refrigerator duty after Znuul leaves."

We take our meal at a place around the way called Café Maspero; a good local place for a belly filling. And considering we have both Vets and Znuul in tow, large affordable portions seem the way to go. We take over a table, and I let everyone know to order whatever they like.

We eat and, in Pffif's case, drink our fills, and we go on a walk about the French Quarter for Znuul's sake. We hit Jackson Square and then cross the street to order Beignets and coffee. We stroll a bit more and drop in on Preservation Hall.

After a short while, we head back home. I am ready for bed. Znuul is ready to check out Bourbon Street.

"I'll pass. It's not my thing, and I'm tired," I say. "You should take Sil with you, she knows the strip."

Znuul perks up and Sil raises an eyebrow at me.

"Who better to take in some decadence with," Znuul says, with a lascivious smile. "Maybe we can take a carnal moment in the shadows of the cathedral, do you like the sound of that, fair Silithes?"

I think we just bought the girl another pony.

"Can we? Can I… Can you?" she says, turning from me to Znuul seriously.

Znuul smiles and says, "My daddy says, I can play as long as I don't hurt anyone or break their mind."

Sil is now standing and damn near shaking.

"Arthur, really?"

"You kids have fun storming the quarter. Just don't hurt anyone." I fix my eyes on Znuul. "And no harming my Sil either."

Znuul stands. Sil takes his arm.

"Nothing even remotely resembling harm is going to happen to her, I assure you."

Chapter 49

The rapping on my door wakes me from my much-needed slumber. I look over at the clock and realize it's very, very early. Being bushwhacked doesn't help with jet lag. Neither does being woken before six in the morning. I yell out, "Coming!" walk to my sitting room, open the door to the hall and find Znuul standing there, looking fresh in a new change of clothes.

"Pilot wants to go early," he says. "Didn't want to leave without a goodbye."

Aww.

"Thanks, big guy, I would have figured you, and Sil would just be getting in about now."

He smiles. "I left her exhausted in her room a little after four. You want details?"

"Heck no."

We stand there in silence for a bit, me more so because I'm tired. Znuul breaks the silence. "No way I can talk you out of your suicide mission? You don't have to do this alone, you know. The whole damn Protectorate will stand by you. Me too."

"Thanks. I have to stand on my own here if I'm going to scare the bully."

Znuul wraps me in a crushing hug. He breaks the hug and looks at me seriously.

"What the hell are you, Arthur MacInerny? You just made me hug you and proclaim you a friend."

"Thanks."

He takes me by the shoulder and basically drags me into the hall to follow him to the door out.

"I can prove my claim of friendship, you skeptical bastard," he says.

We stop in front of the kitchen, and he points at the refrigerator.

"I cleaned your refrigerator. You would not believe the life forms in there."

No way. I walk over and open it – clean as a whistle.

"Damn Z, I'll have to let you play with Sil more often."

"I'm going to miss you, Arthur MacInerny. Please try to stay alive and visit us every now and then."

"You take care of Grey."

He laughs as he turns to take his roller bag in hand.

"That'll be the day… Me taking care of him."

Next thing, he is out on the lift and gone, taxi waiting I presume.

I plant my behind on the sofa in the sitting room and look around for the remote. I turn on the news and smell the fresh coffee in the kitchen. Nice touch, Z. I get up and pour a cup and return to my seat. Hjuul joins me with a plop down by my feet.

I have things to do today. First and foremost, I have to brief the team on the plan. The next thing will be to set it into motion. Once that is done, there's no turning back. I consider my oath to Svea. I remember the violation of my son and his wife.

I remember how easily Znuul brought me to my knees.

I will have only one shot at an encounter on my terms. I will have only one shot at setting the tone for any future encounters.

No pressure.

I get up for another cup of coffee and am joined by Pffif, looking a bit groggy. I get a mug for him and pour a cup.

"No milk," I tell him.

"No worries," he says.

We head to the living room and take in the news.

"It's always the same on this news show," he says.

I agree, and we sit a while in silence, which for Pffif is quite a doing.

Pffif reloads our coffees and starts a new pot.

"Ima guessing it's about time ye wanna talk with us all."

Very perceptive, as he always is.

"You are so right Mr. Pffiferil. Would you get everyone together?"

He gives me an, "Aye" and heads down the hall to everyone's apartments. I reach down and give Hjuul a rub.

Vets and Shey arrive. I get a hug and "Morning" from Shey. Vets just takes a seat in her usual stiff way. Pffif comes with mugs in one small hand and the pot in the other. He sets them out and asks who wants. I hold mine out. Neither Shey or Vets are big coffee types.

Pffif returns the coffee pot to the burner and joins us. "So, whatcha sharin', Arthur?"

"Did you get Sil?" I ask him.

"Aye," he says.

Shey harrumphs.

I turn around to look at the hall and like magic she appears, looking like hell, wearing nothing but one of my dress shirts as a nightgown with the sleeves semi-rolled up. She shuffles into the living room and plops down on the other side of the sofa from me.

"Rough night?" I ask.

"He was insatiable," she says, followed by a long sigh, leaning her head back over the sofa.

Pffif says, "You got some stuff in your hair."

"I have stuff all over me," she says, with a winsome smile.

"Eww!" Shey says, looking like she just ate a lemon, rind and all.

Like usual, our meeting is breaking down. So, it's time to reign it in.

"Glad you had a good time Sil, we need to talk business – Maldgorath business."

That gets everyone's attention. Sil snaps up and says, "fuck, I need coffee – don't start."

She grabs a mug off the table and takes off for the pot in the kitchen. I see her take a huge swig off the mug, then top it off again. She comes back cradling the mug and sits down carefully.

"Okay, ready," she tells the group.

What a diva.

I take a deep breath start in on the plan. "Here's what's going to happen. I am going to ask Maldgorath for a meeting through Arix. We all know he's going to use that meeting time to try to reap me. I can't tell you exactly what's going to happen because I don't know. But when it does happen, you will know. The important things are this: do not kill his dragon unless you think I have a real shot at taking his head. I need everybody on his summonlings, except Shey; I will need you to serve as a nuisance to him while I work the sword."

Vets says, "I do not understand, how is this a plan?"

Sil takes a giant very un-ladylike slurp of her coffee. "It's all about surprise, right? The bigger the surprise, the better?"

"Yeah," I tell the group. "You all know how good I am at deception. I basically have to surprise myself and seize the opportunity. He's going to read me otherwise."

Shey rolls her eyes and folds her arms. "You are a strange one, Arthur."

"It makes sense to me," Sil says.. "Surprise can work. I, personally, do not want to confront that one while he's ready and waiting. But no lie; it makes me nervous – anything involving a confrontation with that one makes me nervous."

"Aye me too, but I'll follow yer lead, Arthur."

Vets adds, "You know I will die for my wielder."

Shey gets up, wraps me in a hug, plants a gentle kiss on my lips and looks me in my eyes.

"You I will follow anywhere."

Sil sneers and gets up. "You should be happy, little pixie, some of us don't get kisses from our wielder at will. Her composure changes rather suddenly, and she smiles, "But thank you, Arthur, for allowing me a very pleasurable night. That was very nice of you."

"You're very welcome, Sil. Okay everyone, let's reconvene in about an hour for breakfast.

Breakfast is going to be the easiest part of the day.

Chapter 50

We take breakfast at the Canal Street Ramada. Sil does not join us, claiming she needs rest and is already well fed; meaning on life energy, I guess. I think Znuul did a number on her; from the sound of it a good number.

We eat our fill and talk about everything except what we we're getting ready to do. It is a pleasant time.

We stroll back home in mostly silence. We all know what is coming. I will summon Arixtumin, make him use that communication talisman and hopefully either encourage or antagonize Maldgorath into a meet and greet.

We get upstairs, and it's time to get this show on the road.

"Alright group, show-time in one hour. Meet downstairs where Vets likes to train. Someone bring a folding chair for Arix. Pffif, make sure Sil shows up."

"I'll be doin' what I can."

I know what he means.

We all break, and I head to my apartment to grab a shower and think through my tactics. Do I just call him out? Do I take a more subtle approach? I review my mental profile of him and decide that an aggressive posture could be less productive than one that indicates some weakness.

Soft sell.

I look around the room, and my eye fixes on the box with the blessed sword. I lay the box on the bed. I grab my leather scabbard and open the box. It is a beautiful weapon: simple, graceful and deadly. I won't be making the call without it.

I strap it across my back and head for the stairs. To heck with the elevator… I get down to the second floor, which is basically an entirely open, gutted area. I stride to the middle of it and kneel.

I close my eyes and try to clear myself of thought. Then I pray. I pray to Dory that she might look over me. I pray to Jerry and Marge for strength. I pray thanks to the Almighty having my family under his grace. I pray for help in this daunting task.

I hear the gate open and stop my prayers. The crew is there in whole. I smile at them and stand.

"You all ready for this?" I call out.

"I am ready to die for my wielder," Vets says.

Not exactly what I want to hear, but I know what she means.

Everyone is here, everyone seems ready. So I ask again with less bravado, "You all ready for this?"

There all say, "yes," in mostly unison.

I reach to the glyph on my arm and say, "Arixtumin, come."

Arix upon manifesting takes to his knees immediately.

"Thank you! Thank you!"

Arix notices the company around him and their demeanor. He looks at me with serious eyes.

"What do you require?"

I am not messing around. I touch my will and say, "Arixtumin you will not speak unless I direct you to." I touch my will again. "Arixtumin, use that coin thing and contact Maldgorath."

He produces the coin and calls to Maldgorath.

We wait. Nothing.

"Call to him again."

This time, we hear a voice.

"You have regained the confidence of the human?"

Arix will not speak unless directed to, so I'm up.

"Not exactly, old friend," I say.

There is a pause, and the voice responds, "Arthur, so good to hear from you. And better yet to hear you call me friend. That warms my heart."

I take a deep breath. The next moments are critical.

"Glad to hear that. By the way, crappy move with my family, you might have done better, just asking for a favor. Heck, the way I saw it, I owed you."

"Now you owe me differently," the voice says.

"I'm not happy with you, I admit. But, what is done is done. I am more concerned with where we go from here. I don't care for having to look over my shoulder constantly."

"You seek to trap and harm me."

"You have my word, upon my honor, that I do not. But, I require your word that you will not seek to harm or trap me either. It's time we speak plainly. I obviously did not fall into your plans. You obviously wronged me. Maybe we can find a middle ground here."

"Fool, you seek to bargain with me?"

"I seek less of a bargain and more of a mutual understanding. I know your strength. Ahtsag Znuul himself has brought me to my knees and showed me how lowly I am. By the way, he told me to send you greetings."

There is a long pause. *Did he break the connection?*

"Ahtsag Znuul is a fool and a puppet for a lowly human wizard. But if he taught you humility, then perhaps we may commune. What is your phone number?"

I didn't expect him to ask to ring me up. I give it to him.

"I will consider your request. You will know if I wish us to meet."

"Thank you."

I make the sign to Arix to break the connection. He nods to me it is done.

I look around at the group, trying to judge their reactions. I see nerves setting in.

"That's as good as it can go. It's up to him now. By the way, what a pompous ass. Who says, commune, anyway?"

"He does," Sil says.

Arix looks at me as if to ask if he can stay. I touch my will and say, "You may not communicate with Maldgorath without my express consent."

I send him back to the white. Bastard. Enjoy the continuous view of nothing.

"Sharpen your swords," I say. "Hell is coming, and its name is Maldgorath."

Chapter 51

There is no telling if or when I will hear back from Maldgorath. I suspect it will be either soon, or in years. I think I played it correctly, showing just enough weakness.

Bullies love weakness.

Regardless, for the next few days, I'm circling the wagons. The blessed sword will not be out of hand's reach. The team will be together. In fact, I plan to hole up on the third floor, taking advantage of what Znuul called our "pretty stout" threshold.

With those petty decisions made, the real issue comes to bear – food. Mr. Stomach is telling me that he is almost empty; I might even settle for a handful of those damn butterflies in a few hours. I envision the look on the restaurant greeter's face; me with the sword and my crew in their natural forms. I chuckle.

I have an empty refrigerator and a hungry hound. Someone's going to need to do a major grocery shop. And somebody's focusing on minutiae because it's easier than dwelling on the real issue – something really bad is coming to call.

So, there's only one thing to do: go grocery shopping. If I strap the wood box with the sword in it to my back - no one would be the wiser. The only mystery left to solve is whether or not the minivan will start after sitting around for two years.

I stroll down to Sil's apartment as she's the best driver of our team. Pffif's legs won't reach the pedals. Shey and Vets never showed any interest. Note to self: make them interested. I knock on the door, which is followed by a lilting, "Come in."

I open the door, expecting the full Sil show. To my relief, she's just curled up on the sofa with the remote.

She looks up at me, "Did he call?"

"No, just need to see if you can start the minivan. We need to get some shopping done."

I pitch the keys over to her, which she deftly snatches from the air. She flicks off the TV and begins to get up.

"Mind if I clean up first?"

Here it comes, not a seduction….

"Take your time Sil. I've got to pull a list together."

"Alright. I won't be long. I'll let you know if we need a new battery. The gas is probably more of an issue."

I close the door and breathe a small sigh of relief. I think about hiring Znuul on a regular basis, Sil seems much less needy when well fed. I make a mental note to talk to her about her "hungers" and if quick trips to the white would help her deal with it better. There have been times where she's asked to go for that reason, and I realize that it must have been pretty bad because she hates that place with a passion.

Maybe I'm not the best warden.

I go about inviting everyone on the shopping trip, assuming the minivan starts.

All are in for the shopping trip. I bury myself in the list. Milk, lunch meat, bread, cheeses, 12 gauge shotgun shells; I really like my newly acquired AA-12. I go to check the freezer, to see what survived. The freezer was mostly empty, and some things had to go that were freezer charred. I fill up a small garbage bag with stuff and walk it over to the door.

I pass Sil in the hall, whose hair is still wet, wearing jeans and tee-shirt.

"Little present by the front door, since you're heading down."

"Lovely," she says.

I figure she must be in some sort of mood as she always dresses to the nines for shopping, enjoying the distraction she generates from our fellow shoppers.

I get to my apartment and attach the carry strap to the sword's box. I sling it over my shoulder to test the fit. It needs some adjustment, so I adjust. Then I head out to the main sitting room to await the verdict on the minivan.

Everyone is there waiting, except Sil, whom I presume is still wrangling the minivan. We're all a bit restless. Patiently waiting for conflict to call is not a collective strong suit, except for Vets who seems rather at ease. We hear the gate to the lift open, and Sil enters.

"It's running, but very rough."

We all pile in, and I take us to the Wal-Mart Supercenter, sputtering and stalling the whole way.

When we get to the store, Sil declares, "Women's wear!" She looks at Shey and says, "Come with me, Pixie and I'll help you lose that little-girl look of yours."

Great. I'm either faced with a Shey-tirade or having to watch Shey model her new "looks" all the while reminding me that Dorothy gave us "permission" to be together.

It looks like a tirade. Shey is frowning and looking around at all the people in the store, arms folded and tapping her feet agitatedly.

"Maybe I don't want to look like a slut."

I start to say something to diffuse the situation, but Sil beats me to the punch.

"Fair enough. But they probably have some cute sundresses for you – come for girly time?"

What's this? Sil, making nice with Shey? I make a mental note to make sure Znuul is on speed dial and do a quick mental calculation of what airfare might be.

Shey's demeanor changes from agitated to questioning. She looks to me for guidance.

"I think I can handle hound chow and groceries Shey."

Now she's all smiles and sunbeams.

"Okays," Shey says. They take off for the clothes.

I look over at Vets. "You want to join them?"

Pffif laughs at me. Vets looks at him with a frown and back at me.

"I have clothing. I do not understand why he laughs."

Pffif walks over and pats her on the waist. "Just canna picture ye in a frilly sundress, big girl."

Yes, Vets has one style of clothing only – military surplus. But she makes it work for her – lots of pockets for ammo and tools.

We head to the back of the store to pet supplies first and then work our way out. We load up the cart quickly. I'm wondering if we need another one.

Pffif begins playing the "you dropped your wallet game." I nip that in the bud – that's the game where he picks peoples' pockets for practice. There are cameras everywhere. Not a good thing for him to do.

Vets is always in awe of the meat section, go figure.

"Go get another cart, Vets, and pick out our meats and eggs."

I head to the frozen food section to pick up veggie burgers, veggie sausage, and stuff of the like for Shey.

My cart now floweth over. Time to head out. So we make our way over to women's wear. Shey and Sil are nowhere to be seen, which means they are in the dressing room. I park the cart nearby it

"You guys in there," I call out.

"In a minute!" Shey's says.

I hear giggles and laughs. It's nice when they get along. Rare, but nice.

After a while Sil's says, "Are you still there? You need to see this."

"Okay."

I walk over to the dressing area, passing a smile along to the grim-faced lady putting clothes back on hangers.

The door opens, and Sil comes out wearing a nice yellow "hello kitty" sundress that barely contains her. Then Shey leaps out wearing a blue bustier and tiny matching panties. Shey does a quick shimmy and leaps back into the dressing room.

"We did a switch," Shey says from the dressing room. Sil puts her hand over her mouth in faux surprise, then rejoins Shey in the dressing room.

"Well, that was kinda fun," says, Pffif. He elbows me in the thigh. "Little fairy's not lookin' too bad, eh?"

That comment deserves no response, even though he's kind of right.

"Just sayin, Master Arthur," he says, punctuated with a wink.

Great, now Pffif too. I close my eyes and send love to Dory, who I know is looking over me. I ask for strength.

My phone rings and buzzes. I jump like I someone put a taser to me. I reach down into my pocket to see who it is. The caller ID reads, "M Collections." Okay. I take a deep breath and answer – "Hello."

"Yes, hello, Arthur. It is your friend Maldgorath; I have decided to grace you with a meeting."

"Wonderful," I tell him "When and where?"

"When will be tomorrow. Where I have yet to decide, you can be flexible I assume?"

"Just for you, sir."

There is a slight pause.

"Sarcasm, it's good to see you're feeling confident. Now, I have your word and oath that you are not seeking to set a trap upon me? You will be alone, with the exception of those in your collection, correct?"

I find it disingenuous he would be asking me for my word when his means next to nothing. All the same, I say, "Just me and my gifts, on my word… My oath. You know how much honor and integrity mean to me. Now, do I have your word and oath that you and yours will bring me no harm?"

He laughs a bit. "Of course, Arthur."

"May I hear you speak that oath, please?"

More laughter.

"I see you understand the nuances, Arthur. Surely. Neither I or mine will harm you. That is my promise and oath."

Now it's my turn to laugh, but I don't. He probably thinks I believe him.

"Thank you. That gives me great peace of mind. I'll look forward to your call tomorrow."

He hangs up.

Vets looks at me with intensity.

"Was that him?" she asks.

"Sure was."

I bellow out to the dressing room, "Come on girls, time to hurry up. We just got a phone call about a meeting tomorrow."

Our pleasant distraction comes to an end. I just hope we aren't facing the same.

Chapter 52

Dinner is very solemn. Uncharacteristically, Vets is the chatty one at the table. Her focus isn't like we're used to, on protecting her food; it's on tomorrow's festivities. Of course, chatty consists of things like, "How can we prepare a battlefield when we don't know where it is?" and "What if he strikes first, before your surprise?"

For a mostly hairless, cat-like creature that just is learning to read, Vets sure understands the nature of warfare pretty damn well.

"Hey, an early night makes sense. The call may come early."

I stop Pffif and hold my hand out.

"Me flask?" he asks.

"Yeps. Need you at one hundred percent tomorrow."

He's not pleased. "Ye can always send me to the white ana I'll heal right up. Don' take me flask tonight - doubts that I'll be fallin' asleep too soon. Ye may be brave, Arthur, but this has me spooked."

I pat him on the shoulder and say, "Try not to hurt yourself too much, okay?"

"Aye, master Arthur."

I go to the shared living room to join Vets and Hjuul. As Hjuul is in wolf form, he jumps up on the sofa and lays his head in my lap. He knows I'm not feeling all that brave. Vets regards Hjuul and me.

"It is normal for some to feel anxious before the day of battle," she says, as if that's supposed to be comforting.

"Thanks."

I scratch Hjuul again, and she continues. "The other females will wish to breed with you tonight, but why I do not understand. As the summoned, we cannot bear young."

And I am not going to explain that either. But her observation, as usual, is pretty much spot on.

I mutter a "Yeah, strange," and wonder to myself how the Vetisghar are so inferior. Maybe it's just that they aren't that inferior to humans.

I remember big Z tossing the Tahoe, and my frame of reference tightens.

Vets stands, bows her head to me, and says, "I shall return."

True to prediction in comes Shey, tiptoeing over to me with her hands behind her back. She sees Hjuul with his jowls on my lap and thinks better for trying to shoo him away. Instead, she plops down in front of me with her chin on my knee.

"Come to my room and make love to me, Arthur."

There it is.

"Not tonight, dear Shey. Wrongest night ever for that."

"Then a kiss? A snuggle? Arthur, tonight may be…"

"Tonight I belong to Dorothy. We need her. I need her. She needs to know that."

A knowing look comes over Shey's face. "You're right. I'm sorry." She looks up. "Sorry, Dory." She stands and says, "hug?"

"Always."

She tackles me in one of her bear hugs causing Hjuul to pull back with a "Rrrr?" She begins to shower my cheeks and forehead with little kisses going from right to left stopping only after sneaking a quick one on my lips. She jumps off of me as quickly as she jumped on me.

"I got my kisses." Then she blows a kiss up to the ceiling. "For you too Dory." For a moment, I am just so stunned by how cute she is.

"And don't worry Arthur," she says, "Tomorrow I'm going to put an arrow in each of that motherfucker's eyes and dance in his black blood once you've lopped the son a bitch's head off."

She lets out some kind of fairy battle cry, blows a kiss and skips back down the hall to her room.

But she was so cute…

I look over at Hjuul, and even he is a bit taken aback. Wolves can be very expressive. We both recover, and he returns his jowls to my lap.

I hear Vets say something to Shey in the hall and the warrior returns with her big black sword in the scabbard. She sits back down, pulls out the sword and a small kit. After opening the kit, she pulls out a small whetstone and cloth. Then she begins tending to her blade.

"This is how a warrior relaxes before battle. You should get your sword, it is calming," she says.

She might be right. But I'm good sitting here with Hjuul, watching Vets tend to her weapon. I find myself admiring her. She's no beauty even in human form unless you are into body-builder types with blunt faces, but she is honest, hardworking and so very loyal. Maybe that's why they are seen as so inferior by the demonkind.

Pffif joins us, plops down in a lounge chair and says, "Ye all be too quiet."

"I am tending to my weapon, Arthur is watching me work," Vets says.

"Naa ye daft thing! He's lookin' at ye like he wants to tie ye to that breedin' stone."

Pffif slaps his knee and breaks out into a bawdy laugh.

I expect the sword to flash and the chase to be on. But instead, Vets gives a smile and goes back to polishing and honing the blade. The small thrum of a purr starts to emanate from her.

"What in the frosty hills of Evermore is that sound?" exclaims Pffif looking at Vets skeptically.

"It means she's happy," I tell him.

"All is as it should be," she says. "The king looks over his warriors, and the fool tries to make everyone laugh."

"Ye hear that, King Arthur?" Pffif says, "She's thinkin' I'm the fool." More laughter erupts from the little man. He jumps down from the lounge chair and walks over to Vets putting his hand on her knee.

"Lookin' forward to dyin' well with ye tomorrow, Lady Vets."

She stops with the sharpening of the sword and smiles at him.

"And I you, fool,"

"Hey, you two – the objective is to make the other guys die. We live. They die. Much better for us."

Pffif flashes a huge grin. "Likin' the way yer thinkin' there. No wonder yer King! Good night to ye all, I be retir'n."

He heads back to his apartment.

Which I think is a good idea too. I get up, excuse myself and head to the hall for my room.

And there is Sil, who has probably been waiting by her door all night for me, wearing this next to see-through number. She points at me and gives me a "come here" with her finger. I shake my head "no" back. She makes a look of exasperation and walks down the hall to me.

"Might be the last chance to come to my room and play cards," she says. She is, if nothing else, at least creative in working around the whole no seduction thing.

"Might be," I reply.

A look of disgust comes over her face. "Had to try."

"Glad you did," I tell her. "It's nice to be wanted." And then I realize the implications of what I just said.

"Yeah, Arthur that would be nice, you must tell me what that feels like."

She starts to reach out to me for either a pat on the arm or a hug but stops after seeing my eyes turn to her hand.

Great, I just offended her even more, involuntarily. She turns around and walks away without saying a word. Most men would kill for a slice of that. Heck, men have. I watch her shapely form disappear into her room and remind myself that Maldgorath gave her to me for a specific reason – to corrupt me.

Tonight's the worst night to jump on the carnal corruption train.

I enter my apartment and latch the door. I open the box with the blessed sword in it and run my finger along the blade, just to feel it. I pull it from the box and carefully insert it in the scabbard and lay it on the bed. Then I kneel and pray.

I pray of thanks for Dory looking over us.

I pray for the well being of my family.

I pray for Grey's long life and happiness.

I pray that there really is a glimmer of light in Znuul's dark heart.

I pray for Svea and her children.

I pray for the resolve to do as I must.

I pray for the strength to endure the foulest torture and not give up my soul, for the sake of those bound to me.

Chapter 53

Dreams are good. They're like pleasant movies you participate in. But being woken from one always sucks. One moment, I'm at the beautiful chateau listening to one of Grey's sermons about how children of the light never fear the dark. The next moment, I'm in a dark room with a cell phone going off.

I grab the phone: M Collections. Time: 2:02 am in the freaking morning. I hit answer and say, "Hello," as perkily as I can.

"It is tomorrow, Arthur," comes Maldgorath's superior sounding voice.

"So I see, where do we meet?"

"Downstairs is good. I am there right now on your very open, unfinished second floor. By the way, that is a most impressive threshold to the living quarters. It's almost a warding. You must tell me how you did that."

Holy crap. He's here. He tried to walk in. I was sleeping. My head reels.

"Are you there, Arthur?"

"Yes, yes, "It's just that, well, I just woke up."

"Tsk, tsk, Arthur. Time is ticking. I came a very long way to see you. Please don't keep me waiting."

He hangs up.

Crap stones. Caught sleeping. Thank goodness our little family's threshold for our living space is intimidating, or I would have awoken to his face instead of the phone. I will have to ask Grey his opinion of why that is, assuming we survive.

I bolt up from my bed and run from room to room repeating "Get ready. He's here. He's downstairs. We need to go."

I run back to my room, throw on jeans, shoes and strap on the scabbard. I look to the AA-12 and as lovely a weapon as it is, know I have to leave it behind.

I literally run down the hall. Vets is already there.

"Dismiss me and summon me back – it will be faster than putting all my armor on."

She is right. So away she goes. Here she comes back, fully armored and looking most intimidating. The others join shortly. I return Hjuul to his regular large size.

Shey says, what we are all thinking, "Let do this!"

She storms the elevator. We follow. The gate closes. I push the button, and we head down. I lift the gate and enter the second floor before the team.

"Good morning!" I call out. "Welcome to New Orleans. Laissez les bons temps rouler!"

I hit the lights to the long and foreboding second floor.

Maldgorath is standing in the middle of the open space claiming dominance of the entire area. He does not look like what I remember. When I was given my "gifts," he appeared imp-like and no more than five feet tall. This creature is well over six foot. He has grey skin, and it appears to be swirling with movement. His face has fleshy tubers where a beard should be. He is clad in a fish scale armor tunic which ties around the waist and extends to a tip below the knees. It is adorned with numbers of what appear to be wooden coins.

Like the ones, he gave Sil and Arix.

I approach closer and see that his skin is not pulsing. There are glyphs all over him, they are moving, swirling, floating about him. His eyes remind me of a lion's eyes, and I see that instead of hair he has snake-like tendrils coming out of the back of his head.

"I see you are taken in by my beauty," he says. "I also see you came armed, I thought I had your word."

"Lord Maldgorath, are you not in and of yourself a weapon? As for my promise, it holds true. The sword is sheathed."

"So it is," he says, beginning to circle around me, causing me to shift to keep him in front. He takes a step forward, so I take one back.

"Cautious aren't you? Is that a Paladin's sword?"

"A gift from a friend, it gives me reassurance."

"So it does."

His smile does not make me feel comfortable.

"One must be of The Order of Light to properly wield that. You are much more nervous than I expected."

He begins the circling again.

Thoughts of sharks circling their prey come to mind. I smile. Sharks aren't very bright.

"It would be disrespectful not to acknowledge your strength – stupid too."

He laughs, changes direction, and walks back to where he was before.

"So, Arthur MacInerny, what do you hope to accomplish this fine morning?"

I smile back to him and take a step forward gauging his reaction. There is none.

"Well, I hope to walk away with a better understanding of what your intentions were, and now are, for me."

His hands suddenly come up from his side, and he claps. Shey skitters to the side and bow appears in her hand with an arrow drawn. He smiles.

"Little plaything, if you shoot that arrow, you break your master's word. I would be loosed upon you all, should I choose to be. Do you miss my most intimate attentions? I certainly miss the sweet taste of your fae blood." His gaze turns to me. "You know, the best part of a fae summonling is that you can eat them over and over again. They're always delicious but do leave you hungry after they disintegrate into nothing."

He begins the slow circling again, clapping.

"Well played, Arthur, find out what I want and give it to me, that way you might avoid their fate. I am impressed."

"Well, until I know what that is, it's kind of hard for me to agree to anything. So, why the Catholic Church, Maldy?"

He bristles at me calling him Maldy. Good. Time for him to be a little off balance.

"Sorry, that's what Znuul always calls you; I thought it was a good thing."

The mention of Ahtsag Znuul bristles him further.

"You would do well to forget anything that one tells you. He is weak. He is a coward and a fool who has given up his very essence to a human."

Realizing he lost his composure, he collects himself, straightening his tunic.

"Poor Ahtsag Znuul, there were so many who thought him great, but now they see his weakness. There are rumors he plays a game for his freedom. That he waits for the wizard to release him at his deathbed so that he may impose himself on this world. That would be cunning and true to the Ahtsag Znuul of old. But, this wizard from what I hear will not release him. Tsk. Tsk."

"Well, that's just terrible for him, isn't it," I say as dispassionately as I can.

Because the truth is, if that is Znuul's game, that is how I feel. I also know he's probably using some form of sight to gauge my emotions. Truth negates the need for a poker face I don't have.

That brings a smile back to Maldgorath's face.

"Good. Good, yes. So, you want to know why the Roman Catholic Church, why you, why now?"

"Yes, Lord Maldgorath."

"Why you – because you have assets of destruction, Why now? Simple. You were an emotional wreck and most vulnerable. A simple push consisting of the death of only two close to you could result in a wave of death and destruction of hundreds. You would take no prisoners. Your passion would take this revenge to the streets, to the news and the public. Of course, the Gratia Potentia would have screamed out because they and the Protectorate don't want people to know about such scary things."

"Likely I would have had no choice, but to come and add you to my collection to remove you from the public's eye."

I give him the what-the-fuck face.

"But, why the church – random thing, grudge, what?"

He claps again and laughs. "Oh, Arthur, I am so proud of you. You have come so very far. There's not an ounce of rage in you right now. After all, I just shared with you. You have changed so much since you were a young drunken man who would screw his best friend's girl just to know he could. I must think I had some hand in the grand change."

"You did, without question, and I thank you for that. But… the church?"

He startles at that admission.

"Yes, I did digress. Sometimes, I just get so pleased with myself. The reason for your target is the size and reach of that institution. You see, with you so publicly bringing devils and such against them I could set into motion another group with just a few strategically placed pushes. I would convince the radical Muslim community that you were a punishment from Allah, himself. I would convince them that their duty to their God is to assist in the eradication of the Church of Jesus in all forms. I would promise them honey and virgins for committing most unspeakable acts. And they would do it because of their need to feel important, their need to feel chosen, their need for hope. And after all, they would have real proof their God wishes them to rend destruction. The chaos would have been glorious. The balance would be tipped, and the gates of Helterezen would be swung open wide with the blood of the innocent and unknowing."

At least he didn't go "Mua ha ha ha." But still, as far as plans for bringing on the destruction of the world go, not bad. Maldgorath is not a dumb one.

"Well? I don't sense outrage or revulsion from you, what are you thinking. Are you blocking me? Did the Protectorate teach you that?"

"Oh, sorry… They tried to teach me that, I can sort of do it. But really I was just marveling at the fact that your plan may have worked had the protectorate not stopped me when they did."

All true. And playing right into his ego, as well.

He begins the circling again.

"So, on to what my plans are for you now. That is simple. You will do my will, or be added to my collection."

He looks over to Shey. "Little one, I think I still may have some of your sister's bones for you to chew on or play with; I can make sure you enjoy that. Remember how I made you enjoy her and so many things."

That tips the scales for me and Maldy picks up the change in my demeanor immediately as he is apparently scanning my emotions.

"Oh! There's something. You have feelings for the little one. Have you tasted her delights? She's quite the wild one."

"Fuck you, Maldgorath," Shey screams at him.

I spin around, "You be quiet, right now. We are speaking."

Shey is snarling and ready to snap. Then I realize I just turned my back to Maldgorath.

"Sorry," I say turning around to see that he's right on top of me now. Damn. I try to add a little levity with a, "She's a firecracker, that one."

He starts the circling again. This time I follow him with my head instead of actually following him.

"So, what will it be, Arthur MacInerny," he asks. "My will be done as a man, or my will done as a summonling?"

So it's on. He's close, he's relaxed. We're almost there.

"Well, before you get all bent out of shape with my answer, I'd like to have some fun and satisfaction."

I step up to him. Again, he doesn't move. He is not at all intimidated by me. That is good.

"You're not in a hurry, are you? This idea would be right up your alley."

"Speak."

I take a step back and begin to circle him, my team following my lead.

"You notice someone is missing? I have to admit, I'm really more pissed at him than I am at you. You're just being yourself. He, on the other hand, pretended to be my friend. You want to have some fun with Arixtumin – want to see him in true mortal despair?"

I hold my arm out with his glyph on it, bring my finger to the glyph and wait for his answer.

"I must admit, Arthur, I am most surprised and intrigued. Let us have some fun at Arixtumin's expense."

I touch the Glyph and call Arix. The air ripples and there stands the backstabbing bastard.

"Okay Arix, tell you what. I think your friend Maldgorath here is going to bring some hurt to me, despite his word otherwise."

I look at Maldgorath, and he smiles a wicked smile.

"Unless you choose wisely, Arthur."

"Take a seat next to him, Arix. He's your buddy. I will not ask you to fight him, you know my weakness for free will."

Vets immediately protests, "He is an asset, you can make him fight!"

Without taking my eyes off Arix or Maldy I say back to her, "He wouldn't make a difference."

This pleases Maldgorath greatly. Arix sits on the ground next to him.

"There, you're where you belong." I turn my eyes to Maldgorath and smile big as day.

"Now for some truth, you don't have any way to turn him back from a summonling, do you? You just played him, and he gave himself to you like a greedy idiot."

Maldgorath lets loose with a belly laugh.

"You see what he could not. I always wanted a sorcerer of his stature in my collection, but they are so intelligent and slippery. I painted such a picture for him and made promises I could never keep." He shoves the kneeling Arix by his head. "All he saw was the prize; he did not even consider the cost. Or the nature of the seller."

I share in the laughter.

Arix looks up at me with contempt.

"Don't be mad at me Arix," I say. "You did all this to yourself. You are indeed that totally fucking stupid."

Now to make my move, my surprise. I say, "May I take…"

"Wait a moment," says Sil, interrupting, pushing her way past me to stand in between me and my target.

Damn it, this is the wrong time. I was setting up for the blow.

"Since you're talking free will, I am going to have to jump in here." She turns to me and continues. "Darling, do you remember the one true law? I know where we're all ending up and I don't want to fight him. In fact, you piece of shit human, this is me rejecting you for a change."

I am beyond stunned. I am reeling. This can't be happening. I am speechless. I hear Shey and Pffif's condemnations, but it's like they are miles away.

"Over seventy years, Arthur" she spits at me. "Constant rejection. Degradation. You reject me? NOBODY rejects me! One true law, Arthur, it says, me before you."

She turns to Maldgorath.

"Baby, promise me after you reap him you'll make him be my kinky little sex toy forever, or until I get bored of tormenting him."

Maldgorath's eyes are upon me. But his words are for Sil.

"That is one promise I will keep, my dear, ever so fine and effective Silithes."

Chapter 54

"Such despair! Such betrayal! Such exquisite pain!" proclaims Maldgorath.

"Sil, what about Jerry? The family…"

I can barely choke the words out. This has blindsided me. I trusted that thing, that succubus.

"One true law, Arthur. Jerry is dead, I don't wish to exist in torment." She turns back to Maldgorath, running her hands across his tunic. "See baby, you ask me for his lust, and I bring you his heart. I am not a failure – that's an upgrade."

"Indeed you are not a failure, most sweet and powerful succubus."

She walks her fingers along his fish scale armor. Then she gets on her knees in front of him, lifts the tunic and… oh no, God… she isn't.

She is pleasuring him.

I feel the beginning of Maldgorath's psychic attic. I am too scattered, I feel weak. But I know I am not weak. I see the frog-faced monster appear. Others start to appear. Vets and Hjuul immediately wade into battle.

I look and see Maldgorath's happy, confident looking face. His hand rests on the top of the rhythmically moving thing under his armor tunic that is Sil's head.

"Arthur, I shall enjoy…" The psychic attack stops. His eyes bulge, and he reels back a step. His face contorts, and Sil pops up like a Jack in the Box from hell. She tosses a grey leather pouch to her side, turns her head and then violently vomits something on the floor making an awful sound. She lets out that banshee scream and starts clawing at Maldgorath's face and neck.

Out of my shock I realize, that's not a pouch, that's his testicles… holy crap! And she vomited up... oh my god she bit his dick off. No wonder the psychic attack stopped.

I immediately go for the sword. Dammit. It's sticking in the scabbard. More creatures keep popping up. Vets, Hjuul and Pffif, are working hard to cut them down before they have their bearings. I tug at the sword again, and it is not breaking free. I swing the scabbard around trying to get the sword out that way.

Sil gets a vicious backhand and goes flying. I see Arix open his third eye and give me a wink with one of his regular eyes. Arix grabs Maldgorath, stopping him from approaching me and a plume of purple flame erupts from Maldgorath's belly. Maldgorath falters, having had a large hole torn through his midsection. A large blue-silver snake flies off his shoulder and takes what appears to be a deep breath – the dragon.

Just like that, a silver arrow sprouts through one of the small dragon's eyes, and it falls to the ground, evaporating in ectoplasmic goo.

"Take him now, Arthur!" Shey cries.

I free the sword and rush toward the prone Maldgorath. Time feels like it's running in slow motion, I am pulling the blade back. I feel the warm crystal feeling of a ward cast upon me – Arix. I take another running stride.

Maldgorath bends up, says, "Enough!" and spreads his arms in a violent motion.

My world goes into vertigo. I have the sensation of circular movement. I stop, suddenly and the wind is knocked out of me. I hear my protective ward shatter. I have the sensation of sliding downward, and my head hits the floor. There is a tinny ringing sound in my ears.

Crap. I've been knocked out. I scramble for my bearings and look up at the not happy face of Maldgorath. The sword is not in my hand. He reaches down and picks me up by my shoulder with one hand, crushing it along the way, causing streams of searing pain.

My vision whites out from the pain as my clavicle, shoulder blade, and arm are crushed in his grip. I start to black out, but a slap across my face brings me around. My shoulder is released.

"This is where the fun starts, Arthur - your pain will be of legend. And in the end, you will be mine," says a rapidly healing Maldgorath. "Let's start with basics first. Give me what is mine!"

It feels as if my bones are being pulled through my skin. The pain is unbearable and all over. I remember this feeling when the ambassador tried to pull Shey and Pffif from me. It goes on and on. I feel my organs rearranging and my brain melting. I can't move or scream.

Then it stops. I am lying on the ground, on my shattered shoulder, which makes me roll over from that pain. Then I feel a thudding pain in my groin and my vision whites out again. Searing pain emanates again in my shoulder as I am hoisted back roughly to a sitting position on the bare floor.

I try to focus my eyes. A slap or two from Maldgorath helps.

"Let me explain the game to you, Arthur. I am going to hurt you rather badly. Over and over and over until either, you die, or I become bored and kill you. That is unless you answer my question the proper way. The question is what are you? The correct answer is I am yours to wield Lord Maldgorath. Give me the proper answer and mean it, I will reap your spirit, and the pain will stop."

I laugh and spit a little blood at him.

"Hell, that's when the pain starts."

He gives me a sick grin.

"Good, this promises to be a fun game."

He tears my shirt open and with a fingernail digs a large vertical rectangle in my chest.

"Now, that wasn't so bad, was it? Now, this … will be much worse."

One hand goes on my crushed shoulder, restraining me and causing excruciating pain. He cuts a rectangle into my skin with the fingernail of his other hand. Once done, he begins pulling the skin off of me, slowly. I think I scream; it's overwhelming. There is no pulling away from his iron grip. I think I pass out again.

A few slaps restores my focus, and I'm looking at him dangling the skin in front me. "What are you, Arthur? Do tell."

"I'm disappointing you, that's what I am."

"Wrong answer," and with that, he leans his head back and gobbles down my skin.

We play at least two more rounds of pull the skin, I think. I'm not really sure how many as shock has set in by this time. I deny him, but my responses get less witty each time.

I remember Znuul's advise to put a gun in my mouth and pull the trigger. He was right. Hindsight is a bitch; I should have brought a gun.

I am hoisted up again, this time by the other shoulder, which is also crushed, causing me to blackout. I am awakened by a warm stream of foul-smelling liquid on my face. The bastard is urinating on me. It stings my eyes and burns where my flesh was torn off.

"What are you, Arthur?" he asks again.

"In pain."

He walks around behind me and hoists me up by both shoulders, causing me to scream. "They say kidney stones are very painful for a human, but kidney fingers are even more so."

I feel his finger very slowly rip through my lower back and into my kidney. The pain is convulsive.

He releases me, and I fall face first to the ground. I am in a daze. I am not in pain; pain is me – all of me. I realize I am sobbing and whimpering. I try to gain control of myself. The realization comes, I will not give myself up. Not for my sake, but for the sake of those who are bound to me. I will not give them back to him. I can endure this for them.

I hear a voice. It's Dorothy calling my name. I must be near death. I'm ready. I feel something like a cool breeze blow across me, and the pain stops.

I hear her voice say "Arthur, you are much loved."

I feel myself heal, shoulders coming back together, skin growing, my kidney sealing itself. I feel more than healing. I feel the love that is bringing me that healing. It is all around me.

I feel connected to all around me. I am connected through Dorothy.

"Well, Arthur," says, Maldgorath "What are you?"

Dory's voice reverberates through me, "Tell him, Arthur. Tell him what you are. Tell him what *we* are."

I am part of Dory's voice, I feel her presence. I sense the room in shades of light. There is a dark swirling shadow standing in front of me.

The dark shadow of Maldgorath says, "Well, Arthur, what are you?"

I sit up, open my eyes and gaze upon the dark swirling entity that is Maldgorath, with the new vision in my eyes. A vision that must be how Dorothy perceives our world. Everything is interconnected. Connected by tendrils of light.

"A nice trick with the healing, Arthur. You know that just means we can play longer, now tell me… what are you?"

I feel Dory and the room and all things good.

"Tell him," her voice prompts me inside my head.

Calm falls upon me knowing that all this pain is only temporary. I look up at him and say, "I am a child of the light."

Chapter 55

I hold my hand up, relax and allow my new reality to flow through me. My hand releases a torrent of bright white light that throws the shadow of Maldgorath back against the wall. The light tears at the shadow, burning it. I feel him struggling against the burning light that so easily flows through me.

I stand and approach Maldgorath, my hand still held outward allowing out the light to pour out.

Maldgorath bellows and tries to cover himself.

I sense a pain, but not the pain of this shadow creature. There is a wounded soul. I look over my shoulder and see Shey's crumpled figure lying at a corner to the wall. I cease channeling the light against him and will Shey healing through the prayers I've learned.

Her pain is gone.

Amidst this battlefield, I hear a single clear note and look to it. It is the sword, ringing. By the note, I know the sword's name - Yayne. I hold my hand out and call it to me, in harmony with its note.

"Yayne."

It flies to my hand and glows bright white, in connectivity with the reality Dorothy shares with me.

Maldgorath begins to stand. The dragon appears over his shoulder twisting and weaving. I run at full speed and swing the sword, with all my might. Maldgorath sees me coming and tries to block the blow with his arm while jumping away.

His arm falls to the ground, and the sword cuts midway through his torso, but not completely through because he was moving. I pull the sword free and see the dragon glowing, preparing to whisk Maldgorath to safety.

A silver arrow pierces the small dragon nailing it to the wall by its skull. Another goes through its head, and it begins to dissolve.

Shey's voice, sounding distant screams, "Finish him!"

I pull the sword back for the final cleaving blow and see Maldgorath break one of the ceramic coins attached to his fish scale armor tunic. I swing through nothing. He is gone. I close my eyes to sense his shadow through the divine connection I have with Dorothy.

He is easily a block away.

A moment later I sense nothing. The dragon must have whisked him off. The bully ran.

I feel my connection to Dorothy begin to disappear. I don't cry. I don't beg for her to stay because I know she can't. Instead, I just take a knee, holding

Yayne in front of me and project love and gratitude for her as long as the connection will last.

Epilogue

There have been no Maldgorath sightings in our realm since our encounter. Certain persons within the Magerium have consulted with their informants through controlled summoning and séances. Those informants are, of course, lesser beings of Helterezen.

According to them, he appears to be holed up there. For how long is the question.

Sil came clean about her behavior. She thought we needed a surprise. When asked about her "One true law claim," she told me she was telling the truth. Her need for revenge came before anything else, and she feels like she got a little. I asked her next time to give us a head's up if she was thinking surprise.

I still get unmitigated grief for not taking his big head after she took his little one.

Given the events of that morning, I have become a bit of a rock star among the various factions of the protectorate. The Order of Light wishes to make me an honorary member, despite my foul company. The Healing Hands, the faction of healers, claims me as their own. The Techno-Mage Guild wishes to study me more and has offered to fit me with one of their magic amplifying apparatus – that could be neat. Maybe I could maybe do boom magic effectively with one of those, but I'd have to wear a bowler or some other skull fitting hat.

Don't know how I feel about the fashion statement. Maybe they can make a Stetson or baseball cap.

Grey paid us a visit after things cooled down, sans Znuul. That meant a lot to all of us. He wanted to know what guild I was leaning toward. I told him I didn't see any reason to be exclusive. In the end, we're all on the same team, and the balance of good and evil must be maintained, or we'll all end up like the Vetisghar.

I had to ask Grey about what Maldgorath told me of Znuul's endgame.

It's not exactly a secret, Grey claimed. His plan to address that game is to live long and die with dignity. I asked about the council's point of view with regards to Znuul's partial free will, being concerned that they may take action against Grey. Grey advises that in the end, Znuul is still bound and not showing signs of rebellion.

Of special note, is that we, as a group, have agreed to parole Arix. Was it not for his quick ward, I'd have been a bloody stain on that wall. He is locked down by some fairly stringent compelling to prevent any nonsense. He is basically the group's butler now and directed not to speak unless spoken to. He'd rather be out in the world as a mute butler than spend more years in his white prison cell of nothingness.

And I'm now officially on call with The Protectorate. The pay will be good. The work will be very rewarding. Travel will be demanding, but I'll see the world, or so I'm told. Karen says she has a globe and puts a pin in every place she's visited – nifty idea. I may have to rip it off.

But before we go on duty, a vacation is called for. I originally wanted to pull the family together at Hilton Head, but schedules didn't work out. So we find ourselves at a very exclusive, very private, Villa resort recommended by Sir Grey himself, located in the Cayman Islands.

The beach is white, the water is blue, and best yet we have our own private pool and chef on call. Pffif spends most of his time at the public beach bar cabana nearby. Hjuul is having a blast crashing into waves and tearing across the sand. Sil has been given hunting privileges with the caveat of no lasting harm, as always.

God help the pool boys - they will be very tired, but happy.

The rest of us, more or less, just enjoy relaxing.

I'm taking in the latest issue of Travel and Leisure and enjoying a fresh pineapple juice.

I spy Shey getting out of the pool. She is wearing an itty-bitty bikini on her human form, and I must admit that she is looking very good. I've never seen her in a bikini before. Her tight little body seems to be made for them, with her well-toned legs, and little apple breasts.

And big golden eyes - looking at me. Dang it! I am so busted and so embarrassed. I just smile and go back to my magazine.

Shey's singsong voice pulls me away from it.

"Arthur, you were checking me out."

Shey tosses the towel aside and walks toward me.

"You think I'm sexy." She gets to my lounge and climbs on, grabbing my magazine and flinging it to the side. "You think I'm sexy and you want me, don't lie." She crawls catlike atop me and sets herself down on my lap.

Now I really can't deny anything.

"You really do want me," she says, smiling and now grinding against the evidence. She leans in and whispers in my ear "I really want you, too."

She leans back, tousles her hair and golden fairy dust falls on me – fairy love dust. Like magic, my hands are on her tight, tiny rear end and the evidence of my arousal is pressed hard against her.

She parts my lips and gives me a tingling, teasing, smiling kiss that sets me afire.

A voice breaks our moment.

"I get nexties!"

Sil.

Shey's body tightens, and she pulls away from our embrace.

Shey's eyes are enraged. She's beautiful when she's angry.

"You fucking bitch," she screams and jumps up from me with balled fists. "This was our moment! You ruined it!"

She looks around frantically and finally spies my pineapple juice. She grabs it and hurls it at Sil who dodges it and blows a kiss back to her.

Shey screams something like "Rrraaaa!" back at her and then grabs the little table I had my drink on and hurls that at Sil too.

I think Sil says, something like "Crazy bitch." I can't be sure because I'm really only paying attention to how cute Shey is when she's furious, and she is most furious. She takes off running at Sil and catches her in a tackle, carrying them both through the sliding glass doors of their Villa.

Damn, that's going to cost me a pretty penny. They are obviously beating the crap out of each other, based on the sounds. I can't have my beautiful fairy getting hurt, so I reach down and dismiss Shey.

Oh … No more fairy love dust effect. I reach down and dismiss Sil too. I take a deep breath and try to find my composure.

The shadow over me takes my attention. I look up and see Vets standing there, holding a copy of Cat in the Hat. She is looking at the Villas' broken door.

"The fairy has issues," she says.

That is an understatement.

MORE?

As independent authors we don't have the luxury of a big publishing house marketing department. In fact, in the case of this hobbyist writer, there's only me.

And you.

Consider taking some time and leaving a review. It doesn't have to be clever, lengthy, or something that sounds like a college professor's thesis. It's just got to be honest and from you.

Reviews help. They help by showing numbers of readers, they help by informing potential readers of what to expect and they help this writer's motivation.

Because it ain't the money that's keeping this keyboard clicking.

So if you'd like to see more of my work, *or any other independent author* trying to find their way - give a review.

They make a difference. And so do you.

Other works in the series

Sworn Vengeance, book two of the series

Death Curse, book three of the series

Fugitive Ways, book four of the series

A Mystery and A Meal, A novella featuring Silithes